DOMINION OF THE STAR

DESCENDANTS OF THE FALLEN: BOOK I

ANGELICA CLYMAN

For Grant

1

Kayla sat slumped against a crumbling wall, gazing beyond the clouds, into the burning pinpricks of the sun's rays. She was trying to stare spitefully into the light, but the defiant star wouldn't cooperate. Its fire had never seared her eyes or flesh before, but she hoped today would bring just a little pain, some small change, anything that would jar her out of this apathetic existence and push her forward. She tried not to blink. Kayla pressed her back harder into the wall, seeking the uncomfortable heat that was generated by the kilns baking pottery on the other side. She held her breath, searching the sky for meaning. Nothing was different.

With her head still upturned, she pulled a thin, worn box out from under her blouse with the grace of a movement often repeated. Kayla tugged on the chain around her neck, her fingers trailing over the wood grain of the locket before she pressed it hard against her chest. It was as if the palm-sized box could be wedged into all those hollow spaces within her.

She sat motionless for a long time before opening the clasp with a quick jerk of her thumb and bringing her head down solemnly to gaze at the photograph nestled in her hands. Kayla's eyes went first to the man with red hair so like her own. His face was turned to meet the wind as it lifted his locks from his shoulders. He was laughing, eyes closed. His arm was around another, younger man who watched him with a look of smiling admiration. Kayla's brow furrowed a bit as she focused on the wiry youth. His brown hair was just long enough for him to pull back loosely into a short ponytail, revealing a boy's face set with intense eyes. Under the photograph was scribbled: *Steelryn and Serafin*. She sighed, her eyes traveling as they always did to the letter set beside the picture.

Michael—

It's a wonder this photograph survived the last four years. Finding it gave me hope, and it makes me remember what our names still mean when heard together. I realize now that when Kiera and Kayla were taken, with them went our reason, our comfort. Tomorrow we fight, and although we can't regain all that was lost, we will lift your wife and daughter up out of darkness.

—Asher

Kayla quickly snapped the hinged box closed so her falling tears wouldn't mar the only relics of her past. Her hand gripped the box tightly, a corner digging into her palm. She didn't understand. She couldn't remember her parents, and no one here knew anything about Asher Serafin. Kayla always thought that one day her history would be revealed to her, but she was more than halfway through her seventeenth year and couldn't wait any longer for a sign that might never come. She had already run out of excuses to stay. Thrusting her treasure back beneath her blouse, Kayla stood up in one quick movement, legs unsteady, and wiped her dirty palms onto her linen pants before smearing her tears away. She wouldn't give herself time to change her mind.

When she reached the small room in the back of the pottery studio, her nervous steps stilled. She looked down at her bed roll in the corner, the few drawings she stuck to the wall and her little trunk beneath the work table. Kayla tried to muster up some heart-swelling emotion for this last visit to the only shelter she could remember, but her chest and head felt numb. The romantic notion of her flight was already dampened, simply by being in this place. She began to fill a bag with her few belongings, but a heavy sense of apathy seemed to come from the air and walls around her, seeping into her skin, slowing her movements.

"Oh my, what are you doing, dear?"

Kayla whirled around, flushed and gulping. "I'm leaving, Miss Helena," she blurted out, the words violently escaping her lips. "I don't belong here. I'm grateful for everything you have done for me, but I have to find out . . . I have to know—"

"Yes, yes, you will." The old woman's words were slow and quiet, causing Kayla's fevered confession to fall, neutralized, into their void. "Explore and know, yes, good. But for now, there is work to be done." She gently extracted the bag from Kayla's stiff fingers as she guided the girl to the door.

"No, I . . . I . . ."

"You have such lovely dreams and they'll all be yours, but first there is greenware that must be loaded into the kiln." Helena released Kayla's arms from the steering clasp of her hands when they reached a shelf of dull, gray pots.

The girl felt her shoulders sag as the rush of independence she experienced just moments earlier was suddenly sapped away. "Do you think tomorrow will be different?"

she whispered.

"Why, each day is."

Kayla barely felt the encouraging pat land on her arm before the old woman left her alone with her duties. She was still for a long stretch before her body began to move on its own, performing this familiar task with delicacy and precision, even with limbs deadened by her bruised spirit. She looked down at the pitcher in her hands. The surface of the vessel was decorated with twisted branches, sprouting leaves as they climbed to the sun. Something about these trees caused her pulse to quicken again. She set the pot back on the shelf with trembling hands. Why could she never hold on to her nerve? Her passion was always cooled before it could start a fire. Still, there were moments when she felt like something braver than herself, when she almost grasped memories that made her feel flooded with life.

She held the vision of those branches in her mind as she ran out of the studio and into the street. She could hear the neighbors calling her name and their voices were what kept her feet from slowing, even as her breath shortened. When she thought her heart would explode, Kayla saw the familiar branches and she stopped, her body suddenly light, her gasps for air triumphant. Her eyes moved over the broad, flat leaves, and then drifted to the darkness beyond, where the trees grew more densely. This wasn't her first time here at the border of the village. The past few weeks she'd found herself at this spot, and somehow, here, she was reminded of her ability to dream. Here, out of sight of the squat buildings and simple faces that inhabited the town, her bones felt restless, as if they wanted to burst through the boundaries of her body and ascend to the sun. Kayla held her breath and felt the air touch her skin with the soft pressure of an embrace. In the rustling of the leaves there was the echo of her name, spoken with some unfamiliar emotion that inspired her to throw off everything she knew for the vision of its source.

She closed her eyes. Here, in this place, it was hard to imagine these feelings disappearing, but she knew if she returned to the village she might never again gather the courage to leave. Hope, fear, and a new sense of urgency beat painfully in her head. She grabbed her locket. It had been years since she accepted that her parents were dead and she was finally old enough to stop fantasizing their return. But if she could just find this Asher Serafin, if he was still alive, she could at least understand what happened to them and what led her here.

Kayla's toes ventured further into the shadows cast by the trees and she saw the beginnings of a road forming between clumps of fallen leaves. She had heard of a city named Madeline, a few miles to the north. It was her only beacon: the notion of a place where there might be news beyond the evasive and blank eyes of everyone in this nameless town she was leaving behind. *Asher Serafin*. Kayla felt the searing force of his image in every pulse beating against her temples, his name in every labored breath. She would find him.

Kayla didn't know how long she had been walking, but as the hours passed, the road dissolved further into swampy ground. The air smelled ominously of fire and ash, and as her surroundings were becoming increasingly tree-choked, she felt as if the gathering darkness threatened to swallow her. Kayla pressed on, too afraid to stop and rest, but too tired to keep up even her slowed pace for long. The righteousness of her cause that served as her driving force was beginning to waver. She fought to control her breathing in order to keep her thoughts from panic, focusing on the simple task of trudging forward.

She heard the sound of an argument before she saw the flicker of a campfire in the distance. A man's voice reached her ears first. "What the hell was that, anyways? A set up? I've never seen a basic relic seize turn into that kind of clusterfuck. When we get back, I promise you someone's gonna pay for this!"

Kayla froze, listening. A girlish voice followed the man's growl. "Oh, stop. You act like we've never run into trouble before."

"I'm not talking about the ambush. In case you didn't notice, we were abandoned by our own, left to die beneath a burning building—" She could hear an edge of pain in his angered snarl.

The little girl giggled. "Lay *down*. I'll watch you kill them later, but rest now, okay?"

Her curiosity piqued, Kayla crept closer, careful to stay off to the side of the pair's small camp. The man sighed heavily. "I hate you."

She heard another childlike laugh. "You're so cute when you're bleeding."

The ground fell out from under Kayla's feet so suddenly that she didn't have time to stop her scream from escaping. She groaned, more from dread than from the aching pain coursing down her backside after her rough landing. She held her breath, waiting for her eyes to adjust to this deeper darkness, and sat helplessly, knowing it wouldn't be long before she met the two strangers. Above her, a small flame appeared and she could hear the young girl calling out, the sound closer than before.

"Jeremy, it's a girl in a hole."

The distant voice yelled back, uninterested. "I know. Girls scream like that."

"C'mon! Let's help her out."

"You told me to lie down." She could hear him rolling his eyes.

The girl let out a snort of impatience. "Fine, I'll do it myself!" A large pair of brown eyes peered over the edge above, the light from the torch revealing a child's form, bronzed skin and long, dark hair sprinkled with thin braids. She extended her small arm. "I'll pull you out."

Kayla frowned. How could she be lifted up by a girl barely more than half her size? Despite her doubts, she slowly stood up and reached for her rescuer. The little girl stretched her arm further into the pit, grunting with the effort, the sound rising to a scream as she inched too far and tumbled forward, knocking them both down to the wet earth below. Before the shriek ended, Kayla could hear Jeremy running towards them, calling, *"Kit!"*

"Down here!" the child yelled back. The torch was still burning on the ground above them, and Kayla watched the girl's eyes shining with expectation.

"Jesus, Kit!" breathed the voice from above. Kayla looked up. She could see a young man's features, transitioning from concern to relief to tight-lipped laughter. No longer fearing for his friend's safety, his gaze then focused on Kayla. His unruly black hair hung down around his face, but his blue eyes were clear and striking, emerging unnervingly from the deep shadows cast over his form. A thin trickle of blood ran from an almost-closed gash on his forehead. His smile vanished. "Alright, Kit, take my hand."

Jeremy leaned deeply into the hole, hoisting out the smaller girl with ease. Then he hesitated, exchanging a long glance with Kit. Sighing, he extended his hand again, reaching for Kayla. His arm was bandaged tightly with white cotton, smeared with blood and dirt, his fingertips naked, the tails of his bandages swinging loosely. She timidly held out her hand, gulping down air in an attempt to slow her heartbeat. He reached for her and she closed her eyes, but with his touch came a sudden, blinding pain, and she was released as quickly as she was grasped.

Kayla fell onto her knees, turning away from the light above. She held her throbbing hand close to her chest, biting her lip to keep from crying out. Her fingers pulsated and burned; it felt as if her bones were pressing outwards. Kayla's eyes widened as she watched a bony protrusion issue out from her palm and land heavily on the ground before her. First she examined her hand, and when she found it unbloodied and whole, she had the strength to lift the strange object close to her face. It looked like the hilt of a sword, formed organically by a fusion of bone. Knowing that now was not the time for further investigation, Kayla quickly hid it in her deep pocket and turned back to face the light her would-be rescuers shined towards her.

Jeremy's eyes were narrowed slits, watching her with suspicion. He extended his hand again towards her slowly, defying her to shock him once more, and determined not to miss what happened a second time. Not understanding what just occurred and afraid of another episode, Kayla hesitated. Whether it was out of the fear of those eyes burning into her now, or just the intense desire to be free, she lowered her head, took a deep breath, and lifted her arm up towards him. Their hands met again and Kayla swallowed a sharp intake of breath. No searing pain came with his touch, but she noticed the hilt in her pocket grow warm and restless against her thigh. She closed her eyes, allowing herself to be lifted from the hole. Blindly grasping this stranger made her ascent feel more like a rescue.

Once she emerged, Kayla lay sprawled against the earth for a moment, finally feeling as though she could breathe easier. As was her habit, she clutched her chest, seeking the reassuring weight of her personal reliquary between her clothes and skin, but she felt nothing but her own flesh beneath a thin layer of fabric. Kayla gasped, her hands frantically searching her body and the dirt at her feet before she grabbed the torch and leaned forward, staring into the pit. She could make out her box lying on that marshy ground far below.

She felt Jeremy's arm barring her from jumping without thinking. "It's that important?" he asked softly.

Kayla searched for the right words to answer, but in her tense pause Jeremy had already leapt down, landing gracefully. She saw him bend low to grab her treasure, lingering a moment before pocketing the tiny box. He stood, drawing a dagger in each hand, and reaching up high, he buried his blades into the pit's steep wall. He pulled himself up, continuing to stab the earth with his knives as he climbed. With only a small grunt of effort he took hold of higher ground and swung his legs over the edge of the hole. Drawing himself up, he wiped and sheathed his blades, and produced the locket. His fingers dragged heavily over its surface before dropping it into Kayla's outstretched palms.

"Where are you going?" he asked stonily.

"Madeline."

Jeremy turned his back. "What's your name?"

"Kayla . . . Steelryn."

She sensed his body stiffen before he started walking back towards camp. "Madeline is gone. You're better off coming with us."

Kayla stood staring at his back, weighing her narrow options, when she felt the small girl's hand slip gently into hers. Looking down, she was met with bright eyes and a reassuring smile.

"My name's Kittie. Don't worry about Jeremy. He just gets a little grumpy after a good deed." She laughed as she tugged on Kayla's arm, eager to follow her friend.

"Wait . . . ! Where are you both headed?"

Kittie turned her face away to the wooded darkness, her voice dropping. "Like he said . . . Madeline is gone." A moment passed before her hair flew in an arc back towards Kayla, followed by her wide grin, shattering the somber mood. "You should go with us. There are worse dangers than holes in the ground since the Eclipse . . . and now . . ." She ran with Kayla's arm in her grasp, letting her last grave words dissolve into the heavy summer air.

2

A fingertip brushed lightly against Kayla's collarbone as she turned restlessly in her sleep, but it was the sharp edges of the bone in her pocket that woke her. She sat up suddenly, straining her dream-clouded senses for recognition of her surroundings and situation. Jeremy was sitting very close to her. He seemed to have been staring into the dying fire until her abrupt movement caused him to glance sidelong at her.

"You okay?"

She instinctively clutched the box around her neck and then nodded.

Jeremy's head absently mimicked her gesture before he slid himself a few feet away from the fire to sit, leaning casually against one of the trees lining their camp. He watched as Kayla twisted her long, red hair into a coil over her shoulder so that the night air could reach the back of her neck. "Why are you out here?"

She looked down at her hair. "I told you . . . I was on my way to Madeline."

"Yeah, I know. But why?"

"I'm looking for someone. Ash—"

"Ssh!" Jeremy hissed through clenched teeth. Then, seeing her wide-eyed confusion, added, "That won't help you find this person. That's how you'll find a predator. I don't wanna know the name, and you shouldn't spread it around."

Kayla turned her head away, her facial muscles tense. She felt as if the world beyond the town she left was already incomprehensible.

When he spoke again, there was a trace of kindness in Jeremy's rough tone. "Listen . . . you seem like wherever you came from, you've been lucky enough to be sheltered from what's been going on out here. But you'll be safer if you keep who you're looking for to yourself. And if that last name of yours isn't a fake, make one up. First lesson in not getting eaten alive."

She didn't understand why she had to conceal her own identity. Why would it even matter? But she couldn't ignore the urgency in his harsh whisper. "Sorry," she mumbled, at a loss. They both sat silently for a while before she braved speaking again. "So what about you? Why are you out here?"

He laughed a little. "All right, that's fair. Well, Kit sort of tells fortunes. We can make pretty good money in the summer doing that kind of thing, and I help her out, provide protection . . . But this time, when we got to Madeline, it was under attack. We ran into some trouble," he motioned to his bandaged arm and head wound with a grin, "but hopefully we'll have better luck in Torin. It's a ways east, but it's on our way home."

She watched Jeremy as he talked. He seemed completely relaxed, leaning casually against the tree behind him, one arm locked, his palm to the ground, while his other hand rested behind his head, his elbow jutting brazenly out of its bandage. His long legs were sprawled out before him, ending in heavy boots that dented the earth. He was clad entirely in black; the only exception the dirty, white dressings that covered his right arm from knuckles to shoulder. The shape of his legs were almost hidden by the wide cut of his heavy pants, weighed down with large side pockets, but his sleeveless shirt was like a thin undergarment, revealing his lean, powerful form. Emerging from his ragged and scorched clothing was his one bare arm, defined by hard lines and patterns of scars, and right above the edge of his collar she could make out the dark band of a tattoo.

Jeremy noted her glance, and with a swift movement that matched the tightening of his shoulders, he pulled his shirt up to cover the marking on his chest. Kayla quickly looked away, searching for something else to focus on. She saw Kittie sleeping close by on what appeared to be a protective overshirt, Jeremy's size. She was lying carelessly on her stomach, mouth open, her smooth and innocent face surrounded by cascades of warm brown hair. Kittie didn't look like she could be any older than eight. Could she really read fortunes? Was it okay for her to be with this guy? Jeremy looked to be roughly Kayla's age, but there was some frightening maturity about him. It suddenly occurred to her that his story about what happened in Madeline didn't completely match up with the snippets of conversation she overheard before she fell.

Lost in this thought, she glanced back at Jeremy, and saw him watching Kittie sleep. His face was very still, but his slight smile was kind. "You know," he said softly, almost to himself, "I think I feel more rested when she's the one that sleeps." He chuckled, his eyes half-closed. "Well, knowing Kit . . ." His voice rose, the harshness returning. "You aren't even asleep, are you? Stop spying on us. The sun's coming up; let's go."

The little girl smiled, her eyes still closed. "Nope, wide awake. Your fairytale nearly put me out, though." She lifted her head and grimaced at him.

Jeremy scowled, rising to his feet. "Get up. Now. We're going."

Before anyone could move, a shrill, male voice cried out from some outlying trees, *"Kaaaylaaa Steeeelryn!"*

Kayla's head whipped towards that strange voice calling her name. She saw two men running towards her with two more lagging behind. The man in the front yelled to the friend at his heels, the words forced out the side of his mouth that wasn't gripping a lit cigarette, "Th' girl with th' red hair! She look'd when we called 'er!"

"Fec, she's not alone . . . !" replied his blond companion, one eye covered with a patch, the other wide open and wild.

The men in the lead stopped short, while the other two slowly made their way closer. Jeremy lunged between them and Kayla, facing the strangers with a drawn sword. One edge of the double-sided weapon was viciously serrated, and although the blade looked polished with great care, it was weathered with scratches and nicks.

Jeremy's face was slightly down-turned, shrouded in the shadows cast by his dark, disheveled hair. His grin was wide and menacing. "No, she's not. You pirates are gonna have to earn it this time."

The blond man leaned towards his smoking comrade. "We really look like pirates . . . I mean, even away from the ship?" he muttered.

Fec sighed, not appearing to hear him, and pulled out his homemade smokes, carefully selecting one. "I hate earnin' it." His scrawny form stretched almost out of its slouch as he lit the fresh cigarette with the glowing tip of the one that jutted out from the corner of his mouth. Switching their places, he threw the used nub to the ground and snuffed it out beneath his sandal. Inhaling deeply, he glanced towards his companion before breathing out a seemingly endless stream of smoke.

The blond quickly pulled some gold and silver coins out from beneath his vest, and Kayla saw them dancing over his knuckles before the darkening cloud of smoke enveloped the pirates and Jeremy, and threatened to take her in as well. She stepped back slowly, covering her mouth and squinting into the thick haze, but the only signs of battle she could make out were a few curses and the violent ring of metal on metal. Each one of those sharp metallic sounds was followed by a shining disk spiraling awkwardly out the pirates' side of the cloud and dropping to the earth.

As the smoke cleared, the two pirates that hung back motionless throughout the encounter sprung to life, dashing into the deep brush and disappearing from sight. Fec glanced around, sweat beading on his pale face. His extinguished cigarette dropped from his lips and he called angrily out to his friends, racing to follow them.

The remaining pirate stared at Jeremy in disbelief, holding his bloodied right shoulder. "You deflected all of them . . . blind."

Jeremy had already lost interest. He was buckling his sword's scabbard across his chest and sheathing his weapon back over his shoulder. "Yeah. Good thing too. Looks uncomfortable," he said, nodding towards the blood that dripped through the pirate's fingers.

The blond followed his glance, and then looked up at Kayla with a furrowed brow. He leaned his head in Jeremy's direction. "It's really her, isn't it?"

"You don't even know what you're saying. Go back to your ship, pirate." Jeremy turned his back and began walking.

Kayla stared at them both, frozen in her confusion. She felt a small hand slip into hers, and she looked down to see Kittie's smile again. The little girl was weighed down with a pack half her size. "Let's follow. We're safe with him," Kittie said happily.

She looked away from the smaller girl to stare first at Jeremy's back and then into the pirate's blue eye. He looked pained and uncertain, almost ready to spring towards her. At that moment, Jeremy stopped walking, his stillness watchful. With a low, frustrated growl, the pirate retreated into the trees after his friends.

Kayla pulled Kittie along with her, rushing to Jeremy's side, struggling to keep his pace. "You knew what that guy was talking about, didn't you?"

He kept walking, staring straight ahead. "They knew your name. *You* explain that. You could at least thank me for saving you from pirates."

She swallowed the angry reply she had prepared. He was right. This might not be her ideal situation, but *pirates?* He did defend her against that strange attack, and now she was free to continue on her journey. "I'm . . . sorry," she said softly, "thank you."

Jeremy didn't reply. He kept striding quickly forward, his face remaining motionless except for a slight tightening of his jaw. They walked in silence for a long time, Kayla's steps determined and breath controlled, refusing to fall behind. Kittie trotted along on her short legs, somehow keeping up and not showing any signs of tiring. After a while, the little girl began to skip and hop happily between stretches of her rapid steps, singing softly to herself. Her joyful spirit seemed oblivious to the tension of her two companions, while their unease was amplified by the glaring contrast.

"Kit, would you just fucking stop!" Jeremy barked.

The violence in his tone made Kayla cringe, her steps

falling out of rhythm.

Kittie was unaffected. "What's bothering you?" she asked, genuine concern in her expression.

Jeremy kept walking, his teeth clenched. After a few more strides he came to a sudden halt, a fierce growl erupting from his momentary silence. His eyes were pale and wrathful as he turned abruptly to face Kayla. "You don't know why those pirates wanted you? You really don't know?"

Kayla became still, her gaze falling to the dirt and leaves at her feet, but she knew she couldn't escape him as she watched his dark, heavy boots approach, confronting her own worn shoes. "I don't. I don't know what my name means to them." She looked up to meet his stare, suddenly unafraid. "None of it makes sense to me. Forget those guys—nothing you've said, nothing you've done, adds up either. And that's fine. There's something out here that I'm looking for, and I'm going to find it."

His earlier fury disappeared as he watched her with quiet interest. "It's that important?" he asked coldly.

Last night he had asked her this same question before rescuing her locket from the bottom of the pit. Kayla reached for her necklace. The familiarity of the burnished wood was a comfort beneath her fingers. Her eyes met his again. "Yes. I have to do this, regardless of the consequences."

Jeremy's lips parted in a dark expression of amusement. "Well, as long as you're willing to face the fallout . . ." He turned his back and began walking again, his steps brisk, but this time, relaxed.

Kayla hurried to catch up, and then found herself easily traveling at his speed. She held on to her locket with a tenacious grip; it was her only connection to the answers she sought. This world outside had already proved to be a place of secrets and instability, not the clear blue realm of understanding she had hoped for. Kayla bit her lip against the memory of her brave declarations. She didn't know if she really believed her own words, but now there was no choice but to feign strength for as long as she could, especially while she was in range of his merciless eyes.

3

Jeremy couldn't remember the last time his heart beat with such anxious excitement. They had walked for days through swamps and trees, wandering from dirt roads, to the unstable remnants of asphalt trails, to ground where there were no paths at all to be found. Some places were pristine examples of nature, others full of pre-Eclipsian ruins, but as they traveled on there was hardly a sign of modern civilization. He knew they'd arrive at their destination tonight, and that knowledge was a burning pleasure in his chest. He leaned against the remains of a wood and wire fence, enjoying the morning air and the sound of Kit's gun going off in the distance.

He knew she was only hunting some small game, but he couldn't help but smile when he heard the loud bang, and not just because he was hungry. Jeremy had given her that handgun years ago, but he rarely saw her fire it except on occasions like this. She was a perfect shot.

"Squirrel?" he called out.

"Bunnnnny!"

Kittie emerged from the brush, holding a brown rabbit by its ears. "Never thought I'd find one out here. What a lucky sign! Maybe we'll even make it back today."

Kayla turned her head towards the girl. "You mean . . . to Torin."

"We were in Torin before Madeline, and now we're going back," Jeremy replied, silencing Kit with a glance. "I think you're setting some kind of record, Kayla. A few days out in the world, and you're already paranoid."

He watched Kayla's face tighten, her eyes coming alive with anger for just a moment, but she let the emotion diffuse out through her limbs as she stood, pacing softly. "Yeah . . . maybe. Would you guys just give me a few minutes?" she murmured, turning away, her steps taking her further from their circle.

Jeremy ignored Kittie's disapproving glare. "Where's she gonna go?" he mouthed.

"It's dangerous out there, Kayla," Kittie called to her. "I'm making breakfast, so Jeremy's gonna have to keep an eye on you. I promise he won't say a word or you have my permission to smack him."

Kayla turned back towards them, her brow furrowed, attempting to meet Kittie's eyes, but the little girl's head was bowed, her concentration now focused on dragging her knife along the rabbit's stomach. Kayla frowned, taking a deep breath before her attention shifted to Jeremy's face. He stared back for a moment, enjoying the way her tawny eyes veiled her fear, before he grinned, lightly pushing himself off the fence and motioning for her to lead the way. Kayla's wide gaze narrowed, tainting that vision of vulnerability, and he wondered if she somehow guessed his thoughts, just before she turned and began walking down the grassy path ahead.

Her stride was slow and without destination, so he only

had to take occasional steps to keep his distance behind her, existing only as a remote guardian. Jeremy regarded her cautious movements with mild curiosity. It was clear that she trusted neither him nor Kit, but she didn't run, which could only mean she was as alone and ignorant as she seemed. Kayla didn't talk much, but the only thing she appeared to know for sure is that she came from some nearby potter's village that he had never heard of. It was hard to accept that her story wasn't a put on, but all the physical evidence was there. Her sleeveless top revealed the muscles cradling her shoulder blades, and the tight curves that composed her bare arms. Her square hands were slightly chapped, and her fingers graceful when in action. Kayla's body carried all these marks of a skilled worker, but what was unusual was the softness of her face and her unmarred skin, all suspiciously innocent.

He watched as she eyed the remains of some downed power lines. It didn't make sense, but it had to be true . . . somehow she was completely untouched by the Eclipse. For an instant, his head swam with the hot breath of his resentment, but his ire cooled rapidly with the knowledge that the world was rushing in fast to meet her. She wouldn't ask him her questions and he wouldn't offer any answers. He'd give her the gift of these last few hours of blindness.

Kayla turned around suddenly, and catching his slight smile, crossed her arms protectively in front of her. "What?" she snapped nervously.

He liked the futility of that gesture. "I was just thinking that you're handling this well," he replied, moving a little closer.

"What . . . ?" She squeezed her arms together tighter, but that only accentuated the fullness of her chest.

"You might be afraid, but you're not letting it stop you."

Her eyes flashed again with a momentary glimmer of

fury, soon quenched by caution. "You say that like it might not be the right thing to do."

Jeremy kept walking forward. "The 'right thing' is never a good motivation anyways." He stopped, just a few feet away from her.

Kayla looked up at him. "You never approved of my reason for being out here."

"What do I know?"

"More than you'll ever tell me."

Jeremy stepped even closer to her, drawing one of his small knives. Kayla stiffened, holding her breath, and he smirked in enjoyment of this unexpected diversion. He turned the knife around, holding it by the blade, and poked the bony hilt in her pocket with the handle of his weapon. "That makes two of us."

She lowered her head, grasping her strange possession through the outside of her clothes. Jeremy laughed a little, backing off and turning away, his interest waning as quickly as it had arisen. "Don't worry, we'll reach our destination tonight. You only have to trust me for a few more hours."

His slow retreat hadn't put much distance between them before he heard her call out, "Is this what you wanted to see?"

He turned around to find her, face pinched and arm outstretched, with a twisted mass of bone in her fist. His curiosity renewed, he came closer, stopping when his fingers almost touched the strange object in her hands. Remembering the shock of pain he experienced last time he came into contact with it, he grabbed her wrist instead, pulling the girl and the thing she held closer. As the hilt was brought close to his face for inspection, they both felt it tremble for an instant before it engaged. A curved, ivory blade cut into the air, covered Kayla's knuckles, and sliced the side of Jeremy's wrist, barely missing his cheek. His fingers twitched, but he didn't release her arm. Kayla's face was hard now, but he had already seen her surprise. "Do you think it's wise to wield a weapon you can't control?"

"My position is no more foolish than yours." She faced him with steady eyes, but he could feel the pulse racing in her wrist.

Jeremy wondered how this potter from some ridiculously peaceful land came into possession of this kind of relic. It didn't matter. She wouldn't hold on to it for much longer. He let her go. As Kayla slowly pulled her hand back, the blade completely retracted; it was just an unusual bone again.

Staring at the blood dripping down his arm, she put the hilt back in her pocket. "I'm sorry."

He shrugged. "I asked for it." He held the wound with his other hand, and began walking back towards camp.

She rushed to catch up with him. "I know it's just one more day, but I . . . shouldn't . . . trust you, should I?" she asked softly.

Jeremy looked down at her. Already, understanding was muddying the clear pools he glimpsed beneath her citrine stare. His throat felt tight, but the necessary words came out anyways. "Kayla, either way . . . we both know you're not leaving."

She nodded. Nothing more needed to be said. They walked back, their eyes trained ahead, and their silence, for once, comfortable.

The sun would be setting soon, they still weren't in Torin, and Kayla was tired of walking. She tried to show no signs of fatigue, but her facial muscles refused to relax, clenching her features into a pained expression. They were walking on the shore of what was once a lake or an ocean . . . she couldn't be sure which. It was dried up, for as far as she could see, and all that was left was sand, trash, and bones. She kept her feet on the shore; to go any further felt like walking on a grave. On the opposite side there was dense foliage, bushes with heavy, sharp leaves, and trees that dropped dark, spiny seeds. Was there a way through that led to the town? After a while, she noticed that Jeremy and Kittie were looking around like they were expecting a signal or landmark, and she hoped that meant they were close to their destination.

"We're here, Jeremy," Kittie piped out suddenly.

Kayla turned her head from side to side; nothing was different. She looked to Jeremy questioningly.

His irritation had been steadily growing in the past few hours, and it escaped now as a tiny explosion. "Well, goddammit, call our ride then, Kit!"

As usual, Kittie was unaffected by his choler. "Okay!" She ran out beyond the border of trees, her large pack bouncing.

Jeremy didn't watch her go. He was staring into the setting sun, on the horizon of the empty sea.

"What now?" Kayla asked softly.

He seemed to have relaxed. When he turned his head back to her, the tense lines were gone. "We wai—" His eyes shifted, looking past her, wrath beginning in his stare and quickly distorting his features. In an instant, his sword was drawn from over his shoulder and brought down in a slashing arc just inches from her right side.

Kayla caught her breath, stiffening. Holding her body still, her eyes followed Jeremy as he swung his sword again, this time to her left, connecting with the two smaller blades of his adversary. Their attacker wore a poncho, loose and tattered pants, and his arms and lower legs were wrapped in strips of cloth, all in various shades of brown and tan. Only his eyes could be seen; he was covered by a long wrap that coiled loosely around his head and neck, ending in a heavy drape between his shoulders. The hair that poked through the cowl as dust-stiffened locks in his face and a long ponytail behind were the same color as his fierce eyes: a weathered brown that was tempered by the desert's sun and sand-strewn winds.

Jeremy pressed the stranger back and Kayla was able to scramble a safe distance away. Out of immediate danger, she quickly noticed the newcomer's manner was vicious, but oddly calm, making Jeremy's rabid approach to battle seem almost sloppy. Each of Jeremy's strikes looked as if they would land, but somehow the man was evading them, usually skewing the attacks to one side or another, leaving Jeremy in a vulnerable position, if only for an instant before he righted himself. She watched tensely, fearing this vagabond that appeared out of nowhere, this stranger who possessed the ability to sneak so close to her before either one of them noticed. What would have happened to her if Jeremy hadn't turned and saw him at that moment?

She heard a gunshot behind her. Whirling around, she saw Kittie running in her direction, her upper body twisted to the side, her weapon trained on the pirates they encountered a few days ago. "Jeremy, it's on its way!" she cried out as she reached Kayla.

The sudden appearance of the pirates was less frightening. They stayed a few yards away under threat of Kittie's weapon, their nervous eyes rarely leaving the hooded man. Still, if Jeremy was defeated, there would only be Kittie's gun to protect them from five strange men. Kayla grabbed the hilt in her pocket, her heart in her throat. Pulling it out, she stared at it, all of her will focused on that bony blade releasing again. Nothing happened. She looked around, searching for a savior from any direction. Emerging from the gathering darkness, she saw a cloud of dust rapidly approaching from the horizon, swirling around two beams of light.

Turning back to the fight, she noticed Jeremy's limbs seemed heavier, his movements slower, but his menacing battle grin was still in place. The man in brown blocked an overhead attack with his blades, angling the sword to the side. Jeremy leaned into the new slant, his knee and elbow continuing the arc and striking his opponent, knocking him to the ground. As his sword came down to complete the movement, the stranger changed direction again, slicing Jeremy's leg with his first kukri, quickly followed by the next curved blade finding his side and arm. Jeremy let out a savage growl, and turning back to his adversary, swung his sword in an upward angle with such speed and force that his opponent couldn't completely skirt the attack. The masked man was wounded on the shoulder, the blade catching his head wrap. He pulled back on the cloth, and used his lowered position to strike Jeremy's injured leg and bring him down as well.

"No!" Kayla's hot blood coursed through her as she ran blindly forward, unsure if she wanted to attack this desert nomad, pull Jeremy out of the way, or test her luck as a buffer. As she approached the fray, the hilt she held vibrated intensely, and as she fell to her knees, the bone in her hands spewed up like a fountain, forming a shield above both her and Jeremy. Something struck their defense and she cried out, falling forward but not letting go. She could hear a pirate yell, "C'mon, get her now! It's almost too late!" as the masked man growled at them, "Stay out of this fight!" and Kittie's gun fired again. She felt Jeremy's arm around her waist before she caught a glimpse of his eyes, strangely soft beneath his tight brow. That vague expression vanished as he turned his head away from her with a snarl and pressed up to run, limping, towards a mechanical sound that was suddenly so close.

He dropped her into the back of a dust-caked metal wagon, and called out to Kittie. She followed, both of them jumping into the remaining seats. The noisy machine had no roof, and all she could tell about the driver was that he was dressed much like Jeremy, but with a mop of blond hair, huge goggles, and fingerless gloves. Kayla looked back at her attackers, bathed in the lights of the vehicle. The stranger's head wrap had come completely unraveled and fell to the ground. Before she could move, Jeremy leaned back over the seat to restrain her, and as the truck carried her away, all she could do was cry out Asher's name.

4

Kayla kept her hands over her nose and mouth, and most of the time, her head down. She was wind-whipped, her face stung by sand, and even all her tears were not enough to wash the dust from her cheeks. The landscape was dark and bare around her, and once in a while she peeked out at her surroundings, but avoided looking at anyone else in the vehicle. Her teeth clenched angrily, unable to escape Kittie's sad and concerned gaze as the little girl sat beside her. *What right does she have to look at me that way?* she thought, *She's just as bad as . . . him.* Kayla's shoulders heaved with a painful wave of silent weeping. She had tried to explain, begging for them to please let her stay with Asher—that's who she'd been looking for—but Jeremy had just held her down, his face blank, as if he couldn't hear. She shut her eyes, huddling into herself, avoiding the unbearable sight of the back of his head in front of her.

With her lids closed, she could allow the memory of Asher's face to become clearer than her current reality.

Much time had passed since the picture in her locket was taken, and she could see the weight of the years in his features, but it was unmistakably him; she didn't need two glances to know for sure. His eyes were narrower, sharper, and there were new lines in his face, but none of these changes, not even his beard, could hide that he was Asher Serafin, the one she had longed to see, and was again torn from. If only she had known it was him, just a few moments earlier, she never would have protected Jeremy. She had to hope that somehow, he would come for her again. Pressing her despair down to a darker place, Kayla tried to hold on to what just earlier in the day had terrified her . . . it seemed that Asher could defeat Jeremy.

The truck began a sharp descent, dropping Kayla's stomach lower and causing her to look up quickly. She saw before her a huge compound of buildings. There was the skeleton of a tower strewn with lights, shorter and broader buildings with more nondescript walls, and lattices of metal poles climbing in all directions. Dust of the dried-up seabed collected in dunes around the stronghold, and bright lanterns shone like low-hanging stars at the highest point of each grouping of buildings. The rare beauty of this place couldn't smother the dread gathering in her chest as she sped closer to its gates.

Kayla was moved by an inexplicable desire to close her eyes and feign sleep. It seemed like a silly plan, almost as futile as playing dead in such a situation, but still she let her eyelids droop and somehow found it within her to relax her grief-racked muscles. After some time, she felt the vehicle stop and heard the driver's door open.

Kittie's voice followed. "She's asleep. I tried to wake her, but I think she's experiencing some shock. That's understandable. So everything else can wait, at least for the night. I don't think Lord Za'in would mind her staying with me until then." She sounded matter-of-fact and careless, like someone accustomed to being humored.

"Hey, I'm just the wheels. He's waiting for your report," the driver replied before departing.

She could feel Kittie's breath on her ear. "I'm sorry. But don't open your eyes now just to spite us, okay? There are worse people than us in this place, so keep up your fainting spell!" There was a new sense of urgency in the child's voice.

Kayla's jaw clenched. She didn't want to do anything either one of them suggested, but Kittie was right. As untrustworthy as the pair proved to be, she doubted they had brought her to a place where there was a better alternative. She tried to relax again, letting necessity rule her.

She heard Jeremy's sigh become a quiet groan before she felt herself being lifted into his arms. Kayla stifled a sharp intake of breath, her limbs rigid, rejecting his touch. With Kittie's words in mind, she swallowed the bitter lump of anger in her throat and breathed her muscles limp, but the hilt in her pocket was still restless and pulsating. She detected a twinge of tension in Jeremy's body as he noticed her weapon's agitation. Kayla searched for a deeper level of peace, focusing on softening her skin, hoping it would soothe the strange object she carried. She sensed it begin to settle, but its watchfulness remained.

Jeremy walked stiffly, but something about his move-ments made her feel as though his wounds weren't what disturbed his normally relaxed gait. She could hear Kittie's usual scampering by his side, but even her steps seemed heavier. Jeremy took a deep breath, and then stopped a moment to angle Kayla towards his torso, folding her arms to her chest and hiding the side of her face with her hair. His quiet voice sounded as if he barely moved his lips. "Stay turned against me. No one needs to get a good look at you."

She was thankful for the freedom to tighten her face in confusion. Would anything ever make sense again? A few frustrated tears escaped her closed lids as she let her cheek rest heavily against Jeremy's chest, breathing in the scent of blood, salt, and sand.

Kayla was carried through winding corridors and darkness, through places where she could see bright spots through her eyelids, and for brief stretches, smell the night air. Often she knew the three of them were alone, but there were also times she could hear the sound of men whispering. She caught only pieces of their surprised murmurings: "the Second Arch is back!" "Saros . . . ?"

No one approached them or addressed them directly. They paused as a door opened, and Jeremy let out a measured sigh, his clenched muscles loosening. They only moved a few steps forward before she heard the door close behind them and she was gently released from his arms, onto a firm bed. Opening her eyes, she saw Jeremy standing over her. In the dim light, his face was divided in deep shadow and his blue irises were shrouded by a cloudy, gray screen. He turned to Kittie. "I gotta go make my report to Za'in. You don't have to go, Kit. I'll sort it all out."

Kittie was staring off, her head turned. "Go," she said softly, "but come back right after. I think it'll take me to convince him to leave her alone tonight."

"I don't know how I let a Malak push me around." He let out a half-hearted chuckle before he left, closing the door quietly behind him.

The little girl remained still, and in the silence that followed, Kayla sat up and looked around the small room. The walls were pale, rough and unfinished. The door was simply fashioned from a dull metal, and the only window was a tall, narrow slit in the wall. There was no evidence that the room belonged to Kittie, or to anyone else for that matter; the place was devoid of any decoration or keepsake, housing only a cot, chair, and hanging light bulb.

Kayla refused to meet Kittie's gaze as she turned around and moved slowly to sit beside her on the bed. "I'm sorry things are this way," the small girl said softly.

Kayla clenched her fists. "Things aren't just 'this way!' You both lied to me . . . kidnapped me! You both knew what you were doing. And I . . . I know this place is . . . evil." She stopped. She didn't mean to say that last part. She didn't know why, but it frightened her to speak it out loud.

"Kayla, don't you know the whole world is in trouble? Don't you know that we all just do what we can to get by? It's not so easy to just go out there alone. Jeremy is my Arch. I had to follow . . ."

"Your . . . Arch?"

A genuine smile returned to Kittie's face, and it was strangely comforting to see it again. "Yeah! In the Second Sphere, he's the head guy! Sure, Za'in is our lord, but I'm in Jeremy's company and get to follow him everywhere." She stopped for a second, her mouth becoming small when she noticed Kayla's confusion. "Okay. So Za'in runs the show. He has us all organized into Three Spheres, with an Arch leading each one. Below the Arch is an Ophan, and then the rest are like me—just another soldier, a Malak. I know, it sounds weird, but Za'in sort of wanted his own twist on Angelic Hierarchy . . . he's obsessed with that stuff."

Kayla's brows drew close together. She had heard of Angels before, but these terms weren't familiar. "But . . . what is he organizing?"

"The world." Kittie didn't sound convinced. "He has plans. And you're a part of that. He's been looking for you."

"Why?"

"You may possess a . . . spiritual power . . . that he desires."

Kayla just stared at her. Beneath her feelings of helplessness, she knew there was at least some power in that strange bone in her pocket, but she kept silent.

Kittie's eyes were pleading, and her voice dropped to a whisper. "I'm sorry you got brought into this. I just wanted to stay with Jeremy and do what he wanted. That's how it's been for so long. Just, until it can be set right, don't give in to Za'in, okay? I'll set things right."

Kayla dropped down heavily onto her stomach, her face buried in the pillow. She was so confused. What could she trust? She just wanted to sleep, in the hopeless fantasy that everything would be different in the morning. She was done running from exhaustion, and let it take her.

She was only allowed a brief release. A new presence in the room disturbed her sleep, causing her to roll over quickly. Jeremy was sitting on the floor, wearily leaning against the wall. She noticed he hadn't washed or changed his clothes, his wounds still in the haphazard dressings he applied during the ride to this stronghold.

"You can go back to sleep," he murmured, his head tilted back, eyes closed. "Right now, Kit is ensuring your opportunity to do that. Don't worry, she'll be back soon, and I'll be gone when you wake up."

Kayla didn't move. "You knew that was Asher Serafin on the shore today. You fought him to keep us apart."

Jeremy's eyelids parted slightly. "I wasn't completely sure it was him."

Her hands balled into fists beneath the pillow. She didn't want to argue about what he did, she just wanted to know why. "So what happens to me now?"

He was silent.

"Za'in . . ." she said slowly, "he's going to hurt me, isn't he?"

Jeremy lifted his head and looked at her. "Just do what

33

he wants."

She remembered that Kittie just gave her opposite advice. "And what does he want with me?"

"What does he want with any of us? We might never really figure it out. And, anyways, it's what you asked for. You said you could take it."

Kayla quickly rolled onto her back and turned her head so he couldn't see her eyes. "You're not the only one who can lie." She swallowed a few times before speaking again. "So how do Angels fit into all this?"

"It's just a metaphor meant to intimidate. Divine order and assured punishment to those that oppose it. Pretty effective psychological warfare, right?"

"But could it be real? Kittie said something about 'spiritual power.' I think he wants that bone I carry."

Jeremy laughed. "Oh, you're one of the Nephilim now, huh?"

Kayla's throat tightened and she sat up suddenly. "Stop saying things that don't make sense!" she cried, her voice hoarse. "I can't stand it! Maybe I am whatever you just said—that's why he sent you to capture me, and now he's gonna kill me—"

"Hey!" He sprung up from the floor, landing on the cot, kneeling in front of her, one hand covering her mouth and the other cupping the back of her head. "He's not going to kill you. But you can't get hysterical." Jeremy's features softened a bit. "If you keep quiet, I'll tell you about some of that stuff, okay?"

She nodded, sprinkling his hand with tears before he slowly released her. He unwound his legs and lay down on his back, his eyes motioning for her to do the same. Kayla frowned, hesitating, before slowly moving to rest beside him. Jeremy watched her carefully for a moment before folding his hands behind his head, his eyes to the ceiling.

"When you hear 'Angels,' it sounds beautiful, right?" he whispered, "but even our legends leave no room for redemption. They say that in ancient times, there was a Heaven above us. There was a God who answered prayers, and Angels who carried blessings to the deserving. But some Angels lost their Grace and fell to earth, unable to return. Some of the Fallen bred with humans and joined their race, but there were others that focused only on discovering a way into Heaven again. They found no forgiveness, so these Angels tried to attack Heaven, to force their way back in, and there was a great battle. Many Angels died, and Heaven fell forever. The remaining Angels fought among themselves on Earth, destroying each other, including those that lived with humans. Maybe none survived. The destruction that this wreaked on Earth angered and frightened the humans of the time. They blamed the Angels for their troubles, so they began to hunt their hybrid offspring, the Nephilim, despite the power of these magical creatures. It was said that even their bones were holy weapons, so a slain Nephil was some trophy. Anyways, they're all gone now, if they were ever even here to begin with. All that's left is the mythology." He paused, as if at the end of a long memorized and repeated recitation. "Most people know this story. Just as a story . . . but they've heard it before. I don't know how you haven't. I don't think Za'in believes it, but he's using it. The world has fallen apart while you've slept in peace. He has power, whether it's ancient or not, divine or otherwise, and he's reshaping this Earth we've been abandoned in." He exhaled, his voice lowering, as if she was no longer there. "Who knows what his creation will be like, but either way, this time I'll be above . . ."

"But . . . this has nothing to do with me."

His head turned towards her voice, his eyes slowly

clearing as he looked at her. "You don't know that. If he wants you, there's a reason." Jeremy's gaze drifted to the little box hanging from her neck. As he reached for it, she grasped the wooden pendant tightly, but didn't pull away. He seized her hand as if it was the locket itself, and tugged gently. "You know from this that your father's name meant something. That's your name too."

A little sob escaped her throat. It wasn't just the mention of her father that caused her tears to flow again, but the confirmation that he had stolen a look into her heart's treasure. This was yet another violation of trust that bound them closer . . . was that how things worked out here? She wearily dropped her eyes and hand.

Jeremy kept his hold on her, drawing nearer. "Kayla, remember when I told you not to be moved by what's right? It's a stupid way to live. Your survival is up to you. Find out why you're valuable to him and use it. One way I kept my existence going was to bring you here, and there's nothing to blame but the world for being the way it is. You're not the only one paying for original sin—I was born on the day of the Eclipse. Don't ask me to explain that. I only said it because it means nothing to you . . ."

His voice was coarse and bitter, but his touch was soft; it was the first time their contact didn't cause the hilt in her pocket to move. Kayla couldn't forget all he had done, but she still found herself pressing closer to him, finding solace in the presence of his wounds, longing to hide in his darkness. She felt his body respond, warm and enveloping, as he angled her face to his, and she opened her eyes to meet his heavy-lidded gaze. Jeremy's arms gripped her, hard. She remembered him holding her down, as they left Asher far behind in a cloud of sand.

"No!" She shuddered, pulling away.

He immediately released her, jarred by her sudden cry. It

took Jeremy only a moment to recover, getting up and looking down at her with his usual cool glance. The door opened and Kittie entered the room, watching curiously as he made an abrupt exit. Before he closed the door behind him, he turned his head slightly and spoke, his voice low. "Remember what I said about survival. But first you have to know what you want."

When Kayla knew he was gone she felt free to move again, curling into a tight ball in an attempt to relieve the pressure in her chest. Soon the room was dark and Kittie crawled into bed beside her. Although there was a comfort to the girl's presence as they lay back to back, Kayla was even more thankful for her silence.

5

Kayla woke before dawn when Kittie was summoned on some official business. The girl assured her that she would be back soon, but when she returned, it would be Kayla's time to meet with Za'in. Kayla watched the sun rise through the narrow window, her stomach tying new knots with every brighter shade of light. She sat up on the bed and began to smooth her hair, lazily gathering it back into one long braid, the familiar activity soothing her nervousness. Her focus now redirected, she looked down at the grimy rags she wore and sighed with regret. The impulsive start of her journey left her with nothing to call her own but these torn, linen work clothes, smeared with dirt and even a little of Jeremy's blood. Kayla's hands dropped into her lap. There was nothing more to distract her from the sick feeling rising up inside as she stared at the empty wall and breathed deeply against her ribs.

She started when she heard a quick rap on the door, moments before it cracked open, but it wasn't Kittie who greeted her. Jeremy hovered right behind the gap, silent, his face closed. Kayla felt a sudden pang of concern for the girl, but her tight throat didn't allow her to voice her question, so she simply rose and followed him. They walked together through bare, dark halls, but he didn't look at her and he stepped as though he didn't care if she kept pace. Kayla set her jaw tight, her fear of Za'in disappearing beneath her embarrassment, as she wondered if what she felt last night was imagined.

They came to a stop before a set of double doors, each one similar to the unadorned entrance to Kittie's room. Jeremy knocked, announcing, "Lord Za'in, Second Arch Saros reporting!"

A few moments later the doors opened and they entered a large, austere room, her feet moving carefully over the smooth floor, as not to scuff the shining wood panels. One wall was a grid of broad window panes, revealing a view of the metal-tangled tower, its lights sleeping in the daylight, as well as some large and idle industrial machinery and more sand. A man stood gazing out the window, and hearing their approach, he turned to them, smiling. He possessed the kind of sophistication that only came with the passage of years, but it was hard to place the age of his youthful face. He wore long, loose clothing, and his hair was short, thick and dark. His eyes were strikingly black, the irises barely a shade lighter than his pupils. "Thank you, Saros," he said.

Jeremy bowed his head a little, then turned halfway toward Kayla, but walked out silently before he met her eyes.

The man extended his hand toward her, his smile gentle. "I'm sorry to hear your journey was so perilous. I would have sent a truck sooner, but I haven't quite perfected my communication system when it comes to Saros. He's a strange case." He laughed, shaking her limp hand. "Sebastian Za'in. I've been very eager to meet you, Kayla

Steelryn."

Kayla couldn't manage a quick reply. Could this be the man both Kittie and Jeremy had spoken of in tense whispers? She was struck by the kindness in his face. "I— I'm not sure why I'm here, Lord Za'in."

He laughed again, waving his hand dismissively. "Please, call me Sebastian. I can't avoid formality if I'm trying to keep my little multitude here unified . . . but it's good for someone to call you by name. I'd be grateful if you humored me." There was a warm modesty to his countenance as he waited for her little nod before continuing. "Why don't we both have a seat and talk a bit? Perhaps the floor isn't the most comfortable spot for this, but there is something beautiful about the light in this room." He moved to the opposite wall, his motions fluid, and sat down on the floor facing the window, with Kayla trailing closely behind.

"Kayla," he continued, "you are here because I've been searching for you, and you happened to run into one of my more . . . zealous Archs. His behavior was unnecessarily dramatic and I don't blame you for feeling like a captive. Still, Saros told me that you came from a place that was very remote—luckily sheltered from what has been happening on this Earth—so allow me to shed some light on the reasons behind his misdirected urgency. Kayla Steelryn, to most people your name is common knowledge. You see, your father was a people's hero, a freedom fighter. 'Steelryn and Serafin' was once synonymous with hope for a better future. Yes, Michael was working towards something not so unlike my goals, although our methods differed. He was so much further developed than most people, although we could never see eye to eye . . ."

"You knew him!"

Sebastian smiled, his eyes closing for a moment. "Yes, I

knew him for some time. He was my student . . . and, for a period, my most trusted and capable Arch."

Kayla watched him carefully. How old was this man that claimed to be her father's teacher? It seemed impossible, but she couldn't deny the simple honesty in his voice. This was the first link to her father in so long. "What . . . did he study with you?"

His features were infused with new life. "It was more than just researching subjects . . . it was carving a path, and walking it. He first sought me out so that I could train him to master his Intercessor—" He paused. "Ah yes. I heard you have discovered yours as well. Can you control it?" His eyes flickered to the pocket that held her strange weapon.

Her mouth opened soundlessly before she shook her head.

"He couldn't either. Not then. Wielding such a unique instrument is not just a matter of strength and will. All aspects of the self must be honed. Michael was a dedicated student and soon found the means to express his true nature. But, Kayla, when I thought of you, alone in the world, without your father's guidance . . . I wanted to have you here as my guest. Still, how you came to be here is regrettable, and I understand if you would prefer an escort back home."

She felt an inexplicable pang of guilt. "No! I mean, it's just that I wanted to meet Asher Serafin. He found me on my way here, but then Jeremy . . . separated us."

Sebastian nodded thoughtfully. "They fought?"

"Yes."

"Asher was Michael's first student, although this was after Michael left my Spheres." He noticed Kayla's furrowed brow. "It was time your father found his independence. But Asher . . . he idolized his teacher to a fault. He has been unable to move beyond Michael's unfortunate passing, still carrying what he thinks was their crusade, rather than finding his own way. I can't imagine him coming here peacefully, but . . ." His dark eyes moved with thought, that candid grin lighting his features again. "I'll send him an invitation to meet with you. I'm sure he will accept, and if anything can prevent future violence between us, it's your disarming presence."

Kayla held her breath. She feared this was some trick, but Sebastian's face was so open, unhindered by the small, sudden changes she observed in those that had to cover and recover their tracks. "Thank you . . . but it seems like a lot of trouble just for me."

His pleasant laugh rang out. "You've caught me! Of course I have my own selfish motivations, but please allow me to explain. Kayla, you possess an Intercessor. Right now you cannot imagine how rare and precious this is. I am willing to train you in the mastery of your weapon, and eventually, open to you the opportunity to enter my Spheres, if it is your desire. It is easy for me to see that your potential is vast, but you are undeveloped. With this arrangement, we can aid each other. Ultimately, my purpose is to restore the world. Many things have contributed to its downfall, but there has been nothing as destructive as this planet's inhabitants shirking the responsibility that comes with the gift of existence: cultivation. They rejected opportunities for personal growth, and this vacuum of spiritual energy led to the decline of society and the environment. Human beings have made this world a prison, but we must not resign ourselves to this fate. The power to heal something as grand as the entire Earth begins and ends with us, and in us. So often we feel that large problems are out of our hands, but I don't see it that way. When we develop ourselves, the world benefits and this allows us to grow even further." Sebastian paused. "We can start your training tomorrow. Here. You know already if you have what it takes to embrace your destiny." Again, he was looking at the pocket that held her Intercessor.

Kayla hesitated for a moment, overwhelmed by the intensity of this vague and serious offer. She thought of her father, of Asher's return . . . and of how, without control, she both wounded and protected Jeremy with her weapon. "Please teach me." Her reply reached her ears before she realized she had made a sound.

Sebastian's eager smile eased the burden of the decision. He stood quickly, pulling her up with him. "Keep this between us. Saros and his Malak don't need to know; I don't offer this to just anyone." His gaze was solemn.

"Yes, Sebastian," she said quietly. Her heart was still beating fast, but no longer from apprehension.

He led her back the way she came, but before they reached the door, he stopped. "One quick lesson before tomorrow . . . why wait?" The corners of his mouth were still upturned, but something was different about his manner. "Draw your weapon."

She felt reluctant to bring it out into the open. Her gaze fell nervously to her feet as she fumbled with the strange object, but when she looked up again to present her Intercessor, she gasped at the mass of twisted bone that gathered around Sebastian's hand. Kayla thought he might also possess this type of weapon, but this was not what she expected. Her hilt was small, and the shape seemed natural, as if it came from the skeleton of some exotic animal. In contrast, Sebastian's looked like a bone that was set haphazardly after a fracture, covered in spurs, and grafted to other similar bones. It was a monstrosity.

He responded to her stare. "If you want to understand and master your Intercessor, you must have true knowledge of yourself. Nothing can be ignored or glossed over just because you don't like what you see."

Kayla nodded. She felt certain that he wasn't going to hurt her now, but she was suddenly afraid.

Sebastian noticeably relaxed, and it was then that she recognized his earlier tension. "Even in an uncontrolled state, your Intercessor is a part of you and may respond in situations when you need protection. When you learn to creatively channel this energy, it can be expressed as an extra surge of power in desperate moments. But now, while you have not yet mastered it, you may call upon its strength to preserve your life." He closed his eyes and drew a deep breath.

Kayla stifled a cry as she felt his body expand, radiating a heat that reached out for her. The room now seemed small and constricting, stuffed with warm air that clung to her skin. Sebastian's Intercessor vibrated before it expelled a stream of more twisted bones, fusing with each other to form a giant, brutal sword. She realized what had changed about his easy grin—this expression relished its own wickedness.

"So do you have it in you?" he murmured, "or if you can't use your weapon, should I just take it from you instead?" He moved in closer, his shadow falling over her.

She held her hilt with both hands, willing it to become a blade, a shield, anything that could protect her. Nothing happened. She thought of Asher, even of Jeremy, but knew she was alone. Kayla couldn't breathe as she watched Za'in's sword descend. She let out a strangled cry, skidding to her knees out of the path of his blade as her Intercessor engaged, shooting out a shower of bone shards, shattering the end of his weapon. Kayla closed her eyes, turning her head to avoid the shrapnel.

After a few quiet moments, the girl knew the violence had passed and she looked down at the hilt still held tight in her grip. It rattled between her trembling hands. Her palms and fingers were pleasantly warm, weak with some unfamiliar, blissful ache. This feeling smoothed away her earlier fear, her ragged breaths now hot with victory. She looked up at Za'in, his weapon now hidden away and his eyes watching her with smiling surprise.

"That was inventive. But let's leave something for tomorrow." He gently took her hand and eased her to her feet before ushering her out the door.

Kayla turned back, looking at the fragments of bone on the floor. "I'm sorry . . . I didn't mean to break it."

"My sweet girl, that would be impossible." Sebastian's hand rested heavily on her shoulder.

She stepped through the doorway, but immediately spun around to see her teacher's satisfied features one more time, her body tired but surprisingly light.

"Saros' Malak will be occupied for a while. I hope you will be comfortable in her room during her absence. I won't burden you any longer with an escort unless you desire one."

Kayla shook her head numbly. "I can find my way back." She managed a weak smile.

His face was lit with the excitement she felt growing within her stomach. "I'm looking forward to tomorrow already, Kayla."

She nodded a wordless goodbye before the door closed. As she walked alone down the hallway, she tried to ignore the regret that their meeting was so brief.

6

Jeremy stepped stiffly through the halls, his scowl spreading across his entire body. He knew where he'd end up again today. It was Za'in's fault for keeping him here without another assignment and separating him from Kit for too many days. He was bored, focusing on meaningless things, and all this walking wasn't helping. That same set of double doors kept appearing at the corners of his vision and he realized that he wasn't wandering, but pacing. With a growl, he changed direction, soon finding an exit that led outside.

Not today . . . he wasn't gonna do it today. He kicked through the sand as he tread a path around the exterior of the building, regretting everything about the last week. It started the morning he brought the Steelryn girl to Za'in, like he was supposed to. He was an Arch and it was his victory. That should have been the end of it. Za'in had a lot of useless curiosities and collected plenty of worthless things; she was no different. Sure, she was famous, there was a novelty to that, but after he delivered her he began to wonder what Za'in had planned for this particular bit of plunder. Jeremy recognized the rewards that came with his find, but didn't he deserve to see what was so special about this girl? He didn't like the feeling of being dismissed.

There he stood that morning, his back to the wrong side of the door, warring with his curiosity, pride, and little bursts of apathy. After a long stretch of stillness, he moved forward, finally deciding it would be some kind of vague failure on his part if he turned back and pressed his ear to the wall. It was then Jeremy heard Za'in's laugh. He froze. The sound was muffled, but it was undeniably . . . affectionate. What was going on in there? He told himself that was enough reason to investigate this meeting as he quietly made his way back to the doors.

Leaning into the wall, he listened carefully, holding his breath. Za'in was going on about something, but he couldn't make out the content of their conversation; it just continued at length with no change in intensity. Jeremy let out a heavy sigh, closing his eyes. He got worked up over nothing. He slid down the wall, sitting on the cold floor and lazily keeping his ear to the crack in the door frame.

The voices came closer and he rose up on one knee, ready to retreat. He was sure he heard the word "weapon," and his face tightened as he strained to grasp the meaning of their exchange. Suddenly Kayla cried out, either in pain or fear, followed by the sound of a rapid series of sharp crashes, and Jeremy was on his feet, his daggers drawn, before he acknowledged his own actions. He caught his breath, looking down at the knives in his hands, and silently cursed his stupidity. What was he gonna do? Kick down the door and save the lamb he brought to slaughter? No, he'd only end up being the one butchered. He worked too hard and struggled too long to jeopardize his position.

The doors parted and he flattened against the wall

behind them as Kayla and Za'in exchanged pleasant goodbyes. Jeremy's agitated awareness barely caught the two significant portions of their farewells—Kit wasn't coming back any time soon, and Kayla would return here tomorrow. His body remained rigid and motionless as the doors closed and he watched her walk slowly down the hall, her form relaxed and her skin lightly glistening with sweat. She disappeared around the corner and he sheathed his knives. For a moment he considered following, to coax and threaten the answers from her, but after what happened last night it was probably better to stay away. He said too much then, and what's worse, he didn't know why. At any rate, it ended with her acting like she'd been attacked, even though just moments before her protest, she was yielding to his touch, drawing closer to him with her eyes closed and lips parting . . .

Jeremy shook his head, attempting to clear it from last week's memories, as he stood beneath the sun, his boots buried in sand. That was how it started. He had returned the next morning, quickly realizing the ear-to-the-door technique would provide no answers. On the third day, he woke before dawn and walked out into the yard, regarding the braided tracks of metal above his head that connected various parts of the compound. Without another thought, Jeremy began to climb a latticed column, his long limbs quickly bringing him to the top. He followed the beam as it bent at a right angle, forming a bridge to a huge pipe. He straddled the cylinder, sliding across its surface until he reached another rail, and then he carefully balanced his boots over its narrow width before stepping foot over foot along the gradual ascent. Jeremy leaned forward to keep his equilibrium, his eyes trained on the broad, flat surface where he would soon be landing.

Once he was safely on the roof, he lowered to his belly

and inched over the edge to see a thin row of windows, tucked right beneath the overhang. They were shuttered, but it didn't take Jeremy long to find his way in. It wasn't until he was nestled in the steel rafters that he briefly considered the consequences of his actions. He relaxed into a dark space, wedged between a support post and a dense collection of cross bars, and made a conscious decision to ignore that nagging call for reflection. At this point, there was nothing left to do but wait.

Jeremy watched the warm brown of the wood floor far beneath him gradually come into view, the rich color emerging as the sunrise slowly entered the room. The shadows shifted, making way for bright shapes to form an orderly pattern over what earlier resembled a void. His eyes softened as he allowed all his thoughts to recede. He didn't know how much time passed before he heard footsteps, but now he could see Za'in walking below, his usually relaxed movements a bit tighter and more energized than ordinary, displaying an energy similar to the anticipation of battle.

There was a short, nervous knocking sound, and Jeremy shifted in his seat to steal a better view as Za'in made his way to the door. When Kayla entered the room, Jeremy took hold of the metal beams surrounding him, resisting the urge to move closer and give up the cover of the shadows. She was dressed in a deep green top that hugged her form closely from the sleeveless straps down to her slender waist, ending in loose, delicate panels around her hips. Her charcoal pants were heavier cotton, widening as they reached her ankles, where a knot connected the front and back of the garment below a small slit along the side of her calf. He was struck by her long hair, shining like a trail of flame, and it was then he noticed that he had never seen her so clean. There was something else too, something different. He wondered if her new glow meant she was happy.

Jeremy clenched his jaw. He missed some of their conversation already.

"Now you understand that a sense of self-preservation, or even a firm resolve, will only bring you so far," Za'in said, guiding Kayla into the center of the room. "The vessel that holds those precious jewels must be strong. Part of this training is physical. If we align our bodies so that energy can flow freely, the expression of our will is pure and uninhibited. However, it takes time and effort to find and maintain this structure. At first, it is uncomfortable, painful even, and may not feel natural, but with consistent practice it will be difficult to imagine your previous forms of movement or stillness."

What the hell was he talking about? Jeremy watched as Za'in instructed Kayla to bend her knees, and he then adjusted her posture by lightly touching her thighs, ribs and shoulders. He smoothed her stiff fingers and laid her hands on her stomach below her belly button, one over the other. The pair stood together, side by side, breathing deeply. The silence in the room was thicker than when Jeremy was alone in the rafters. He understood the challenge of their modest posture when he found it difficult to remain as still and quiet as they were.

After a while, they widened their feet, sinking deeper into their stance and raising their arms to hover in the air. He could see Kayla's limbs quivering, but that was the only evidence of her strained muscles. She didn't complain or fidget. Za'in arranged her into a new pose and touched his palm to hers, then applied some pressure. Kayla stumbled back, but quickly assumed her previous posture and tried again. Jeremy leaned forward, enjoying the spectacle of the girl struggling to find a strong position, falling over again and again, and he wondered when she would accept defeat.

As soon as that thought entered his mind, her body appeared to transform, taking on a beautiful shape that he was sure wasn't present earlier. His eyes followed the lines of her legs, descending like roots, before his gaze doubled back over her torso, regarding the two graceful limbs that met Za'in's force with stability, but no resistance.

There was some sudden movement near Kayla's face and Jeremy's body jerked in response, his tight grip on the surrounding rafters barely preventing him from springing to action. Soon his heart slowed as he realized the tiny explosion wasn't a blow directed at the girl, but something projecting from her own hand. His features tensed, both in frustration at his reaction and in wonder of the gleaming, bony sword she held to Za'in's chest. Was all this activity about training her to use the relic? Why didn't he just seize it?

Kayla's form continued to be tested, and she managed to retract and release the weapon a few more times to Za'in's approval. The lesson ended with his arm around her shoulders, and exchanged whispers that Jeremy couldn't decipher. When they were gone, he made his way out in the same manner he entered, but with even more caution beneath the blazing sun.

Jeremy's musings scattered with the wind-blown sand. Over the last week he found plenty of excuses to return to his hiding spot in the rafters, but ultimately he knew it all came down to his own weakness. Swearing oaths of damnation on his own head, he hurried up and over the metal beams, holding his breath against the knowledge that his hesitation might be what would give him away this time. Jeremy entered the room as soundlessly as he could, his eyes scanning the space below as he settled onto his shadowy perch. This was the first time Za'in was already present when Jeremy found his way in, but he seemed too focused in his standing meditation to notice the stealthy Arch.

Jeremy watched his lord, frowning. He thought about the contents of Kayla's locket and wondered what it felt like to be Asher Serafin. It's not that he didn't respect or fear Za'in, and he couldn't complain about his position just a few rungs beneath the man that ruled almost everything worth having—but he couldn't forget that tiny picture and the admiration on the boy's face . . . he couldn't forget the familiarity and shared pain present beneath those written words. Jeremy lifted his gaze, directing it towards the shadows. It didn't do Serafin any good. Michael Steelryn was dead, and Kayla . . . well, she was out of his reach now. Jeremy's heart beat faster with the memory of her screaming Serafin's name.

He closed his eyes, steadying himself against the metal bars. This was ridiculous. Maybe he could just leave now without being noticed. In a tiny, involuntary spasm of movement, his boot slipped on the beam below him and his eyes immediately shot downward, only to be caught in Za'in's black stare. Before he could breathe, there was a knock at the door, but the man below didn't move. Jeremy was unable to swallow, speak, or flee while he was held by those dark eyes, and even after Za'in turned to answer the door, the Arch knew he had been commanded to stay put.

"Is something wrong, Sebastian?" He heard Kayla's voice before he caught sight of her.

"I didn't want to burden you with the conflicts that sometimes occur in my organization here, but recent developments have moved me to accelerate your training. My responsibilities may limit our time together, and your safety is my paramount concern."

"What happened?" she asked, nervously crossing her arms.

Za'in moved to the window, assuming the simple stance

that always marked the beginning and end of a session. Kayla quickly followed. After a few long breaths, he spoke again. "Saros has killed his Ophan."

The girl turned towards her teacher, startled. "Jeremy?"

"Is that any reason to abandon your posture?" he said softly.

Kayla's mouth opened, but she shut it without a sound, her body falling back into position, bending her legs even deeper in penance.

Jeremy angrily turned his head away. What was the point of telling her that? He was within his rights. His Ophan went against orders, leaving him to die in Madeline, and if he wanted to return as an Arch there would have to be a confrontation. It was the strongest that led, not the most forgiving. He knew trial by combat was not only outdated and had little to do with justice, but in this case it was also a bullshit excuse for revenge. Jeremy called for it anyways, and Za'in sanctioned the battle. It was a long time coming. He held his breath, steadying himself against the dizzying memory of his Ophan's dark form falling to the earth.

Looking down, he saw Za'in and Kayla had already begun the day's lesson. They stood facing each other with an extended arm, their bodies making contact at the wrist. He could feel the tension of possibility between them, the heightened pulse of the inevitable.

It reminded him of his first night back at the compound, just before dawn. The desert air was cool as he stood beneath the electric lights, facing his Ophan, acutely aware of his men watching from the perimeter of the yard.

Now the pair below him had made some space between them, each holding aloft their own bony hilt. The twisted mass in Za'in's fist expanded, transforming into a short sword. Kayla's face was hard with resolve as she drew a ragged breath, moments before she stumbled backwards, moved by the force of her own almost identical sword releasing. Za'in didn't give her a moment to recover, immediately changing the form of his weapon to a blunted spear. She grabbed the wrist of her sword arm with her opposite hand, choking back a whimper before she expelled a growl along with the extension of her relic. Their staffs clashed and she closed her eyes as she threw her body into one wild swing. Za'in yielded to the strike, and then snapped his weapon in half, drawing each shard into a thin trench knife.

Jeremy squeezed his temples as the memories returned. He knew he could defeat his Ophan, but he had to make it seem fair. He discarded his sword in favor of a steel pole as defense against his opponent's bladed knuckle dusters. The small knives danced in quick succession close to his face, his hands, his side, but he blocked each attack with quick swings of his makeshift staff.

Kayla was backing up, protectively waving the jagged rod in front of her. Her face was twisted in concentration, but the relic refused to transform. "No, stop! I . . . can't!" she cried as Za'in approached.

His Ophan said nothing as Jeremy was forced up a set of stairs and back along a metal beam, high above the ground. He remembered that wicked smile . . . was it eager to kill or to die? His adversary shot low, catching Jeremy's leg with the edge of a trench knife, and he stumbled, dropping his weapon, but he used the opportunity to pull his Ophan down with him, wrenching one of the knives from a surprised grip as they fell together against the girder. It had to end here. Trial by combat really was an excuse—not for revenge, but for control. The eyes that watched them didn't matter, and what happened in Madeline was nothing in the face of the knowledge that being an Arch didn't make him free. This was the only way to end the struggle of the past five years. He dragged the weapon's barbed knuckles along his Ophan's back, and then turned his wrist, pressing the blade through flesh, all the way to the hilt. He released his grip on the weapon and shoved the writhing body off the beam. Jeremy stood, regarding the still, twisted form that lay in a patch of dark, wet sand, wondering if he'd ever feel the relief of a lifted burden, even as his men raised their voices in his name.

A girl's scream brought him back to the present. Kayla was on her knees, holding her staff above her head as Za'in's blades made contact with her weapon. Her opponent took a retreating step, bringing his hands together and conjuring a sword that was the skeletal twin of Jeremy's blade. The Arch watched as Kayla's eyes widened, her hands dropping into her lap. She lowered her head, gripping her relic tightly as the staff began to glow, shrinking in size and collecting in her right hand. Kayla raised her face, her eyes wet and shining, her teeth bared in rage. She flung her arm up into the air, throwing an explosion of light towards Za'in. He shielded himself with the massive sword, and she fell forward, collapsing to the ground.

Jeremy swallowed hard, staring as his lord stood over her, motionless and silent. Za'in then knelt down beside Kayla, gently resting his palm on her back, and he looked up to lock eyes with his Arch.

"When we push our limits, we find they are further than we think. However, this is dangerous without the proper guidance. You survived today, and such a trial need not be repeated." Za'in turned his full attention to the girl, gathering her trembling form into his arms.

Jeremy's face stung, and he lingered for one more moment, catching a glimpse of her eyes fluttering open. He quietly crawled out the window into the blinding desert light, a pale imitation of the brilliance that escaped Kayla's right hand.

7

The giant bulbs above each metal structure outside Kayla's window were shining brightly, every one throwing out four radiant beams in separate directions. Some cast a bluish, others an orange tinge on the surrounding concrete walls and sand dunes. The only sound in the night was the ever-present wind, cooled by the fallen sun. She had brought Kittie's chair to the narrow, tall window, and sat resting her head against the single bar running vertically through the opening, while she stared out, her eyes unfocused. She was lonely.

Kayla recognized that the dull pain in her chest wasn't the same longing that moved her to leave the potter's village. There was a sense of accomplishment and thrill that came from her lessons each morning with Sebastian. Even now, the muscles in her thighs and shoulders ached, and her right hand tingled and burned, but those physical reminders of her training brought a blissful grin to her face. In each session, Sebastian revealed that she was more than she thought she ever could be. The little trials he put her through were meaningful challenges, and his approval was a true reward.

Still, she recognized that he was a busy man, and she didn't try to meet with him outside their appointed time. Kayla practiced her exercises and contemplated the mysteries he revealed to her, but there were so many empty hours left in the day. She hoped Kittie would return and bring her cheerful energy into this gray room, but nearly two weeks had passed since she last saw her wide and smiling eyes. It had been almost just as long since she followed in Jeremy's cold shadow to meet Sebastian for the first time. She liked to think the Arch was on another mission, somewhere far away from the compound, so she wouldn't have to consider other reasons behind his absence. With a sigh, Kayla closed her eyes.

She didn't know how much time had passed before she opened them again and saw someone walking alone in the sand, dwarfed by the industrial equipment around him. Kayla could tell by his relaxed gait that it was Jeremy. She was at the door before she even acknowledged her desire to run out into the night. There, thoughts of Sebastian sobered her, causing her legs to go rigid. He told her that she wasn't a prisoner, that she'd find no guards keeping her locked away in the room, but the entire world was dangerous, every part of it, down to this place and his Archs, especially . . .

Kayla shook her head, bolting from the room and hurrying down the corridors, looking for a door that led outside. This part of the stronghold was eerily quiet, and she felt as though her breathing was thunderously loud. Holding her next inhale high in her chest, she spotted a way out and, stumbling into the sand, she found Jeremy sitting against the building she emerged from, looking up at the sky. Kayla walked towards him, and although she was sure he noticed her presence, he didn't move. She sat down at his side and turned her gaze toward the moon, neither one of them speaking for a long time.

Jeremy was the first to make a sound. "You're okay." His whisper was almost carried off by the wind.

"You haven't come to find out."

She felt his body stiffen. "What happened with Za'in?"

"Nothing . . . we've just talked," she said, the volume of her voice dropping at the end of her statement.

A bitter smile flickered over his features, but he didn't say a thing.

Kayla dug her bare toes into the sand, certain he knew she was lying. "Have you seen Kittie?" she asked loudly, hoping to change the subject.

His head whipped in her direction. "What did he tell you?" Jeremy growled.

"N-nothing! That she'd be gone for a while . . . but I missed—"

He turned away, his shoulders slumping. "You wouldn't know anything about it anyways," he spat. "Don't start thinking he's telling you the truth about stuff." Jeremy paused, taking a shuddering breath, and when he spoke again his voice was soft. "Za'in is preparing her to be my new Ophan. It's all my fault . . ."

"Is that bad? Isn't it a promotion?"

"It's an excuse." He dropped his head into his hands.

Her fingers hovered in the air, stopping before they touched his shoulder. "Jeremy, what's happening?"

In two sudden, violent movements he opened up his armored vest, pulled his undershirt over his head, and faced her bare-chested. His arms and torso were traced with scars, but it was the tattoo on his chest that he was presenting to her. It was a cross with pointed ends; the vertical arms were short, but the horizontal line was long, almost reaching his armpits. The ends of each cross arm were intersected with a perpendicular line. "I took this willingly. I did what I had to. Kit always found a way around it. But he's not going to stop now . . . Fuck!" he cried out in frustration.

"Because she's going to be an Ophan . . . ?"

Jeremy let his head hang. "I said it's just an excuse. But I let it happen. If I didn't kill my Ophan, she'd still be here with me. I should have known he'd do this. She's good enough to have been an officer a long time ago, but he didn't trust her without the cross." He looked up at Kayla. "He hasn't tried to mark her for years. But you've renewed him. Finding you . . . has driven him further." His irises were hard and translucent.

Kayla tried to ignore his last two sentences. "You're afraid . . . because of what it did to you?"

He laughed harshly. "This thing I carry—I've been lucky. Each one of us that took this had to make a choice. Lie down and die out in this world, or be a part of something that will win. The answer is simple. And he even sweetened the deal. Let this ink and blood pierce you, and who knows what new power you'll obtain. It wasn't a lie. But never mind about your soul, if you have one. You'll never be free of him . . ." He stared into the sand, speaking to himself now. "Maybe I can dodge that bullet. Even now, he can't command me through this mark . . ."

She tried to piece his words together. "He hasn't perfected his communication system with you . . ."

Jeremy looked up at her sharply. "He told you that?"

Kayla didn't answer him, her mind racing. "He uses these marks . . . to send orders? He can talk to you through them?"

"That's one way they're used. The thing is, that part doesn't seem to work with me. It almost stopped me from becoming an Arch. But I guess it can be overlooked when you're some Saros kid . . ." He must have seen the question flicker across her face because he paused, sighing. "It's a wonder you've survived so long, you know that? I bet you still don't even know about the Eclipse."

She shook her head and he moved closer, his eyes still trained on the heavens. "Stars are all fire and pressure, exploding ceaselessly in the abyss," he whispered. "The world teaches us that violence is natural, but the sky pretends it's beautiful too. Stars die like we do—victims of their own mechanisms of survival. We don't notice when it happens; we only see what we can't avoid."

"The sun?"

"Yeah, and it went dark once, almost eighteen years ago. It was a simple matter of the moon moving into the sun's path—it's happened before and it'll happen again—but this Eclipse was different. The world noticed. Less than eight minutes of darkness, and it wasn't the sun that exploded, but everything below. They say mountains sank into the earth and oceans rose over cities . . . the ground shuddered and split open, and the deserts expanded. The years that followed were worse. If there was ever order before, it was finally gone. People didn't rebuild, they destroyed. Some acted out of fear, others embraced their primal impulses, while some just seized opportunity. Kids like me didn't know what the world really was like before, but we were blamed anyways, just for being born at the wrong time. Superstitious bullshit. It was the first total eclipse of this ill-fated Saros series, so we were branded with that title." He paused, shaking his head. "What am I saying, 'we?'" he muttered, "it was just me where I came from, and the other Saros kids around the world are probably all dead now . . ."

Kayla was afraid of the desolation in his eyes. "You said it was going to happen again?" she managed.

"In less than two months, yeah. The next Eclipse in the series will be identical, but fully visible in a different location. West. Little more than a week after my birthday." His eyes cleared and he looked back at her. "Hey, don't be scared," he scoffed. "It's superstition, remember? Sure, the masses will freak out and cause the destruction they're afraid of, but you're here with us now. No one fucks with the Spheres."

"So it was a coincidence?"

"I dunno. Doesn't matter."

Kayla's brow tightened. "No . . . it does. Sebastian wanted you to be an Arch because you're a Saros child. That same thing other people hated you for—he finds it valuable. He was looking for me and I have a relic; you know that. That's tied to the story of the Angels, inhabitants of Heaven, realm of the sun. He wants to change the world. You said it yourself in Kittie's room! And there's a sense of urgency here . . . I know you can feel it. Something is going to happen during this next Eclipse."

"Shit happens all the time, Kayla."

"He didn't tell you, did he?" she murmured.

"Of course Za'in has something planned," Jeremy snapped. "He always does. But I don't care what happens when the sky darkens. I don't live under its shadow anymore."

Kayla cringed. She didn't know how she hoped this would go, but she didn't mean to keep hitting his sore spots like this. "I'm sorry. I'm talking about things I don't understand. I'll ask him about Kittie; I'm sure she's okay—"

Jeremy roughly grabbed her wrist, stopping her from fleeing. "Hey, relax. This got weird quick. Forget it. And you're right, even though you don't know it . . . Kit always ends up on top. She's a tough girl. It wouldn't be the first time Za'in went for her. He knows she's different, and he doesn't like people to keep their own secrets." There was a trace of a smile on his face. "But he doesn't know what he's getting into with her—she always gets her way. I'm the one that's having a hard time with it. She'll come back laughing and I'll just be glad she's my Ophan."

Kayla watched him visibly relax. The pain, rage, and fear in him had boiled to the surface, and then sunk beneath his cool exterior again as quickly as it arose. Jeremy seemed cleansed by the rapid-fire release of those emotions. He glanced back at her a few times when her gaze was fixed on the stars, and something about the quality of his attention made her feel as though he recognized her place in that process tonight.

She was moved by a strange sense of belonging. This wasn't what she expected when she ran away in search of answers, but wasn't she finally uncovering truth? The feeling first emerged in Sebastian's studio. Each day under his tutelage she became stronger and more able to express herself through her Intercessor. She was told a few stories about her father, and there was still the promise that Asher Serafin would be here soon. She wasn't troubled by Jeremy's ominous statements. Sebastian was a leader, and she knew that required him to make difficult choices. Whatever those actions were, it was the Earth's welfare he had in mind, so couldn't his sins be forgiven? Even now, her lingering resentment towards Jeremy was being washed away by her new understanding of his circumstances.

As she watched the clouds moving past the stars, Kayla could feel the vastness of the heavens and the earth, and the pressure of the two of them sitting right in the rift. She thought of the empty spaces she still needed to fill between the past and the present, and she wondered if her father had ever been in this same spot before.

"Jeremy, you're the Arch of the Second Sphere, right?"

"Mm."

"Do you know which Sphere my father commanded?"

She could feel the tightness return to his muscles. "I thought you didn't know anything about that."

"I don't. Not really."

Jeremy wouldn't meet her eyes. "First Sphere. Now don't ask me any more of those kinds of questions."

Kayla let out a frustrated sigh. "Fine, I'll just ask Sebastian."

His hand closed over hers instinctively, as if he was going to pull her away from harm. "Don't. You're playing a dangerous game with him, Kayla."

Her voice raised a little, defensively. "What else am I supposed to do? You brought me here and then left me alone with him." She looked down at their hands, hers almost completely obscured by his long, calloused fingers and heavy knuckles. His touch was gentle again, like it was that night . . . "How long has it been since I've seen you?"

He didn't let go. "There were things I had to take care of. Besides, I thought it would be better if I stayed away."

She understood what he meant by that, and she closed her eyes in embarrassment. "Can you blame me for not knowing what I wanted?"

"Look, you're lonely. Stay with me until Kit comes back." He kept his face turned from her. "But if you don't know what you want, then you still won't be able to tell if I'm trapping you or saving you."

"Either way, I can see now that you're lonely too."

Jeremy's features were hidden by the shadow of his dark hair. Kayla could only see his smile, both resistant and resigned. He stood up suddenly, pulling her with him. Led by her wrist, she stumbled in the sand, catching her balance against his chest. He looked down at her, grinning. "Even the stars look peaceful from a distance, right?"

He didn't let go of her hand as they walked silently over the desert floor and through darkened corridors, beneath the shadows cast by the crisscrossing iron bars above.

8

Jeremy had quietly left the room before dawn, careful not to rouse her, but Kayla had noticed him leaving her side. She could hear him slide into his boots, and softly pull his shirt down over his head. The next sound was the gentle tug of his body armor being tied into place. He moved like someone used to taking extra care to be silent, even now in his own room. It was just another sign that pointed to Kittie.

Without her, Jeremy seemed ill at ease. Last night's display of vulnerability was the proof that a piece of him was missing. Kittie's constant presence at his side was natural, unobtrusive, and something he had maybe even taken for granted. For the first time, Kayla saw clearly that the energy for each of his relaxed movements was circling around empty space, and his simple consideration for her was routine, as she served as a substitute in the void that Kittie left behind. As he lay beside her in those early morning hours, Kayla noticed how effortlessly he kept to his side of the small bed; it was natural to not disturb a companion beside him.

Now that he was gone, she recalled the image of him stretched out on his back, his eyes closed, one arm lying limp beside him while the other draped across his forehead. With both of them protected by the darkness, he was able to say the words that weighed so heavily on him.

"Kit . . . we've never been apart. Almost twelve years together, more than five of those with Za'in, and she's never been afraid of anything. Before I met her, I thought I was tough—I didn't know any better. It's weird thinking about it now. I was just a little kid, but I can't remember a moment of innocence. I always felt like me. Even then, I didn't want to admit that it hurt . . . everyone in that place calling me 'Saros' every god damned day, no one letting me forget what I was or teaching me anything at all. Some of them were too young to even know why they should hate me. Maybe the world is fucked now, but I don't know if I believe things were ever really better. Not really. Not that I would know. But then Kit came." There was a smile in his exhalation. "And with her, it was never about escape, and she thought things were beautiful. Sure, when we got outta there things were even harder for a while, but I felt free and clean, no matter what I had to do for us to get by. I never thought it was strange that she didn't get any older. Kit was Kit. She was right as she was. I knew there were things about her that she hid from me, and that was okay. She had her reasons. I always tried to take care of her, but it was probably the other way around, no matter how much I fought it . . .

"But it just built up in me. I was sick of being on the short end of the stick. Sick to death. Nothing changes except who's on top, so I knew I had to be on the winning side of the struggle. I had to be stronger. So I joined Za'in, took my mark, and I got stronger. I was climbing, and Kit was with me. I can't even say that I did things I wasn't proud of, it was never a question of that. I was backing the right horse. Nothing else really mattered. Still, I'd be lying if I said I wasn't happy that she couldn't be marked, that Za'in couldn't figure her out. It was what he deserved for trying. What did he need to know for anyways? She did as she was told, she made herself useful—she knows how to survive. But I've seen what he's capable of. She's been gone for too long, and if anything happens to her . . ." He trailed off, the hand at his side curling into a fist. He didn't move again until later that morning when he left the room.

Kayla had wanted to reach out for him then, to touch his clenched fingers, but she was afraid of any of the possible consequences she could imagine for that action. Her frozen indecision led to a fitful sleep. Now, as she lay there alone, she felt even further from rest.

Light had started to enter the room through two small windows. She noticed that although his room was larger than Kittie's, there wasn't much of a difference between them. Kayla rolled over, her face pressed against the pillow that Jeremy had given up to her last night. She told herself that her stillness in this position had nothing to do with the scent she caught in each deep breath.

She knew she had stayed here long enough daydreaming, and soon it would be time for her lesson with Sebastian. Kayla's fingers trailed over the creased sheets, wondering if her emotional responses had become twisted in some way, but she knew that it was useless to feign horror at lying in a killer's bed or training with a man he feared. Her concern for Kittie was real, but it was hard to connect those feelings with the ones regarding either of these men. She allowed her thoughts to drift a few more moments before straightening her clothes and rushing to meet Sebastian.

By the time she neared his doors, Kayla was already late.

Jeremy's room was not too far removed from Kittie's, but from this new starting point it was difficult to find her bearings in a place where so much looked the same. Rounding a corner, she stumbled at the unusual sight of Sebastian sitting on the floor of the hallway, right in front of her destination.

She rushed toward him. "I'm sorry I'm late," she called out, smiling.

He rose slowly, his movements deliberate. Kayla's steps halted, an inexplicable threat of violence causing her body to tense into stillness, her grin vanishing.

"Was your room uncomfortable?" he asked quietly.

"No!" She stopped, flustered, then tried speaking again more softly. "No."

Sebastian came closer to her. "I understand the burden of training in isolation, but I suggest that you don't linger in any of my soldier's rooms tonight."

This was the first time since their initial training exercise that she was truly afraid of this man. "I'm sorry." She didn't understand why she felt so ashamed.

He rested his hand on her shoulder and spoke with his face close to hers, his voice quiet. "Saros is an excellent Arch, but he's not the sort of man I thought you would give in to. He doesn't act on principle and isn't motivated by morals. You wouldn't be his first conquest, but you would be convenient, for now. Drawing you in with the romance of a somber face and a clenched fist . . . Kayla, remember how we spoke about guarding your unique energy against those things of the world that would ensnare you?"

She turned her head away, feeling foolish. In the morning light, beside her teacher, last night's events seemed reckless and unnecessary. "Yes, Sebastian. You're right."

His smile spoke of his forgiveness as he ushered her through the double doors. "Don't be too hard on yourself.

These are the mistakes of youth. But we don't have to accept that mistakes just happen. We must make the best decisions we can, hmm?"

Kayla nodded.

They took their usual places, standing in the light that streamed in through the large windows. She began to concentrate on her breath as she had been taught, feeling the energy expand inside her, flooding her entire body with warmth. Aligning her inner forces with her outer form in this way filled her with the awareness of potentiality. She was learning to express this promise with her Intercessor, and Sebastian claimed she was moving forward in her training even faster than her father did. Still, sometimes Kayla wished their lessons didn't have to go beyond this point, so she could continue to drift in this familiar flow, without the lurking threat of darkness and her duty to clear it away.

Sebastian spoke then, as if he sensed her thoughts. "Kayla, I was hesitant to reveal this to you so soon, but I can see that you need to know now."

She froze with her intake of breath, her eyes opening, watching him cautiously.

"That was not an invitation for your structure to crumble," he said sharply. Immediately, she lengthened her spine, closed her eyes and continued to breathe deeply, although she couldn't seem to relax her face. He continued, his voice even. "Have you ever wondered how you came to possess an Intercessor and why you're able to wield it? Have you considered what ultimate purpose it serves?"

Kayla forced her breaths deeper, her facial muscles tightening.

Sebastian didn't wait for any further reply. "You felt lonely last night. Was it because you were alone, or because you knew that you would still be alone, even in Saros's bed?

You're different . . . far removed from these ordinary creatures that crawl over the surface of the Earth. Your blood flows from a separate source. You are of the Nephilim, as I am."

Kayla's posture was suddenly perfect, relaxed, her breathing full and even. She opened her eyes slowly. She had never heard that word before her first night here, but it resonated in her like something that had been sitting on the tip of her tongue.

"Yes . . . inside, you've always known. Your ancestors are Angels. That is why you can Intercede, and that is why you've been lost. I've found you, Kayla. I've walked this ground for longer than you can imagine, and I know how hard it is to be without your equals. Your past was out of your control, but now you have a choice. You can grope in the darkness as a human or you can forge yourself into a powerful and free Nephil. You can be a person that merely survives, like Saros, or you can be someone whose life reaps the rewards of a higher purpose. I have spent my life cultivating my mind and body—" Sebastian pulled up his sleeve, revealing a complex network of dark tattoos, "—and my world." He turned his head, his eyes meeting hers. His gaze was solemn, but she felt the return of his usual kindness.

"Sebastian . . . you know by now that I want to do my best."

His eyes smiled. "And you know that's what makes you so dear to me. It's been so long since I've seen someone want to soar. Thank you, Kayla."

Her face burned, but both that heat and the pressure in her chest were pleasant. Still she avoided his gaze, trying to catch another glimpse of the strangely familiar symbols on his skin.

"I know this is a lot to process. All of our lessons have

been accelerated and I'm sorry that we must move at this pace, but so much time has been wasted. If I had found you sooner, I would not burden you with any exercises after such a revelation, but nothing we can do will slow this current . . ." He guided Kayla to the center of the room, his touch raising the hairs on her arms.

"What would happen if you lost your Intercessor, Kayla? This is something we must prevent. It came forth to protect you, to remind you of your true nature, but it was never meant to be outside of your body for this long."

She remembered the pain she felt when it first pushed through her skin, but she still took hold of her weapon as he instructed, despite her fear.

"Feel the base of your palm become soft, your skin enveloping the end of the hilt. The bones of your wrist may ache a bit, but there's some pleasure in that, isn't there? Your flesh remembers; your skeleton feels the loss. Let it return and don't be afraid. It is your destiny to be whole."

Kayla didn't let her beating heart drown out her thoughts. Sebastian had taught her how. At this moment it was so clear that every exercise he led her through didn't build some new ability, but instead cleared away anything that blocked the shining of her own light. She could do this. There was no pain, only a warm and almost wet feeling sliding up her arm. Looking down at her hand, her Intercessor was gone and her body was unmarred.

Her eyes excitedly sought Sebastian's, and the pride on his face was almost a greater reward than her achievement. "Now can you draw it out again?" he asked softly.

Kayla focused her energy as she had been trained. It took an explosion of will to extend her weapon when she held it in her hand . . . what would it take to force this bone out of her body? She pressed harder, everything within her driving towards this one intention. Her Intercessor was unmoved—could it be that this task required a different technique?

He noticed her struggle. "Recall the memory of when it first came forth."

She was back in the darkness, looking up at Jeremy's face as he reached his hand down to her. Her breath caught in her throat, just as it did that night. Lost in the vision, her weapon's handle burst out from her palm, followed by a glistening, ivory blade projecting through the hilt. Kayla's muscles felt cool and light. Gripping her Intercessor, she playfully met Sebastian's sword a few times before effortlessly calling the bone back into her body.

With an affectionate laugh, he led her to the doors, his arm around her. "Kayla, you always exceed my expectations." A little smile was all she offered, but his praise meant more to her than she could express.

A quick embrace was their usual goodbye, but afterward, his eyes held her still. "Please return to the Malak's room tonight."

"I thought Kittie was going to be an Ophan."

She was surprised to see him hesitate, his face stiffening. "As with the rest of us, her future depends on her own actions." The doors closed, but she imagined Sebastian's gaze guiding her back to Kittie's room, careful to notice if her steps faltered.

9

Kayla stood facing the narrow window as she practiced projecting her Intercessor from her palm and drawing it back into her body. Her hand and wrist were dark and swollen from over-exerting herself in training, but she felt like she finally discovered the subtle channel through which to direct her energy. With this precision, it was becoming effortless; soon there would be no signs of stress in her face or breathing. Every few tries, she would release a weapon from the hilt, but she still found it difficult to control exactly what came forth.

The sound of the door behind her slowly creeping open caused Kayla to quickly draw her hilt back in, whirling to face the intruder. She saw Jeremy sliding through the opening in the cracked door, smiling at her. "Hey . . . you're here. I wondered what happened to you."

Kayla avoided his eyes, silently searching for some excuse that would save her from this exchange.

His grin dropped, but as he came closer he was still speaking softly. "Don't be mad. I know it's been a few days, but you didn't come back that night and Za'in hasn't given me a break since. I didn't mean to leave you here alone for so long."

She didn't speak.

Jeremy's face darkened. "What is it?" he snapped. "Stop being so damn cryptic and just say it already."

"I . . . I just want to be by myself right now," she managed, turning away from him.

He was quiet for a moment, before laying a hand gently on her waist. "Are you alright?" She hoped he couldn't feel her trembling beneath his touch, but before she could pull away, he gripped her shoulder, spinning her back to face him. "Jesus, what happened to your hand? Za'in . . . !" he growled.

"He didn't do anything! You always assume he's up to something terrible." She couldn't shake this sick, guilty feeling, and she wondered if her words could make him leave, and take this emotion away with him. "If you hate him so much, why do you bother being his Arch? Just to have power? Isn't there more to life than that?"

He spit out a short laugh. "Nice deflection. So he told you to keep away from me, huh?" The stiffening of her body told him his words hit on the truth. "What about what *you* want? Do you have any of your own thoughts left?" She looked up at him with tears in her eyes, but he only laughed again. "Oh yeah, I forgot, you have no fucking clue."

For a moment she was blinded, but her vision cleared after a few frantic blinks of her eyelids. He was no longer standing before her, so she followed the sound of his angry steps as she ran down the hall. "Wait!" He kept striding away from her. "Jeremy, stop!" She felt ill. She knew what she wanted to say, but dreaded the words. "Would you just listen to me?" He had reached his door, but he stopped, his back to her. Her voice was hushed. "It's not about what I want. There's more to it. I know you don't care about what's right, but we both know that we . . . shouldn't—"

"Are you going to believe everything he says?" His voice was flat.

Kayla's face burned. "I bought your shit, didn't I? What happened in Madeline, Jeremy? Are we in Torin yet?"

He was suddenly facing her, his fingers bruising her arm below the shoulder. "Christ, are we not past that? The last time I saw you . . . *everything* that night was real!" He looked as if he wanted to say more or simply let her go, but he just stared at her, his limbs and face rigid.

The pain of his grip wasn't in her arm. In that tight band that circled around her, she could feel his bewilderment, his fear, his need. Kayla closed her eyes, leaning into the hurt he pressed through her flesh and into her bone. She couldn't get Za'in's words out of her mind, but she knew she needed this too. She remembered what Jeremy said that night, under the stars. He was right. *Do I know what I want? Will he trap me, or . . .* "Save me . . ." she murmured, surprised to hear the words spoken aloud.

Those two broken sounds barely hit the air before his mouth was on hers. He held her tightly to him, the pressure in her arm spreading to include the rest of her body. Jeremy turned around with her, pushing her against his door, leaving her no escape from his passion. Kayla let herself give in, forgetting this place and any of the circumstances that led to this moment. She stumbled backward as the door behind her gave way, Jeremy catching her fall while he continued pushing her forward. She heard the door close heavily as she landed on his bed, his body never losing contact with hers. Kayla lay breathless, accepting his touch, his kisses, wanting to consume anything he would give her. She didn't realize until this moment how much she had longed for this—his simple desire for her. She let her fingers tangle in his hair, her other hand reaching up his back, feeling herself trapped between his skin and the weight of his armor. Her cool touch against his flesh sent a little shudder through him. Jeremy curled her thin shirt forward, his palms moving up her waist, over her ribs, his mouth claiming her breast.

There was a short, sudden knock on the door. They both sat up quickly, their legs entangled, Kayla immediately straightening her blouse and smoothing her hair. Her frightened eyes searched Jeremy's face as he looked toward the sound, his features hardening. In the dim evening light that came through the window, his slow walk towards the door seemed to her like something out of a dream. She held her breath as his hand clutched the knob, his body tensing.

Kayla heard Kittie's voice ring out, "Geez, you could look happy to see me!"

Jeremy pulled her into the room, slammed the door behind him, and fell to his knees, putting his arms around her. "Kit . . . you don't even know . . ." he breathed.

"You're such a baby," she laughed. "What's the worst that could have happened?" Kittie looked up. "Oh, hi, Kayla! I—aagh!" Her words ended in a strangled cry as Jeremy pulled the neck of her shirt down. "Hey, stop! You're going to stretch it out!"

"That bastard. Dammit, Kit, how did we let this happen?" His voice was soft. Kayla was surprised that the sight of the tattoo on Kittie's chest didn't pull a more violent reaction from him, but she knew this wasn't the worst scenario he had imagined and prepared himself for.

The girl just giggled again. "It's a rub-on!" She licked her finger and wiped it firmly against the mark, leaving pigment on her small digit.

Jeremy stopped mid-laugh, staring at her. "Kit, I don't know how you've gotten away with it so far, but that's never gonna work."

"Don't you know me any better by now? I have a super-special-super-secret-technique! He thinks I'm a good girl, and I'm your Ophan and we're on the strong side of things, so all is well."

He shook his head. "Heh, little favors, right? Alright, so act like an Ophan and give me some kind of report." He shifted from kneeling to sitting, pushing himself backwards and leaning against the bed. His anxiety was gone; his earlier passion traded for a poised watchfulness.

Kittie pulled his chair closer and sat, her legs swinging. "Well, it's been a really tiring couple of weeks! Za'in is serious about getting all his ducks in a row. He had me talking to the stars, listening to stones, and dreaming into events halfway across the planet. It's the usual stuff, I know, but it was never this much, and he was never so insistent! He tried looking into me too, to see what was really there. I don't think he found much, and the tattoo proves it. Oh well. Hmm, what else . . . ah yes, you're vexing him quite a bit too!"

Jeremy frowned. "I shouldn't be, not anymore. What's his problem, anyway?"

She looked embarrassed, covering her face with her hands. "Jeremy, Kayla's in your bed!" she whispered.

Kayla flushed, tensing to jump up. Without turning around, Jeremy grabbed her wrist and held her still. "So what?" he asked, his voice low.

Kittie peered at him through parted fingers. "Don't look at me so scary! *He's* the one that's bothered!"

"So what did he say?"

"You know him—he didn't say anything to me. I just know that if you keep this up, both of us are going out somewhere without her. It's been years since we, or hardly anyone, have gotten to just hang out here for more than a few days, but we brought Kayla with us, so we get a little vacation. Get too close, though, and poof! We're out looking for some relic or quashing some unorganized rebellion. Yuck."

Kayla struggled against Jeremy's grip. He wouldn't release her. "I don't know why it even matters to him," he growled.

Kittie blinked, her head tilted to the side. "You don't? If you think about it, it'll come to you. Kayla, I'm sure Za'in gave you some version of his reason, right?"

She turned her head away, just as Jeremy looked back at her sharply.

"Something to do with your . . . identity?" Kittie asked quietly.

Kayla didn't answer.

"Well, either way, we'll all have to make some decisions soon 'cuz I hear that Asher Serafin is really on his way."

Jeremy let go of Kayla's wrist and crossed his arms, and she wondered if he could tell that this news was no surprise to her. "Good," he muttered, "we have something to settle."

Kittie watched them carefully before jumping to her feet and, grabbing Kayla's hands, she began to drag her towards the door. "But for now, you should come with me, Kayla. It's getting late. We can all talk tomorrow in the light."

Jeremy scowled, but followed them out. Kayla turned around, driven by her desire to see his face again before she left, despite her fear of her eyes meeting his.

He stared at her, the coldness leaving his gaze even as he tightened his brow to keep the chill from escaping. "Maybe you're smart to keep your secrets from me," he whispered, "but I still wish you wouldn't."

She had no answer for him, her eyes helpless. Kittie pulled her down the hall, calling over her shoulder. "See you tomorrow, Jeremy. Don't think I didn't miss you!"

Jeremy turned around, avoiding the sight of the girls disappearing around the corner. He let out a long sigh, allowing his forehead to rest against the cool wall.

"You can learn some things from your Ophan, Saros," said the voice behind him.

Jeremy whirled around, standing straight. "Lord Za'in."

His dark eyes were still. "I can see now that Kayla has a . . . weakness for you. However, I am expecting you to show more self-control in the future."

"Yes, Lord Za'in." His jaw tightened.

"Saros, I have sympathy for you. She is a truly unique creature, and I understand your desire. But you know how we've been searching for her. She's a treasure, and not only must she be kept safe, but it is necessary to polish this jewel. That can only happen in a very controlled environment, without the ups and downs of passion. Yes, she is very precious . . ." he trailed off.

"Because she is Michael Steelryn's daughter, sir?"

Za'in raised an eyebrow. "It's not that man's legend that makes her valuable to me." He paused. "I see you are invested. I'll give you an opportunity to use that energy constructively. Keep an eye out for Asher Serafin—you have first crack. That's my gift to you, Saros."

"Thank you, sir." Even in his frustration, this news brought up the corners of his mouth.

He rested his hand on Jeremy's shoulder. "You're a good soldier, Saros. You've fought hard for me, and I know you've seen some of the rewards already, but soon things will change again with the return of the Eclipse. If your lust survives the passage of these next crucial weeks, I'll let you have Steelryn."

He didn't reply, his eyes meeting Za'in's steady gaze.

"For now, rejoice that you have been reunited with your new Ophan. Spend your time here training. The state of the world is shifting, and I want both of you in top form. Don't mistake any of this for disapproval of your performance. You are one of my best and I expect to see you standing when the former world passes away. The change may be more violent than you imagine, and only the strong will survive. I anticipate turning my head and seeing you when the sky darkens again."

Jeremy choked down the warm feeling of pride in his chest that came from those words. He didn't believe the biblical nonsense that drove Za'in, but he respected the man that was strong enough to bend the world to his will. If Za'in had faith that plagues were coming, then they were certain to appear, but they would be of his own design and crueller than those of any vengeful god. If something was really going to happen, this man would be the source, and Jeremy would be a dark Horseman. "Yes, Lord Za'in. You'll see me there."

Za'in smiled. "I'm counting on it." As Jeremy was left alone, he felt for the first time in weeks that it was the way it should be.

10

Kittie pressed through the ceiling hatch, shielding her eyes from the sunlight. As the two girls climbed out onto the roof, she pulled her goggles down from atop her head and adjusted the brown shades on her face. She handed a pair of wide, dark glasses to Kayla. "Careful, that's an antique!"

They sat down on a stretch of concrete underneath the iron skeleton of a sloped roof. Looking out, they could see the entire compound from above—every metal beam and every sand dune—and all around that, nothing. Kittie leaned against a post, trying to squeeze herself into a cast shadow, and she sighed as she took in the view. "Can you imagine, all of this was water, once."

Kayla smiled wistfully. "I bet it was beautiful. Do you think it will ever return to how it was?"

"You mean with this next Eclipse?"

She avoided Kittie's gaze. Should they be talking about this? Kayla began to wonder what parts of her training were secret and what information was common knowledge.

"Well, I don't know," Kittie continued, "because the last Eclipse didn't do this."

"It was humans then . . ."

"You say that as if you don't belong in that group."

Kayla kept her eyes on the horizon.

"The first Nephilim were as much human as they were Angel. You can imagine the split in the modern variety."

"I wasn't supposed to say anything . . . I didn't!" she whispered. "Did Sebastian tell you?"

"Of course not," Kittie snorted. "I think he takes joy in watching me figure things out. You know, to prove that I really am good at seeing what others don't. But I know what you are."

"Who else knows?"

"Oh stop, Jeremy wouldn't believe it if I told him."

Kayla felt her face grow hot. "That's not what I meant."

"You're sure famous, all right—or at least your dad was—but people don't believe in the Divine anymore. So that answers your question, sort of. But you *were* thinking of him. It's really pointless to try and fib me."

"I wasn't!" Kayla stood up quickly and went near the edge of the roof, the wind nudging her to cling to one of the metal poles. "I wasn't . . . conscious of it. I've been training, meditating; I don't want to think about him."

"You both like each other a lot. I don't see what's so bad about acting like you do."

Kayla glanced back at her sharply. "Just a few days ago you told him to keep his distance from me!" Her gaze drifted back to the sand and sky. "And he has," she said softly.

"For his own safety and for yours. We can't forget where we are and we certainly can't ignore our circumstances, but if we become disconnected from our feelings, well then we're lost!"

"What if our feelings lead us in the wrong direction? I have to think about what's right." Kayla was speaking now to the emptiness that surrounded her, suddenly finding a voice for every moment she spent alone since she came to this place. "Sebastian has helped me so much. I don't want to make him angry. I'm afraid he'll end my training, and I'll be adrift again. I want to be whole and free, in a restored world. I can't forget the responsibility I was born into, and I can't ignore what my father would have wanted."

Kittie stood up and quietly made her way to Kayla's side. "Did Za'in ever tell you about your father's life after he was no longer an Arch?"

"We don't really talk about that. I know it sounds stupid, but I feel like I *can't* ask. He gets close to telling me, but I think it's too painful now that my father is gone. Asher will be here soon and I know he'll fill in all the gaps that Sebastian can't. He wouldn't come all this way just to leave me in the dark."

"Za'in's already asked you to make a choice between him and Jeremy. If you try to bridge that space with Asher, you might have to choose again."

She looked down at Kittie, her eyes cold. "If I had everything figured out as well as you do, then I suppose I wouldn't have to worry about that."

The little girl grinned. "If you could see what I can, you'd be halfway there. I'll let you have a peek if you want!"

Kayla just stared, surprised by Kittie's answer and taken off guard by her smiling enthusiasm. Kittie used her momentary hesitation as an opportunity to grab her hands, and she pulled her away from the edge so they both could sit, facing each other. Kittie shook her goggles off her head, and deftly slid her glasses off Kayla's face. Her voice was hushed and eager. "A tattoo like this is nothing to me," she said, glancing quickly down at her chest before locking eyes with Kayla again. "I can do what it does without this business of ink and blood and whatever else it contains. I can pull it out of my skin, or spread it back again—it doesn't matter. So look what I can do!" She rose up onto her knees, and leaning forward, she pressed two fingers between the other girl's eyebrows.

Kayla felt the ground beneath her give way, and she grabbed the rails on either side of her in a desperate attempt to conquer the dizziness that left her reeling. She could hear Kittie's voice as if from a great distance, calling, "You're safe. It's like a dream, okay? Just breathe. I'm here with you." Kayla couldn't feel anything around her, but after hearing her voice, she did notice a cool pressure between her eyes. The haziness that shrouded her vision began to clear, and prompted by the floating sensation she was experiencing, she looked down. Kayla could see the warm, familiar floors of Sebastian's training room and she felt the tightness in her chest subside.

As the corners of her sight sharpened, she recognized Jeremy's dark shock of hair below her. Although she couldn't see his face, his unconsciously insolent posture gave him away. He was sweating and panting, sword in hand, as he faced Za'in. Her teacher was also holding a weapon, but she noticed it wasn't his Intercessor. It took a moment for her ears to adjust, but soon their faint voices began to clearly reach her.

"You'll have to do better than that if you want a victory without your Sphere." A slight smile played over Sebastian's face.

Jeremy rushed at him, swinging his serrated blade up-ward. Sebastian's weapon met his, and angling to the right, Za'in continued the arc and brought his own sword forward. Jeremy slid back, and then shot at him from the side, taking Sebastian off balance. As Za'in fell, he grabbed

Jeremy's arm and twisted it hard until he lost his grip on his weapon. They rolled and Sebastian landed on Jeremy's back, pressing his face against the smooth floor.

"Are you sure I can leave this one little thing to you?" asked the dark-eyed man.

She could see the side of Jeremy's face, frustration contorting his features. "I won't lose, Lord Za'in," he managed between clenched teeth.

Sebastian released him and stood up. "That's enough for today. I'm sure Serafin will find a clever way to let himself in, but I didn't give up my location just to see him walk out of here with Steelryn. If you fail, I'll step in. But when the time comes, I hope to witness a better performance from my Second Arch."

Jeremy stood slowly, collected his sword and sheathed it. His muscles appeared tight. "I'm training, sir. I swear I won't let him defeat me." It seemed difficult for him to get the words out.

Sebastian stood at the window, watching the horizon intently. "Good. Now bring Steelryn to me. Time really is running short," he said absently.

"Yes, Lord Za'in." The soldier turned to leave.

"And Saros?"

Jeremy froze.

"Please keep in mind that although she is promised to you, she's not yours yet. I don't think I need to remind you what happens to those who try to take what's mine."

"I understand, Lord Za'in," he said quietly before leaving the room.

Kayla felt her stomach drop steeply as weight returned to her limbs and she could feel the sun on her shoulders again. She opened her eyes to meet Kittie's excited stare.

"I'm pretty awesome, right?" the little girl sang.

Kayla shook her head, her body trembling. "Did you

hear what he said?"

Kittie's mouth grew small. "Well, yeah. It's my ability you were using."

"How could Sebastian say those things?" Kayla jumped to her feet, holding on to the metal beams to steady her wobbling legs. "He's saving me as some sort of prize for Jeremy . . . he's using me as bait to trap Asher!" Her right hand twitched and burned, and unshed tears stung her eyes. "Has he been lying to me this whole time? How could he?"

Kittie watched her, unmoved. "You need to pull yourself together. Right now."

Just as she spoke those words, the roof hatch opened and Jeremy pulled himself up. "Za'in wants you." His words were a moment too late, delayed by his attention on her apparent agitation.

Kayla took a cleansing breath and composed herself. She didn't say anything, but moved towards the opening in the roof, her steps even.

Jeremy stopped her before she climbed down, grasping her arm gently. "Let me walk with you."

She met his eyes. Between Sebastian's words and her own misgivings, Kayla had hoped she could discard her muddled fervor for this man, but it was a useless fight. She was sure he experienced a similar surrender, since the anger and pain she saw in his eyes at their last meeting was now gone. She searched his face, and it was clear that the passion he expressed to her that night was still present, but it was shrouded beneath a thin veil of control. Kayla felt weak at his touch. Although Jeremy held her arm in just an effortless, protective grip, her entire body responded, ignited by this simple contact. His eyes spoke of his intentions, and she knew then that her reaction was not excessive. If she couldn't resign herself to duty alone, then the expression of her emotions at least had to be restrained and the two of them could only convey their feelings in the most imperceptible ways. Kayla realized she let too much time pass to keep their exchange unnoticed by whatever hidden eyes have kept watch on them before. "Yes, that would be best," she said softly.

Kittie put her goggles back on and relaxed against one of the rusting posts. "I'll catch up with you guys later."

Kayla barely heard, descending back into the compound. The pair walked through the silent halls, their steps slow and measured. Kayla felt stunned, not only by today's events, but by the sudden plunge into this dim light. Though her steps fell strangely weightless, she knew she could walk alone and unaided, but she still rested her fingers against Jeremy's forearm, in the crook of his elbow. She followed his lead, letting her fingertips press her swirling emotions through his shirt's thin fabric, into his being. He kept walking forward, his gaze set straight ahead, but she could see her message was received through the jerk of his fingers that ended in the warm loosening of his arm.

When they came to Za'in's doors they stopped, facing forward, neither one of them moving to knock. Jeremy spoke quietly, his lips almost still. "Nothing's changed, Kayla. To me, you're not a weapon." Before he finished the last syllable, he rapped on the door, freezing Kayla's movements before she could turn to him questioningly. He glanced at her quickly, then retreated down the hallway and was almost out of sight before Sebastian granted her entrance.

11

This was the first night in a long while that Kayla's dreams had been haunted by Asher's face. Her sleep was fitful, and on each frequent awakening she was disoriented, finding herself gasping in the momentary, breathless fear of being vulnerable in a strange place. Now she was determined to fend off sleep for the remainder of the night; it was easier than continuing this violent cycle. She closed her eyes against the unfamiliar shadows around her. She didn't want to be here in this room, so far removed from Kittie and Jeremy. But Sebastian had insisted.

She didn't know how she should feel, as she re-examined the events that led her here. Nearly a week ago, when Sebastian had opened the double doors and beckoned her in, his usual warm smile was not enough to ease her fears. It was the first time she had met with him later in the day, after their morning training, and she could only assume that this audience with him meant that he was displeased. Maybe he knew she had seen his exchange with Jeremy, through Kittie's strange power. Kayla took her usual stance in the sun-lit portion of the room, being very careful to keep her shoulders relaxed, concentrating on not showing any physical signs of tension that she knew he could easily detect. She understood that she had to put her feelings of betrayal, anger and apprehension out of her mind. Sebastian always knew what she was thinking by observing a tightening muscle, a kink in her posture, or a fluttering eyelid. Staring out through the full-length windows, they were both silent for a long time. It was becoming more difficult for Kayla not to unconsciously give anything away.

When Sebastian finally spoke, it was almost as if he was continuing a conversation that had already started without her notice. "Kayla, I have reason to believe that Asher Serafin will be here very soon. Unfortunately, my sources also inform me that he intends our meeting to be hostile. If it was a simple matter of him coming in with his guns blazing, it could be easily handled. I would see to it that he was subdued, unharmed, and then I would comfortably count on a reunion with you to soothe his wrath. But I'm afraid it won't be as straightforward as that. He has sided with four men that are in possession of stolen Nephilim relics. This could be very dangerous for everyone involved, especially if they are not capable of understanding and controlling these sacred objects. All of that aside, those relics are our birthright, and I intend to take back what is ours."

He turned to her, his face earnest. "And Kayla, I must confess, I have other, more personal reasons for my concern as well. You've never been a prisoner here, but it's difficult for me to think of Asher leaving with you. I haven't had a pupil like you—no, not since your father— and your spirit, not just as a child of the Nephilim, but you, *you* have brought me much happiness. I had nearly given up hope. I thought perhaps that the days of those eager to learn, better themselves, and strive for the highest within them had set with the Eclipsed sun. You've given me a gift that you cannot imagine, just by being you. I admit I have found myself growing very protective of you, perhaps to excess. Please forgive my offenses; I just don't want to lose you to this world, and without you, I don't think this world can help but lose." He paused, searching her eyes for a response.

Kayla tried to control the stiffening of her shoulders. How could these words soften and dissolve what she had just witnessed with Kittie? Still, they did. Her heart felt heavy in her chest, expanding with pride. Here, beside him, she felt as if she was soaring above the mundane world, and with Sebastian, she was a part of something important, something she was chosen for. Kayla suddenly reached for her locket. It was a strange impulse; she hadn't grasped for it in so long. "Sebastian, I can't thank you enough for everything, but please, let me speak with Asher. And I beg you not to hurt him."

He looked a little wounded. "I brought Asher here for you, Kayla. But, as I just mentioned, I don't intend to let him snatch you up in the night. That is not the proper road to your meeting. Please, stay in my chambers for the next few nights. You will have your own suite—I assure you privacy—but I need to know that you are safe with me. Please, humor a tired, old man." His smile reached out to her.

Kayla felt herself giving in, and she struggled to hold on to what she heard Sebastian say to Jeremy. Could it be that Kittie's vision was false? She didn't really witness it in person; it was some sort of strange episode. No, she trusted Kittie. Was it possible for that cruel Sebastian to be the same one that had always been so kind to her?

"I am afraid that I must insist, Kayla." His voice was

gentle, but with a slight edge that gave her the impression that he was irritated by her hesitation.

She nodded.

Sebastian's uplifting smile returned. "You're a strong girl. When the world is so precarious, I know it can be difficult to make decisions. One's emotions can easily rule him in times like this, but you always seem to keep what is important in mind. It is precisely in times like this that a higher purpose is most needed and most difficult to follow."

Kayla's eyes closed tightly, and opening them again, she was jarred from her reverie. She was back in the darkness, and the warmth she had felt from his words spoken in the daylight had faded now, as she lay there alone. She told herself that he hadn't been wrong so far, and there was no doubting his wisdom. Perhaps the contradiction she detected was just a simple matter of his manner being harsher with his subordinates. He seemed constant. To keep an organization like his running in such troubling times forces a man to hold an iron grip. Kayla considered the present necessity for someone to put their own comfort and desires aside in order to lead, and she felt sympathy for Sebastian.

Still, that knowledge didn't ease her burdens. She spent her days in training, and her nights alone in a room that never seemed to become familiar to her. It appeared that each passing day brought more urgency, and with it, more scholarly and physical tasks. Kittie and Jeremy were kept busy as well. Often she didn't even recognize her own loneliness except when chance allowed her to see Kittie's smile or feel Jeremy's hand brush against her arm or back as they passed by one another. Kayla pressed her face into the cool pillow and thought of his eyes. They exchanged no words this whole time, but his gaze remained the same. She didn't want to be his promised prize for defeating Asher, but she couldn't deny the pleasure of witnessing how his passion for her did not fade with their lack of contact.

She suddenly experienced an overwhelming desire to see the moon. Although she didn't want to be in this room, she was thankful that the window here was a broad, glass-paned expanse, unlike the narrow slits in Kittie and Jeremy's quarters. Kayla moved the heavy curtains aside, but instead of the calm, cool sands she expected to see, there was a storm on the horizon, swiftly moving in towards her. She watched, transfixed, as the heavy winds, thickly strewn with sand, beat against the steel beams outside, pressing them closer to the mysterious lighted tower that the compound centered around. Kayla saw no signs of life. Was she the only one that noticed this strange phenomenon? No, although she couldn't hear or see anyone scrambling about, if she concentrated, she could feel the panic in this place. She could sense preparations being made and defenses reinforced.

A strange instinct moved her to hide behind the curtain again, shielding herself from the events outside. She felt exposed. Kayla hurried to the door, and she wasn't sure if she was comforted or threatened by finding it locked from the outside. She stood there, frozen, listening to the howling of the wind, the sand crashing against metal and concrete, and the whine of iron and steel slowly bending to an unnatural force. Kayla rushed behind a tall cabinet as she heard the door rattling open. Even hearing Kittie's distinctly soft, prancing step was not enough to free her movements again. The man with her was one of Za'in's soldiers, and although his head was covered to protect him against the storm outside, she was sure he wasn't Jeremy.

Kittie was dressed in the dark, slick armor Kayla was familiar with, but she had never seen the small girl wear it before. Both she and this soldier were wearing similar headgear. Kittie pulled her goggles up and her dust mask down. "C'mon, let's go! This diversion isn't gonna last forever, you know!" She threw some black clothes at Kayla, and then looked down at her bare feet. "Do something about that. I got a covering for your head."

Kayla watched the masked man next to her. "Kittie, tell me what's going on."

She frowned, turning to her companion. "Well, hurry up and say hello—we're running out of time!"

Kayla felt relief instead of surprise when she saw Asher Serafin remove his helmet. The only astonishment she experienced was the realization that, as soon as she saw the storm, she knew he was the one that brought it in. His hazel eyes were sharp, and she felt as if nothing escaped his vigilant gaze. He didn't smile. His voice was quiet and softly harsh, as if he spoke rarely. "I had no doubt we would meet again."

For a moment she wondered if she should feel injured by his seemingly cool reply, but she knew it was as it should be. Regardless of how it appeared, he shared her feelings on their reunion. Kayla reached for her locket. Something deep within him had changed since the picture was taken and the note was penned. Her heart soared at finding the man she searched for, but as she examined his face she also felt as though she should mourn for him. "There were times I wasn't as sure as you," she whispered, "and all I could do was dream."

Asher bowed his head. "We are awake, and so we must move."

Kayla felt renewed, throwing on the soldier's uniform and putting on her boots as Kittie tied on her armor. As she began to secure her headgear, her excitement melted into uncertainty. Wasn't she supposed to meet with Asher under

Sebastian's supervision? Isn't this what he warned her about? She looked to Asher. No, it was this man that she had been searching for. She wouldn't make another mistake like the one on the shore, where she was lucky that her Intercessor only acted as a shield. She squeezed her locket once more and pulled her goggles down over her face.

They made their way swiftly and silently down the halls with no incident. As they approached some unfamiliar doors, she whispered to Kittie. "Where does this lead?"

"The Beacon." They continued into the next room, which was nothing more than a darkened stairwell.

"That lighted tower?" Kayla asked breathlessly as they ascended.

"It's just a recycled ruin, once a part of a cement plant. It's been altered to retain its appearance, but to function as a more traditional structure. Now it exists as a place for Za'in's . . . research." Kittie's movements were almost wrathful.

"Why are we going there?"

Asher came close to her. "We need the key to our way out." His gentle growl was laced with an edge of irritation that Kayla could tell was not directed at her.

She found herself winded, losing track of how long they had been climbing. Kayla had expected Jeremy to meet them, but the further they went, the more her worry grew. "Are we running away?"

"It's not safe for you here," Kittie said, her voice low. "Have you forgotten how you felt the first night in this place? You weren't wrong. We were terrible to bring you here. When I was away, preparing to be an Ophan, Za'in had me listen to some stones. Oh, the stars understood too, and even the wind tried to tell me, but it was the stones that made me realize . . . I know what he has planned for this next Eclipse. It's horrible. He'll use you, Kayla, just like he used—"

She grabbed Kittie's arm, stilling her forward motion. "Where's Jeremy?"

The small girl pulled her sleeve out of Kayla's grip. "There wasn't time! I—" Kittie shook her head, hard. "He'll come. He always does."

The storm still raged outside, and the strained groan of the metal beams was dangerously close. A loud clang shook the building, forcing the three of them to cling to the walls. Kittie scrambled to the next door, pushing it open, with Kayla and Asher at her heels.

The room they entered was cold, chilled by the violent gusts that blew through the broken windows to their right. The rare and precious electric lights flickered. Jeremy stood before them, his sword drawn, his eyes moving quickly over Kayla, then back and forth between Kittie and Asher. His muscles twitched, frozen rage darkening his down-turned face. It was impossible to say who struck first, but when their blades met, the tower shook, shrieking against the storm.

12

Kayla clung to a table that was bolted to the floor. She didn't know what to fear more: the outcome of Asher and Jeremy's fight, the probability of the tower coming down, or Sebastian's wrath. The sinister atmosphere of this room thickened the air. What was it that Sebastian "researched" here?

She turned around quickly as another loud thud sounded from the window behind her. Four vaguely familiar men dressed in ponchos were attempting to get up from the floor, using each other to balance themselves. They pulled off their goggles and head wraps, and Kayla realized they were the pirates she had encountered when she first traveled with Kittie and Jeremy.

Kittie ran to the blond pirate. "You have it, right? Give it to me!"

He scrunched his face at her. "Serafin can beat that guy. Then I'll give it to him."

Her expression was a tiny mirror of his. "You want to get out of here alive? Then at least hand it over to her." She flipped her hair in Kayla's direction.

The blonde's scrawny comrade frowned. "Well I guess sh' could ak'shly *use* it, Cap'n . . ."

He glared at his friend. "Givin' away treasure now, Fec?"

"You were gonna give it to Serafin! And he came here for her," chimed in the bejeweled pirate that stood behind him, fiddling with his dreadlocks.

The Captain's shoulders slumped and he pulled on his short hair. Turning his head, he saw Asher wrestling with Jeremy on the ground, their weapons out of reach. He tensed his body, ready to rush to Asher's aid.

His tall, somber companion laid a heavy hand on his shoulder. "Bruno, he said if it came to *him,* to stay out of it."

The Captain nervously yanked on his hair again. "Okay, okay!" He muttered under his breath as he retrieved a bag from underneath his poncho and reluctantly handed it to Kayla.

She pulled open the drawstring, her hands shaking with the inexplicable knowledge of what was inside. Her hands closed around the bony hilt of an Intercessor, recognition flooding over her. "This was my father's . . ." she whispered, shocked by the words escaping her lips. "Where did you get this?"

Kittie moved in closer, her eyes intent. "What's important now is what it does. When two Intercessors are brought together with one purpose, they say even those without wings can fly. It's our only way out of here. I can't say where we'll end up. But if we stay here, Za'in won't let us live. Not now."

Kayla couldn't speak. Her chest felt like a gaping wound. Holding her father's Intercessor against that void, she watched Jeremy and Asher fight, and she was no longer sure if the shudders that racked her body came from the trembling of the tower or from some closer source.

The bitter taste in Jeremy's mouth could only be described as "pain." He had let that sensation drive him before, and now it was his only comfort as he met with the reality of the three of them coming here, all dressed like that—exactly as Za'in had predicted. When his weapon clashed against Asher's, that taste covered him, saturating his body and expanding his lungs. He remembered Asher's angular defenses and attacks, and enjoyed appropriating them, tossing them back carelessly. "You think I'm gonna let you take what's mine?" Jeremy's sword raked against Asher's armor.

Serafin's face was calm beneath a fierce expression. "Those aren't even your words." His kukri caught Jeremy's gauntlet, tearing it off and pulling him forward.

Jeremy let that force carry him towards Asher, swinging his sword down violently, as if that rush of steel could drown out what was just said. He didn't know how Serafin knew, but his opponent was right. He felt sick when Za'in used those words against him; why was he repeating them now? The cross on his chest felt like a razor cut. "Shut up. There's no way Kit could really be on your side. And Kayla—" Jeremy didn't know how to end that sentence, and he was almost thankful for being silenced by the sudden need to dodge Asher's blow.

"—doesn't belong to you." Asher's eyes caught his, as all three of their blades locked together.

The anguish that had been tracing jagged lines through Jeremy's insides finally cut something loose. A savage growl escaped his throat as he kicked Serafin down to the ground. He twisted his sword up, not caring that it forced the weapons out of both of their hands. They struggled on the floor as the whole tower shook, each of them vying for a dominant position. Jeremy's knee landed against Asher's ribs before he grasped his adversary's hair with one hand, his other fist smashing into Serafin's face. Keeping a tight grasp on his hair, Jeremy secured his hold of Asher's head by seizing his opposite ear and then slammed him into the ground. A strangled cry broke through his clenched teeth as he bashed his enemy's head down again.

Another scream pierced through the fever that gripped him. He didn't need to turn his head to know he would be faced with Kayla's panicked eyes. The momentary slackening of his grip was all Asher needed to draw his legs in and kick Jeremy over. The soldier's agonized cry couldn't drown out the sickening crack that came from Asher wrenching his arm on the way over. He landed on Jeremy's back, pulling his head up at another awkward angle. Before Asher could complete the jerking movement, Kayla's hands were on his, desperately prying his hands back with her fingernails.

"If you do this, you leave here without me," she whispered, her voice wavering.

Asher let go, but not before pulling Jeremy back far enough so he would collapse against the floor, instead of into her arms.

Kayla didn't know who to comfort: the man with the twisted arm who lay crumpled on the ground, or the one that staggered, bleeding above her. She squeezed her eyes shut, drawing out her Intercessor, and held one in each hand. "Help me use these. Let's just go now!" she cried out.

As the others crowded around her, she could hear Jeremy mutter, face down on the floor, "You're not leaving. . ."

"I have to, and I want you to come with me," she whispered back hurriedly.

Asher knelt down beside her, and Kayla tried to hand her father's Intercessor to him. He shook his head, pushing it back at her with an open palm. "I'm just a man," was all he said.

She looked around to find six faces watching her, all tense and breathless. Kayla closed her eyes again, adjusting her grip on both hilts. The only thing she could do was breathe deeply, hoping that some of her training could be applied to this situation. She felt a pang of guilt when she thought of using what Sebastian taught her in order to escape him. Kayla pressed that thought back down; it was too late now. Her right palm grew soft, enveloping her Intercessor, but she felt the hilt ramming hard against her left palm. It just wasn't hers.

"Are you wondering why that isn't working? Perhaps you are questioning if it's even possible." Sebastian's voice felt very close to her ears, but she looked up to see him standing a few feet in front of her, next to Jeremy, who was slowly finding his way to his feet.

Kayla's heart beat hard and fast. She opened her mouth to speak, but fear and shame silenced her.

"Did I not offer you enough, Kayla? Freeing you from your terror and ignorance wasn't adequate? Opening you to a sense of purpose, and presenting you with a better world wasn't sufficient? Or maybe you're just nothing more than a weak-minded girl who was easily persuaded by these two." He cast his gaze on Kittie and Asher. "I thought that it was Saros I had to worry about. Instead, it seems that it takes very little convincing to sway you. And now look at what you're trying to do. Your left hand offends me."

She froze. There was something strange about his last sentence. Kayla turned to the sudden movement at her side, and saw Kittie rushing toward her with a small knife, her eyes dark and torpid. Kayla dropped her father's Intercessor and instinctively raised her arms to cover her face. Kittie slashed her left hand before Asher smacked the small girl hard with the back of his arm, sending her to the ground.

"Serafin, do you now see why you can't conspire with my Ophan? All of my men have made the choice to belong to me. Even in the midst of betrayal, I have the power to enforce loyalty." Za'in smiled grimly.

Asher stood, shielding Kayla with his body. "You think I could forget that? But I also recall that your methods didn't work with all your soldiers."

There was a slight break in Za'in's cool demeanor, but he ignored Asher's words. "How many of your kind are you going to sacrifice to your vengeance, Serafin? Do you think that's what he would have wanted?"

Asher's expression contained a violence tempered with tranquility. "He never would have wanted her to be with you." His movements were so swift that they were difficult to follow, but when his kukris made contact with Za'in's throat and abdomen, no cuts appeared. Asher noticed the strange toughness of his skin immediately, and started for a retreat. Za'in's Intercessor was released only a moment later, and it scraped Asher's side, breaking through his armor, its barbed and craggy edges catching in his flesh.

Kayla cried out, dropping the cloth she had pressed against her wound, and impulsively reached for her father's weapon. As her bloodied hand closed around the hilt, a throbbing pain spread from the point of contact, through her entire being. She felt her bone fuse to his Intercessor, a warm vibration lightly shaking her body. Kayla brought her palms together and she was sure that she was a circle, a conduit of energy, a ball of light. There was no reason to be afraid—or to fight for Asher, or to be hurt by Kittie, or to long for Jeremy, or to mourn for Sebastian—or to doubt that this would work.

She pulled her palms apart, and the air felt taut between them, as if she was drawing a bow. The pirates were crowded protectively around her and she turned to them, eagerly. "I've done it! I'm the way out."

The pirate with the heavy locks stared at the space between her hands. "It's true," he called out, and the four of them grabbed ahold of her arms.

Asher staggered backward, his side bleeding. Turning his head quickly back to Kayla, he straightened, and then rushed at Za'in, who had also noticed the girl's heightened energy. Knowing his blades couldn't cut him, Asher caught them against Za'in elbow and shoulder, and pulling down, tripped his enemy against his hip. Za'in fell gracefully, easily taking Asher with him.

Another shudder shook the tower, and Kittie stirred. She crawled toward Kayla and then wrapped herself around her leg. Her distressed squeal rang out in cries of "Jeremy!"

For a long time Jeremy had stood motionless, holding his arm, but Kittie's calls brought forth an automatic reaction. He moved a step forward before he stopped, forcing himself into stillness.

Kittie noticed his struggle. "Come *on!*"

Jeremy's eyes darted to Za'in, but he was still occupied with Asher. "Kit . . . what did you do . . ." he whispered brokenly.

"Jeremy, hurry!"

"It was always us, Kit . . ." His expression went flat.

Kayla tried to move towards him, but she was weighed down by the five people holding on to her. "Jeremy . . . oh Christ, I don't know how this happened! But, please, just come with us! We need you. I . . . I . . ."

His eyes were wet and shining, but his stare was cold. "You've made your choice, Kayla." He took a step backwards.

The room shuddered, and a pulsating flare of energy between her hands moved her almost like an aftershock. She felt Asher grab her ankle and kick himself free of Za'in for a moment. Kayla knew that if she didn't let this rising force rule her now, it would be too late. The heat between her hands coursed through her, and she almost didn't care if she ignited. She fixed her swiftly blurring eyes on Jeremy, determined to let him be her last sight, if that was what this had to come to. Her voice rang out over the roar of the world crashing down on their heads. "Damn it, Jeremy! Whether you trapped me or saved me, you're still what I wanted—" There was a strange and sudden silence, and she didn't know if anyone could testify that her last words were "I love you."

13

There were endlessly repeating shadows on the wall, in the form of circles enclosing tri-pointed knots. Kayla's eyes rested wearily on the dark shapes, her body weightless and her head heavy. She didn't know where she was, and she had lost the desire to investigate her surroundings. It was hard to say how much time she had spent here in this place, but in between fits of sleep the shadows always returned, cast in various shades and hues.

Kayla knew she wasn't alone. There was always someone with her, but she felt as though there was a screen between the two of them that couldn't be penetrated without at least the effort required to turn her head and face her companion. It didn't seem worth it. Sometimes she knew that she was touched or spoken to, but her inner burdens pushed the external world far into the distance.

A sudden warmth brought feeling back to her flesh, and a sense of substance returned to her body. The film was removed from the world she viewed with her opened eyes. Kayla was then aware of the discomfort that came from lying on her side for so long, but when she moved to turn, she could feel a gentle pressure along her shoulder and down her back. This hold was comforting, awakening, but she knew she wasn't in Jeremy's embrace.

Kayla's body stiffened. "Please . . . let me go."

She was immediately released. "You don't know how relieved I am that you're speaking again." Asher's voice moved from behind her, and soon she saw him sitting at the edge of the bed. He was back in his desert garments, but his head wrap was replaced with a bandage that wound around his brow. The skin surrounding Asher's eyes was dark, his features drawn, and his beard unkempt. He rubbed his cut and bruised face before he offered her a little smile, which she noticed was expressed more in his eyes than his mouth. "What you did back there . . . your father would have been proud."

Kayla looked away, shifting her soft focus back to the shadows on the wall. "I wish I could honestly believe that, but I don't know the nature of the ghost I'm chasing. So many of my actions are an attempt to be close to something that is constantly changing in form." The words were spilling out, and her tongue felt loose. "I wanted to find you, and I knew there was something wrong about that place. The Sebastian that lifted me up wasn't the only Sebastian there. I know that. But still, I don't feel right. And Jeremy—" Her voice broke. "We cornered him. And then I left him there, as that tower was on its way down . . ." Her aching limbs pulled her eyes to her palms, but they were smooth and unmarred.

Asher took her hands in his, and she watched her fingers splay out with the tender squeeze of his scarred and sun-browned fists. "Kayla, it was either that tower falling, or you." He knelt at her bedside, holding her eyes in his steady gaze. "I know all the information you have collected has been second-hand. I will do what I can to prove that what I say is true, although there are things that I pray you will never have to witness. I know you want to see with open eyes, so I will try not to shelter you . . . even if it is my first instinct, even if it was the job he charged me with." She could tell that it was a struggle for him to keep his voice even and his features still.

Kayla's head cleared and her breaths came easier. She held on to Asher's hands tightly. At this moment they were all that was keeping her from going adrift again. "You can't hide your hatred for them. They've done something terrible, haven't they?"

She was interrupted by Kittie's squeal, beginning somewhere out of sight and ending in her arms. "Kaaay-laaa! You're awake, you're awake!" The small girl jumped onto the bed and crawled close to her, knocking her hands out of Asher's grip. Kittie's usually bright face was red and tear-streaked, her eyelids swollen. "Do you think he'll ever forgive me? I did such a bad thing. I didn't think it would end this way!" She burst into tears, sobbing against Kayla's chest.

"He's alive then . . ." Kayla murmured, remembering Kittie's ability to watch events happening elsewhere. She sat up against the wall and pulled Kittie's face to hers. "You've seen him?"

Kittie sniffled and frowned, eyeing Asher suspiciously. "He can do anything he wants to Za'in, but I'm not gonna give him any information he can use to hurt Jeremy."

Asher sighed heavily. "We've been over this. It's not the boy I'm after. But as long as he keeps acting the Arch, I—"

"I know!" Kittie slumped against Kayla's shoulder. "I *can't* see him, okay? He's not gone, not completely. Maybe he's blocking me out, or—no, there's no way . . ."

"What is it?" Kayla straightened herself, pulling Kittie up

with her.

"Well, he could have finally given in to Za'in. Jeremy's tattoo never seemed to work right, and that was just chalked up to him being a Saros kid, but I think he was always just too stubborn, you know? If he handed himself over to Za'in completely, he's out of my reach. But he wouldn't do that, he wouldn't! He's just blocking me, right?" Kayla had no answers to offer, and Kittie's words dissolved again into weeping.

Kayla clenched her fists and rested her head back against the wall, her eyes closed tightly. Jeremy didn't die in the tower. That's what mattered. She didn't want to hear any more, and she didn't want to think about what Kittie's words might mean for the future. She set her jaw and didn't move again until the little girl had sobbed herself to sleep in her lap.

When Kittie was finally quiet, Asher moved closer, clasping Kayla's hand once more. "Do you know where you brought us?" he asked gently.

She shook her head, her brow furrowing with the effort to yank herself back into the present again.

"This place . . . many had searched for it, but here it was, hiding in plain sight. It was one of the nine spots where the Angels first fell to earth."

Kayla opened her eyes, his statement prompting her to really look around for the first time. There wasn't much to the room beyond the worn mattress covered with a poncho—only a window and crucifix adorned the dusty space that enclosed her. Outside, she could see a concrete wall, cut with openings shaped as the repeating circles and knots she had known earlier as cast shadows.

"I know, it looks like an ordinary enough place. For quite a few years before the Eclipse, it was a modest church. Although it's abandoned now, it's still very much intact.

Perhaps we can thank Za'in for that. This is where he rang in the New Year, after all . . ." Asher's eyes dropped for a moment, his brow tensing and releasing as he struggled to push back his sudden sarcasm. "I apologize. I'm not going to make you ask. Whatever he told you, the catastrophes that tore the world apart almost eighteen years ago were not an act of nature. He brought this down on us and he's ready to initiate the next stage of his plan with the coming Eclipse. God is dead, Kayla, but he thought he was the next best thing. As one of the Nephilim, alive for centuries, he felt superior. The failings of humanity were all he could see in people. If only he could kill the humanity in himself, and in everyone around him, then some great new era could begin. He excludes nothing from his methods—magic, religion, science—anything to serve his purposes. What went on here? I can't say that I have it all figured out. But this was a place of high spiritual power and, according to his calculations, the Eclipse was the beginning of a Saros cycle that was identical to the one at the time of the Fall. Both of these factors determined the time and place of his actions. And then, all he needed was Kiera . . ."

Kayla clutched at her locket with the hand that wasn't lost in Asher's grip. "My mother . . ." She hung her head, laughing bitterly. "Everyone is a part of this, huh? What did he do to her?"

"He used her as long as he could. In some ways it was easy—Kiera was devout. But she had reason to be a believer; maybe she was more Angel than woman. He wanted her. And if he couldn't have her, then her energy would become just another mark on his body and another barb on his weapon . . ."

"Did he kill her?" Kayla's hair hid her down-turned face.

"Kiera had the strength to do what I couldn't. She gave her life to save Michael's." Asher's voice was thick with emotion.

Kayla raised her head and saw his face turned from her. She leaned against his side, unsure if it was an attempt to comfort him or to soothe herself. "Tell me about her."

His muscles tightened, but she could see a smile beneath his closed lids. "She wore her hair long, like you, except it was very dark. You have her eyes, too. I met her here, outside. She would sit in the banyan trees and pray to God. I was just a child, but she was almost a woman: a strange mixture of learned maturity and naïve wonder. I'd come here with my friends to simply waste time—playing ball, skateboarding—but she always looked like she was having more fun than I was, just sitting there, dreaming. Sometimes I would come back alone to talk to her. She had one foot in some eternal realm, but she also burned with a sense of urgency and desires to accomplish important things. She considered becoming a nun, only because sainthood wasn't a real job, although she thought it should be. She was ready to go to university, and because she knew she could heal, she had half-hearted plans to become a nurse, but that didn't satisfy her spiritual needs."

Asher was silent for a moment. "I know some of these things won't make sense to you; so much has changed since the Eclipse. But I wasn't the only one that saw Kiera sit in trees or lay in the grass. She called him Sebastian too. He told her she was special and that wasn't a lie. He told her that she could use her powers to help others, that she could mother a world that accepted her fully. Her beloved stars would be within reach, and maybe she would feel more comfortable in her own skin if she could just spread out her wings. Soon, I found myself spending more time sitting in the banyan alone. Then everything changed. But I can't feel too much bitterness. Without Za'in, I never would have met Michael."

As she leaned against Asher's form, Kayla could sense the weariness he kept inside beginning to come to the surface. "You don't have to tell me everything now," she whispered, "I'm still very tired and weak."

He looked down at her quietly for a while before speaking again. "It's true you're tired. Thank you . . . you won't need to spare me again. We have one more day of rest before we must move. We'll speak more tomorrow."

Kayla settled back down into bed, her movements slowed by her aching body and her care to not disturb Kittie. "Asher, I'm sorry that I helped fight you off, that day on the shore."

He stopped in the doorway, his back to her. "Don't be. You didn't recognize me. And you were protecting . . . the one you love."

A pained silence was all she could offer. She wondered how much Jeremy knew about everything Asher had revealed.

"Za'in knows your feelings. If you see Saros again, he will have orders to use them against you."

Her sight became unfocused and she grounded herself by stroking Kittie's hair. "There must be something wrong with me . . . to miss them both like this."

"It's the burden that those with a heart carry. You can't let your emotions rule you, but don't cut them off. Your feelings are not a sin against any of us."

Kayla called out to Asher one more time before he closed the door behind him. "I know if you didn't come to rescue me, something terrible would have happened to me there."

He didn't reply until she looked up again to meet his gaze. "It may make me sound like less of a hero, but I had to stop that from happening because of what it would have done to me."

When the door shut, Kayla closed her eyes. As her dreams swallowed her consciousness, she imagined a world where those were Jeremy's words.

14

The inside of the banyan tree was rotted away, but it was still standing. Kayla crawled into its trunk and looked up at the canopy above. She was no longer able to sleep on that old mattress. The only dreams it allowed were more awful versions of what happened in that tower, so she had wriggled out of Kittie's small arms and walked the halls. The plan of the church was based on boxed-in circles, and she enjoyed wandering through the open corridors, watching her shadow pass through those of the tri-pointed knots. When she reached the back yard, she knew immediately which tree was the one Asher had mentioned. As soon as she touched its bark, she was sure she could rest there.

Kayla's head bobbed sleepily, and then she couldn't tell if she was down in the trunk or up in the branches. It was hard to remember what color her hair was, or what clothes she was wearing. But she knew she saw Sebastian, and although he was dressed in black as usual, there was something different about his style.

"Good evening, Kiera. What are the stars saying to you

tonight?" Her heart jumped at hearing that friendly and soothing voice again.

"Mintaka is laughing at me," spoke a voice that wasn't hers. "He says I don't have any time to waste. I don't know what he means, but I'm glad to see him. It gets harder to see stars out here, but Orion's belt is always around."

Sebastian smiled, sliding his hands into his pockets. "I really must take you south sometime, so you can see Alpha Centauri."

"Would you?" Kiera asked, not looking down. "I never get to go anywhere. Maybe that's what Mintaka means."

"Perhaps he thinks you should start thinking of your future. Like what we discussed yesterday."

Kiera frowned. "I don't know about that. You sound like a cult leader sometimes, Sebastian."

Kayla was able to recognize the slight tightening of his face that could only mean he was controlling his anger. It was almost imperceptible, but she had become acquainted with it. Kiera didn't notice.

"Isn't that what they always say about someone that comes with new ideas? When the world changes, you'll hear no one say that," he murmured.

"Will the change be good?"

"Nothing better."

Kiera laughed. "Well, I got nothing better to do!"

As she jumped down from the tree, Sebastian's smile was just how Kayla remembered it best. They walked together, and Kayla could feel her legs moving, but she clenched up against their momentum. Her vision blurred as she fought, and although her wrists and ankles felt anchored to the ground, her head was pulled to dizzying heights.

When Kayla's eyes cleared again, she could see her hands passing over some cards laid out on a silk cloth. Her fingernails were painted a dark color. "*The King of Swords,* reversed," announced Kiera's voice from her own throat. "You don't want to know what *that* means," she laughed.

Sebastian sat across from her on a carpeted floor. He was looking down at a small screen, his smile cast in its artificial light. "I always want to know," he said absently, lost in his own research.

" 'This card indicates destruction, separation, sudden change. A cunning and manipulative man that disdains any form of weakness. His strong will to succeed by any means possible may lead to supremely evil acts. Absolute dominion and abuse of power.' " she recited. "You know that card is supposed to represent *you*, right?"

He was still absorbed in his work. "Is that what you think of me?"

Kiera laughed again, her words playful. "Yes, Sebastian equals 'supremely evil.' " He made a little dismissive noise, and she was quiet. When she spoke again, her voice was sober. "You do disdain weakness. And you are working to bring a sudden change."

He looked up at her, and Kayla could see something stirring restlessly in his dark eyes. He turned off his device and gently pushed it aside. "This is a world where it is acceptable for a worthless human to throw rocks at an Angel dreaming in a tree."

Kiera flushed, turning her head away.

"This is a world where your talents go unrewarded. A damned *nurse*, Kiera? You hunger to be a saint. But there's no insurance plan with that, is there? You have to be practical in times like these, while every day there are more people on the streets, or going off to war . . . clean air or clean water or clean *anything* is growing more scarce. You're just one more storm or act of violence away from being taken out, and you know you'll have to stop dreaming. In a world like this, dreams are just delusions."

"That's no reason to tear it all down," she whispered, bracing herself against the air between them.

"It's more than enough reason to create something new in its place." He looked down at his exposed arms, covered in patterns of dark intersecting lines, knotted forms and symbols. "Aren't you lonely in this kind of world? I know I have been."

The tears standing in her eyes kept reality safely indistinct. "But you have your students! They look up to you. And we're never really alone—" Her voice ended in a sob, and she drew her legs up to run to the window. She needed to see the stars.

Sebastian seized her wrist and pulled her towards him. His voice was low and harsh. "Kiera, your outlook is beautiful, but we *are* alone. Hopelessly alone. That knowledge has driven me to seek out the other solitary souls that possess this blood. You know what we're building. It seems that everything is finally within my grasp." His other hand touched the back of her neck. "But still, it's you that I need." He pressed his lips against her forehead, and lingered there before seeking her mouth.

Kiera let her tears fall, and accepted his kiss. He rose up onto his knees and leaned into her, and although his pressure was soft, she pulled away from the hungry insistence that threatened to drag her in. "I'm . . . not ready." Her limbs shook, but her voice was even.

He closed his eyes for a moment, his lips frozen in a tight smile. Sebastian rested his hand on her head, and let it slide down her hair before standing and walking into an adjoining room. As Kiera moved to the window, Kayla strained against the body she shared with her. She broke through, feeling it first in her fingertips, and then quickly followed by the rest of her being weightlessly sliding towards Sebastian. Something wasn't right, and she was

determined to witness what he would do next. She passed
through a door, but didn't understand why she collided hard
with his form. Kayla reeled, holding on to his shoulder for
support, and at the same time, cringing away from him. She
craned her neck to see his profile as he bowed his head.
Sebastian spit into a little glass jar, snapped the lid shut, and
although he wiped his lips, his satisfied smile couldn't be
smeared away. Kayla cried out, unsure of why she was so
horrified, as the world around her dissolved into dull white
vastness.

When color began to return to her sight, she thought at
first that she was floating above her body, but it was Kiera
below her in the morning sun.

"I've changed my mind. I'm not doing this, Sebastian."
The resolve on her face didn't match the fear in her voice.

They were joined at both palms by their Intercessors,
blood trickling down their arms. "You no longer want to
make this world Heaven?" Sebastian looked far away and
blissful, as if he didn't care to hear the answer to his
question.

"No, that can't be it! The Angels are gone, Heaven is
gone. Only the Nephilim remain—you've said so yourself!
If we call down the void that once was Heaven, it could, it
could. . . Don't you see what would happen to the world?"
As she watched his smile widen, she screamed, desperately
fighting to free her hands.

"I already accepted the disappointment that you
wouldn't have the vision to see this through with full
knowledge. But really, Kiera, what a time to come to a
realization. It's too late, you know." The sky was beginning
to darken.

"No!" Kiera yanked herself back, hard, and though she
fell alone to the ground, her Intercessor was still lodged in
his hand. She held her bleeding palm, no longer able to keep

her tears inside. "How did you . . . ? Give that back!"

"What a waste." Sebastian brought his palms together, the marks on his bare torso and limbs glowing in the gathering darkness. He seemed to expand, and the light between his hands was like a new Sun.

Kiera collapsed in the grass, clutching her right wrist as the symbol on her shoulder shined brighter, while she grew pale and still. A boy with shaggy, brown hair ran to her from somewhere beyond Kayla's limited vision. He tried to pull her away from the light that swelled towards her threateningly, but he stumbled in its brilliance. "Kiera, get up!" he yelled in between hard breaths, only able to drag her a few feet before falling, unconscious, atop her body.

"Not anymore, Za'in. I'm not going to take your word for it anymore. Drop her Intercessor. You have no right to take that. You have no right to do this." A man emerged from the darkness, his angelic weapon trained on Sebastian like a gun. A few locks of his shoulder-length red hair hung in his face, casting shadows over his hard-boned features and his determined, narrowed eyes. He looked as if he had just been roused from sleep, wearing only some loose, thin pants.

Surprise was expressed on Sebastian's face as only a momentary spasm, but his eyes stayed fixed on the cross that adorned the intruder's bare chest. "Steelryn, I trust that you won't do anything foolish. This is what we both worked towards."

Michael was close; the backs of his fingers almost brushed against the unearthly light. "Drop it. I'm not going to tell you again."

"I know." The radiance that surrounded Sebastian flared up and suddenly burst out further, engulfing Michael as he fired his Intercessor repeatedly.

The blistering light scorched Kayla's vision, slamming

her back into the banyan tree and waking her with a choked cry. She trembled from the cold that stung her skin from within and without. She stood on wobbling legs, holding on to the tree as her sleep-clouded eyes searched her surroundings. It was so much like the setting for her dream. Could she have imagined it all?

"I wouldn't be surprised by anything you saw in that tree." Kayla jumped at the sound of Asher's voice, turning to see him leaning against a large concrete tube lying in the dirt. Their eyes met. "You saw her," he said softly.

Kayla tried to run to him, her legs weakening halfway through the short journey. Asher was there before she fell, raising her up in his arms. "You all survived that day, somehow," she whispered. "If someone took your Intercessor, what would happen to you?" She let Asher support her, but she spoke to the sky, her arms aching and restless.

"You would never be the same." His grip on her tightened.

"You were very brave to stay by her side." Kayla's voice was almost inaudible.

"They say it was a miracle that I lived, that no ordinary human could have withstood being so close to that energy. There were times that I wished I had died that day. There were times that I tried to make up for my sin of existing, and moments when I wanted to set the universe right by letting it finish the job it started. My survival didn't make sense then, but now it does. If I had got my wish, I wouldn't be here with you."

Kayla held her breath; his words felt like blows to the chest. Neither one of them moved for a long while, until he set her down on the ground, both of them resting their backs against the concrete tube.

"You must be more conflicted than I ever was," he said softly. "Za'in trained you, nurtured you. You have no memories of a world he didn't construct, you have no memories of Michael and Kiera, and . . . you love his Arch. But your unique ancestry makes you a weapon. I can't deny that you might be the only one that can prevent this coming disaster or make it possible."

She turned her face to the sky, and she could almost see the stars through her closed lids. Jeremy told her that she wasn't a weapon, and although she didn't understand it then, she knew he didn't believe his own words. Did he realize what Za'in had planned for her? "This next Eclipse . . . we can't avoid the darkness, but we have to stop whatever he intends to bring with it. I know that now. But I feel like a loaded gun, waved around by a child. How can I live up to the expectations created by my blood? Where do I even begin?"

They sat beside each other in silence, drawing comfort from the gentle sound of each other's breathing. After some time, Kayla could no longer ignore the pain in her left arm that had arisen when her last question left her lips. She felt as if the only thing that could relieve the burning pressure was to release her father's Intercessor. She freed the hilt, letting gravity pull it down to touch the dirt at her feet. She held the bone in her palm, but the heavy sensation didn't subside. His Intercessor stirred in her grip, dragging its edge through the soil. *Where do I even begin?* The question kept repeating in her mind, driving out all other thoughts, even her attention on the hilt. When it became motionless again, the sudden break in movement brought her gaze down involuntarily. The words *Look up* were etched in the ground. *Where do I even begin?* This was her answer. Above her, Orion's belt shone brightly.

15

The pirates stared longingly at the television in the corner while Fec frantically tried to pull a nail out of the wall. "There's *got* to be a penny in tha' sofa!" he cried out. "Viiic! C'mon, *look!*"

The broad-shouldered pirate sighed. "You can't make a battery. You don't even have lemon," he droned as he half-heartedly rummaged through the cushions.

"That's where yer wrong!" Fec abandoned the nail, drawing three lemons out of the deep pockets inside his calf-length coat. "An' there's more where tha' came from. I found a'tree!" he cried out gleefully, letting the fruit drop to the floor as he brought his attention back to the nail again.

Vic handed a few copper coins to the pirate with the heavy dreadlocks. "Give these to him, Kerif. It'll keep him distracted for a little while at least. Not like it would power a TV . . ."

Kerif offered his hand absently, his gaze fixed at the blank screen. "There aren't any stations left to watch anyways," he sighed with regret. He passed the pennies along to his left, into Bruno's hands.

"It wouldn't hurt to try, right?" His blue eye was hopeful.

Kayla lingered in the doorway watching them, while Kittie sat on the floor with her eyes shut tight and her face strained, searching for Jeremy with her unusual viewing ability. Bruno and Fec were busy piercing lemons with nails and pennies, pulling wires out of their pockets and abandoned appliances in the room, and then stringing it all to the television. She couldn't help but laugh at their antics, but she still felt uneasy, remembering when Jeremy stood between them in the swamp. It seemed like a lifetime ago.

A hand on her shoulder made her breath catch, but when she felt its weight and stability, she knew it was Asher, and she relaxed.

"They're harmless," he said, his voice low and staid, as always. "I'd rather do this without them, but they've seen to it that they enmeshed themselves." When Kayla turned to see his face, she was almost sure there was a smile beneath his stoic composure.

Her gaze followed him as he moved to the window and stared out. The light shone on Asher's straight, assured form and pensive face. He tightened and unclenched his fists before brushing strands of his hair from his face and rubbing his jaw. She could tell he was making a decision he wasn't satisfied with. Kayla felt weighted to the ground, unable to look away and unwilling to move forward. She was afraid of what would come next. At this moment, nothing seemed more constant than the man beside the window, but she also knew that Sebastian once held that place in her mind. The past month seemed like an endless circle of searching for trust and crashing against betrayal. Kayla couldn't hold on to a sense of wounded superiority; the thought only deepened her guilt and served to sharpen the memory of Jeremy's face as he stepped away from her under those flickering lights.

"Kayla. Kayla?" She shook her head, fighting to find the voice that called her. Asher was watching her from the window. "We don't have to do this now," he said softly.

"No . . . we can't stay here long, right?" She didn't understand why she suddenly felt so weak again.

"That's right."

She turned to Kittie, who looked up to meet her gaze. The small girl's face was pinched anxiously. "He's too far away," the child whispered brokenly.

Kayla sat down beside her on the floor, letting Kittie crawl into her arms, both girls holding on to each other for comfort. "Asher, please begin." She spoke with her head bowed.

The pirates had all fallen silent, their eyes darting between the disconsolate pair and their expressionless leader. "This's awkward," Fec whispered loudly, wiping lemon juice from his face.

From his place on the couch, Kerif kicked him in the back. "Shut up! Let Serafin say what he has to!"

Asher closed his eyes for a moment, his brow furrowing, and took a deep breath. "We have a little less than a month before the next Eclipse occurs," he announced gravely, his eyes fixed on some point outside the window. "There's no more time. It's certain that Za'in is going to use that moment of power to commit an even more heinous crime against this world. He has to be stopped." He looked to Kayla. "This is not how I wanted it to be, but I've found you a place as safe as any, and you'll have four capable guards. I promise to come back for you."

"What? No!" Kayla halfway rose up, gripping Kittie tightly.

"We swore to follow you, Serafin!" Bruno fought to stand amid the tangled wires. "Didn't we prove ourselves back there?"

Asher turned from Kayla. "I never asked you to follow me!" he growled quietly at the pirates. "I foolishly assumed you'd eventually scatter. You have nothing to do with this, but if you insist on holding some unnatural attachment to me, then at least honor my wishes and protect her when I go." He paused, holding his breath briefly, as he clutched his side where Za'in's weapon caught him. The other four men were silent, as if they couldn't release their breath until Asher did. He noticed, and that knowledge only increased his agitation.

Kayla dragged Kittie along with her as she made her way to stand before Asher. "I don't understand. Last night you said it was my mother he needed last time and now I was the one—that the outcome depended on me. Please, I have to go with you."

"That's precisely the problem, Kayla. He needs you. But this time the goal is different, and I can't guess at his method. He may have already taken from you what he wanted, but if he hasn't, then I don't want to deliver you back into his hands." He turned his head, his eyes distant, and spoke quietly, as if to himself alone. "He may have what he needs already. Is that why we were able to leave that tower alive? He had to know his Ophan wasn't acting on orders. I didn't realize it then, but he had to have known . . ."

Kittie drew herself up, no longer limp and despondent. She tore at her clothing, pulling off every article of Za'in's uniform she was wearing, and stood before Asher in her green striped underclothes. "I'm *not* his Ophan! Not anymore. This wasn't some sort of game for any of us. I lost my best friend. It's true we survived on Za'in's arrogance. It happens at surprising times, doesn't it?" She dropped her head, letting her angry tears fall. "I never took his mark, but I was able to make him believe it for a while. It was a risk. He doesn't miss much, but he's not infallible. And he was drunk on Kayla. By his estimations, he had already won. But he misread her too."

Asher laid his hand lightly on her shoulder. "Kittie, I'm forever in your debt for bringing Kayla back to me. My intentions have never really been lost on you."

They exchanged a tense look before Kittie lowered her eyes, a regretful smile pulling on her face. "I know. Za'in must be stopped. It's simple. We can't let anything else move us now. Not our pride, not our grief, not our desire. If we don't stand now, there will really be nothing left this time. Only abominations. I know." The tears standing in her eyes weren't those of a wailing child any longer. "But Kayla should go with you. I know there's a risk of recapture, but didn't you notice that your kukris had no effect on him? If you want to strike down the most powerful of the Nephilim, you'll need one of their own."

"I can't allow myself to risk Kayla that way."

"You want me to . . . kill Sebastian?" Kayla's whisper rose louder, her voice lost somewhere between fear and resentment. "Just because I don't want to be his pawn doesn't mean that I'll be yours."

Kittie looked at her dispassionately. "Without that threat of violence, Asher is just walking to his own death. You wanted to go with him. What did you think you'd do?"

Kayla matched her cold stare. "I'm a part of this. I'm not going to hide."

"Well, that settles it then." Kittie turned back to Asher. "You feel she's safer with these guys? If Za'in finds where you hide her, do you think they can stop him from taking what he wants?"

"Hey!" Bruno cried out, while Kerif muttered, "uh, we're sitting right here . . ." Before Fec could protest, Vic rolled his eyes at him. "He'd kill us."

Asher looked momentarily defeated. "I suppose you all want to come. And you think we'll sneak by as an army of seven?"

"It was Vic's strength and my illusion that got us into Za'in's," Kerif chimed in.

"An' if it wasn't for me an' the Cap'n, you'd be without yer precious Inte'cesser," Fec mumbled dejectedly.

Asher rubbed his jaw again, glancing down at Kittie's discarded uniform. "Collect yourselves then. We need to put some distance between us and this place by nightfall."

The pirates were already celebrating their victory with lemon slices as Asher stalked out of the room. Kayla ran after him, meeting him in the hall. She grabbed his forearm, and he froze, his back to her, waiting calmly for her words. "Please, don't be angry with me," was all she could think to say.

"I'm not. You have reason to go. I can't deny that."

"But still, I'm sorry if I made anything worse. I can see that you don't want to continue your companionship with those pirates. I thought, that day on the shore, that you had been working together."

He breathed a quiet laugh, turning to face her. "No, they were looking for you on their own. We both caught up to you at the same time, but it seems that Saros had easily defeated them in an earlier battle. He had really put some fear into them. They watched me fight him and close in for victory, until you entered the fray. They were excessively impressed and I've been unable to shake them since. The way they idolize me is maddening." He looked exhausted, his bent spine giving away the wound in his side.

Kayla couldn't ignore his injury. "It was an Intercessor that hurt you. Do you think that I might have the power to ease your pain?"

Asher's body tensed slightly. "Your mother did have the gift of healing."

"Would you let me try?"

"Save your strength for the journey. I've traveled further

distances in worse conditions." He looked at her with kind eyes before turning and continuing to walk down the hallway.

"Wait!" She grabbed his arm again, pulling him towards the opening in the wall that led to the yard. "If we sit in the banyan, I'm sure I could help you."

Asher gave in, silently following her. It was a tight fit inside the rotted tree trunk, but Kayla pressed close to the perimeter, giving him room to sit. He reluctantly pulled off his poncho and the thin shirt he wore beneath, his eyes never leaving the familiar bark that surrounded him. Kayla gingerly removed his bloodied bandages to see the twisted, purple lines that were only interrupted by dark pools of skinless tears. Asher held on to the tree with his elevated left arm, allowing her to inspect his wound, his head bowed patiently.

Kayla's lungs never felt lighter as she breathed in the damp odor of the banyan's heart. Her right hand slid down the warm wood, the tip of her Intercessor catching the bark and holding her still. When the palm of her left hand gently made contact with his side, she felt her shoulders pull inwards involuntarily before she experienced a stabbing pain in her hand. She drew back to see only bruises lightly marking his ribs and a few welts on her palm.

They stared at each other for a long time, almost forgetting the injury in the glow of recognition they both felt here in this place. Asher let his head loll back, gazing up into the branches. "Thank you for not allowing me to let you disappear again. I've done this alone for so long. After Michael was gone, I led alone . . . but I led. It seems I guided death too; it always followed close behind. And then I just couldn't let anyone get caught in this inevitable cycle any longer. So I left. And then no one had to die except for the ones I chose. But now there are barely more than three weeks before the next Eclipse, and if that's all we have left, I want to live. I want to take the chance. I want to tell you everything I remember. I want to see Michael's smile on your lips and Kiera's tears in your eyes. I want it to be Steelryn and Serafin again, saving the world, or remembering it in the next one, if that's what it has to come to. I want to help you fulfill your destiny, or your will. I want Za'in to see justice, but I know it can't be my justice alone. Not anymore."

Kayla was still, watching the rising and falling of his chest as he spoke. The movement became slower and fuller, and then he was silent. When she looked to his smooth, sleeping face, she was certain she was witnessing a rare sight. She hesitated for a moment, then crawled out of the tree and sat among its roots, leaning against the trunk. Her heart was beating hard, and she closed her eyes. In her sudden and panicked need for comfort, she tried to conjure up Jeremy's image, but she could only imagine his back. Kayla drew her knees up, resting heavily against them, and as her hair fell along her side, she could feel the sun touching her neck. She was certain that wherever Jeremy was, he was without this warmth. She suffered the sensation anyways, and the guilt that came with it.

16

Jeremy wished every star above him would burn out so that he could finally be alone in the darkness. The knowledge that some of the glowing points in the distance were just the ghosts of dead stars only made him close his eyes against everything that hung in the night sky. The light felt piercing and watchful, and he told himself that was why he was lying still in the sand.

He couldn't feel his body anymore. His last memory of sensation was experienced as heaviness, his form sinking halfway into the sand while he imagined his spine fusing with the center of the earth. The desert dust collected in his upturned palms, and he surrendered to the wind's power to move his stiff fingertips. He remembered pain, but like everything else, it was gone. The only irritating reminder of existence was the constancy of the bright spots above his head.

Jeremy was falling in and out of sleep, and although each malformed dream that carried him was the essence of horror, he didn't mind. He knew his dreams weren't his reality, and that was the only condition of his preference. Only one question remained. *Am I dead?* He was numb. He wasn't sure if that meant he was cold. *Am I dead?* He could only begin to answer that question if he tried to remember how he came to be here, under those damned stars. His head dropped involuntarily to one side, as if it was compelled to shake against that notion. But still, it was movement, and that brought back a wave of pain. It was hard to distinguish if the hurt was physical or otherwise, but when it rose up in him, it was all-encompassing. He had to settle for it eventually subsiding into a dull ache that sharpened in spasms in concentrated locations.

He tried to fight his awakening, but he realized he couldn't forget the flash of white light and the tower coming down. He couldn't forget what brought that light. Jeremy gasped for breath; his mouth and lungs felt clogged with sand. He remembered jumping from an open stairwell and falling hard against the dried-up seabed, unsure of which bones were left unbroken. Every electric bulb that Za'in had kept running was out, and the desert floor was littered with shattered concrete and twisted metal beams. Jeremy crawled towards the horizon on pulled joints and fractured bones, his blood mixing with the sand, leaving behind a trail of thick and gritty sludge. He had lost track of time, dozing every few yards, until he was on his feet again, falling to his knees between shaky steps. He didn't know where he was going or why, only aware that he had to put some distance between himself and the destroyed compound before the sun rose. It wasn't long before he collapsed, supine, to the welcoming ground of the wasteland.

It was night again, and he still was here. He didn't understand why he was alive, why he was no longer bleeding, and why he was certain he could now move any of his limbs, if he could only summon the desire. He couldn't say that he was truly surprised. It wasn't the first time something like this had happened to him, even if this was the most extreme case. Regardless, he had never examined the phenomenon.

Jeremy struggled to remember why he had crawled away. He did it without thinking, but there was still some motivation behind it. Za'in survived the fall; he didn't even need the pain that crossed his chest to tell him that. Jeremy couldn't return to him as an Arch, not now. He knew he had been used by Za'in, but he never felt like a puppet when he thought of the benefits his status allowed him. Even so, now all that would be waiting for him at the end of his servitude would be death. The only way to get back on top and ensure his best chance of survival would be to capture Kayla on his own, and deliver her to Za'in before the next Eclipse. Jeremy remembered when he was promised ownership of her, while he promised himself he would be standing that day, when the sky darkened again. The thought of the former oath only increased his awareness of the sand in his throat, while the latter lent him the strength he needed to draw in his elbows, plant the heels of his palms against the ground, and painfully sit up. He didn't care anymore if the stars were shining. Let them go on burning. Soon they'd have no choice but to watch what fires he'd be setting, down below their gaze.

It was almost dawn when he found his way back to the compound, experiencing only mild surprise at how far away he had dragged himself in his injured state. There were few traces left of his flight, but it was easy to fall back into his own steps, his subconscious guiding him as if he was a sleepwalker. He could sense that Za'in had already left this place himself, and although he was certain that his former

Lord couldn't track him or speak to him through his mark, Jeremy knew that Za'in was most likely aware of his continued existence.

He walked through the halls of the only undamaged building. Nothing he expected to find within the ruins tempted him enough to test his ability to survive by lingering anywhere near crumbling concrete or creaking beams. Out of old habit, he entered his room and stared at its emptiness for a while before he sat down on the bed. His hand reached for his pillow, and as he began to pull it towards him, he stopped, holding it at his side. He fought with himself, weighing the consequences of his potential action. His mind raced. There was a time he had wanted to save her, but he was trapping her all the while, wasn't he? She was just doing what she set out to from the beginning, before he captured her. Jeremy remembered the last words she cried out before the flash of light took them all. She couldn't have meant it. Even when she held on to him, her eyes frightened and hopeful, the whole time she was planning this. He had bought her act so thoroughly that he was moved by her cries, costing him his victory against Serafin. Jeremy flung the pillow back down. There would be no traces left of her presence here anyways. It didn't matter.

Jeremy abandoned his bare room and found his way to Kit's. He couldn't suppress a sad smile as he stood in the doorway, his hand stiffly clutching the knob. He dropped his head. Could he blame Kit for leaving? She never wanted to be involved in any of this; she just went along to survive. No, that was a lie. Everything she had done was to stay with him, and he knew it. Za'in took her, tried to mark her—this mark that was an abomination, this mark that should never mar someone like her—and he knew he just sat back and waited. She came out unscathed, or so she said, but he never stepped in and rescued her. He thought of all the things she took on her shoulders for his sake. Jeremy grabbed a purple scarf off her bed and stuffed it into one of his deep cargo pockets, his movements quick and automatic.

He turned his back on the room. No. They were supposed to stay together. She should have warned him, instead of backing him up to the edge of a cliff to see if he would jump at her request. And what was she doing with Serafin? She dressed him in uniform and brought him up to the tower. Kayla didn't have the knowledge of this place or the freedom from Za'in's watchful eye to pull off something like that. Not alone. Not without Kit. He walked back out into the hall, his legs rigid.

As a curiosity before he left, he opened the door to Za'in's quarters. On his simple bed were two masses of bone that loosely resembled claws. They weren't the same as Za'in and Kayla's weapons, but they were obviously related.

Jeremy's fists clenched against the memory of Kayla's mastery of her Intercessor. It was all true, wasn't it? This whole time he never minded the thieving of relics, the destruction of cults. He never understood Za'in's attraction to dead religion, but he admired his willingness to crush what he didn't collect. When Jeremy first saw Kayla's hilt, he assumed that relic was just a fortunate bonus to capturing the daughter of Michael Steelryn. Sure, he had heard the rumors that Steelryn was part Angel, but he never believed in God anyways. If Michael was so powerful, how did Za'in take him down? He always thought the Angel legend was just the result of the mistaken retelling of a story that began with Steelryn's former rank as the First Arch in Za'in's Spheres. And Za'in was just a man. He used a weapon that matched the description of an Intercessor, but he was obsessed with the old cults, steeped in magic, and drunk on drops of science. He could achieve amazing things, but so have countless men before him. He was just a man.

Jeremy shoved the bed over, sending the two bony claws skidding along the floor, as an enraged cry escaped his raw throat. It wasn't just tricks and tradition. They drew their weapons out from their own flesh, and he witnessed Kayla use two Intercessors to Deliver, just like the myth described. Were all the superstitious rumors true? Did the Eclipse really destroy the Earth because Za'in brought down the void that was once Heaven? On the rare occasions that he considered what really went on the day he was born, he always put more stock in the theory that the poles shifted. He thought that what happened was all that mattered, not the why. Nothing could change the past. But this changed everything.

Was Kittie part Angel too? What about Serafin? Is that why they blew everything up and left him to die out here? He felt duped, like the only human left on earth. Jeremy stared at the bones at his feet. Were they claws or something else entirely? He squatted down and held one to the window, examining it in the light. It twitched very slightly in his grasp, so he held on tighter. With his opposite hand, he ran his fingers up its base until his palm lay flat against its center. The claws shuddered, clamping down between his fingers and along the tender part of his wrist, the ends of each protrusion fusing together around his forearm. He felt a momentary pain in his palm before the claw unwound, relaxing its grip and returning to its former state.

Jeremy wiped the drops of blood from his hand onto the side of his pants, a grin spreading darkly across his face. "So this is how you catch an Angel," he whispered hoarsely. He pocketed his treasures and paused at Za'in's door. He looked around, almost expecting to see that dark Angel descend. He laughed, crossing himself mockingly before exiting, taking pleasure in leaving his door wide open.

He hurried to the garage, his feet light and his energy renewed. He didn't care what state he would find the building in, he would brave it. As he ran, he considered that perhaps all this was part of some plan. Why else would Za'in leave behind these fetters? He shook off his doubts, dashing to the gate and pulling it open violently. Jeremy stopped short, staring at the one truck left in the empty garage. It only mattered *what* was, not why. Reasons were just excuses, and he wasn't going to let them start paralyzing him now. Jeremy jumped into the driver's seat, pulled the goggles off the rear-view mirror, and drove out into the desert, high on the knowledge that he would never have to see this place again.

17

"I figured it out! It's gonna take almost a year to walk to the location of the new Eclipse," Kerif complained, separating his dreads as he walked.

"If you weren't playing with your hair, you'd get there faster," Vic called from over his shoulder, yards ahead of him.

Kayla followed as Asher led them through the outskirts of a ruined city, preferring to watch his back rather than her surroundings. She knew she'd feel safer by his side, but she lagged behind to stay close to Kittie. The small girl wasn't moving at a pace that was unusually slow for someone her size, but Kayla remembered a time when she never had trouble keeping up with Jeremy's long strides. Kittie's eyes were clear again, her face was composed, and even some of her cheerfulness had returned, but Kayla couldn't ignore the momentary clenching of her chest that gripped her each time she held her hand. They had been walking for two days, and in that time, Kittie had not mentioned Jeremy's name, nor was she seen attempting to locate him.

"Serafin's got somethin' up his sleeve, mos' definitely! We won't be walkin' much longer . . . right Cap'n?" Fec's confident tone slid into an uncertain whine as he stumbled in his sandals.

"Well, yeah. That's what I've been figuring." Bruno pulled nervously on his hair, his eye troubled. "Miss Kayla is probably gonna spirit us away again!" He nodded, satisfied that he banished his own doubts.

"Sorry, we decided against that," Kayla said softly.

They were silent, meeting her uneasy glance with hopeless expressions.

"It would be dangerous for all of us," Asher said as he kept walking, his steps slowing just enough to allow the gap between them to close in a few feet. "In the tower, we had to let her Deliver us—there was no other way out. It didn't matter where she took us; few places would have been darker. Za'in may be the only one left who really understands the process of how to Deliver using two Intercessors. I can't teach her. If she makes another attempt like last time, we might end up further away from our destination, or worse. I won't take that chance. But that doesn't mean we're going to walk forever." Asher didn't glance at any of them, his eyes intent on the horizon, his gaze sometimes flickering to the brush and debris that surrounded them, as his careful steps seemed guided by urgent certainty.

Fec frowned, kicking the rocks at his feet. "This'is worse than my batt'ry not workin'. If I got to watch even little TV, I'd walk th' whole way there!"

"You've watched TV before?" Kayla asked.

"Oh yeah, lots!" Fec's sallow face brightened. "I was four when the sky wen' dark, so I still r'member. Hey Vic, you 'member that Batman cartoon?" he called out ahead.

"How could I forget? You never stop talking about it." He didn't turn his head, his irritation carried to them by the wind.

"Aww, ignore m'brother. He acts like things were always this way! But I'm not bothered, 'cuz it'll all come back soon." He winked at Kayla.

She stared back, unsure of what he assumed she was a co-conspirator to.

"Oh yeah, she was stuck in that shithouse town near Madeline, whatever-it-was-called, for like her whole life. She doesn't know, Fec!" Kerif smacked the back of his friend's head, and then resumed his grooming as he walked.

"Who even tol' you tha'?" Fec scowled as he attempted kicking Kerif with his scrawny legs.

Bruno side-stepped them, continuing his walk at Kayla's side. "Technology is coming back. The world had some major issues right before the Eclipse anyways, so then when *that* happened, it was too much to recover from. It was basically anarchy for a while there, what with nature turning on us and none of our gadgets working! I mean *nothing*. All the power was out. I guess it doesn't seem like much now, but at the time . . . Everything was built on it, see? People just went crazy. As if one wave of destruction wasn't enough, right? Well, we get by now, but it's like another Earth. It wasn't an easy adjustment. But lots of time has passed and some of that old stuff is returning. It's underground, of course. If Za'in knew anything about it, he'd take it for himself, and no one would ever see it again—not in a way you'd want to see it, anyways. But alls we gotta do now is take Za'in down!"

"Revolución!" Fec and Kerif cried out in unison.

Bruno ignored their outburst as if it was a common occurrence. "So now you see why we were looking for you, right? We have a coupla relics, but you're a *real* Nephil."

"Yeah, and we gotta win now, 'cuz we have Serafin too!" Kerif grinned, fidgeting with his rings now. "I bet he even

has a little Angel in him—just watch his powers of ass-
kicking! Yeeaahh, we're so close . . . You can have the TV,
Fec; I'm waiting for *air conditioning!*"

Kayla was overwhelmed and she looked down at Kittie
for help.

The little girl appeared tired. "I think your best bet is to
walk up front with Asher. If you don't, they might never
shut up." When Kayla hesitated, she forced a little smile.
"I'm okay, really."

Kayla squeezed her hand before letting go and running
timidly to Asher's side. Vic noticed her approach and slowly
fell back to walk with his comrades, but Asher's eyes barely
moved in her direction. They walked together quietly for a
long time, as the pirates' chatter behind them dissolved into
a vague mass of distant noise. Kayla looked down at her left
hand; the bruises were almost gone. She clenched her fist
tightly, the pressure keeping her question about his wound
unasked. She knew the answer already, and any time she
thought about that morning, a wave of some uneasy feeling
hit her. It was frightening, and she always banished the
memory quickly before she could either examine it or be
harmed by it.

"Thank you. It really has made traveling easier. Don't let
anything within you try to smother that ability—it's too
precious." Asher spoke quietly, his eyes never wandering
back to her.

She caught her breath, marveling at how natural it felt
for him to pick up on her thoughts. She could only nod in
reply. Kayla felt the sun warm her shoulders, and although
her feet ached, her steps felt light. She breathed in the
silence between them, almost forgetting why they were
walking out here.

As soon as this thought relaxed her face into something
like a smile, Asher spoke again, breaking the illusion. "They

were right. We're not walking the whole distance there, but our options aren't good. The way we're going, we'll end up drawing attention to ourselves. It can't be helped. But if Za'in is watching, he'll let us come. One way or another, he'll see to it that you return. We have to be ready for it."

Kayla nodded again, still unwilling to make a sound.

"You don't want to fight him." Asher's voice was almost inaudible.

"It's not just that," she began, her voice cracking beneath her wish that their quiet moment didn't have to end. "I don't even know how. He opened my eyes, he taught me, and not only does he understand everything I can do and hope to do, but he can read me. However I intend to act, he'll see it coming." She let out a low growl of frustration. "Don't you see? He knows what I'm capable of, even when I don't."

Asher let her anger settle into the air, leaving only a vacuum of silence. When he finally spoke again, nothing had changed in his voice. "I'm not talking about him."

Kayla turned her head away, feeling as though it was pulled by a string tied to whatever was tightening in her chest. "No, I don't want to fight *him*. I won't."

"The only way out of that is if I do it for you. I will."

"No, you're wrong. It doesn't have to come to that." Her voice was too even, and she felt as if her words echoed back to her, hollow.

Asher didn't speak again, and Kayla found a lump gathering in her throat. She watched him as he walked beside her, his movements purposeful, his face resolute. She didn't want to imagine having to fight Jeremy, but she had to confront the reality that he didn't walk like the man beside her. What she may have mistaken for purpose in Jeremy's steps was simply anger or insolence or spite. Did anything drive him beyond a search for relief or a flight from pain?

Kayla remembered his blank eyes as he held her down against her reunion with Asher . . . she remembered the pained tightness of his face that night when they talked beneath the stars . . . she remembered the fevered breaths she felt between his kisses . . . and she remembered the disconnected rage that held his body stiff as he finally stepped away from her. She watched Asher move. It was effortless, as if each movement remembered every one that preceded it and was conscious of why its turn was next. If Jeremy was moving towards her now, he'd be running on passion, following it in any misdirection it pointed. No matter which way it went, it would end in a fight.

The air stung Kayla's throat. "You're really asking if I'll stand with you against him."

There was the slightest movement in Asher's eyelids. "I'm planning. And the details rest upon where each of us stands. Make no mistake—Za'in will use your feelings as a weapon . . . and he'll use mine."

She struggled to catch her breath. "Asher . . . I—I won't let you down."

His eyes finally met hers, if only for a moment. "I know that." His voice was reassuring, even if it was still a little distant. "Relax . . . there is nothing you have to tell me. I have what I need to decide now. It doesn't change that our options are few." His smile was thin and grim, but gentle.

Kayla's heart raced. Her reaction to his words was enough for him to read what he wanted to know? She felt exposed, afraid of this ability that was another aspect he shared with Sebastian. She decided that was why her breathing was shallow and her chest ached.

Forcing her focus back to the world around her, she noticed that their environment had begun to change. Heavily overgrown ruins began to make way for smaller, abandoned buildings that weren't as severely damaged. She realized that the long, flat stones at her feet that existed between sprouts of grass, gnarled roots and little flowers, were stretches of concrete. That material must have been ground down to the pebbles and dust they had tread over a few miles back.

Kayla could only see dark, broken windows, sagging roofs, and faded paint between all the green that craned upwards towards the sun. They were just rows of houses, left behind. "Is there no one here anymore? Not everything is gone, so you would think, maybe . . ."

Asher was paying careful attention to the houses they passed, and it seemed like a struggle for him to form a reply. "This close to the eye of the storm, no one is left and no one wants to come near. I don't know if they even know why anymore. But there is one exception, which is why we took this road."

It was getting dark, and although the rest of them dragged their feet, Asher's movements were quicker and sharper. His head turned right and left, his eyes sweeping over the houses on either side of the road. He suddenly rounded a corner onto a street even thicker with foliage, and the others scrambled to follow. When they caught up with him, Asher was opening the door to a yellow house that sat between two overgrown, empty lots. "Quickly, in here," he called over his shoulder. "We go no further tonight."

The fear of standing in this vacant street under the gathering darkness was stronger than the apprehension Kayla felt for entering the ramshackle house. She hurried to Asher's side, and although his eyes were still reaching for distant points even now, he pressed his palm lightly between her shoulder blades in a steadying gesture of comfort. They stood beside the door as the pirates dragged themselves inside the dark house. Bruno and Kerif leaned on each other, their jaws jutting out cheerlessly. Fec followed them with only slightly more energy, calling out, "Anyone 'ave fire?" Vic was last, carrying a subdued Kittie on his back.

When the others were inside, Asher finally let his eyes meet Kayla's. "Go inside and try to sleep. They're going to protect you for the measure of the night."

"What? Where are you going?" She impulsively reached for his arm.

He looked down at her hand. "I'm going to ensure that, starting tomorrow, we cover more miles. But I have to go alone. It wouldn't matter to this man who you are—he wouldn't trust me if I brought anyone along. He barely tolerates me as it is." Asher faced her again, a tired smile almost brightening his features. "Don't look so worried. I doubt Za'in has recovered enough by now to have located you already, and those boys can guard you against most everything else. I know it doesn't seem that way, but they can handle themselves, and I've seen you do some pretty remarkable things too. Still, I'll be back before dawn." He turned to leave, his steps sure, even on the crumbling walkway that led down into the yard.

Kayla lunged forward, grabbing his hand. "Something is going to happen while you're gone," she blurted out.

Asher froze. "Is that so?"

"I don't know why I said that." She dropped his hand, her embarrassment something akin to being caught talking in her sleep. "I feel like something is close. Like I'm being watched. Or maybe I'm just afraid to see you go."

He didn't turn around. "I tore down Za'in's compound to get to you. I'm coming back. Just stay with the boys and stay inside."

Kayla watched him walk out into the darkness as she clung to the column that supported the porch's overhang.

She closed her eyes against the rising sting of tears. Something was coming for her. And she wasn't sure she'd be able resist its pull.

18

Through the screen door, Kayla could see tiny flashes of light sparkling between Bruno's fingers as he played his coins over his knuckles. She watched for each reoccurring metallic glint as she lay there on the wooden floor, wrapped in a blanket they found in an upstairs closet. Fec had first watch, and she hadn't slept then either. She just lazily observed the nervous motions of his toes and the trails of smoke he expelled. Now she turned her head to see Kittie, nestled in the reclining chair beside her, her face smooth and untroubled by dreams. Kayla had chosen the floor as her place of rest for reasons she didn't fully understand, but the wood seemed warm, and it was certainly more appealing than the furniture that sagged unhappily.

Her hands ached, the pain running halfway up her fore-arms. She remembered seeing a banyan tree across the road, and she thought that if she could just climb into its boughs and see the stars, maybe this uneasy feeling would leave her. Kayla closed her eyes and thought of Asher. He wanted her to stay securely inside, but was this place really safe? The pirates had searched it before they settled down for bed, and although there was no threat of danger, this house was not a fortress against Sebastian or anything else that might intend them harm.

Kayla pressed her palms together, the force relieving some of the pressure in her limbs. She opened her eyes and searched for the sparkle of Bruno's coins on the other side of the screen. The tiny glimmer was still as the coin lay on the porch, steadily reflecting the glow of the moon. The Captain's limp fingers hung above it as he slept in the chair they had pulled outside from the kitchen. Kayla glanced back quickly at the others. Kittie hadn't moved from her position all night; her cheek was still pressed against her fist, her mouth open. Kerif was sprawled out on the couch, the blissful expression on his dreaming face no doubt the result of winning this coveted spot in a game of rock-paper-scissors. The pirates told her that Asher had previously given the order for all of them to sleep in the center of the house on the ground floor, but Fec didn't let his loss at the game stop him from finding a soft resting place. He slept in a similarly triumphant pose on a bare mattress he brought down the stairs. Vic was sitting on the floor, propped up by the corner walls, his arms crossed and head drooping. He sat facing his brother, still the silent protector even in sleep.

She held her breath as her eyes passed over each of her companions again, watching the rise and fall of their chests in an attempt to gauge if they would awaken easily. Kayla rose painfully to stand, her body aching from days of walking, but her arms and hands throbbed even more intensely. She didn't bother to slide into her boots; it would be easier to quietly make her way out barefoot. The screen door creaked as she exited the house, but she had timed the sound to blend with the singing of the crickets, and even then she froze, making sure the noise didn't rouse anyone from sleep. Kayla crept past Bruno, who was slouched in his chair, snoring quietly, and she crossed the road, her eyes searching nervously for the banyan tree.

The sky above her was strewn with stars, but she wouldn't look up—not yet. She had to find that tree. It wasn't where she remembered it. Kayla ran in the grass beside the road, clutching onto the blanket wrapped around her shivering form. She felt exposed out here in the open, but she was certain that if she could climb the banyan she would be safe, and every doubt and fear that plagued her would be relieved. She wouldn't feel watched or pursued. She would be able to dream in peace until Asher returned for her. Nothing else mattered or made any sense.

Ahead of her, she could see the tree, cast brightly in the cold light of the moon. It was further than she thought, but as long as she could find her way back to the yellow house, no one would know she ventured this distance. Kayla fell forward onto her knees and pressed her palms against the bark of the tree. The wood felt cool to her burning flesh, soothing her body and pulling her eyelids downward. She tried to climb, to crane her neck towards the sky, but her joints were loose and her chin was heavy. The moon was just too bright. How would she ever see the stars? Kayla used the last of her waning strength to release one of her hands from the tree's trunk and shield her face from the intense light.

It didn't make any sense. The rest of the world seemed to have receded, but this brilliance still pierced her. She turned her head to see two orbs of light shining towards her from the road. "No . . . no! Asher . . ." she murmured, backing away on her hands, her heels digging into the dirt as she kicked herself away from the harsh glow. Kayla tried to rise up on one arm, releasing her Intercessor with the other. She stumbled a few times before she finally stood, looking again towards the light before attempting the run back to the yellow house. The two bright points that dazzled her sight were the headlights of a truck, stopped right in front of the tree. Kayla slowly focused her gaze, afraid of whom she would see in the driver's seat.

Jeremy pulled his goggles down to fall loosely around his neck. He watched her silently, his rigid features thinly veiling what seethed beneath, and she stood frozen, unable to let anything move her but his next action. His movements were slow and measured as he turned off the engine and then the headlights, his eyes never leaving hers. Jeremy jumped out of the roofless vehicle and walked deliberately towards her, his limbs stiff, his form dirty and disheveled, and as he approached, Kayla felt like a storm was about to collide with her body.

He stood only inches away, looking down at her coldly. "It didn't take him long to leave you here alone in the ruins."

Kayla retracted her Intercessor, her relief and dread collecting to form a sob. "Oh God, Jeremy, it's really you—" She wanted to fall against him, to press her cheek to his chest, but as she tried to reach for him, she could barely make her arms obey.

"Don't touch me," he said flatly.

Her hands hovered in the air before she drew them back limply to her own heart, her head dropping and her tears falling against his dusty boots. "I'm so sorry . . . about everything! I didn't want things to go this way . . ."

"What did you expect?" His rage had begun to thaw his icy expression as he spat the words at her. "You're glad I survived what you did to me, and now what am I supposed to do—forget? You think I'd believe anything you said after you . . . you—"

"No, I can't expect you to believe that since the

beginning of this, I wanted to stay beside you!" Kayla looked up at him, her angry tears challenging even the threat of violence she knew he carried with him. "It doesn't make sense, does it? You captured me, used me, put me in danger . . . I was supposed to hate you. I tried to forget you, Jeremy, but I was always thinking of you, always! But, fine, don't believe it. Take me back to Za'in. Kill me. Offer me up. Or do what you really want to, if you even know what that is anymore."

Kayla couldn't breathe, and for a moment she was sure Jeremy had taken his revenge on her. The pain of a dropping impact stung her back, but her head was cradled in his hands, caught between his coarse palms and the driving pressure of his mouth. His weight pushed her further into the grass and dirt. Jeremy released her from the protective grip he held her in as they fell to the earth, so that now his hands could forge rough paths over her body. Kayla could feel the cool night air against her breasts, followed by the wetness of his kiss, and just as suddenly she was trapped beneath his sand-beaten armor. She reached for him, pulling on his shirt, conscious only of her desire to feel his skin upon hers. Jeremy pushed her hands away, rising up just enough to wrench off his armor and peel his soiled shirt from his torso. The moon's cold light cut deep shadows into his chest, his scars shining as clean white lines and the black cross receding like a narrow, intersecting void. Kayla could barely see the glint of his half-closed eyes beneath the dark hair that hung in his face, but his mouth was loose, fervent, and wrathful. She closed her eyes and turned her head, knowing then what would come next, her longing and fear endlessly feeding on each other.

Jeremy fell upon her again, pinning her arms above her head with his one hand, and she marveled that even now, he didn't realize that she wanted this. She forced the tense muscles in her thighs to relax, offering him her weakest defenses, and he didn't hesitate. The acknowledgment of pain was momentary, and it became indistinguishable from the acute intoxication that filled her with each wave of assault. She felt his teeth in her flesh and she cried out, struggling against his grip, yearning to reach for him, but his hold only tightened, preventing her embrace. Kayla strained to bring her face closer to his, wanting to claim his eyes and mouth as he took possession of her now, but his eyes were closed, his features lost and unaware, completely cut off from the moments before this and what the aftermath would bring. His eyes suddenly opened, and for a moment there was recognition in his stare, and bliss, but then the lines in his face gathered tighter together and he kissed her, hard, the movements of his body reflecting the fury that contorted his features. This time she couldn't return his kiss, her mouth opening stiffly, quivering as her breath caught almost soundlessly in her throat. At nearly the same moment Jeremy let his head drop beside hers, the side of his face resting against her cheek.

They were both still and silent for a few moments and she felt him become heavier as his body relaxed, although his grip on her wrists never loosened. He rose up onto his knees and, without meeting her gaze, adjusted their clothing to cover their bodies again, his movements slow and casual. Jeremy looked towards his own shirt and armor beside the tree's roots, but they were too far to reach without letting go of her. He pulled Kayla up and sat behind her, trapping her forearms together behind her back and wrapping his arm around her chest, pulling her close. She could feel his heart beating fast against her shoulder blade. His embrace was unyielding. Kayla rested heavily on him, deciding it was too late to fear danger. They were both motionless for a long time, until he abruptly dropped his face into her hair,

nestled in the crook between her neck and shoulder. "Kayla
. . . I . . ." he began, his voice choked and muffled.

She stiffened as Jeremy's hold around her tightened and
suddenly something cold and sharp constricted against her
palms, between her fingers and down the backs of her
hands, around her forearms. Kayla slumped in his arms, a
bitter pain numbing her flesh and stealing her breath. "What
. . . did you . . . do?" she gasped.

"Just like you said, Kayla. I did what I wanted to. You
know what that's like, don't you?" Jeremy's voice was harsh
and labored. She knew the words were his, but they felt
foreign.

Every part of her clenched tightly, and even the tears
that welled up inside couldn't reach her eyes. She could feel
her two Intercessors beneath whatever Jeremy had clamped
on her hands, but instead of the slick, clean sensation she
usually experienced, they felt barbed and brittle, and thick
with poison. "You're . . . killing . . . me."

"That was another option you gave me, remember?
Right after 'taking you back to Za'in.' How about we try all
of the above?" Jeremy stood, yanking her up by the arm. He
pulled her over to the truck, stopping to steady himself
along the door, coughing and closing his eyes as if against a
dizzy spell.

Kayla felt herself being lifted into the passenger seat, and
then she sat slouched, her head lolling back. She watched
Jeremy walk back over to the banyan, pulling his keys out of
his pocket before he bent down to gather his belongings,
but she wondered why he froze, halfway stooped to the
ground.

She heard a voice that wasn't Jeremy's. "You're going to
wish you were still beneath that tower, boy." Her vision was
failing her, but she was certain it was Asher who spoke.

19

Jeremy's face was lost somewhere in the shadows that gathered beneath his unruly hair, but his smile cut through the shroud, glinting sharply. "I'm thinking . . . if you wanted to kill me, you wouldn't have given me any warning. You want to fight. Okay. Then let's fight." He began to straighten up when Asher's boot slammed into his head, knocking him into the dirt.

Asher pressed his foot against the side of Jeremy's neck as he looked back towards Kayla. She was slumped in the passenger seat, semi-conscious, while Bruno struggled with the door, attempting to lift her. "No, I gave you warning for her sake. But now you're only alive until I find out what you've done to her."

"I only did what you've been wanting to," he laughed out of the corner of his mouth.

Asher dug his knee into Jeremy's back and pulled his head up by the hair, a kukri to his enemy's throat. "What did you put on her hands?" he growled quietly.

"Oh, that? That just makes her easier to handle. Don't

worry—I only cuffed her afterwards. It's been my experience, if I let the girl fight a little, it's better for both of us." Jeremy chose his moment carefully, sliding out of Asher's grip at the exact instant his hold was loosened by a tiny shudder of rage. Jeremy wrenched Asher's arm on the way out of his grasp, causing him to drop his blade. Asher pressed forward, slicing down with his other kukri, but Jeremy dodged, bent over and stumbling on his hands, but soon he righted himself and ran to the truck. His grin dropped when the vehicle didn't react to the key in the ignition. He turned the key again, panicked, before he was forced to give up on it, only dodging Asher's next blow at the last moment. He found his weapon beside him and yanked it from its sheath as he jumped into the backseat.

Jeremy turned his head wildly, unable to find his enemy. He felt the back of the truck bounce before a stabbing pain in his right arm caused him to drop his sword, and a sharp pressure against his throat prevented him from reaching for it.

Asher's voice was still low. "Remove those bones from her hands."

"Just kill him! Look what he did to Miss Kayla! We can get these things off ourselves!" Kerif screamed. Kayla lay on her side, half in Bruno's arms, as Kerif frantically tried to pry the bones away from her hands with some small tools.

"No, we can't. Only the one who put these on can remove them." Kittie spoke quietly, standing barefoot beside the trio on the ground. Her face was pinched as she watched Jeremy caught helplessly in Asher's deadly grasp.

"You'd know that, wouldn't you, Kit? Look around. Has everything gone according to your divine plan?" Fury choked his voice to almost a whisper.

"And you didn't know, did you?" Kittie stepped closer, stopping beside the truck's door and staring up at him.

"You didn't know what would happen if you used these on her. And you did it anyways."

"Yeah. And I don't know how to take them off." Jeremy couldn't turn his head away from her, so he just lowered his eyes.

Asher yanked him down off the truck, pulling him through the dirt towards Kayla. "You're going to figure it out, right now."

Jeremy struggled violently against him, his resistance causing him to superficially cut his throat. "I don't fucking know how, okay?" he snarled.

Asher fought to keep him under control. "God damn it, stop! Do you want to die?"

He was suddenly limp and still, a short laugh falling dryly from his mouth. "This guy doesn't miss much, does he, Kit? Real sharp. I see why you threw in with him." A sarcastic grin twisted his face, but his voice was quiet. "But if I just fell forward, would that ruin your plans?"

"Stop. It's disgusting." Kittie's voice was cold and resonant. Jeremy looked up suddenly, unnerved by the change in her tone. "I was prepared to throw myself at your feet if I found you again, to apologize for the sudden nature of that night . . ." She shook her head violently, her own voice breaking through. "You want revenge? I'll face you, Jeremy. But just look at her! You won't, will you? Because if you do, you'll have to face the fact that you were only able to hurt her this way because she loves you—"

"Shut up!" He thrashed wildly as Asher drove him to his knees, facing Kayla.

Kittie dropped down beside him, her breath hot on his ear. "She doesn't deserve this. And you don't deserve what you're doing to yourself. This isn't some kind of punishment you have to endure to pay for your feelings."

Jeremy was suddenly calm. "Listen. I'm not the person

you think I am. And I don't pretend to understand you. But this makes sense: there's a knife to my throat. And we both know that's how things get done." He reached for Kayla's hand, and pried back her cold, stiff fingers. He studied the bones attached to her palm and he trailed the dark mark that deepened in the center, growing lighter as it spread out down her arm. He wedged his fingers between the rough protrusions and her flesh, pulling outwards, but he couldn't break the seal. Jeremy brought her hands closer so that he could examine them both with his head bowed, keeping his face from the scrutiny of those crowded around him. He listened to Kayla's labored breathing, but he refused to turn and see her face, staring harder at the blackened tangle of bones that choked her limbs.

He didn't know what to do. This strategy was supposed to be simple and the details were never decided. It wasn't a surprise that things turned out this way. Whatever the conclusion, it's all the same. He ran his fingers over hers. This wasn't what he wanted, but his desires were unrealistic and sentimental. In the end, the world moves according to its nature, regardless of your agenda. There was no such thing as destiny, and it was useless to make plans. All you can do is make it to the next moment, and sometimes, just hold off death. He squeezed her hands, his fingers intertwined with hers, their palms pressed towards each other through the layer of bone.

When Jeremy felt an icy spine puncture the inside of his hand, he held down a shudder. He didn't know what was happening; he only knew he just had to take it. He set his jaw tightly as he felt the bones lifting off Kayla's hands and clamping down around his. Each point of contact was experienced as a tiny, but penetrating, sting. His limbs felt cold and constrained, but he couldn't ignore the pulsating rush that pushed upwards towards his temples. He raised his head, meeting Kayla's gaze with his sharpening vision. Although she was obviously weakened by these fetters, her tired eyes were clear. There was no threat of tears as she studied his features, carefully, as if she was trying to catalogue every detail of something she would never see again. Her mouth opened slightly, but closed again with an almost imperceptible frown as she accepted the small regret of being too drained to speak.

Jeremy threw back his head and closed his eyes. His chest throbbed, his head swimming and arms tingling. He had never felt this way before. He couldn't tell if he was going to die or shoot straight up into the heavens. He closed one hand around Asher's blade, while scraping his other forearm down his captor's arm. The bony spurs tore Asher's flesh, and with a savage growl he was forced to let go of his prisoner. Jeremy ran to the truck and grabbed his sword, then turned around for a moment. A fleeting realization sent him lurching back abruptly—for an instant there was nothing else steering his body but the thought of scooping Kayla into his arms and running into the ruins with her. But like everything else, that desire passed too, and as always, he was immediately gripped by another compulsion.

He stretched out his arms, slowly adjusting his grip on his weapon, feeling the bones caught between his hands and the hilt. Every long, tense movement of his fingers sent sharp paths upwards, searing his limbs. He repeated each action, a strange attachment to the pain keeping him in a loop of motion and sensation. He stared down at the dark, twisted masses that coiled jaggedly up his arms, his own flesh only escaping at the fingertips and up from the elbows. "I know you're curious. We both want to see what happens next, right?" Jeremy's eyes were closed against a momentary wooziness that swayed him, but he knew Asher would understand he was being addressed.

"I already know the outcome. I won't let you return to Za'in as a puppet that snatched some power from a wounded Angel. I end this now." Asher spoke between clenched teeth as he held his bloodied arm.

Jeremy watched his enemy hovering protectively over Kayla. Her weary body was limp and motionless, but her eyes followed their exchange carefully. He felt the ache in his arms reflected in the cross on his chest. "The end . . . You can't bring that, Serafin. That never comes." A mangled smile twisted his features as he tore forward, his sword's arc leading his movements.

Asher dropped low, pressuring Jeremy's leg, and at the same time catching his weapon with his blade as they made contact. The splitting movement brought Jeremy to the ground and he let go of his weapon too easily, almost as a novel afterthought. He rolled around the tightening circle of momentum, flailing his arm towards Asher, his skeletal gauntlets slashing his adversary's thigh. Asher let the force pull him down, his knee landing hard against the side of Jeremy's neck. The former Arch coughed, spitting, and skid out from under Asher's weight as that knee continued to slide to the earth. He righted himself, controlling Serafin's movement by catching the gauntlets' ridges in his flesh. Jeremy crossed his forearms against the other man's throat, just one pulling movement away from a warm comfort drenching his frozen and constricted limbs.

He felt something cold against the base of his jaw just moments before he heard her tiny voice. "You won't heal from this, I assure you. Get the fuck out of here, Jeremy." He held his head still and strained his eyes towards the sound to see streams of water falling over a brown cheek.

"We never get to finish this. How many times will you all interfere? It doesn't matter who wins . . . it just needs to end. Why can't you let it happen, Kit?" He spoke evenly, already resigned to the incessant loop he was caught in.

Kittie's voice was low and deliberate. "I won't let you incidentally tear down the world just because you're blind to anything beyond this moment."

"I see. You prefer him, too."

"For Christ's sake!" She pressed her gun harder against him, struggling to bring her tone back down to that cold, even murmur. "I'll do it."

"Oh, I know." He didn't move.

Her voice softened a little. "You need to get those things off your arms. If you don't, you'll wish I blew your brains out here."

"I know," he said again quietly as he loosened his hold and began to withdraw.

Kittie kept her weapon trained on him. "Get your armor and go."

"What are you doing? You can't let him go. Shoot him!" Kerif yelled. The pirates were gathered around Kayla, frozen by fear of Jeremy as well as Asher's standing commandment to stay out of their fights.

Kittie didn't stir, silencing them with her quick reply. "Say that again and I'll turn this on you."

Jeremy moved sluggishly to collect his possessions, pausing for a moment to consider the truck. A little laugh pulled his head down as he walked out into the ruins. He looked back once, unable to deny the pleasure of watching Kittie hold that weapon with the intention of firing, even if he was the target. The burning cross on his chest drew him towards the horizon as he turned painfully away again.

Kittie waited until he was out of sight before flinging the gun into the darkness and dropping down hopelessly into the dirt.

20

Kayla just had to survive the length of this day. Then Asher's commands would come and she would know the right path to walk. She sat slumped in the recliner, her forearms to the ceiling, her upturned palms hanging off the armrests. The cool air that circulated through the open windows soothed the raw wounds in her hands. Her eyes closed with the memory of pain. Kittie had cut shards of blackened bone from her limbs and thoroughly cleaned the punctures in her palms. Kayla tried half-heartedly to press her Intercessors outward, but they felt swollen and jammed. Kittie had told her that she would regain her abilities, but there was still a sluggish threat of panic below the surface; she didn't realize until now how much these newly discovered aspects of her being truly completed her. She felt empty. No, clogged with filth.

She let her head drop. It was a thought she tried to keep hidden deep in her subconscious so that no one would be able to detect it . . . but perhaps this was almost worth it. For a moment, she had what she wanted, even in an imperfect world. Kayla let a shudder of pleasure move her, her inhalation catching in her throat. She held her breath as long as she could, as if the air held her memory. She thought of Jeremy's face as she saw it just hours ago with her blurred vision. It wasn't an unspoiled recollection, but she wanted to keep it, since it could be her last. She wouldn't hope for a reunion. The only faith she could hold was that he was satisfied they were even, and if they met again, he would at least have the decency to walk away. With those parasitic bones, he had taken a part of her with him. She had recklessly endangered their cause, but she hoped taking this chance allowed her to pay for her sin against him. The lines had been drawn. Her weakness was exposed, and she had to bury it again. Kayla remembered the cross on his chest. Jeremy never belonged to her.

From the kitchen's open door, she could hear Kittie softly talking to Asher as she tended to his wounds. Her shame drowned out all her earlier thoughts. He had carried her back to the yellow house, despite his injuries and the knowledge that their source was her carelessness and disobedience. Kayla's body jerked; she had forgotten that it was too painful to attempt clenching her fists. She let a little sob escape before she realized she was stumbling across the wooden floor, skidding to her knees in the kitchen. Asher was stretched out on the dining table, and he stiffly sat up on his elbow to look down at her.

She averted her eyes. "You were right to want to hide me somewhere safe while you defeated Sebastian. I'll go wherever you say. This is all my fault, and you don't know how sorry I am."

He breathed out a small laugh and slowly lowered himself back down onto the table. He didn't speak.

Kayla's fingers gingerly gripped the kitchen table and she pulled herself up to stand, wobbling. Asher lay there bare-chested, his pants cut up the sides to gain access to his injuries as Kittie deftly pulled gnarled, black shards out of his torn and bloody skin with some small tools. He looked up at her, and although his brow was knit with discomfort, his gaze was tranquil. "You haven't already forgotten the words I spoke in the banyan, have you?" he whispered.

She froze, caught somewhere between clutching at his hand and turning away. "No, of course not. I just—"

He closed his eyes in pain as Kittie extracted more shrapnel from his leg. "So we're both a little worse for wear. But these trials give us certainty. I trust you'll move forward."

Kayla lowered her gaze. He couldn't know everything that happened last night. Would he be so calm if he had full knowledge? "You said Za'in would use my feelings against me. I don't know why, but I thought, hoped . . . Jere—" She shook her head. "It doesn't matter. I'm sorry we disagreed yesterday. I was wrong. In the tower, I took steps toward my own freedom, foolishly believing he would follow my path, but my decision became a personal declaration of war in his eyes." She looked down at her hands. "Now every choice we've made stands between us and . . . and I'll stand with you . . . against him."

Kittie abruptly left the room.

Asher gripped Kayla's wrist and held her still as a choked cry caught thickly in her throat. "Don't go after her. She won't be able to really hear your words right now," he said quietly.

She sat heavily on the hard, wooden chair beside the table, letting her arm lie outstretched beside Asher, her head drooping on her shoulder. He released her wrist, allowing his hand to rest lightly on hers. "Asher, what he's carrying on his arms right now, what I let him take from me . . . What will he do with it?"

"He'll do what it tells him to do." Her body stiffened and he let go of her hand. "Did you let him put those on you?"

Kayla didn't move. Her lids were heavy as she let the words seep out of her loose mouth. "When I left here last night, I wasn't looking for him and I didn't know he would find me. Something was pulling us there, but I think we were both surprised to find each other. I can't deny that I wanted to see him. I wanted to offer my penance for the suffering I brought on him, and I expected pain, but not this . . ."

"As I approached, I heard him speaking to you. Did you suggest returning to Za'in? Did you offer up your life, Kayla?" Asher's voice seemed slightly labored.

"I wanted to depend on what I thought was inside him. I wanted to trust him, and if I could save him or if this was truly our final meeting . . . either way, I didn't want to fight. I . . . wanted . . . to give in."

"And you did."

She imagined the cold force of his words stinging the wounds in her palms. "Yes. It was my last act of need for him. I can't tell you that I don't still love him, but I also recognize that he reached inside of me and almost took everything." Kayla clenched her fists and accepted the hurt that came with it. "He won't take the Angel out of me. I can't let him use what's mine as a weapon against this world."

Asher stared up at the ceiling. "From that day on the shore, I knew you loved him. After all those years of hoping to find you again . . . watching you look at one of Za'in's Archs that way . . ." She felt his muscles contract and release. "It hasn't been easy to accept. Still, I knew he was just a boy, and how could I blame the young for doing what they could to survive in such a world? But what he did this time—Kayla, it's unforgivable." He gently grasped her hand again, unwinding her throbbing fist and smoothing out her tense joints. "After this, how can you still stomach the thought of him? How can you feel concern for what will become of him?"

"Just because I can't afford to have feelings that Za'in can use against me doesn't mean there's nothing left."

"When he becomes an abomination, he won't be able to blame those shackles without first placing responsibility on his own actions. He did this to himself."

Kayla began to draw her body up in a violent motion, but stopped, already weak when she sat erect in her chair. She steadied herself with her elbow against the table, settling for just turning her face away. "What's going to happen to him, Asher? It's too late to keep feeding me information in tiny bites, in some effort to protect me. When I met him, I just wanted to find you. Your face was the symbol for every answer I needed; you were my release from ignorance. There was nothing else. But now, everything I learn comes with its own darkness, its own weight. If I have to bear this load, then at least tell me everything. Please, Asher. We only have three more weeks before the Eclipse, and if I'm supposed to become a hero, we're out of time. I have to know now."

"The only thing he knows about those fetters is what I've been able to tell him." Kayla hastily pulled her hand from Asher's grasp and turned towards Kittie's voice. She was standing in the doorway, holding strips of cloth bandages. Her dull eyes stared out from a pale and fatigued face, and her worn voice matched her appearance. Kayla didn't remember Kittie looking this haggard when she treated her wounds, and that shock held her still and mute. The small girl softly stepped into the room and continued caring for Asher's injuries silently.

After some time passed, she began to speak again. "If Jeremy wasn't the man he was, he would have died that night when the tower fell. If he wasn't a child of the Saros—it's funny how *that* alone has led both of us for so long. Running from that fact, or being pulled to wherever, whoever, was able to accept it or use it. I was different too, and he never asked questions. He liked to be with me and that was enough. I wasn't alone anymore. But now, Za'in is just using him again, using him up until there's nothing left. And he won't even stop to realize it. Za'in counted on that. I looked into Jeremy's eyes. He really didn't know what those fetters were. I knew then that he wasn't given direct orders. A suggestion was more than enough. And now . . . now he's Za'in's. No matter what, he'll always be too far away." Kittie rubbed her eyes with the back of her hand and murmured almost inaudibly, "I lost."

Kayla watched Asher's closed face and eyelids. "So . . . those bones," she asked, "bind him to Sebastian? If the tattoo didn't work, why do the bones?"

"It's not so easy to control a child of the Saros . . . or a Nephil. He needed to raise some more power and these Ruiners were the perfect plan. Za'in knew that Jeremy would survive the fall, and that he would be more torn up on the inside than anywhere else. He knew Jeremy would be desperate to win back his position as Arch—"

"He's not an Arch anymore?"

Kittie kept her gaze lowered as she worked, the movement of her hands slowing. "What did you think would happen to him? Instead of finishing the job he was charged with, he heard your scream and, for you, he released his hold on Asher and was defeated."

Kayla couldn't ignore Asher's tightening features, so she pressed her fingers against her forehead, hiding her eyes with her wounded palms. "I see."

Kittie waited a moment before continuing. "How could he return things to the way they were before they got so complicated? Just capture an Angel and return her to the one that rules the world. Za'in just left the method lying around and Jeremy found it. But I know a bit about such traps. They never lose. You see, they're activated by the blood of the captor. These fetters are made from the bodies of Nephilim and will only attach to one of its own kind. But Za'in perverted the bones of the creatures he destroyed and they've become parasitic. Once they pierce the skin and connect to an Intercessor, they feed off the Nephil's power and pollute her blood. Eventually, they will be saturated with the Nephil's life-force and leave her an empty shell. But the one that unleashed these bones is also able to release his victim. If he does so prematurely, the Ruiners are programmed to continue to be useful. They will join with the one that activated them. That is what has happened to Jeremy. From the moment he touched those bones, I know he hasn't been the same. I'm certain that he's Za'in's eyes and ears now, and for the first time, Za'in can reach into him like never before. And the more that happens, the more those bones will crawl over his body and taint his spirit. But Jeremy and Za'in aren't the only ones in the loop. It's a part of *you* that has been stolen and twisted through that blackened mass that grips him. Can't you feel Jeremy, even from this distance?" Kittie raised her eyes, her last question hopeful.

Kayla sagged wearily against the table. She didn't want to try. Not now. She shook her head, the tiny movement swaying her whole body back and forth. "So you're saying that Jeremy is coming back for us again, next time fully as Za'in's agent. What will you do?"

The bitterness on Kittie's face was new and unfamiliar. "I'll keep playing this role." She was finished dressing

Asher's wounds, and she walked towards the doorway.

"Wait!" Kayla stood, clinging to the table. "What does that mean? Will you fight him?"

"Jeremy knows that when I shoot, I don't miss. He knows I've only killed once and he knows what it does to me. He knows I made a choice last night, when I . . . when I . . ." She shook her head, hard. "I know what I have to do. Make sure you can say the same."

Asher sat up slowly, and then found his way to stand, straightening with effort. "Is there a way to free him from those Ruiners?"

Kittie watched him with wide, wet eyes, the softness returning to her face. "There's no way I know of, and even then . . . But, Asher! I removed those fragments of toxic bone from your wounds only now, you shouldn't be walking yet—"

He had already moved to the door and was kneeling at her side, his hands on her shoulders. "If even you see no redemption for him, I can't hold back next time."

"Redemption isn't the question. You can't lose. I didn't come this far to give up on the world." She offered a tight smile. "All pain fades, right Asher?"

His grip on her shoulders tightened, their shared gaze steady. "Most things do, Kittie. But nothing stops you from moving. Your eyes tell me you understand that."

Her smile was sad, but genuine. "There was a time I forgot. I stood still for too long."

"Me too. It's over now. Let's forgive ourselves."

Kittie rested her head against his for a moment before she pulled away from his grip and disappeared up the stairs. "You first."

21

Whatever wasn't frozen and numb was incessantly burning, and all Jeremy could do was lie face down in the dirt. He rose up on his elbows, retching, and then crawled away a few feet to collapse in a slightly less filthy spot. *What have I done?* He tried to remember the night's events as he hid his face from the sun that slowly rose in the haze-choked sky. Every time he attempted to recall the image of a face or some remembrance of words spoken, his limbs were strangled with a tight coldness, and the dense line in his chest smoldered, pushing acid up into his throat.

Kayla. That one word repeated endlessly through him, as he tried to remember its meaning. He tensed his muscles, straining to dredge up any connection he had to these sounds, to either understand why he kept hearing them or to finally drown them out. *Kayla.* His fingers moved, unexpectedly thawed and flexible again. The remembered warmth that flooded him wasn't the searing burn that held him prostrate against the earth. *Kayla.* The sensation of softness was jarring, but familiar, as if from another life.

Jeremy dragged himself forward, his eyes closed, reaching towards some unknown resting place. *Kayla.* It was her. She was the one that did this to him. He shook his head hard, swallowing that stabbing pressure. No. No, there was something else. Something worth saving. He could see the radiance of two eyes, golden and wet, and he was sure they recognized him. He cringed, shielding himself from their gaze, but he was unable to drown out the remembered awareness of their bodies touching. His joints went slack, tears stinging his eyes. They weren't the only ones here, inside. There was one Other. Jeremy tore at what constricted his arms, scraping them against his chest. This memory was for him alone; he wouldn't let the Other have it.

It's useless. Jeremy froze, lying still again. This time the words didn't echo in his head, but they resonated from within his chest. He knew the Other had witnessed everything. He could see her, weak and pale and desperate, and he knew he was to blame. *Why?* He didn't understand. *I hate her, I hate her . . .* He struggled to remember what she did. There was a flash of light, the stars were falling, everything was falling, and he wanted to be the only one. Maybe he had this coming. He was nothing but her captor, after all. It started out as duty, a step towards glory and power, but hadn't there come a time when he kept her prisoner for himself?

Why? Why does it even matter? Jeremy painfully dragged himself up, planting his palms against the ground and pulling himself up onto his knees. He let his head hang and didn't try to explain to himself the drops of water he saw falling, or to find a cause for the trembling of his body. "Because . . ." he whispered, his voice coarse and broken, "because I . . . love her."

An agonized cry wracked his being as he collapsed again to the earth, the cross on his chest piercing him like never before. He struggled to breathe as the images he couldn't remember just moments ago now flooded his brain. He could see that desert vagabond and his still, sharp eyes—that man with the maddeningly impassive face and composed mouth. Jeremy could see her hands on Serafin's, see her standing beside him with her head raised to glimpse his face, hear her wailing his name as the truck sped away. He could see Kit. Those familiar features that brought him comfort for so long were now twisted in anger, disappointment, and desperation. He could feel the barrel of her gun, cold, digging through his jaw line.

"It's what I deserve!" he screamed, rising up just enough to slash his chest again with the sharp bones that covered his arms. He caught his throat with the barbs, and then lay motionless, wanting to feel the blood leave him, hoping against reason that perhaps he could finally die. He painfully rolled over onto his back, running his fingers over his wounds, and felt nothing but smooth skin. His tortured laugh was like a sob. Jeremy had never healed this quickly before; this change was new, its activation instant. He lay quietly, paralyzed by this crushing helplessness.

The mark on his chest began to grow almost pleasantly warm. It wasn't the harsh burn that had ravaged him earlier. The voice of the Other softly reverberated through him. *Look at you. This is what happens when you go alone in this kind of world. Start acting like an Arch again, Saros! My offer still stands. Call it what you will . . . you want her. After the sky darkens, you can still claim her. Just make sure she finds her way to me first, with her retinue broken. This isn't a curse, Saros. You've been chosen to wield this new power you possess. An ordinary human couldn't bear it. You alone haven't forgotten the realities of this life. You know the rule is strength. Look at your arms . . . the playing field has tilted your way, now.*

Jeremy groaned. "Za'in . . . ?"

169

There was no answer. The pain and the conflicting temperatures in his body began to fade to a comfortable distance. The sun still rose as it always did. He lay still, letting his eyelids hang heavily, his sight unfocused and passive. He didn't try to determine his location, or decide his next move, or entertain any other thought. Any motion of his mind would be perceived and analyzed by Za'in. *Eventually you'll have to think again.* "Shut up," he muttered quickly. This time, the decision not to question the source of the voice was automatic.

It was safe to focus on sensation. Jeremy tried to feel his own arms and hands, but he couldn't tell where the bony shell began or what happened to the flesh that disappeared beneath. He felt a surprisingly deep regret that he couldn't touch the dirt with his own down-turned palms, so he let his naked fingers be saturated in the experience. He breathed in the damp smell of wet leaves and barren soil. If he could forget the past awareness of her hair against his nose, maybe he could lie here indefinitely. If he could forget the comfort of her lying beside him that night, when he had to say things out loud to be sure that he still could, maybe he could just sink into the earth. If he could forget her defiant and fearful eyes, if he could forget her body on fire . . . Za'in was right; it was useless.

Jeremy dug his elbows into the ground and pushed his chest skyward. He slowly stood, his boots sliding on the damp blades of grass. It *was* useless. He couldn't stop thinking or stop feeling. Za'in would know his every intention, his every move, but he would keep moving. His steps were unhurried as he walked back the direction he came, the strange weightlessness of his limbs keeping his motions warily gentle.

What will you do? He couldn't be sure if it was his own thought or Za'in's question. His body felt disconnected, and it was difficult to separate the sources of these inner sounds. Jeremy kept walking. *What will you do?* He briefly considered that this was all madness before he found himself speaking aloud. "I'm going to find them. I'll find . . . her."

You're . . . killing . . . me . . .

"What?" Jeremy stopped short. His heartbeat was a painfully slow, heavy throb.

You're . . . killing . . . me . . . He could see the panic frozen on Kayla's face, and the soft twitching of her body that was the strongest fight she could manage against those fetters. *That was another option you gave me . . .* Jeremy heard his own voice echoing back to him coldly.

"Stop!" he yelled out.

Today you claim to love her? Don't pretend you didn't do it . . .

"No! There was something . . . different about last night. My head . . ." He reeled, his mind spinning. His arms and chest felt tight again, a bitter taste returning to his mouth.

Those were your actions. You can make excuses and apologies, but you wanted to hurt her for leaving you there, to be with him—

"I . . ."

They won't forgive what you've done. She won't forget.

"I . . ."

You love her? Does that mean anything . . . love? Wasn't that the line she used when she delivered her final blow? It was a clever tactic, at least . . .

"I wanted . . . to take her to Hell . . . with me." The words were torn from his raw throat as he stumbled down onto his knee.

That's what I thought. So do it.

Jeremy's eyes felt dry and swollen. He struggled to maintain his equilibrium, his body unbalanced by his stunted desire to release his emotions. He stared down at his blackened limbs, rendered speechless by the horror of what just escaped his mouth. How could he be so unaware of his own desires? That voice inside was right—if that was what he had confused with love, then he just wasn't capable of such an emotion, if anyone was.

This kind of confusion comes from fighting your nature.

He closed his eyes. What was his nature? Wasn't it his nature to fight . . . everything? Was he held helpless to the circumstances of his birth? His body stiffened with the memory of . . .

Saros!

He dug his fingers into the dirt to stop himself from cringing against a beating he knew wouldn't come. That part of his life was over. He escaped that. They escaped it, both he and Kit. And then he tore that place down. He was born into darkness—that was the reason they gave him for his suffering. Every form of alienation, anguish, and humiliation was his to accept as punishment for an existence that began at that one sinister moment. He remembered trying to discover the secret as to why they didn't just kill him. If he was such a curse to that village, why let him shame their ruined streets? It was a disappointment to realize that the only thing keeping him alive was their cowardice.

Kit made him see that. They feared her too. Four years passed and she never changed. She looked just the same as when she first came into town selling fortunes. He was ten when he left with her and he never asked how old she was. She may have been willing to take the blows for him that night, but he wouldn't let anyone who would strike her live. From the day they walked away, it only took him six years to become an Arch.

He was young and fragile, and it would have been easy to die where he was born. He could never forget that he lived because the others were too weak and afraid. That's why burning that place to the ground was the easiest decision he ever made. It was his first act as an Arch, and the most troublesome part of the whole thing was convincing Za'in that such a pitiful town could house anyone that could ever be a potential threat. His new lord probably never believed it, but he had the kindness to humor the youngest soldier ever to reach that rank. It was the beginning of something. Jeremy never again had to taste blood after hearing that word *Saros* spoken. Za'in gave it new meaning.

It was you who made that name yours. Rise and continue to forge your path.

Jeremy stood. "What will I do . . . ?" He echoed the voice's initial question.

You know what you'll do.

"If you know me as well as you pretend to, you know that can't be true." He walked with his head down, his hands tearing holes in his pockets. He felt constricting pressure above the bare flesh in the crooks of his elbows, and he struggled to recall if the bones had reached that point last night. He couldn't remember. It didn't benefit him to try and hide any of his thoughts. He had to admit that his own sight was too muddled to be of much use to anyone. The only thing he knew for sure is that he would keep moving. He would find her.

22

"No school today?" There was amusement in Sebastian's earnest voice, and Kayla moaned softly, struggling against this vision. Every time she tried to sleep he dominated her dreams, and even now in her own subconscious, she found herself again the helpless captive of his soothing manner and his seamless arguments.

"What?" Michael raised his gaze from under his furrowed brow, his dark green eyes glinting sharply through the screen of his lashes.

Kayla couldn't feel her body and she didn't know exactly where her tension was held, but her stress immediately dissipated when she saw his scowling face. She clung tenaciously to this vision, determined to remember every detail of her young father. He was different from the mature man in her locket, or even the coldly determined youth she had seen in her vision. This boy seemed to be almost her age, his tangled red hair pulled back into a ponytail, the sides of his head shaved. He sat on the floor, slumped against a bookshelf, his limbs bony and his posture insolent.

He was surrounded by open books, a ragged notebook smeared with scribbles held tight in his grip. This had to be before the Eclipse. Michael's clothing was disheveled, but this affect was achieved with great care. After a few of these visions, she was becoming accustomed to the difference, although she didn't understand many of the motivations that moved people in the Pre-Eclipse world.

Sebastian looked down at him from over an open book. He was young—the same undefined age he appeared at present. He hadn't changed at all since then, except for perhaps the addition of more dark marks on his arms. Za'in wore black then just as he did now, but instead of the understated, smooth and clean clothing she was used to seeing him in, he was dressed more similarly to Michael. "I'm just wondering why someone would skip school just to study."

"And I'm just wondering if you would mind your own fucking business." Michael turned back to his books, uninterested and unthreatened.

Sebastian was quiet for a moment as he glanced at the titles Michael had collected. "Astrology, yoga, anatomy, psychology . . ." His voice dropped to a whisper. "None of those things can stop you from hurting someone again."

The boy stiffened. "Are you a cop? You have to tell me if you are."

"It's nothing like that. I'm someone that understands the power the right hand can wield."

Michael gripped his notebook hard, but it still trembled. "If you understand that, then you know to leave me alone."

"I'm not afraid of you, Michael. And if you come with me, I can teach you to no longer fear yourself." His voice was comforting, and Kayla's heart clenched, rejecting the emotion that sound still arose in her.

"I don't know how you know my name, but there's no

way I'm letting you pick me up. Seriously, dude, I've seen enough after-school specials that warned me about guys like you." Michael grabbed his backpack and leapt to his feet.

"Whose blood will be on your hands next, Michael? Will you be able to stop yourself when your bones move according to their own purpose? Will you even want to, when you know how easy it is to strike them all down?" Sebastian's words were low and hard. Although he didn't touch him, the boy appeared to be frozen still, his face straining with his halted movement.

"What do you know about that?" The panic that twisted his features wasn't fear of the dark-eyed man. Michael clenched his right fist, his left hand holding his wrist tightly.

"I know that feeling. It isn't wrong. You don't have to fight it. But it would be a waste to let it destroy you." Sebastian met his eyes to see two light green rings pushing his terror outwards, leaving only defiance.

"And you can stop that from happening?" Michael's question was thick with sarcasm, but it didn't completely obscure his need.

Sebastian's smile was both the guarantee and the bait of a man with answers. "I can show you a way."

Kayla let the vision soften and dissolve. She didn't want to see this anymore. She didn't want to remember how much she too needed a way, a place to belong and be understood, a guide to angle her to the sun. Michael needed it too. She didn't want to remember how it turns out when you give yourself over. It already happened. She couldn't stop it.

She felt her arms, chest, and back knocking hard against an enclosing pressure, and it was then she realized how violently she was trembling. It took some time before Kayla discovered it was Asher holding her body still, but she still couldn't understand what he was murmuring along the side of her face. She watched a trickle of water run down his forearm and collect on his elbow before it fell, leaving dark spots on her dirt-smeared pants.

"I could never ask you what happened. I can't even ask now. I could never . . . I can't . . ." Kayla kept letting the words fall, repeating endlessly.

Her ears began to clear, and she could finally understand the sounds Asher breathed to her. "Wake up. It's over . . . it's over. Wake up, Kayla. I should have never made you ask. I'll tell you everything and free you of your dreams. Just wake up. It's over."

Kayla shook her head, pushing herself to fully awaken. "It happened that way, didn't it? Who did my father hurt, to make him want to follow Sebastian?"

"That's not the question that we've been avoiding." Asher stopped, steadying her as a new shudder shook her body. She felt him grow heavy against her as he released a long breath. His voiced dropped, hard. "Who was I protecting, not telling you from the beginning? I wanted you to choose, without my emotions swaying you. But it's damaging both of us. Nothing needs to be feigned. Not strength, or duty, or inner peace. You've drawn your own line, even though you've only sensed the truth, even if you've hoped otherwise. Kayla, why do you think I chose this path? Za'in ki—"

"Both of them?" Kayla's words collided loudly with his in a desperate attempt to keep what she already knew unsaid.

He nodded painfully, finding no relief in their unspoken understanding.

"Everyone knows." Her voice was flat with realization.

His silence stung. She lay still in Asher's arms, thankful that her weakness allowed her to remain enclosed in his embrace, sparing her the sight of his face at this moment.

He was right. She sensed it for a long time—no, she *knew*—but she couldn't ask anyone, least of all him, the one she sought out for answers. Her uncertainty seemed preferable to the strange gentleness that softened his face every time he had come close to telling her the truth. It was then she discovered that the body's reaction to real pain was sometimes surprising and often unnerving. She found that witnessing that response in someone strong could hurt more than the knowledge of its source.

Asher spoke again suddenly, but his voice was soft and tranquil, letting the words wander with his memory. "It made sense to me that Michael stayed with Za'in for so long. They were similar in that they both wanted to know . . . everything. But first, Michael wanted to know why he was different. Why his anger hurt those around him. There were times that, because of his own pain, he didn't even care, but when that weapon tore from his palm, he was always remorseful afterward. His Angel blood must have come from his father, but he never met him. No one knows what happened to your grandfather . . . maybe Za'in took his Intercessor too. Michael's mother was fragile and couldn't protect him or herself, so the first time his power surfaced, he didn't try to stop it . . ."

Kayla wasn't sure exactly when Asher's words became images, the sound of his voice lost beneath a loud crash and a muffled scream. She could hear a man's labored breathing, and she squinted her eyes in the dim, yellow light. "Fuck you, fuck you, fuck you . . ." a child's voice spat out, over and over. Kayla didn't want to venture any closer to the sounds, but the vision seemed to rush in her direction. A woman was on the floor, hugging the corner of a sagging couch as silent sobs rattled her thin frame.

"Go away. Never come back." The red-haired child held his right arm with his left hand, struggling under the weight of the sharp bone that protruded from his palm. The boy couldn't have been older than ten, but she got the impression his staring, green eyes had seen more than a decade of suffering. He watched the man before him with an expression that was a strange fusion of wonder, satisfaction, and apathy.

"Fucking freak . . ." the man drawled through his cut mouth, both hands holding the wound that traveled from his cheek down to his hip. He stumbled backwards towards the door, dragging his body around the kitchen counter, leaving smears of blood in his wake. He glanced for a moment at the woman on the floor, his face reddening with an embarrassed anger that drove out his fear. Impulsively, he lurched forward, skirting sloppily around Michael's small frame, violence loosening his swinging limbs.

The boy whirled around, letting his weapon lead his movement. The sharp bones twisted forward, slicing a jagged wound across the man's back and thickly catching the flesh behind his knee. The man fell forward with a low cry, rolling onto his side to stare up fearfully at Michael.

The child was unmoved. "You should leave. I don't care if I kill you." He closed his eyes for a moment. "I don't care," he said again softly to himself.

The man slid across the linoleum floor on his own blood, avoiding the boy's piercing gaze. Michael kicked the door open and watched dispassionately as he crawled out into the night. The door creaked closed as the boy's Intercessor retracted, the sensation sending a visible shiver through him. His eyes were intent on the smears of blood that marked the floor. He had finally stood up to him. That's all it took. He'd never have to see him again, he was sure of it.

Kayla recoiled from the scene, less disturbed by the red-streaked floor when confronted with the horror of that severe expression lingering on her father's young face. She struggled to escape the vision, reaching out for Asher's voice again, for the awareness of his touch. Her body wasn't flailing about like her thoughts; she could feel once more that warm pressure holding her still and his words falling back down to earth.

". . . but he was wrong. You can't change everything so simply. It's true that his mother's boyfriend never came back and its true Michael saved them both that night from the usual treatment, but although he took a stand, it was still just another thing that happened to them. He didn't know he had that within him and it moved without his conscious will. You know. It happened to you on the shore. A vague emotion, no matter how intense, isn't enough. It's a poor guide for one's actions. But at that time, he had nothing else that could steer him. He—"

Kayla tried to make a sound, to pull her hands up to her face. Maybe if she could, it would stop these images from flooding in, but the visions still came. She could feel everything that Michael had endured. He was so alone. As he grew, so did his rage, and the power that fed off it. How could they not see that wasn't his true nature? It seemed so clear to her, even as she watched him wound those who opposed him, even as she watched the boy ensuring his isolation by every act of fear he committed. No one could console him. Not even his mother . . . she kept making the same mistakes. It was always the same damn thing, over and over, the same thing, always. She just didn't get it, she just wouldn't see, and he couldn't hold it in anymore. But that dark red line across her hand, beading up and spilling over . . . she didn't deserve that. He had to finally stop this, somehow. This all started out with his desire to protect her; he couldn't let himself hurt her again. He'd find a way to control this curse, or he'd never come back. She'd be better off without him.

There was that man with the answers—the first person he'd ever seen that looked like he knew anything for sure. That's why he sought him out after their first meeting at the bookstore. He promised Michael he would tear down all his present constructions, and build him into a tower one hundred stories tall. That was his only chance: to gleam like a skyscraper instead of mirroring that dirty house with the kitchen counter stained with blood, his mother always reminding him they'd never get their security deposit back now . . . as if they would ever leave. There was no place else for him to go, until now. Tear it down. That's how it should be. He never liked things the way they were, anyways. Make something new. Anything would be better than this.

Kayla watched a dark mark spread across his chest—a sharp black cross that seemed to draw in and swallow the light. She couldn't bear to see it mar her young father's body. The darkness threatened to consume her, but when she pulled herself free, it was Jeremy that stood in Michael's place, his arms covered with those blackened bones, but this time, they reached almost up to his shoulders. Kayla returned his bitter stare with desolate eyes, struggling to escape the vision so that she could delay the inevitable battle between them. Desperate for a way out, she dug her nails into her own flesh, cool air flooding her nostrils and clearing her sight. Kayla was in Asher's arms again, the morning light stinging her eyes. She had seen enough. It didn't seem right to do this in the presence of the sun. She felt suddenly trapped by Asher's embrace, her face warm, her eyelids heavy with shame. Kayla had been wounded, cast aside, and she consciously understood there could be no sin in taking comfort from this man, but still she felt as if she was revealing to the world her participation in some grand betrayal. She opened her mouth, unsure if she just was in need of air or ready to cry out, but regardless of the reason, she was immediately released. Asher stood and gathered his travel gear, his movements stirring Kittie and the pirates from sleep. He didn't speak or look at her. It was as if he knew who suddenly had crashed her thoughts and shattered her vision, as if he could sense which memories spoiled the solace they found in each other.

" 'A vague emotion, no matter how intense, isn't enough . . .' " she whispered, letting Asher's words replay over her tongue.

He stopped moving for a moment. "You understand that?"

"I've seen where it leads." Kayla stared down at her palms.

Asher's voice softened. "I never meant to further complicate this for you."

Kayla closed her eyes. All she could see in the darkness was that black cross. She fought to raise her gaze, breathlessly wondering which Arch's face she would see above that mark. The cold determination in Michael's features as he walked towards Sebastian on the night of the Eclipse was the same look that often held Jeremy's face still, and for both of them that expression was edged with the potential to explode.

She stood. "I'm not going to be caught in this crossfire. I'm going to stop Za'in. It's my feelings that have led me here, in every victory and every mistake. I can't help that. But now there's a purpose behind those emotions. Za'in won't take from me what he stole from my parents, and he won't darken the world again. I won't allow it."

Asher's eyes were weary, but clear. He raised his voice to be heard by the others, but his gaze was fixed steadily on her. "It's time to go. Hold fast to your convictions. Where we're headed, they'll be tested soon enough.

23

"I know, we rock." Bruno's proud grin couldn't be darkened by Asher's scowl.

Kittie jumped into the vehicle, bouncing on the passenger seat and peeking out of the open door. Za'in's black truck was no longer the sleek machine adorned only with his long-armed cross. It had been transformed into a pirate's vessel: a colorful, ragged landship, meant to rattle through the dust, replete with trinkets and charms, as well as sayings and pictures scrawled on its exterior. "Well, it's pretty, but I thought it didn't run?" Kittie said, sitting with her arms crossed, the corners of her mouth drooping with the memory of how this truck was left with them.

All eyes turned to Fec, who was giggling wildly. Kerif kicked him hard, but when he hit the ground, his laughter only grew more raucous. The other pirate sighed, nudging him with his boot. "Fec stole the battery while Serafin was fighting that Arch. He was hoping we'd find another TV. But we made him put it back."

Asher was rubbing his jaw, his brow knit in irritation.

"We can't ride in this. It'll attract too much attention and we'll be recognized. I already made arrangements for Kayla and me to take this motorbike I bargained for our first night here—"

"Hey!" Fec sat up, a sober expression awkwardly freezing his face.

"Not this again . . ." Kerif breathed, shaking his head.

Bruno began to rush towards Asher, ready to argue or plead, but Kittie's scramble was quicker, dashing between the two men. She pulled down on Asher's poncho and he stooped slightly to face her. "It would be unwise to go without me," Kittie said, her voice low. "You saw what happened last time, and he'll only get stronger. If he doesn't finish the job, Za'in will send other Archs. I'm the only one here that's seen them and knows what they're capable of. He has an army. We only have each other. We can't split up now."

Asher closed his eyes for a moment, a tight smile gripping his face as his head was pulled down by a slight nod. "I understand. But you're not the only one, Kittie. It's been some time since I've seen the Arch that took Michael's place, but I haven't forgotten him."

She blinked. "Of course. You know Tregenne. So then you know I'm right."

He straightened, letting out a long, fatigued breath before exchanging a steady gaze with Kittie, visibly one of trust and shared knowledge. There was a solemnity to the growing bond between them, and the fusion of their skills and mysteries brought comfort to those that traveled with them, even though it was clear that their relationship was a constant reminder of what they both had lost.

"Kittie, even you will agree that *this*," he motioned to the truck, "is a bulls-eye on our backs."

"There are other pirate vessels . . ." she replied slowly,

turning her head back toward the boys.

Fec removed his hat and they all cast down their eyes in mourning. Bruno yanked angrily on his hair. "Goddamned Za'in! And that Arch, burning down our ship . . ."

"I told you it was too dangerous to search for the same treasure as Za'in," Vic offered in his usual cheerless manner.

Kayla had been passively watching the scene before her, but the last two statements sharpened her awareness. "Wait! Sebastian destroyed your ship? Why? Because he didn't want others to have mobility?"

Kerif turned toward Kayla, spinning the ring on his thumb with his forefinger. "Well, not necessarily. We rode around for a long time before he took us down in Madeline—"

"When was that?" Kayla interrupted, her voice urgent and low.

Fec rubbed his knuckles over his eyes and tried to laugh. "Well, tha' was th' las' time *anyone* was'in Mad'line!" His forced chuckles sputtered out into coughs as all eyes turned to watch him with appalled or pained expressions, followed by another of Kerif's smacks.

"Was that almost six weeks ago?" Kayla asked quietly, turning her stare on Kittie.

"Yeah," Bruno muttered.

"The night I met you both . . . what did you do?" She eyed Kittie accusingly, and then paused, dropping her head. Kayla's soft laugh was bitter. "But the next morning was even more interesting." She turned to the four men. "You came for me, 'searching for the same treasure as Za'in.' You were scared of Jeremy already and he knew you were pirates." Kayla's eyes darted as she remembered. "And then, he told you to go back to your ship . . . I'm sure he thought that was very funny, since he was the one that burned it down." She shook her head, hard. "*Why*, Kittie?"

The small girl's eyes were genuinely bewildered, as if there was something, for the first time in years, she didn't understand. "I . . . wanted to be with him."

"Christ! Why is that so damn important?" she cried. Her face was twisted in pain, a low sob escaping her throat as her Intercessor reflexively tried to release, but was caught in her swollen palm. Kayla recoiled from her own violence, knowing that question was as equally directed at herself.

Kittie closed her eyes, remembering. "Sometimes, when you set out to do something and you've been alone for so long, you just keep moving. You forget why. All you can recall is that you're trying, you're really trying, and you can't let it all go. But then someone reaches out to you, and he needs to stretch out his hand as much as you need to grasp it . . ." She paused, silently reminiscing as Kayla pulled further away, unable to shake the vision of the first time she saw his face. She could see his eyes emerging from the darkness, his insolent mouth, and his rough, bandaged hand descending to meet hers, to pull her out into the world.

"I didn't kill anyone!" Kittie's voice was quiet and fierce. "Not for Za'in. I also have my own reasons to stop him, okay? I had to get close to Za'in, I did what I had to do as a soldier, but I didn't kill anyone for him. We had orders. There were pirates in Madeline's harbor and we had to get rid of them. Sure there are others, I know gangs exist all over, but these four, they had Nephilim relics. He wanted them gone. Otherwise he lets it go, usually. Even if they have some technology. There's a lot he'll overlook, especially lately. He's been concentrating his efforts on preparing for the second Eclipse. Eighteen years ago he 'brought down the wrath of God,' as he's fond of saying. Even if it was really just his own wrath, in the absence of our Creator. Even if all he did was play with the physics of a supernatural disaster. But this time, it's different. It's worse.

He's going to build a new race to 'fall to earth.' And once that happens . . . the former Earth really will pass away."

"Is this common knowledge?" Kayla asked.

"You mean 'does *he* know?' " Kittie glanced at Kayla's flushed face. "I'm sure Za'in is satisfied that his hints have been enough notice. But, of course, he purposely misleads too. And you know Jeremy—this isn't even on his radar. Now when I think of those things on his arms, I wonder if there was anything I could have said . . ."

Kayla's eyes were still and hard. "I apologize for causing us to linger here, when we should be moving. It's useless to do this now." She turned to Asher. "Kittie said there are other vehicles running; there are pirates and gangs that Za'in ignores. We should take this truck. If we don't, we may have more than just Za'in to worry about."

Asher was watching the two girls carefully. "Alright. How much is left in the Core?"

"Far more than we'll need," said Vic.

"Fine."

"What should we do with the bike? Return it?" Kerif asked regretfully.

"There's no time. Destroy it."

Kerif nodded and stalked back to the yellow house, leaving the rest of them caught in a tense silence.

"Shotgun!" Fec cried out.

Kayla stared through the streaked, plastic window at the miles of abandoned suburbs they left behind. She kept her head turned and chin tucked; even with the convertible top, attached with the pirates' embellishments, enough wind and dust still found its way inside. Kittie sat beside her, her expression distant and troubled. Asher was behind the wheel and Bruno was at his side, poring over hand-drawn maps, some of which were on vellum, laid over antique diagrams. The other three sat in the back, cheerfully exposed to the elements. Kayla kept her fists balled tightly. The pressure caused her wounds to throb painfully, but she didn't ease her grip. It was a reminder.

She unzipped the rear flap between their seats and pulled back on the first arm her fingers brushed against. Half of Kerif's body followed. "Whoa!" He steadied himself, and then glanced down, grinning at Kayla's hand grasping him above the elbow. "Hey there, lady."

"You have to tell me about your relics," she whispered, her head bowed.

Kerif's discomfort was expressed in a grimace. He forced Fec's head into the window with him as a needed backup. "Um, well, we had this ship . . ."

"Th' *Ugh* was more like'a boat," Fec muttered, trying to get comfortable in this tight spot.

Kerif hit him somewhere on the other side of the fabric wall. "We had this *ship* for a really long time—we pretty much built it and everything! It's been hard getting on without it, actually," he sighed. "But before it burnt up, we survived by hunting treasure. There's a lot of Pre-Eclipsian spoils out there if you know where to look, and there is always someone willing to pay. We never had dealings with Za'in. Shit, we wanted to stay away from that guy! But we knew the kind of stuff he was after, and it was kind of fun to try to find it first." Kerif paused, looking up carefully at Kayla before he continued. "Then there was this old guy, Gabriel. He had a place in Azevin and he'd buy a lot of the stuff we got our hands on, especially the really worthless junk. But he was particular. At first he wanted busted electronics, car parts, jewelry—typical. Then he started requesting certain things, easy things, like stuff abandoned in old churches. Hell, everything was just left sitting in those kinds of places. Also, he was interested in bones and objects that used to be buried with the dead. We weren't ever really grave robbers before, but we can't afford to have moral dilemmas like that. Plus, that sort of stuff, you can just walk in and take without a fight. Easy. I don't know if he used to be a priest or a scientist or what, but he was different. Peculiar, right?" Kerif glanced at Fec who was nodding. "He was powerful, though. He didn't pay by trading with anything we were used to receiving."

Kayla searched his face. "What do you mean?"

"You've seen what Fec can do with his smokes, right? And the Cap'n with his coins? Well, he paid Vic and me the same way too."

"Yeah, so get back to it, Kerif!" Bruno barked, his anger ending in a sigh. "We sat you back there for a reason, you know."

"Okay, okay, I know." Kerif retreated back into the bed of the truck, but motioned for Kayla to follow.

She peeked outside, shielding her eyes from the swirling dust. Vic was leaning against the side before he looked up, watching Kerif move to sit opposite him. They exchanged a glance, and then Vic raised his arm and pressed his palm forward in the air. Kerif performed a similar motion, but his hand was facing downward as it flicked a short, sweeping gesture. They continued to repeat these actions, their faces subdued with a mixture of concentration and boredom, as they kept their eyes on the tracks the truck left etched in the ground behind them.

Kayla stood hunched over, leaning further towards them as she tried to decipher the meaning behind this strange ritual. She followed the direction of their gazes, and it was then that she noticed the trail they left behind was being swept away, completely disappearing. With the forward motion of Vic's hand, the wind near the tires strengthened, followed by Kerif's smoothing gesture scattering the sand. Her unbelieving eyes darted between the boys and the ground. "How are you . . . ?"

"Like I said, it was a trade," he called out, his concentration unbroken. "You asked about our relics, right? Take a look at Fec's wrist."

Kayla pulled back as his scrawny arm was thrust suddenly towards her face. She noticed three raised lines running parallel to each other along the top of his forearm. "What is this?"

"Ol' man Gabe put som'thin' under our skin. I tried it first." Fec grinned. "He said it would jus' help us do wha' we already do *better*. I did'n get it at first, but then he show'd me how to use m' smokes. M' brother, he's strong. So, see, he's movin' the wind here. And Kerif, he changes th' way things look."

"Who is this guy? He sounds like—"

"Nah, nah, he's jus' a guy. He's no friend of Za'in, I'm tellin' ya. No way."

Kayla stared off into the clouds of sand. "He told you to look for me, right?"

Fec frowned. "Well, yeah. But ev'ryone—"

"Kayla, leave it alone for right now." Asher's voice was severe, strangling her questions, but she was calmed by its strength. She settled back into her seat, zipping up the rear flap, again separating her from three outside. Her eyes rested on the raised lines that adorned Bruno's left arm before she searched Asher's face. She could only see a portion of his profile from her seat, but there was no ignoring the tension in his jaw and the weary recognition weighing down his sharp, forward-looking gaze. Kayla tried to relax into the gathering stillness. There was something familiar about the intensity that held Asher's face motionless. She breathed deeply, as if that action could slow time, even as she understood it was a weak protection from the weight of the knowledge she'd have to bear when his silence was finally broken.

24

The smell of damp leaves and living wood filled Jeremy's senses as he rested the crown of his head against the banyan tree. He pressed his palms to the wide trunk, the blackened bones piercing the bark as his bare fingers lightly stroked the rough surface. This was the place he saw her last. What happened to both of them after their moment here? His chest was tight with the memory of the pain that had kept him frozen that night as she stood before him, just moments before he had let it go and allowed whatever he was holding inside to rule him completely. He gripped the bark. He could see her face, pale and luminous beneath the moon. Her eyes were closed, but the pull of her brows expressed pleasure, he was sure of it. *Is that how you remember things?* Something was warmly constricting his fingers. "What?"

His memory dissolved and was replaced with another. The vision was inescapable and insistent, and although he wanted to reject it, he just let the images flood over him— he was becoming accustomed to these new additions to his reality. There were tears in Kayla's eyes as she turned her head away. She was trapped beneath him, her hands bound together in his grip. She struggled in vain against his violence . . . "No!" Jeremy drew back fiercely, tearing handfuls of the banyan's trunk out with each wild jerk of his arms, as he attempted to retreat from this image of the past.

He fought to control his breathing, to steady his shaking body. "Fine. I'm crazy, right? Possessed? Okay. I'll talk to you . . . I'll fight with you. Maybe I'll even end up doing what you want. But leave that alone. Don't give me any fucking commentary on that night." His anger fed on the knowledge that his apparent inability to die left him nothing with which to bargain or threaten. This sort of talk was useless now. But the Other remained still and silent.

Jeremy released a long, heavy breath, then raised his head and turned his back on the tree. His truck was gone. He walked slowly out into the dirt, kicking up dust with his boots. The tracks he made that night were still there, but there were no other imprints left in any direction. It was as if the vehicle had lifted gently into the sky and disappeared. He was strangely untroubled as he continued moving forward, giving in to the pull of some unknown destination. Jeremy walked through the empty streets, his dull eyes sweeping over the lonely, dark houses. An acute pain suddenly gripped his spine, traveled up to his neck and shoulders, and stiffly pulled his chin towards the yellow house at his right side. He turned sharply, treading over the stone-strewn path that led to the door, even as each step sent a tremor up his legs. His breath caught in his throat when his hand closed around the doorknob, but he swallowed back that tightness and stumbled inside. She had been here.

The worn, wooden floor seemed inviting, and he no longer wanted to battle his unsteady legs. He let himself fall to his knees in the center of the room, the bones on his arms scratching the wood panels as he bent to feel the cool floor against his forehead. That chill stung his brain, freezing his eyes wide as another vision flooded his consciousness. She was lying in that man's arms. They were huddled on this floor, in this same spot, and he was stroking her hair, whispering gentle words that had the power to stop her tears. Something warm was pulling at Jeremy's chest. He could feel the ache that lived in Kayla, not disappearing, not healing, but being pressed against something soft and clean, as if her anguish was being packed with gauze. Serafin could comfort her. His hands were steady against her body, but he wasn't restraining her movement. She reached for him too. He wasn't trapping her, unlike . . .

It took a sudden burst of violent movement to break the illusion. Jeremy sat back on the floor, slumping into the sagging couch. His laugh was weak and bitter. "You really are an asshole."

Have I shown you anything that wasn't true? You can evade reality for only so long, Saros.

"This isn't my memory. How do I even know it's real? It's bullshit," he said quietly.

The power you carry with you came from an Angel. You're tied to that Nephil now. You'll follow where she goes and, at times, you may suffer some of the same things she experiences. You want to be free of it? Bring her to me.

He stared down at his blackened palms. "Even before this, wasn't she—"

She was never yours, Saros. Even with your reckless, emotional insubordination, I still gave you this gift. You finally have the power to defeat your rival, to claim everything you've wanted on this earth, but you know there is only one way skyward. You've seen where going against rationality has brought you—to the disorder and fearfulness of an animal. You've seen where you'd still be now, without my intercession.

Jeremy was silent for a long time, his unfocused eyes blurring the sharp black patterns that wound up his arms. "You're counting on my . . . hatred . . . to destroy both me and her."

His body was moved by the warm vibration of a chuckle from somewhere deep within. *Saros, your simple logic is so—*

". . . charming."

That voice momentarily froze the movement of his neck, and he was unable to look towards the sound. "Ev."

A husky giggle immediately met his reply. "Oh, you remember me, do you? You don't match my fond recollections at all. Saros, you look like shit."

He didn't stir.

"Don't be like that. I guess I should be fair. I can see that certain parts of you have been enhanced. C'mon, at least look at me. You'll see I've improved too."

"I don't care, Ev. What do you want?" Jeremy made his way slowly to his feet, his eyes regarding her dispassionately.

A little frown pulled down the corners of her mouth, but her gray eyes were content, bright, and peacefully heavy-lidded. "Your heart is beating too fast for you to act so disinterested."

"What do you want, Ev?" he asked again, slowly. Jeremy knew she was right. His pulse was pounding in his head. She shouldn't be here. But she was also fishing for a big reaction, and he was determined to not let her have it.

"Stop calling me that!" she growled before taking a deep breath and beginning again with that composed smile. "I'm not your Ophan anymore—or your anything else, for that matter. If you won't call me 'Fiora' as you probably should, then at least call me Evangeline. That 'Ev' business was never cute."

Jeremy eyed her coolly. She was almost the same as the last time he saw her. Her face was pretty, but at almost thirty it was too old for the childish moods that moved her features. Evangeline's blonde hair was still short, with pixie-wisps sweeping down at the borders of her face, but now it shone with a strange pink cast. She was dressed like an Arch of the Third Sphere, but she had altered her uniform so that the volume of the full curves above and below her narrow waist wouldn't be concealed. There were still the raised lines crawling up the length of her arms, and he could see the familiar symbols scrawled behind her ears that, he knew, wove down around her spine. But now, there were some blackened bones, much like his own fetters, that coiled about the base of her thumbs, wrapped over and around the heels of her palms, and ended jaggedly right above her wrists. "Alright. I get it. Za'in raised you from the dead, made you more of an abomination—" He seized her hand before it struck his cheek, keeping it caught in his grip as his eyes pierced hers. "—and let you be an Arch. Good for you, Ev. I'll ask you one last time. What . . . do . . . you . . . want?"

"You never killed me," she hissed between clenched teeth. "You think Za'in would let that happen? Leaving you to die in Madeline, your inevitable, pathetic attempt to murder me, it was all a part of his plan. You would have known that if you were capable of understanding *anything* he's achieving through us . . . with us! Instead, you've always been a weak child, recognized only because some woman shat you out on the day of the Eclipse. And now, you've thrown everything away for some clueless twat who isn't worthy to . . . to . . . God, she *trained* with him!" Evangeline's eyelids fluttered for a moment before a spiteful smile curled her lip. "You fucked her yet? Is it out of your system? Was it worth it, Saros? Now that she traded up for

Serafin—"

He let her go. "Jesus, Ev, you're still boring. And you still can't answer simple questions." Jeremy turned away from her and started to head into the kitchen.

Evangeline pressed her body against his back, coiling her left arm around him, her hand resting lightly on the cheek she wasn't able to slap, while the spiny heel of her other palm was forced against the cross on his chest. "I know that right now I can't kill you," she whispered into his ear, "but I can see to it that you suffer."

"Your only tricks are what Za'in gives to you. What is it? Physical pain? Visions?"

"Of *her?*" she snorted.

"There's nothing you can do that I'm not already living with right now."

"I'll tell you why I'm here, Saros. That's what you want, right? Here's how it is: you're going to follow that girl and when you find her, it will be my pleasure to do what you don't have the nerve to carry out."

Jeremy shrugged off her embrace and continued walking again.

"You can evade reality for only so long!" she called to him.

He only hesitated for a moment when he heard Za'in's words ring out from her throat. "I see some things never change," he laughed dryly before he stepped into the kitchen. There was something pulling him there, something beyond the desire to put some distance between Evangeline and him. He was beginning to realize these insistent impulses that had been moving him were each stepping stones leading him back towards Kayla, through these fetters and Za'in's will. Since she was caught up in this loop as well, since the tool of his destruction was the distorted pieces of her he carried on his arms . . . did she ever feel this too? He caught his breath, knowing he only had another moment to lose himself in thought before Evangeline would follow him, and Za'in had been silent for too long. Wherever Kayla was, could she sense him? Jeremy closed his eyes, focusing his concentration on one word. If he could choose just one sound to say everything to her, if she could hear him . . . *Run.*

A sharp pain against the back of his skull sent him to the floor. *How generous of you to feel sympathy for the one who betrayed you. You think you can't die, Saros? Don't try that again. You know how I detest needless sacrifice.*

The air stung his lungs. "You think I care . . . if I die?"

Your desire to survive—until you can take everything down with you—is why you're even hearing my voice right now.

"I'm not doing any of this to fulfill Ev's need to please you. If you really wanted me to do this, why did you send *her?*"

Za'in was silent. Jeremy fought to regain control of his body again, willing the pain that washed over him to recede. He could feel Evangeline standing in the doorway, but he ignored her as he crawled toward the glint of metal that came from beneath the moth-eaten blanket covering the kitchen table. His hand trembled as he clutched the fabric— a fleeting vision of Serafin lying on that table, healed by Kittie's hands and Kayla's tears, assaulted his senses—but when he pulled the blanket away, there was a relic of a motorbike lying on its side.

Curiosity left Evangeline's voice without its fury and forced sweetness. "Oh, good. I didn't want to have to tow you around. It looks beat up, though. Does it even have a Core?"

Jeremy removed the fuel cap, but he could see nothing within except for dark, gritty remnants. "It was adapted. But the Core is gone now."

"I'll give you one. For old time's sake."

He turned to look at her. "You'll do whatever you have to do to get his approval, even if it means helping me. You don't want revenge at all, Ev?"

She laughed. "For what? You brought me closer to him."

Jeremy watched her carefully. There was something here he almost wanted to understand. "Lend me a Core, Ev. I'll go get her. But let me handle it. If you touch her, I really will kill you this time."

Evangeline smiled sweetly as she knelt beside him. She gently took his hand and laid hers over his. From the heel of her palm, a small, twisted mass of bone grew and released from the fetters she already wore, before it fell lightly into his hand. "You can only destroy, Saros. See this Core I made for you? My energy is productive. And you can't kill that. You're on the wrong side of things and I don't answer to you anymore."

His fist tightened around the barely vibrating mass. "You're not an Angel. You're a puppet."

She kissed his forehead before she stood and turned around to leave. Jeremy could see a blissful smile smooth her face as she looked back for a moment. "Of course. I'm his Arch."

25

Run . . . run . . . run . . . Kayla was light-headed as she gasped for air, pressing her hands to her chest and feeling irregular beats beneath her palms. *Run . . . run!* Fuzzy, black masses began to overtake her sight, and she rested her head along the dusty side of the truck to keep her balance. Ever since she had taken in her father's Intercessor, visions moved her frequently and she had accepted the toll they took on her body and spirit, in exchange for the fragments of knowledge they brought her as she pieced together her past. She wasn't sure if she could call it a "gift," but still she was thankful for the burden. Without it, she wouldn't have this certainty. She wouldn't have been able to heal Asher's wounds back in the churchyard's banyan . . . Kayla held her breath, her face warm with the memory of his bare chest, rising and falling, the words he spoke that yielded to fate and challenged the past that tore them both from their comforts.

Run. She shook her head. This wasn't one of those experiences. This wasn't about her father. Kayla's arms tingled from the inside out. "Jeremy . . . ?" she whispered, brokenly. The word tasted bitter. She glanced up quickly at the pirates, guilty, but they hadn't noticed her shameful utterance. They were stretching their legs and staring into the distance, waiting for Asher and Kittie to return from town, their thoughts only on what supper they would enjoy, cold, here on the outskirts.

Run. This word was Jeremy's, she was sure. The grasping blur of her memory couldn't reconcile the existence of two banyan trees.

Run. It wasn't a threat. But why would he warn her? He would have coolly taken his revenge on her if it wasn't for Asher and Kittie. Could it be some kind of trick? *Run.* No. This was something familiar . . . sincere desperation. Kayla stared down at her nearly-healed palms. She didn't want to be tied to him this way. There was no denying that she had been fighting the persistent compulsion to call out to him. The war she raged against her weakness was complicated by the impression that he would be easily within reach, if she only let her longing resonate in his direction. She swallowed hard. It was too dangerous to attempt a response; she couldn't take the chance of revealing their location. Still, she needed a release. "Jeremy . . ." she breathed again. That was it. She wouldn't allow herself to speak his name again. The desperate wish that she could keep a foothold in both worlds was unsafe and fickle. She could only hope that severing her connection would ensure the success of their mission and maybe, over time, her desire might fade.

Kayla reached for her locket. It was a comfort she hadn't needed for some time, but the reminder of the broken trust between them drove her to her unchanging personal relic. The picture and words within never shifted, and she could always depend on the invented memories of her father. And the boy that stood beside him . . . now there were no doubts that the man he became was as constant as the stars that were beginning to appear in the darkening sky. She held tight to the tiny box. It didn't even need to be opened.

The haze that held her drooping form to the side of the truck finally lifted. She was able to breathe deeply again, each intake of air strengthening her muscles and steadying her frame. Her hands felt whole and her bones were solid as the familiar elements of her training with Sebastian moved her. Since the tower came down, she had been sorting through too much sorrow to practice what he'd taught her, but now, even as she felt that this state was natural, healthy, and even useful to their cause, a crippling self-reproach crashed against her elation. Kayla held her breath, allowing her brow to furrow, her returning tension breaking up and dispersing the divine energy that moved within.

"My God, this is so dumb. Have you really thought about it? I mean, *really?*" Kerif's voice burst from the quiet hum of the pirates' conversation, the sound yanking her from her introspection.

Kayla looked up to see Bruno staring at him in disbelief. "What? Nonononono, I'm not hearing this."

"Listen, we all agree Serafin's awesome, right? For one, he's pretty much the only guy who could stand up to that psycho—" Kerif paused, cringing against his friends' stares, *"whose-name-we-do-not-speak,"* he whispered. Kerif coughed before continuing. "Hey, it's not that I don't wanna stick around—it's not that! But we have no idea what we're doing! We know our coordinates, but what kind of place are we going to? And what are we supposed to do when we get there? You saw what happened in that tower. Za'in can't be killed! And what's with this new Eclipse? I don't get what's supposed to happen. Why should we bother trying to stop it? If we just lay low, we'd probably survive it fine. We always do!"

Vic was eyeing Kayla nervously. "Guys . . ."

Bruno lifted his eye patch to double his ability to stare Kerif down. "It doesn't even matter! We're not leaving Serafin to do this alone. That's it, Kerif. You've lost your privilege to speak!"

"Hey, guys . . ." Vic mumbled.

Fec had been watching Kerif with a puzzled expression for some time. "You r'member that Eclipses are *bad,* right?"

"Oh shut up, Fec!" The dreadlocked pirate kicked his pale, bony friend before stomping off a few feet. "We're gonna get killed, and for what?" he called over his shoulder. "It was fun at first, yeah. Breaking into Za'in's," he grinned a little before shaking his head and continuing. "Okay, it was fun. I admit that. But that's it! We should get out now before our luck runs out."

Fec's face fell. "Wha' about *Revolución?*"

"Guys, seriously." Vic's voice was getting steadily louder with irritation, his gaze continually darting back into the gathering darkness.

"You got something better to do?" Bruno yelled.

"Yeah, not get dead." Kerif was a few feet away, sitting cross-legged on the ground, his back turned to his friends.

The Captain's expression softened. "This isn't anything we can't handle," he offered, gently.

"Yeah, 'cuz we have *so* much experience dealing with Angels and Demons and girls with Stockholm syndrome and their deranged boyfriends who try to kill them. Next time he shows up, I'm gonna stay out of it or I gotta worry about that little girl threatening to shoot me again!" Kerif sat still in the silence that followed his outburst. When no replies or arguments chased him, he turned around to see all eyes fixed on Kayla.

"You're scared. So you have some sense after all." She was regarding Kerif with a cloudy stare.

He turned his head, hiding his hot cheeks with his heavy locks. "I-I'm sorry. I—"

"No, you should run away. Some of us are already cast into this, but you're not. He's right. We should all run." Kayla's voice was hard and distant.

"Who's right?" Kittie called out.

"What?" Only Kayla's head moved, slightly jerking in the direction of the sound. The others jumped at her sudden intrusion, their surprise emphasized by Fec's choked cry and shaky lighting of a cigarette.

"Did someone suggest that you run?" Kittie asked quietly as she moved closer to the girl.

"I'm not taking suggestions right now." A constricting chill began in Kayla's palms and ended somewhere in her chest.

A flare of light appeared among them, a shelter from the deepening darkness. Vic knelt down beside Fec, his calloused hand considerably strengthening the glowing ember at the tip of the cigarette that burned slowly between his brother's fingers.

Kerif shuffled to Kayla's side, hanging his head. "Hey, I didn't mean to . . . I'm just freaked out by the both of them. I guess Za'in is sort of like a legend. He doesn't seem real, even after I saw him. But he's gotta be pretty intense if his Archs are so . . ." He shivered. "Fec and Bruno didn't see Saros sink the ship, but Vic and I, we didn't stand a chance. And then later, he put those weird cuffs on you, even though you guys were like . . . um, well, you really could have died, right?" He trailed off, coughing before trying again. "But, uh, I'm sure you've seen other sides of him . . ." His voice was cracking under the pressure of forced tolerance.

Kayla turned from him. "Thank you for trying to help me that night. But you don't have to worry about our misplaced affections anymore. Kittie won't threaten you again."

"I'll try to contain myself," the smaller girl mumbled.

"So, for once, you boys want a plan. Fair enough." Asher stepped into their dimly lit circle. He passed a large, ceramic pitcher to Kittie, and then sat on a broken, concrete pillar that was lying on its side. He rested his elbows against his knees, leaning heavily on his own structure.

Kittie handed Kayla a tin cup before serving the others their portion from the pitcher, but the Nephil didn't notice the lukewarm soup in her hand, her eyes fixed on Asher. His weariness wouldn't cause him to falter, and that gave her strength. She held her breath, awaiting the comfort that would come from her willingness to obey whatever strategy he laid out.

Asher glanced up to meet her gaze, as if he sensed her thoughts. "The truth is we're going into this without that luxury. I can lay out my approach for you, but I never tried to conceal the fact that this is a last, desperate attempt. We're going to have to improvise." Something akin to disappointment pulled his eyes down as he bent his head to drink a mouthful of soup. "The totality of the second Eclipse will be visible from an area around Velsmere. He mapped this out too well." Asher's knuckles went white around his cup. "Even the rock formations in that place will aid him in his plans." When he raised his face again, his eyes were narrowed, determined and clear. "But we're going to give ourselves a fighting chance. We're stopping in Azevin on the way."

"You wanna g'see ol' man Gabe?" Fec asked, an awkward smile freezing his features.

"Za'in has grown more powerful with each passing century: tattooing himself with angelic script and sacred blood, grafting other Intercessors to his own, and imbedding Nephilim bones beneath his skin." He paused, his gaze sweeping over the pirates. "We need some spiritual armor of our own." Asher's voice dropped to a nearly inaudible whisper, his eyes distant. "We have to go there. Either way, I must face him. I won't wait for him to come to me."

"Spiritual armor," Kayla repeated softly. She pressed her palm against her chest, remembering the cross that damned both her father and . . . "Is that the only way?"

"I'm not advocating such extreme measures. But I am certain . . . Gabriel . . . possesses relics that will aid our cause. I even have reason to believe we might find some of your mother's belongings there."

"How?" Her features were painfully twisted. "Who is this man?"

A tight, cheerless smile seized Asher's face and he extended his hand towards her. Kayla reached for his unyielding grip as if it was the only thing solid in this swaying world. His reply arrived with his touch. "Like me, he's just a ghost of the past, but he sees himself as a man of the future. There was a time when Za'in only had one Arch. That was all that was necessary. But everything was different after the Eclipse. Michael had walked away and Gabriel Tregenne had changed. He was ready to lead."

Bruno was pulling on his hair. "Oh God, we are incredibly stupid."

The brilliance and direction of the light was fluctuating erratically as Fec began to nervously smoke. "Tha' ol' guy was an *Arch?*"

Kerif had been spinning his rings around his fingers, but now his hands were stiff and still. "We brought him so many relics . . ."

"I suspect you also were experiments. Maybe even research in the development of those fetters that were used on Kayla." Asher's voice was quiet and without accusation.

"Jesus!" Kerif stomped out to the edge of their circle and paced, muttering angrily to himself.

Asher kept Kayla's hand firmly in his as he calmly observed the pirates' agitation. "We'll be in Azevin in another day and a half. If you're planning on running, do it now."

"No way!" Kerif yelled to them. "He took that shit off us under false pretenses. I'm taking it all back!"

Run. The warning still resonated through Kayla's body. She breathed deeply, pressing clean energy down her arms. It didn't matter if that voice was right; she could just as easily offer him the same advice. In the end, this was a desperate attempt for the both of them.

26

The slick, glazed surface of the pitcher was comforting under Kayla's fingers as she ran her hands over the curving planes of the ceramic vessel. She lay there in the backseat of the truck, unable to sleep, fighting off the oppressive heat with the cool, glassy jug against her cheek. The construction of similar pots occupied her empty reality for so many years. It suddenly struck her that, this whole time, she hadn't longed for the days before she stepped out onto the swampy road to Madeline. She didn't exist until the moment she made the decision to leave.

It wasn't easy to remember the details of the life she left behind; it was as if those memories belonged to someone else. The detached glimpses that she could still recall weren't unhappy—just gray. She couldn't complain. No one was unkind to her and all of her needs had been met. Well, no, not all of them. She was fed and sheltered, she received presents on her birthday and was encouraged to be creative with the clay she worked, but something was missing. The first time she could almost name that void was the same instant she found herself in a dark pit, reaching skyward towards something she had never seen before, in his eyes.

Kayla's hands slipped, the pitcher dropping heavily beside her. It was also the first time her bones released to be her guardian. Somewhere within, she knew she wasn't like everyone else, she wasn't like him, and she needed to defend herself. She gripped the wide mouth of the jug. Her background offered her no help in dealing with any of this. She recalled Asher's words to her the night before. *Spiritual armor* . . .

She didn't realize she had fallen asleep until the creaking door woke her with a start. "Asher?"

"It's okay, it's me. I'm just going to sleep up front for a few while the boys cover us. Try to rest."

Kayla could make out the hard angle of his jaw, but his gaze was lost in the shadows. She abandoned the pitcher to clutch at his arm, pulling herself up and leaning towards him. "Asher, do you know why I was in that place for so many years?"

He paused for a moment before slowly making his way over the front seat to sit beside her. "Michael's final act was to see to it that you were kept safe from Za'in. We are 'wandering stars for whom is reserved the blackness of darkness forever . . .' "

"I've heard that, somewhere . . ."

The long sigh he expelled sounded like a wistful smile. "Kiera carried a Bible with the word 'star' highlighted, every time it was mentioned. She said that passage was written for us. I wonder if that was what Michael was thinking of when he saved you—to send you someplace too dark for Za'in's sight."

She closed her eyes, letting a warm, fluid sensation slide up her arms before it found its way to her throat. " 'The fifth angel sounded his trumpet, and I saw a star that had fallen from the sky to the earth. The star was given the key to the shaft of the Abyss. When he opened the Abyss, smoke rose from it like the smoke from a gigantic furnace. The sun and sky were darkened by the smoke from the Abyss.' "

When the words spilled from her mouth, her eyes burned with each release of hot breath. Kayla could see herself as a very small child, with her arms around her father's neck. His limbs were bloodied and heavily marked with Angelic script, and the red smears across his face and clothes were difficult to distinguish from his long, wild hair. Michael's palms were together, compressing a familiar ball of white fire. The determination on his face was edged with tender sorrow and triumphant spite. A kiss wet with tears was her final goodbye before she was Delivered into the sleepy Abyss of a potter's village, an ordinary inferno of endlessly burning kilns. "How did he . . . ?" she whispered, falling weakly along Asher's frame.

"Michael was the Arch of Za'in's First Sphere, Kayla. He stood at his right hand when there was no one else. He absorbed all he was taught, but Za'in wasn't the only one who made discoveries and developed techniques to bend reality. All of Michael's hopes were with you, and it was left to me to protect you if you ever made it back into the sight of the enemy." His arms enclosed around her, shielding her from both present and remembered darkness.

Kayla's heart beat fast against his chest. He was what she needed. Asher was unwavering and enduring, and she had no doubts about his motivations. He was driven by purpose. At this moment, she could sense the solace her existence brought him. He needed her too. Kayla kept her eyes shut tightly as she pulled herself closer to him, reaching for his warmth and moved by the wish to stir the dying fire within him that he managed to keep flickering for so long, alone. She clutched at his dense shoulder blades, her fingers caught and bound together by his hair, and it was then she felt the pressure of her body against his wasn't completely self-generated. He remained still, but she could feel the sharp bristle of his beard, warmed by his breath, raising the tiny hairs on her neck. She could sense the question raging inside him, and she wouldn't make him ask. "You can . . ." she sighed fervently.

Asher didn't move, his inhalation frozen in his throat.

"Please . . ." Her muscles tightened in anticipation and fear.

He hesitated for another moment before she felt his lips brush over her throat. There was a careful tenderness to the way his mouth moved along her neck, until she felt her skin burn behind the force of his teeth. Her body went limp for a moment before her chest swelled forward, her fingers gripping him hard, a cry almost escaping her throat. Before it began, the sound was smothered by his ardent kiss. She surrendered to his passion, surprised by the intensity he had kept carefully reined in. Kayla held tightly to him, her symbol of strength, unmarred by this evidence of emotion. Asher was everything that *he* wasn't. Asher was everything she admired, everything she reached toward, so then why . . . why . . . ?

Her stomach lurched upward as she pulled away, unable to escape the accusations of betrayal that tore at her insides. "I thought—I thought I could . . ." Her body was trembling violently.

"I can't help you forget him," Asher sighed heavily. The shadows were drawn into the weary lines that held his features still.

Kayla stared at him, an overwhelming sense of shame briefly stealing her recognition of the man before her. "I was trying to understand! You've defended the truth and remained constant in the face of Armageddon. You've protected me. I know what I'm feeling is real, even if it's not fair to name it. So why is he always here in my thoughts? It's horrifying. Especially when I know I have to forget him if I want to survive this—"

"I can't do that for you!" Asher's voice was harsh and jarring. "This whole time, I've been willing to lay down my life for you! I'd still do it. I'd do it now. But there are some things you can't ask for! Some things mean too much to be misused."

She recoiled from the unfamiliar, explosive suffering in his usually restrained words. Her thoughts were frozen by self-loathing as she reached for the handle behind her, spilling out of the truck and blindly running into the night. Kayla could hear Asher call out to her, the sound followed by a gunshot and Fec's groggy voice screaming, "aband'n ship!" She whipped her head back in the direction of her friends, but a pair of gray eyes obstructed her view.

"Hey there, darlin'," the woman breathed, smiling as she reached for Kayla's wrist. The Nephil felt the cold tendrils of rutted bone begin to constrict around her flesh and she pulled her arm back hard, ignoring the blood that splashed against her cheek as she began to run again.

The blonde woman let out a high-pitched growl and lunged forward, but her pursuit was halted by Kittie, who blocked her path with a pole twice the girl's height. "Hi, Evangeline. Wow, you look pretty good for being dead and all."

"I'm not dead, you half-grown bitch," she snarled as she drew her jagged trench knives.

"Oh. You sure? 'Cuz it looks like Za'in dragged you all the way here, face first."

"Cute. You wanna see a real clusterfuck? Then stick around and catch a glimpse of your beloved Arch, fallen from grace. On second thought, I'll just cut your throat and spare you the sight, k?" Evangeline sprung at her, slicing down with the bladed knuckle duster in one hand while stabbing forward with the spike that protruded from the other.

Kittie's only reaction to Evangeline words was a hardening of her face. Kayla watched with relief as Kittie sidestepped the attack and countered with a tight swing of the pole. Kayla turned away again, standing behind the cracked, vine-covered wall of the roofless garage where they had hidden their truck for the night. Her arm was bleeding from the gouges Evangeline inflicted, but she was still able to release her Intercessor and grip it tightly. As much as she didn't want to face Asher again, she needed to return and help in any way she could. She wouldn't hurt him again, this time through a different expression of her cowardice.

"Kayla."

She didn't move, unable to raise her head to see the man she had both dreaded and longed for. "What are you going to do?" she asked, her voice faint.

Jeremy laughed dryly. "That's the question, right? I'm beginning to wonder if we have a choice at all."

She swallowed hard and released her father's Intercessor from her opposite hand. Kayla allowed herself to finally look at Jeremy, carefully stifling any physical reaction to the sight of the blackened bones that completely covered his arms, ending in branching veins over his shoulders. "I'm not going to be your victim again, Saros."

His scornful and resigned smile vanished. "What did you call me?" A tiny, painful shudder moved him.

She ignored his question as two gleaming, ivory blades emerged from her hilts. "Thanks for your warning, but I'm not running from you."

His cold eyes softened with surprise. "You heard me."

He was staring down at his hands.

Kayla's face burned with the recognition of how often she had repeated that familiar action as she thought of him. "Yes, and it's not going to work. I won't lose."

Jeremy didn't hear her. "So it's not all bullshit," he murmured to himself. He let curiosity move him, rushing forward, yanking one of her weapons from her grasp and flinging it to the ground, while her other blade made contact with his armored shoulder. It cut a clean slice through his fetters, but the surrounding bones grew around the blade, catching it in a solid grip. He slipped his arm around her waist and held her firmly, the fingers of his opposite hand seizing her chin. Jeremy's blue eyes pierced her. "I've been pursuing you this whole time. I've been . . . consumed with you. Can't you see what *these* have done to me?" His eyes flickered briefly to his arms. "It's a part of you. Do you ever feel anything I . . . ?"

Kayla closed her eyes and held her breath. She knew it would hurt to see him again, but this was unbearable. His stare was wild, his face sallow, his bare chest filthy and wind-whipped. Jeremy looked crooked with pain and weak with hunger, but too deep in this sleepless torment to notice. She braved sight again, hoping she was facing him with clear, assured eyes. "It's not me that's doing this to you. It's Za'in."

He hung his head for a moment, smiling bitterly. "I know that. And, to a point, it's not even him . . . it's me. But you heard me call out to you. Did you even try to reach back?" He brought his face closer to hers, probing her eyes for answers.

"There's nothing to reach for anymore." Her voice wavered slightly with effort.

"Shut up!" he growled after quickly turning his face away.

Kayla froze nervously, certain that outburst wasn't meant for her. "Please, just . . . let me go. We've already hurt each other so much. Can't we call it even and walk away?"

Jeremy's fingers bruised her face. "Was it a lie?"

"W-what?"

"God, I'm so naive. I knew it. Was it a fucking lie, Kayla?"

She was trembling as tears sprung to her eyes. "You want to know if I really love you? If it was a lie, could you have used it against me like you did? It suddenly matters to you?"

His mouth was hot on hers, searching, and it was then that a vision seared her senses. She could see herself, writhing in Asher's embrace as she accepted his devotion in the warm pressure of each kiss against her neck. Kayla knew Jeremy could see this too, even if she didn't understand why he could draw her memories from her this way.

He pulled back violently, raising his hand in the air as if readying to strike her. His face was pale and tight. "I knew it was a lie. But, yeah, it matters. Don't you shudder to think what would happen to you if it didn't?" he whispered unsteadily. Jeremy wrenched her weapon from his arm and threw it down, leaving a shard of her blade imbedded in the blackened bones.

Kayla watched his jerky motions. Each shift of his body was halted before it could continue, as his desire to hurt her was thwarted by this abrupt helplessness in the center of his being. She wondered why she could feel his inner conflict, until her eyes settled on the tiny sliver of white caught in his Ruiners.

A sudden gust of wind blew her hair towards his face. Jeremy felt the soft, red strands against his fingers before he yanked on them hard, driving her to her knees. Her pained cry steadied his shaking legs. He now had the strength to leave her here and run back into the darkness. She was quietly crying, and he breathed in the calming sound of her misery before he departed. "I know you're going to Azevin. You'll wish you ran. Tregenne doesn't give a fuck. And maybe by then, neither will I."

27

"Say something, goddamn it," Jeremy muttered as he stalked through the abandoned garage, prying the ivory fragment from his fetters and flinging it to the ground. "You were right, okay? Is that what you want to hear?" His voice was steadily increasing in volume and degree of despair before his footsteps suddenly halted, and when he spoke again, his quiet words were deadened by their heavy fall. "What do you want me to do?"

Fiora is making herself a disobedient fool. Get her out of there and follow them all to Azevin. If you want to win this, stay out of sight until I give the word. The impersonal authority in Za'in's reply was soothing; by ignoring his humiliation and anguish, it was slightly eased.

"If she ruined your plans, it'd be what you deserved. You should have never sent her." Jeremy knew his scornful words were just cover for the relief he expressed in his fluid movements. It had been so long since he experienced the comforting, dulling sensation that came from following orders, and even longer since he enjoyed it. He knew his thoughts gave him away, but he couldn't let his words allow him to appear tractable. "I tried cleaning your mess up for you before, but apparently I wasn't in on the grand design. That's okay. I just get to do it again."

He stopped when he heard that familiar, shrill battle cry, keeping himself hidden within the shadow of a heavy column. Jeremy watched Evangeline's frustration as Kittie kept her at bay with her skillful evasions and compact swings of her weapon. He smiled. The small girl knew the Arch she faced wielded trench knives, so she chose that metal pole to keep her enemy from getting too close. If she would only use her pistol, this would all be over. His grin vanished with the certainty that Kittie would never allow herself to seriously wound her. Jeremy's brow furrowed, remembering the last time he saw his once constant companion. Would she really have killed him to protect Serafin? His limbs tightened and he refused to move, even as he felt Za'in rush nervous energy into his legs. "I'll do what you say, but not yet."

A stabbing pressure gripped his chest, as if something was being wound tightly around his heart. "This won't . . . make me move . . . faster," he breathed with difficulty. "Are you afraid . . . to let their combat . . . decide?" Jeremy fell down on one knee, holding fast to the column. The pain paralyzed him, but beyond that discomfort, it didn't seem to matter. He raised his head, dazed, to see those four pirates huddled together beside that ridiculous truck. A few heavy jerks of his body were the only expressions of his silent laughter. The sleek, ominous surface of Za'in's vehicle was now a colorful hodgepodge of absurdity. He looked for the cross that marked the hood, just as his tattoo marred his chest, but he could barely make it out beneath the image of a comically grimacing face, sloppily painted over the symbol. They truly made this their new ship. It was an even trade.

"Something scary . . . something scary . . ." Kerif was repeating nervously, his eyes shut tightly.

"C'mon, I'm ready! Now!" Bruno's eye was wide as his body shook with growing intensity, his fingers jangling the coins in his pockets.

A twitching grin moved Fec's face as he toyed with his lighter. "Vic 'n I ar' ready t' back y'up, Cap'n!"

"Something scary!" Kerif yelled, "got it!" He jumped back into the cloud of smoke that was gathering around Fec, his bejeweled hand stretched towards Bruno, as Vic's arm mimicked the same movement.

The raised lines on their forearms slightly swelled as Bruno's hair grew dark, his body becoming harder, paler. He looked down at his hands. "Aah!" The Captain whipped his head back towards his friends. "Kerif! I never asked you to make me look like Saros!" he wailed.

"You said 'something scary!' " Kerif called back defensively from the mist.

Bruno sighed, staring down at the cross on his chest and the fetters that crawled up nearly to his elbows. "Scary is not the same as creepy," he mumbled. He looked up to see Evangeline's lithe frame bending around Kittie's makeshift staff, her sharp knuckle duster barely catching the girl's round cheek. "Okay, that is not cool. Vic, I'm counting on you!" he shouted as he ran towards them, trailing smoke and launching his razor-edged coins with an unnatural force.

In the tense moments before his tiny weapons met their target, the markings behind Evangeline's ears blazed softly, pulling her head towards the direction of the attack. In that brief instant, she turned, brought her wrists together, and then dragged the heel of her left hand down her right arm, stopping at the inside of her elbow. She had created a gauntlet just in time to raise her arm, a handful of coins embedding themselves painlessly in the blackened bones. Bruno didn't hesitate, continuing to rush forward, drawing an imitation of Jeremy's sword before the gloom of the smoke cloud completely enveloped them.

"Careful who you pretend to be. I might not have killed you if you didn't look like such an offensive person," she said, her voice untroubled as his blade caught in her gauntlet. "Why would you want to look like him? Without the illusion, you're actually sort of cute, really." Evangeline pulled her arm down and Bruno stumbled as he was dragged towards the ground by his sword.

The Captain's eyes widened for a moment before he let go of his weapon, flattening himself to the ground. "Vic, now!" he yelled out before his sudden, powerful sweep to her ankles slammed her to the broken concrete below. He scrambled away from Evangeline, struggling to stand as he covered as much distance as possible. "Kerif, she can see through it! Change something else! Fec, it's not gonna work as cover—try another! Vic, stay with me!"

Kittie jumped back into the fray, bringing her pole down to strike the momentarily dazed Arch. Evangeline caught the weapon, pulling her adversary down with her, a sharp kick sending the small girl skidding over the rocks and weeds.

Evangeline giggled as she slowly stood, turning her attention back to the pirates. "Appearing like Saros in a fog . . . was that supposed to do something? You still can't fight for shit." She pulled the sword from the blackened bones, casting it aside, uninterested, as it transformed into a splinter of wood. The Arch eyed the raised lines on the pirates' forearms. "You've got Mods. Hmm, I thought only Tregenne was into imbedding Intercessor frags."

Kerif dropped the rest of the illusion, sighing, while the

other three exchanged uneasy glances.

Her sweet chuckle erupted into raucous laughter. "You're really them? Who knew the world was so small? We really did an awful job wiping Madeline off the map if not only Saros and his tumor there walked away from it, but you pirates too? I'll have to remedy that."

As she rushed towards Bruno, a look of resolve hardened his features. "For the *Ugh!*" he screamed as he launched two more sets of coins from his knuckles.

"No new tricks?" Evangeline snorted as she moved to block the attack with her gauntlet. Her intake of breath caught in her throat as she coughed, her head jerking away from the acrid smoke that suddenly curled around her face. She kept her arm raised, shaking as she blinked hard with her red, watering eyes, but the blackened bones were a weak defense.

The coins followed the path of Vic's outstretched hand, colliding with the gauntlet, grinding through the bones, and splashing over the obstacle like water, finding their way into her flesh. She shrieked in pain, stumbling back as Kerif came forward, his fingers brushing against her eyelashes. "See through that one!" he laughed, peering at her to admire the results of his illusionary handiwork.

A broken grin distorted her face. "If you insist," she whispered between her painful coughs. Evangeline lunged towards Kerif, who was only saved by Vic yanking him back by his hair. The dreadlocked pirate howled as he fell, while Evangeline nearly collapsed in his lap as Kittie struck her from behind with her metal pole. The small girl dropped to her knees, gasping for air.

Fec quickly put his cigarette out beneath his sandal as they all stared down at the fallen Arch. "What do we do now?" Kerif asked softly, rubbing his head.

"Don't take this as a sign that you can win." Jeremy

stood above Evangeline, his voice toneless and his eyes distant.

The pirates jumped at his sudden appearance. Bruno plunged his hands into his pockets, grabbing for more coins. "Don't underestimate us. We've taken down an Arch on our own!"

Jeremy stared back at them dispassionately. "Tell him, Kit."

Kittie was looking down at the concrete below her. "We haven't won anything."

In that moment, Jeremy fell down on one knee against Evangeline's back, pulling away her gauntleted arm as she nearly dragged the sharp edge along Kerif's throat. The former Arch pressed his jagged palms to the mark on her chest. "If this is what you want me to do . . ." he whispered to Za'in before she collapsed beneath his touch. Jeremy hoisted her up over his shoulder, stood, and turned his back on them without another word.

Kittie choked, the sound full of sorrow and unshed tears. She crawled towards him, wincing as her scraped knees dragged against the ground and her bruised palms made contact with the uneven surface that held up her trembling, twisted form. "Why are you doing what he says? That was never why we got into this in the first place!" she cried at his back.

Jeremy stood still for a moment. "Kit, the voice that led me then has failed me. So now I'll give him his chance and see where it takes me."

Kittie stood, wobbling, and with the last of her waning strength, dashed towards Jeremy, falling down again at his feet. She looked up at him. "If you took your revenge on me, would you stop all this?"

"This is stupid," he breathed, beginning to walk forward again.

She held on to his leg, stopping his progress. "You want to know where Za'in will take you? You're going to die, Jeremy. Right now you don't care about that, but I do. I'll submit to your wrath if you just stop this. Please!"

"Were you always so vain, Kit? Ending your life wouldn't change a thing." His eyes were closed, his facial muscles taut as he took another step.

Kittie could see a familiar piece of purple fabric poking out of his cargo pocket. "Don't forget who you're talking to. We both know you don't mean that," she whispered. The hopelessness was driven from her eyes, her warm brown irises ignited with determination.

Jeremy's brow tightened, the tense movement somehow loosening the rest of his face. He looked down at the girl that had been the only bright spot in his world for so long. He couldn't remember why he let go of her. Her hand was outstretched towards him and all he had to do was to let his fingers touch hers. The sound of someone approaching to his left pulled his head in that direction, and then he saw something that froze the movement of his hand.

Kayla was leaning against Asher as they entered the garage, the girl holding a piece of cloth tightly to her bloodied arm. She looked up, flinching as she met his gaze, her hand coming up to touch her bruised face. Asher's arm tightened around her protectively.

Jeremy adjusted Evangeline's unconscious body over his shoulder, laughing bitterly. "How did I get stuck with this trade?" he muttered to himself. He took a deep breath before pulling Kittie off his leg and turning back to Asher. Jeremy eyed his enemy's swiftly drawn weapons, shaking his head. "Don't bother, Serafin. You already beat me senseless tonight. Enjoy your victory. Next time I won't go down so easily." He raised his hand in a derisive wave as he walked away, the others too exhausted by their own battles that night to do anything else but helplessly watch him go.

28

Kayla sat very still, watching through the window as the barren, dusty landscape made way for familiar slash pines and dark patches of ferns. "Kittie, are we close to where I first met you and . . . ?" Her mouth snapped shut, the movement sudden and heavy.

The small girl had almost disappeared beneath her bandages and blanket. "Not really. Everything looks the same. You'll get used to it." Her voice was blunted, her eyes desolate.

"It's my fault."

Kittie closed her eyes tightly. "I can't take this right now, Kayla. Not everything is—"

"You would have gotten through to him if I didn't hurt him just moments before," Kayla whispered coarsely.

"You fought him?" She opened one eye, which quickly focused on the bruises on the Nephil's face. "Who got the worst of it?"

"I tried to stand up to him. I drew my weapons with every intention to—" She shook her head. "He's stronger than before. And he can see everything . . . inside me . . ."

Kittie sighed. "I get it now. So he did get the worst of it." Her gaze rested on Asher's profile.

Kayla followed her stare before her head snapped back towards the other girl, her face hot. "I don't owe him anything! Faithfulness is wasted on him. He got the worst of it, Kittie? Whatever it was he *got*, he deserved."

"You don't have to tell me what he deserves."

"Do you have something you want to say to me?" Kayla asked, her voice low.

Kittie grimaced at her, her eyes slowly traveling between Asher and Kayla.

"Stop acting like a child!" Kayla snapped.

"How should I act? How old do I look? Eight? Nine? Take a good guess. But I'm old enough to recognize what's going on here. Have you forgotten what you said to Jeremy in that tower? I thought that would be what he could hold on to, if he could only believe it. I wished he would, but you make me think he never should have! He wouldn't have come all this way just to let you go again if he didn't love you too—"

"He loves me?" Kayla laughed harshly. "I don't think I can survive that kind of affection from him. Do I have to pay for it with my life or with the lives of anyone else that happen to be in his path? I don't need any reminders of what happened in that tower. Do you think I wanted this? You're the one that brought us all up there that night without one word of warning to him. When he lived through that, you're the one that held a gun to his head. Sure, he deserved it. But you don't want to hear that, remember?"

Kittie's eyes twitched closed, turning her face away as if she had been struck. When she raised her gaze again, her eyes were wide and soft, and all traces of her earlier severity had vanished. "I've failed him," she whispered before her sudden tears drowned any other words.

A deep discomfort numbed Kayla's body, keeping her unaware of her hand covering her own loose mouth. Just moments earlier, the girl before her was cold, critical . . . old. Even her anger was experienced, expressed in her inquisitive and long-suffering eyes, and in each trenchant word. But now she was a child again, moved by the desperate anguish of someone unable to see beyond this moment. "Kittie, he chose his own path," Kayla murmured as she reached her hand towards her sobbing companion.

"Free will," Kittie gasped through her tears, her eyes growing to dominate her drawn face, her words slowly maturing her features as she spoke again. "You're talking about free will. And it's not as simple as that. You made choices, Kayla, but is this where you wanted to end up? Most things, in fact, occurred without your consent. From where you stand, your paths aren't infinite. All our choices are limited. I had goals, I had purpose! But when you look around and find that your options are short and narrow, sometimes you stand still. You stop acting and you just let things happen. But I wasn't supposed to let this happen to him. This all isn't some mistake, some chance, it's . . ."

"Fate?" Kayla murmured.

Kittie paused for a moment as if she was awakening from sleep. She slowly looked down and gently took Kayla's offered hand. "Fate, free will . . . do any of those things exist? Sometimes I wonder if Za'in will really take God's empty throne, since it seems that it's only his will that finds fulfillment anymore. All I know for sure is that I wanted things to be different. I never wanted to see Jeremy like this."

"Then you have to know that I feel the same. I didn't want to exact some revenge on him, I just can't . . . I can't . . ." She stared helplessly at Kittie. "I just *can't*. Not anymore."

Her tiny brown braids shielded her down-turned face. "Yeah." Her sniffles disappeared into a few deep breaths. When Kittie raised her head again, her eyes were clear. "I'm sorry about Evangeline. I should have sensed her approach and I should have been prepared to see her again, this time stronger and more zealous than ever."

Kayla ran her palm over her bandaged wrist, her fingers twitching with the memory of that woman's unconscious body draped over his shoulder. "Who is she?"

Kittie nestled close to her side, resting her cheek against Kayla's cool arm. "Evangeline Fiora is dressed like an Arch now, but she was once Jeremy's Ophan. That is, before he—"

"She was the one he killed? But how is she . . . ?"

"That's the thing that's not sitting right with me. I'm certain he would have made sure he finished the job. And she was never powerful enough to be an Arch before, no way. Which makes me think that Za'in's been setting up something for a long time now. Something I haven't noticed before. If that's the case, then Jeremy is in more danger than I could imagine. If that's the case, then we've all been his pawns and we're just moving towards our destruction according to his will."

Kayla swallowed down the tremors that threatened to shake her. "What do you mean?"

Kittie shook her head as if she drew a simple comfort from her face sliding along the alternating softness of Kayla's skin and blouse. "There's still a piece missing. When we get to Azevin I might find my answer, even if I hate that our hopes are riding on that place."

The brief silence that followed stung Kayla's wrist. "He protected her. They were working together so that she could capture me?" She shook her head. Even though Evangeline tried to seize her, he had let her go. But then why did he carry the Arch away with him?

"Jeremy might be a mess right now, but there is no way he'd ever be interested in working with her again," she snorted. "Yuck."

Kayla closed her eyes. She needed to know the nature of their relationship, even if she didn't want to search for the reason why. It was safe to seek him out through this infected bond they shared, now that she was sure that both he and Za'in already had knowledge of their current position and destination. She wouldn't be giving anything away, so it was okay to do this, right? Her hands were cold and she found she was now unable to move them. The chill traveled up her arms and into her chest. Kayla took a deep breath as she went under, her psyche swimming in his direction. She broke hard against something that stung her entire being, leaving her too stunned to even bring her hands to her ears in some feeble attempt to quiet the noise that flooded her head—a chorus of muddled violence. She strained to find his voice amongst the sounds that pierced her, but she couldn't isolate it. He was there somewhere, but no single part of him remained untouched and whole. She was sure that he didn't even know what voice was his anymore.

As Kayla tried to navigate through this strange labyrinth of turmoil, her senses slowly receded, leaving her floating in a terrifying absence of attachment. A glimmer of remembered warmth pulled her towards some hint of movement that appeared on the fringes of this sudden stillness. She made her way towards that point, beckoned by his pained breaths, racing pulse and turning stomach, and she knew he was trying to drown his fear, doubt and loneliness. She swallowed hard with her new knowledge of what people are capable of in that state.

Kayla could see that woman's blonde hair brushing against his skin, even as his brow furrowed under the lightest pressure of her touch. He was concentrating on the curve of her neck and the heat of her body. He wanted to forget why they were here, who she was, who he was. It was supposed to happen and he knew it should have been his desire all along. It didn't matter. She wanted this and he just wanted to forget. It would be easy to go along with it if he could keep his mind unfocused and his awareness narrowed. He could do this. Kayla felt her eyelids burn as he pulled that woman into his lap, his arm rough around her waist, his other hand gripping her thigh. She felt her cheeks and lips tingle with icy pinpricks as she struggled to see his face. It wasn't enough to be shown these shadowy fragments of flesh, to hear his splintered thoughts. This time his eyes wouldn't lie to her, this time she was sure she would be able to understand all of him, if only she could be doused in his cold, blue gaze.

Kayla could feel water choke her lungs, but she pushed forward, her fingers reaching to brush aside the dark shroud of his hair. Her eyes blurred as she felt herself slip away, but at that instant, his head lolled to the side, revealing a younger boy's face. A jolt of surprise held her consciousness tight to this vision for a moment longer as his eyes opened lazily, seeming to focus on hers. Here he was, years before she ever saw his face, but his piercing eyes were the same. They weren't windows, but fortified gates. He had built the wall so that virtually nothing could penetrate his defenses, but it also served to keep his wrath from spilling out in diluted, random streams. She knew she was really seeing his stare for the first time, even though it was as unchanging as her reaction to it. That familiar helplessness gripped her, intensified by the frustration of her inability to escape it.

His face kept falling in and out of focus, and it was hard to distinguish the difference between his memories and his current incarnation. Kayla had to remind herself that she was swimming in the space between their thoughts, and that she too must be constantly shifting in his sight. She struggled to keep her attention trained on his gaze, hoping it would give her answers. Was this scene something recent or remembered? His expression hardened as soon as she felt the question quicken her pulse, and it was then that his features aged, each familiar scar crisscrossing over his flesh before the fetters reappeared, swallowing up his arms. A spiteful look darkened his countenance as he reached out, snatching her wrist. The thick air silenced her scream before she fell headlong into the dark cacophony she first waded through. Flashes of light on the edges of her vision pulled her eyes this way and that, but when she found something her sight could focus on, she immediately struggled to turn back into the black abyss. With every apparition of his past she was forced to experience, he had given her the answers she asked for, and everything else she never wanted. As she plummeted down through this dense atmosphere, an uncomfortable heat was dragging her back to reality, and a tearing sensation seared her skin.

Kittie's fingers gripped her arm as she reeled, choking on the suddenly lighter air. "What did you just try?" the small girl cried out. "Don't you do that again!"

Kayla tried to rub the numbness from her tingling arms with her freshly bruised palms. "I just wanted to know . . ." she murmured before her voice rose defensively. "You've asked me to search for him before! It's wrong to do it now?" She didn't understand why her speech was so strained, cracking and squeaking hoarsely under the thin weight of her words.

"Look at your arms," Kittie said quietly.

Purple marks spread out from her hands, over her shoulders, and ended in tiny dots around her collarbone. She reached for her throat, feeling tender flesh beneath her fingers, and she huddled into herself, holding her arms in sudden shame. "I . . . I just wanted to know . . ." she repeated.

"You won't be that reckless again." Asher's severe voice was very close to her ear, and she whirled back towards him. She hadn't noticed that the truck had stopped and he had moved to her opposite side sometime before she fell into Kittie's arms. Bruno was also missing from his usual spot in the front passenger seat, and she could sense the uneasy, restless movements of the pirates on the other side of the screen that separated her from the bed of the truck.

"I thought—" Kayla began to protest.

"You shouldn't have run last night. It was dumb luck that he wasn't in the mood to really hurt you then, but you can't count on that to save you. It was the second time, Kayla! Don't let something foolish separate us again. Not until you find your own strength." He twitched slightly as if he was suppressing a desire to move. "You're not just flesh and blood, and the sin of thought is just as dangerous for you. There are places you can't let your mind wander. You have to promise me."

Kayla let her head rest against him, even as he stiffened slightly at her touch. "How can I make any more promises? How can I tell you that I won't fall again into weakness or danger? Every time I've sworn to cast him aside, my heart hasn't obeyed and my mind has found its way back to him. I'm responsible for the sin of thought? Suppose your dark imaginings could bring down this whole world. How would you handle that?"

Asher grabbed her by the shoulders, one strong shake painfully raising her head. "I'd have to grow up quick. There would be no other option. Indecision can be deadlier than making the wrong choice. You'll understand that soon enough. Tomorrow we'll be in Azevin and you'll find that if you try to straddle the fence, it will tear you in two."

29

Asher maneuvered the truck through the broken streets of Azevin with the same urgent speed that had delivered them through the wastelands surrounding the sprawling city. He rounded each corner with certainty, finding his way between buildings and over the detours of uneven pavement and packed dirt without hesitation. His familiarity with this place wasn't pleasant. Kayla could hear a low growl growing hot in his throat, the almost inaudible sound repeating like a sigh every time they encountered a collapsing, wide-gapped overpass or a toppled train car. Even though these overwhelming spectacles on the other side of the window demanded her attention, her eyes were pulled clumsily back to Asher's face. She could clearly see his profile as she sat in the Captain's usual spot, while Bruno joined his friends in the bed of the truck for some homecoming celebration. The tightness of Asher's jaw and the angle of his brow still expressed his constant, purposeful thrust forward, but in his gaze, everything was torn away by some inconsolable memory.

She was certain that these curving ramps above her head had once met in some graceful way, back when travel was easy and constant. Now they just arched over in incomplete trajectories, the missing pieces sometimes lying in cracked fragments below them. Kayla wasn't surprised to see power lines, always disconnected or downed, but the signs that dominated the skies were new. Some of the large poles led nowhere, reaching up only to be adorned with the fluttering trash that wanderers left behind after their climb. Others were broadly crossed with large boards proclaiming some unrecognizable messages from the past, and still others were hand-painted with cryptic warnings, snippets of philosophy and profanity, useful directional arrows, crude drawings, and other simple affirmations of human existence. Asher never looked up.

The most captivating and frightening aspect of this new empire was their sudden break from isolation. Kayla could feel that the city was absorbed in its separateness, unsympathetic to their cause and unthreatened by Za'in's. Whether it was a metropolis of ruined machinery or a village lazily warm with molded earth, she realized that much of the world must be the same way, by either virtue of defiance or ignorance. What made Azevin stand apart was the simple presence of a few other ragged vehicles, kicking up dust and grinding against the cracked pavement in irregular hiccups.

She didn't know why a sudden, fearful impulse caused her to reach for Asher's arm. "The people here are . . . dangerous," she whispered.

His gaze didn't flicker back in her direction, but his irises trembled slightly with the gathering pressure that branched out from his temples. "Why do you say that?" His words seemed to be quieted by his precarious grip on some precise control.

"They have no idea." Kayla's still-raspy voice left the last syllable silent.

"None whatsoever."

"Hey, Serafin! Follow that blue scooter thing. He knows where we can park without trouble!" Bruno's head vanished behind the back flap as soon as it had appeared to make his cheerful announcement.

Asher turned the wheel sharply, as if he was eager to find his way out from under the open sky. An unusually broad, double-storied building came into sight and his breath released with a slackening of his cheeks. He finally glanced at Kayla, his expression less tense, if not kinder. "They don't understand who the players are or what is at stake." She could tell that there was something about the arches that crowned the boarded-up doors, something about the way his eyes followed each one as they repeated around the exterior—his familiarity with this place didn't bring him pain. "For once, I'm glad their loyalties and concerns are so ordinary." A grim smile started a reaction of deepening lines carving his face, the darkness once caught in those grooves spreading to cover his features completely as the truck moved up the building's ramp and into the dimly lit garage.

Kayla held her breath, closing her eyes with the knowledge that soon she'd have to face a reality that was quite separate from the cool, dreamy echoes that bounced off the concrete walls and landed against her body in soft vibrations through the truck's secure shell. Her fingers rested on the latch. This was a city that Asher knew well; her father must have been here too, once. This was the world. Beyond that gray place that she couldn't call home or the empty streets beneath where her mother once perched, this was really the world. Not an artificial oasis of stars in the desert or some swampy pit with steep, dirt walls. It wasn't a sad story about her parents or orders to breathe deeply or his damn eyes . . . This was the idea that was worth saving, and they'd never even been introduced. Her fingers tightened around the handle.

"No." Her wavering grip disappeared beneath Asher's rough hand.

That warm pressure halted her forward movement and was a sobering reminder of another warning that followed a far less gentle embrace. "He told me—" she began before a dizzying warmth between her eyes made her catch her breath. She didn't want to repeat that warning, but . . . "They know we're here anyways. Tregenne—"

"You're not going anywhere near him. He's not to see you. Tregenne is for me to handle, understand?" His voice was low and sharp, edging the silence that followed with a painful, quiet whir.

Kayla watched through the window as the pirates exchanged embraces and playful blows with the two men that led them to this place on their bike. "We have a better chance doing this together," she whispered. "How many times do we have to argue about it? I want to prove that I can be a help to you; I know that I can. I'm sorry I've broken promises before, but please just let me show you—"

"You've shown me enough, Kayla. This isn't time for a test of faith. If there is even one life here that you value, just do as you're told." Asher's eyes were fixed on a distant point, his words rigid and toneless, and she imagined the crisscrossing lines of his immediate plans catching his thoughts in a momentary stranglehold.

Her fingers left the latch to absently probe her own throat. Kayla's hoarse voice was suddenly too weak to form a reply. She waited passively for his commands, fully experiencing this punishment, the sore spots beneath her touch circling around her senses as a kind of final punctuation.

Enclosed in the truck's airless silence, it was the

distorted, hollow sounds of voices and laughter outside that kept the world from completely receding. The heavy sound of quick footsteps boomed closer before a jaunty series of knocks on the driver's side door brought reality back into close proximity. Asher cracked the door open wide enough for Bruno to slide his head through, awkwardly bumping into the frame in his joyful agitation.

"Serafin! So, yeah, I know you didn't want to meet anyone, but if you ever change your mind . . . I mean, Lester and Jax, they're good to keep their mouths shut, you know? They know something's up and they're still helping us, no questions asked. But, shit, I wish I could tell them we've been working with *you* this whole time!" A nervous cough cut off the beginning of a giggle. "But, yeah, uh, awesome— we're doing this guerilla style, I got it. So, pretty much, Kayla is safe downstairs, as safe as anywhere in Azevin. We'll see to that." He nodded soberly, eager to show his hero that in his uneasy excitement he hadn't forgotten the importance of his task.

"Fine. Please ensure that we remain out of sight." Asher's demeanor was still cold, but he briefly grasped Bruno's forearm in recognition of their comradeship.

Kayla ignored a sudden, blinding twinge of pain, blinking lazily against the blurring of her eyes as she watched Bruno trot back to his friends, throwing his arms around the two Azevinians and walking towards the sunlight. Fec followed close behind, casting one look back at the truck and raising his thumb in the air before disappearing out of sight. She shifted in her seat, glancing behind her to make sure Kittie was still sleeping peacefully, giving her one last moment alone with Asher before Vic and Kerif returned.

He sat beside her in complete stillness, remote as an outlying star or an untouchable ideal. "You've been here before," she whispered, inching closer to him with painfully slow restraint.

"Many times."

"I'll do as you say. I'll wait for you down there, but can't you bring me to that place yourself? If all I can do for you is sit still, hidden from the world and my own failings, then I want you to be the one that seals me away. I know this place has significance for you, for us. I know I can't walk its streets. If you only have a few moments, please let me see just one memory of Azevin, through you, in your own words."

Asher's only response was a brief lowering of his eyelids.

"I see. You have to go now. Time is running out, and Tregenne—"

He abruptly left his seat, shutting the door swiftly behind him and making his way to the passenger side with a speed that didn't match his relaxed strides. Kayla's door was opened suddenly and soon she was on her feet, hurrying to some unknown destination, with only his hand around hers as a guiding force. She was barely aware of the two remaining pirates stopping short, bewildered, as they passed them by, approaching the door of a dark stairway.

A damp, sharp odor was her strongest sensory experience as she descended, her footsteps unsure and falling heavy with unnaturally resonating thuds. When they reached the bottom and the door was flung open wide, a comforting, stale air reached her before her sight adjusted to the changing light. There below the high ceiling was a ring of mirrors and golden bars, chipped paint and frozen horses.

When Asher heard her catch her breath, he released Kayla's hand and she cautiously made her way towards the still stampede, reined in by so many elegant lines.

"There was a time when the most insignificant amount of money would make this thing move. Sing too," he whispered behind her.

She turned back questioningly for a moment before she dashed forward, grasping a bronzed, spiral-etched pole, and swinging her leg over the side of a horse, she carefully slid her feet into the double-tiered stirrups. "What was it like?"

Asher walked slowly towards her, his voice gentle. "The horses would be pulled up and down in tiny waves, as they rode around the circle. The music was loud and jarring, but sweet. Familiar songs. The lights would glow and flash, and you would just sit there, passively bobbing on your steed at a safe, steady pace. There was no destination. You only knew that eventually the ride would slow and then it would be someone else's turn." He stepped onto the platform, leaning back against the horse beside Kayla.

"Was it really such a useless thing?" She smiled, running her fingers over the deep grooves of the curling mane.

"This is a perfect resting place for a monument to futility. The grandest of all wastes of time . . ." His eyes were closed as if he was listening carefully for the details of a quiet sound.

"Then I guess it's the right spot for me to wait for you." Kayla attempted a little laugh, to shrug off the discomfort of his melancholy. It was lost somewhere in the ribbed canopy above. "I can't complain. You'll return before I know it. You've always come back for me."

He held out his hand and helped her down off her mount. She let him lead her over to a brightly painted bench nestled between the rows of horses, and they both sat huddled together, their backs awkwardly unsupported and their knees too high in the small seat.

"Asher, just tell me you'll—"

"The end of the world stopped me from coming back here for so long. It was the only thing that ever stopped me. My own personal Eclipse. I could deal with Za'in's Apocalypse, with that world falling down. But what I lost in

Azevin . . ." He let a heavy breath stir her hair. "If it ends here again, if there is even a chance of that happening . . ." Asher unclenched his fist, letting his fingers move slowly to her temple and across the line of her cheek. The soft motion of his touch dissolved into a trembling grip, a spasm of his hand that pulled her face to his. His tender kiss soothed her restlessness, unwinding the tightness in her throat and limbs. Her body loosened in his arms. It was okay to let go, to let it all go, and resign herself to some dark and peaceful sleep where neither one of them would remember their struggles.

"No!" She was on her feet, crying out streams of memories that weren't hers, stumbling over curling ribbons of brass and unlit bulbs. "Just because Sebastian killed them and Gabriel gave you all up, just because everything was lost in Azevin—everything, everything gone—just because you were happy here once when this place was ordinary, and you were happy here when it was the shattered backdrop of something greater, and now it's a reminder of everything that's wrong and irreversible . . . just because you think you can't beat him . . . you won't just kiss me goodbye. You're coming back and we're finishing this together." Kayla fell down on her knees and palms, her eyes wide and dry with the futile effort of attempting to hold on to her fragmented visions.

"Whether I'm coming back or not, I'm leaving now." He was standing above her, his sorrowful warmth now driven out by his purpose. "Kittie will stand by you. Even those pirate boys can be trusted. And if we're broken and all you can do is run, then I want you to do it."

She closed her eyes, the memory of that same warning to run echoing through her, with another's voice as the source. "I didn't do it then," she whispered. Kayla stood unsteadily, keeping her balance against a hollow stallion. When she raised her eyes to make another proud declaration, with the faded glitter of the carousel as her romantic backdrop, she found there were only the darkened windows of the gutted shopping center staring back.

30

From the ground, it was hard to imagine the original Pre-Eclipsian design painted on the water tower, but up close it was almost decipherable. Jeremy took the time to examine the curving surface, his eyes following the rounded, once-sleek letters. It took some imagination to fill in the gaps of graffiti-covered script, but eventually he pieced together *Welcome to Azevin: Star of the Gold Coast.* He laughed soundlessly at the slogan, buried beneath rust, paint and soot, as he stared morbidly at the giant *A.* The futuristic look of the past always made him uneasy. It was just another reminder that the order of the world was senseless and backwards. He walked halfway around the circular platform, eager to escape the faded catchphrase. On the other side of the tower, there was once an image of a white bird—he could see the pointed wings—and a giant sun . . . or maybe it was an orange. It was hard to tell. Not like it mattered anymore. He couldn't picture a time when this filthy, disordered city could have ever been a tropical paradise. He didn't even like to think about it. This world really deserved an Eclipse.

Jeremy leaned over the railing, his gaze sweeping over ruined buildings, useless train tracks and all the petty, oblivious people crawling over the surface of the whole damned trash heap. She was here, somewhere among all this garbage. Somewhere in the dying light of the Star of the Gold Coast, she existed—just another star that wouldn't let him sleep, a distant and incessant radiance that glowed softly but was surrounded by a continuing violence, and that ceases to burn long before he could ever accept it. She was here, but she wasn't alone. He crushed the rail beneath his grip.

Go find Tregenne and be patient. You're wasting your energy. She'll come to us. He closed his eyes for a moment, drawing his brows together tightly as he released his breath in a rumbling hiss. "Fuck Tregenne. I can do this without that elitist asshole. And why would she show up there? If Serafin has any sense, if he—" Jeremy paused, tearing free the crushed piece of metal beneath his palm before he sat, heavily, staring down at the potential drop below him. He began again, soothed by the steel fragment shattered in his tightened grasp. "I just know he won't let her go near Tregenne."

"He won't? Oh yeah, you know that because you both share a hobby, right?" Evangeline was standing over him, smiling, her wounds wrapped neatly as if they were accessories to compliment her outfit.

"Calm down, Ev. Your eyes bug out when you're jealous. It's disturbing." He sighed, turning his gaze to the horizon, the flaming orange circle that descended reminding him of the decoration painted on the tower at his back. "Why are you here anyways? Go follow Tregenne around. You can congratulate each other on being in Za'in's good graces." He threw the shrapnel in his hand out into the distance. "This is so stupid. Three Archs to catch one girl—"

Evangeline giggled as she sat down beside him. "You're not an Arch anymore, Saros. And I'm just here because I like to watch you talk to yourself."

"He shuts up when you're around. What do you think that means?" He hung his head, letting a short, dry laugh fall from beneath his hair.

"Maybe he's just leaving us alone together," she murmured, sliding closer to his side.

Jeremy raised his head sharply, and then immediately froze, regretting his strong reaction. "You can't be serious."

"Well, why not? There were some times with you that were worth remembering . . ."

"Just spit it out, Ev. What is this all about?"

"Why does it have to be—"

He stood suddenly, turning his back to her. "He wants you to do this? Don't even bother." He could feel her rise and step behind him, her fingers traveling gingerly up the backs of his arms, stroking the blackened bones that had begun to gather between his shoulder blades. A cold shudder moved him, and then held his body still. "What are you doing?"

Her lips brushed against the dense mass of fetters on his back. "You're not the same man, Saros. You're not just a *man* anymore. Both of us, we're something better now. Forget that mongrel bitch. There's nothing special about her. She was just born with some ancient blood, and was oblivious to it her whole life! She didn't earn it. We know what to do with her resources; she might as well be a tree or a cow. Let's just finish this damn mission." She pressed closer, tightening her grip on the fetters as she released a breathless sigh. The bones bruised and scraped her hands, but her yearning only grew as she caressed them, breaking her voice into short, husky gasps. "Oh God, you don't even know what you're becoming . . ."

Jeremy broke free from whatever internal force was deadening his limbs and he pulled violently away from her. "And *you* know what's happening to me? Watching whatever it is killing me, it's exciting to you, Ev? I might be fucked up, but I'm not about to join you in some master race project. This, all of this, is nothing to be proud of." His disgust left him helpless but to stare at her, the outline of her form shifting in the changing light of the rapidly setting sun.

Evangeline regarded him coolly, disappointment quickly dissolving her earlier passion. "Well, now you're getting ahead of yourself. You have such strong opinions for someone that can't see the beauty of his new potential. No one said you're dying. So far, does it look like either one of us can be killed?" Her eyes left him to gaze down at the broken railing. "It's such a waste, but you can be faithful to her if that's what you want. I just thought I might help you relax; it looks like you could use the release. But please, Saros, no matter what new feats you can perform or what voices you hear, don't mistake yourself for Lord Za'in. You can remember the past however you'd like, but I was never in love with *you.*"

He threw his head back for a moment, stretching his shoulders and spine. That cold, sharp fear that had paralyzed his body and distorted his perception had cleared, leaving only a sleep-clogged sense of embarrassment at his earlier weakness. "Yeah, and I killed you, Ev. Whatever sick acts of violence you treasure as your only connection to Za'in . . . don't mistake my unkindness as evidence of affection." He turned around, making his way to the curving ladder that would lead him back to the earth below.

She frowned. "If you hate me, then why did you carry

me safely out of that last battle?" she cried out to the shadow he had descended into.

"I never claimed to be too fond of myself either," he called back.

Jeremy ignored her indignant chattering as he made the long climb down. He was determined to evade her, at least for the next few hours. Even with their mutual dislike, he knew he had wounded her pride enough for her to temporarily keep her distance from him. He sighed, almost satisfied. Walking faster along the darkened roads of Azevin was a useless defense against the uneasiness that his encounter with Evangeline had reawakened.

He didn't want Ev. But that didn't mean that there wasn't a time when . . . well, it was never that. It was never her that he wanted, but a simple moment of oblivion, giving up control, just for a short time, to whatever basic, animal compulsions he could indulge. Then he could forget he was human. He could stop all the damn voices in his head. But now things were different. He wasn't sure what kind of creature he was, and those internal voices weren't his own anymore. The memory of all the excitement, frustration, and fleeting peace that Evangeline once offered now left him with the nauseating sense that every event in his life, even before his almost five years as a soldier, was a part of someone else's plan. It was as if all he could do was react to these uncontrollable forces, while every choice he made just reinforced this predetermined order. Every time he tried to climb out of that choking web, he found himself more isolated. The last time he felt any connection at all, to anything real . . .

Jeremy suddenly stopped walking. The day before, he was certain he felt her. Kayla had reached out, fought through the boundaries between them, and found him. But he was sure it was some kind of strategic move on her part.

Drawing out his memories of those nights with Evangeline . . . she was just searching for information about her new enemy. Not that it helped her. It was so long ago and it was worthless. Ev was an excuse and he was a novelty. It ended just two years after it began, when he became an Arch. She longed for that closeness to Za'in and he was just some kid, ten years her junior. With her limited abilities, she was lucky to be an Ophan. It was jealousy that broke their bond on Evangeline's end, but he was freed from her by a new sense of control. As an Arch, he might be making the world darker, but he'd get to stand above it as the sun crashed down. He could sleep easier at night, without using her to dull his faculties.

It wasn't a pleasant reminder of his past, but still, Kayla reached into him. She wanted to. His legs were shaky as he began walking again, the movement meant to ease the sudden ache in his chest. He'd find her here, just as she found her way into his thoughts. Jeremy closed his eyes, his lids twitching with the acknowledgment of the pain that their connection brought him. She was looking for something that she had no right to drag out, and just a few hours after he discovered how easily she replaced him. Her energy was questioning; she wanted to see. So, fine, he gave her what she asked for. She could have everything that tore him up, if that's what she wanted. His breath caught in his throat as another stabbing throb shot through the nerves beneath his fetters. He didn't anticipate his aggression having negative effects on his own body. Did this mean that Kayla won that battle, or was she in even worse shape?

"So you're not gonna object to this? As long as what I do leads her to you and I don't tell her to run, right?" he muttered. Za'in was silent. Jeremy's steps quickened with his sudden anger. The inconvenient moments that voice chose to give orders, information, encouragement, or to disappear completely, were maddening. He had no plan and Za'in knew it. Whatever happened when he saw Kayla again would be twisted by that foreign force within him, and his actions would never be completely his own. Nothing could be done about it. He kept moving forward, losing track of everything except for the steady impact of each step, letting that rhythm drive out the details of the outside world.

Jeremy tried to remember her face. Last time he saw her, it seemed like her features just wouldn't come into focus. He struggled to recall how it felt to touch her, but her warmth died somewhere past his fingertips. His ability to experience physical sensation seemed to fluctuate wildly between dulled, callous perception and painfully intense awareness, and he was beginning to doubt if his own will ever held dominance over his body. The world was falling away. When was the last time he was ever really with her? That night, beneath the banyan tree, he could feel her against his skin, but that sensation was now some alien and dreamlike memory. What was it like before those fetters swallowed his limbs? He searched for an earlier encounter, before he found her there, alone, among the ruins. It was then, when the tower came down. But his vision was blurred that night, and he couldn't remember her features under the flickering, florescent bulbs.

So this was all bullshit, right? Jeremy's chest felt as if it would burst under the pressure of his frustration. He couldn't forget her, he was consumed with this need for her, but he couldn't even piece together one clear memory. Was this emotion he'd mistaken for love fabricated by Za'in with the purpose of manipulating his actions? He was being used, just because she was . . .

. . . *Steelryn.*

His brow contracted as he remembered when she first told him her name. She was so oblivious. He couldn't believe that just moments after meeting a stranger, she'd reveal something like that. At the time he wanted to laugh. It would be too easy to get what he wanted. But it didn't really turn out that way. Kayla was different. She was once some legend, some crystallized idea of the perfect prisoner that would earn him the perfect reward as he delivered Za'in's perfect weapon. But she just wouldn't fit into that role he had imagined. She wasn't this inanimate treasure he could just hand over. Nothing he ever saw before had eyes like hers. Those golden eyes took in the entire world, regarding it as if it was something new, as if it mattered what happened to it. He found a strange fascination in that, even if it meant she was impractical and doomed to fail. Her eyes watched him too. He liked the careful way she stared; she was untrusting, but she understood her own helpless-ness. That kind of honesty was something jarring. It was an uncomfortable surprise, like being shaken awake, and she kept catching him dozing. He saw how she ran towards him on the shore, the first time he fought Serafin. Her one thought was to protect him, and she didn't care what happened to herself. Why? Why would she do that for him? Why, after he tore her from her goal, did she then listen to him talk for hours, under the stars, in his bed?

He couldn't breathe. She was sitting on a golden floor, surrounded by delicate floating hooves. She couldn't see him. She was alone in the darkness, below a high ceiling, in an abandoned building. She couldn't see him. Kayla was there on the carousel that must still be in the old Azevin Mall. The world came crashing back and he was on familiar ground again. He was running down the boulevard towards her. She was there. All his awareness was focused on her, but she couldn't see him. Because, like she said, there wasn't anything to reach for anymore.

Jeremy stopped. It never made sense anyways. He was

nothing but Za'in's tool from the beginning. Once she got a wider look at the world, her eyes were clearer and he lost whatever luster had earlier caught her attention. He looked down at his hands. Ev was right. He didn't know what he was becoming, and although he was tied tighter to Kayla with every breath, their worlds were growing so separate that they were destined to tear each other apart if they tried to inch closer.

He knew where she was, but he couldn't just swoop in and take her away. Even if he ignored her resistance, where would they go? Jeremy began to slowly walk again, each painful step ending in a numbing sensation. There was nowhere to take her, because the only place he had to go right now was Tregenne's. Za'in had been too quiet for too long. "There was no reason to try to stop me, because you knew it had to end up this way."

My hope for you has always been that you'd find your way by simply opening the door, instead of hurling yourself through the wall.

"Heh. You're known for those gentle nudges towards personal growth." Jeremy laughed bitterly, scraping his fingers along his jaggedly bound arm. "That's why you gave me these?"

They've only been fetters for you because that's how you've labeled them. But, for once, you're going in the right direction—to Tregenne's. That might be just the place for you to learn that if you stop resisting your gifts, you might discover their true nature.

"So it really matters to you that she comes to us, instead of me going and getting her?"

You saw her. She was alone, wasn't she? Where do you suppose that Serafin has gone?

Jeremy found that it was easy to breathe again. "Sometimes you don't have to convince me to do what you want. The least you could do is shut up for a while." Now that Azevin's skyline was completely obliterated by the darkness

left by the fallen sun, he could step forward with his head
raised and his eyes wide open.

31

This wasn't the Azevin that Asher remembered. He walked in the shadow of the winding, raised rails that once supported the long streak of silver carrying passengers through the city in orderly patterns. The sight of those trains gliding above him never failed to pull his chin skyward. There had been something comforting about their movement, as they snaked between buildings, dwarfed by the skyline, unaffected by whatever chaotic business played out below. But that all occurred in a place that didn't exist anymore. He wouldn't look up to see dismembered steel doors, a row of discolored seats, or a vestige of the Metro's bold and simple logo, now stripped of its function. He could find his way to Tregenne's without using corpses as landmarks. It was painful enough that his whole body remembered the way after all this time. Still, the sureness of his steps as they followed a once familiar route somehow soothed the tightness of the gathering dread that held his form rigid.

It wasn't the Eclipse that ever hurt him. It took very little away from his life, and in return, it gave him purpose. It was something he could handle. The days of watching the trains go by above him had a nostalgic charm, but they were far from idyllic. There were moments of peace when he visited his grandfather in Azevin, but he always knew those trips were a simple matter of sharing the load of an unwanted burden. Even at a young age, he understood how it all worked. It was useless to wish for things to be different, so he was very careful to enjoy the pungent smell of the stained sidewalks, and the way he had to cautiously cross the streets, ignoring the red and green lights like every other pedestrian and vehicle. Asher had made sure he loved his daily dose of strong coffee and overly buttered toast from the corner café, and the too-sweet orange concoctions that sustained them during their Saturday morning walks through the mall. He knew that the warm, beige haze on the horizon that hung below the blue sky was unhealthy, but he truly believed that no two colors ever were so beautiful, resting side by side.

Everyone called his grandfather "Duke," so he did the same. The old man was his only living relative, besides his Aunt Tara who had taken him in after the accident. He wasn't angry about any of it and never was. Not really. It was an event that occurred sometime before his solidifying personality gave him a grasp on memory. Without the recognition of exactly who it was that he would never see again, it wasn't hard to be comforted by the simple knowledge that sometimes planes crash in this world. Even if they had lived, things still would have changed, eventually. He could never be sure when he'd wake up to rain, or an empty house, or on a bus headed to Azevin. Whichever way it went, he knew he'd get along. People were always talking about the end of the world, but Asher wasn't worried about it. It wouldn't be something he could plan for, so he'd take it as it came his way.

Tara tried the best she knew how. She never expected to
have to take in her older sister's child, and dealing with
change was never her strong suit. It's not that she didn't
care, but there were just too many obstacles barring her
sight and bending her will. He couldn't help her; no one
wants to hear a child tell them how to manage the difficul-
ties of their lives. Duke was different, though. He wasn't the
parenting kind and there may have always been the sharp
scent of alcohol on his breath, but he would listen. He was
just as set in his ways as anyone else, maybe more so, with
his strictly followed daily rituals, but he didn't seem to
realize that Asher was just a child. Every night, Duke would
sit with him in front of the television, beer in hand, only
halfway watching the game shows, using them only as
starting off points for rambling observations on life.
Whenever Asher would reply with a carefully formed
thought of his own, his grandfather would listen, his eyes
half-closed, which always meant he was at full attention.
Duke never responded with matter-of-fact corrections on a
naïve viewpoint, but took the boy's insights when they were
offered and argued loudly when he needed the stimulation.
It would always end with Asher falling asleep in the stiffly-
padded wooden chair, and in those sleepy moments, bathed
in the television's blue light, he was safe in the knowledge
that between some people, differences were of no consequence.

He didn't consider attempting a permanent move to
Azevin. Duke was glad to see him for each short visit, so
Asher never tried to prolong his stay. He was determined to
ensure that he would never see Tara's weary and martyred
expression set into his grandfather's features. There was no
one to talk with back home, and there were no reasons to
look towards the sky. It made Azevin that much more

precious. Keeping that place sacred was the only reason left to stay in the town where he was born, until he discovered an Angel in a tree.

"It'll get infected." That was the first time he heard her voice, calling out to him somewhere behind the tangle of branches. There was both disapproval and concern in the melodic laugh that descended like falling leaves.

He stopped at the sound while the other boys continued forward, dragging their skateboards behind them, too close to the empty parking lot to pay attention to some voice spouting random warnings. "What will?" he asked, moving closer to the tree.

"Your foot." The foliage above him rustled, but he couldn't see who spoke to him.

"Huh?" Asher dropped his skateboard and started to climb.

"You're not wearing any shoes. You're just asking to step on something you'll regret."

He pulled himself up onto a branch with an abrupt movement, anger silently pulling his brows together. The boy was tired of this lecture from Tara, his friends' parents, teachers, and even strangers. He wouldn't take it from this disembodied voice, whether the source was a tree sprite or some perverted stalker. As he propelled upward, a bare foot was suddenly in his sights, dangling just inches from his nose. Asher grabbed the slender ankle and yanked hard. "What about you?" he called out triumphantly.

She slid down against the bark, twigs catching her with stinging flicks along the way, one of them scraping a red line down her leg. She barely caught herself from falling, but her tawny eyes held no rancor, watching him only with curiosity. "Well, I can't climb trees if I'm wearing my sandals," the girl said simply, gesturing to the flip flops discarded at the base of the trunk.

Asher stared at the girl, her long, dark hair hanging over her pale arms, her shorts and tank top smeared with marks from her fall through the branches. He had never seen anything so beautiful. Before his breathless surprise could cause him to lose his balanced position, he stared down at her dirty feet. "Aren't you too grown-up for climbing trees?" he mumbled.

"I'm only seventeen!" she cried before sighing. "I guess to a sixth-grader, I must look really old."

He raised his head hastily. "No! I mean, it's not that. Shouldn't you be . . . *out?* I dunno. I don't think I'd be hanging around here if I could drive." His eyes drifted to the delicate curves that composed her knees. "Hey! How did you know what grade I'm in?"

"You look it," she replied plainly, watching as some struggle darkened his features. "Where would you drive to, Asher? You'll always be underneath the sky, and you'll always be inside your head. Love what you have here. Eventually, everything changes. And you'll miss even the worst of it when it's gone."

"What, this place?" He frowned. It was something he always understood, but never put into words. He could tie that emotion to Azevin, but he never wanted to admit that vague feeling could apply here. "Wait! How did you know my name?" He turned his head away from her in his confusion, and it was then he could hear his friends calling out to him. They must have been yelling for a while now.

When he looked back up at her, she was smiling. "I gotta go," he said quietly. She nodded, but he didn't move. Asher was sure this rare and fragile creature would just disappear, never to be seen again, if he let her out of his sight. He blinked hard against the jumbled thoughts that filled his brain. He was distracted by the mental image of a night-blooming flower.

"My name is Kiera. I'll see you again. I'm not so ready to leave my home as you are, Asher." She looked down at his filthy feet and grinned. "Be careful out there."

He left her regretfully that afternoon, but came to see her every day after. She was always around when he needed to see smiling eyes or to hear a genuine laugh. She was there to interpret the stars and read his fortune, to both tell and listen to stories with equal wonder. But things changed when Sebastian started coming around.

Asher had to admit that she shined brighter in those days. Maybe it was because he spent so much time alone among the branches, waiting for her return, that when she would climb up to him, satisfied and weary, she seemed that much more luminous. But it wasn't only that. She had new stories and new hope, and she had acquired an air of peace that came from a tenuous hold on secret knowledge. She wasn't standing still anymore with him; it was as if she finally was discovering her own wings. He had tried to tell himself that it didn't hurt, that this was just a natural progression, but he could never fully swallow down the burning pressure below his throat that always appeared as he watched her walk away, smiling up at her new teacher, who was most often flanked by a red-haired boy and a quiet, well-dressed man.

Just a few years later, when the world came crashing down, he felt honored to care for her. Those days saw many horrors, but Asher was unmoved. There were things to be done, and there wasn't any time for mourning or longing or fear. He finally understood the emotion behind the gaze Kiera had devoted to her mentor, as he now looked to Michael as a symbol of strength.

"Wake up! Hey kid, wake the fuck up!" Asher's eyes had opened on the first morning of a new world to those words, paired with some dizzying blows to the head. He looked up into the tempered wrath in Michael's eyes. "You're alive," the man growled quietly. "Why's that?"

Slowed with pain, Asher sat up from the tile floor and looked around the room, darkened by barricaded doors and windows. He remembered the flash of light. "Kiera!" He tried to stand, but he stumbled before he could reach her huddled form in the bed.

Michael immediately moved to block his forward progress. "How did you survive? There's no Angel in you; I can see that easily. You should be dead like everyone else." He coldly grasped Asher's arm and probed his neck, limbs, and chest, carefully examining him with rough impatience. When he discovered nothing unusual, he lightly shoved the boy back with a sigh and sat heavily down on the bed beside Kiera. "You know her," he said softly, looking down at the sleeping girl.

Asher was swaying a bit, but he was finally on his feet. "She's my friend."

"You must be Asher." He ran his fingers through his hair, taking a deep breath. Michael now regarded the boy with steady eyes. "Thank you for watching out for her. I apologize for treating you suspiciously, but she's dearer to me than this whole damn world, and even that contributed to what went on this morning. I've lost a lot today—we all have—but her safety is my first concern. Do you know what just happened?"

A strange whirring sound quietly clogged his ears when he heard Michael speak his name. He had a hard time concentrating on the rest of his words, wanting only to see Kiera's face, but she was hidden beneath the blanket. "I know who you are, Michael Steelryn. I've seen her go off with you and Sebastian and Gabriel. Whatever happened, Sebastian did this. So what was your part in it?" Asher returned his severe stare.

"My part was that I didn't see this coming. I didn't let myself see it. I should have told her to leave, but I wanted this all to work. I . . . didn't want to be without her. I wanted to believe that our child could live in the kind of world she deserved." He followed Asher's stunned expression back towards Kiera's cloaked form and gently laid a hand over her belly. "It took all this for me to really see Za'in. He saved my life, but he thought he built me. There's a difference. I could say that I let this happen. It's true, but we all did. Angels, Man, Nephilim. All of us. Anyone you had here is dead, Asher. I don't know about the rest of the world, but I intend to discover the extent of the damage. Your survival has given me hope, even if it was only Kiera's energy that shielded you. But first, I need to find Gabriel. He can't be far from here. I know I can trust you to protect her while I'm gone." In the following silence, their eyes remained trained on each other, two fierce expressions crashing against unyielding forces.

Asher couldn't smile about that now. Not here, in Azevin. How many times had they locked stares, exchanging a vast complexity of information in one look? Some of their gazes were power struggles; others held more comfort than an embrace. The last time their eyes met, in this place, Michael forgave him for his failings and apologized for leaving him to fight alone. Everything they worked for together was shattered in that moment and he couldn't even mourn, not until he had stumbled down the back stairways and ran out into the streets, finally stopping safely beneath the shelter of an overpass to weep. For seven years, it was Steelryn and Serafin. It was in penance and for the love of an Angel that they began their rebellion, but soon they found their purpose in securing a world for Kayla. Their reality could never return, but they wouldn't let Za'in's flourish. Not as long as she lived.

But the next ten years were dark. Michael and Kiera were gone, and Kayla's whereabouts were unknown. Asher was truly alone. He left the resistance to wage his war in solitude. Although *Za'in* was the name he repeated with every vengeful step forward, Tregenne was the ghost that followed him. Asher didn't realize until it was too late that the gentle, pensive professor was acting as a double agent, with not even Za'in's agenda in mind, but his own. Tregenne's physical changes should have been a clue to his true motivations, but it was hard to see his intentions after receiving his aid for so many years without betrayal. It made his final treachery that much more excruciating and effective.

Asher stood in the shadow of Tregenne's citadel, as it cut a black swath through the surrounding pavement, the deep darkness it created threatening even the light of the moon. Whatever happened tonight, it wouldn't end with him cowering beneath the lifeless freeway. This wasn't just an opportunity for his own atonement, but possibly his final chance to shield the last Steelryn from this world and the embodiment of its viciousness.

32

There were no traps laid to prevent a siege of Tregenne's fortress. There was no need. No one in Azevin knew he was Za'in's first Arch, and if they did, they wouldn't care. If any poor resident of the city ventured close to the building, moved by desperate thoughts of theft or shelter, the ominous aura surrounding the place would drive them from beneath its shadow and force them back out into the resurrected area of town. Gabriel lived and worked in self-imposed exile, secluded in the heart of one of the last persevering cities, safe in his brazen secrecy. Whatever weakened force of rebellion remained after Asher left it leaderless had never attempted coming back to this place. No one had. Only in his panicked dreams had he returned, endlessly walking the narrow, checkered hallways, chancing the unreliable elevators, and struggling for breath in every windowless room.

Asher banished those fearful memories from his mind with the steady motion of his eyes following the horizontal ribbing that separated each of the building's stories. When he counted all nine, he turned around to face the vacant structure across the narrow street. Instead of forcing a door—passing by the formerly fashionable glass entrance-way and the rusted roller shutters—he decided to find a more discreet and familiar path. As he easily slid the wood panel from a window of the decaying building that faced Tregenne's, he found that the structure still wasn't in use. It wasn't a surprise to see all the desks and computers untouched and useless. In the darkness, he felt his way to the far wall and reached for a doorknob. As he made his way up the stairwell, he tried to walk softly on the steel tread plate steps, but every movement upward sent a booming vibration crashing against the wall. Asher ignored the ominous sound and continued his swift climb.

When he reached the top, he pressed his way through the double doors, blindly taking five more steps before releasing his gathered energy in a hard kick that made contact with the boarded-up passageway. This narrow corridor hung high above the street, connecting the two buildings for the ease of some unknown business that took place years ago. Now he made his way forward, his body tense in anticipation of new obstacles, bracing himself against the stale air. Asher found his way more gently through the door on the other side and, as he entered, there were no doubts that he was truly in Tregenne's domain. The softly glowing emergency lights cast everything in a menacing red tint that seemed appropriate for his reunion with the realm of his nightmares. The silence was oppressive, but he was certain that Tregenne was somewhere in one of the floors below, so he had to make haste. Asher knew his drive for a confrontation, which would end just as satisfactorily in revenge as it would in the unfinished business of his own rightful death, had to be restrained. Although his true terror was leaving this place without finally facing what had been haunting him these ten years, he knew there was a wider goal. He didn't promise Kayla he would return this time, but that didn't erase the pledge he made in her name, for every year of her life. This was never fully about vengeance. This was never about the world, for its own sake. He had to locate the spiritual armor they required for victory, and then he had to return to her side. Asher knew what he was. He was just a man, cursed from the moment that he fell in love with an Angel. Nothing would change that. No amount of death, here in this place, would erase that crushing force that held him standing through every disaster. He hurried past the elevators to Tregenne's stairwell, and descended, counting the floors as he made his way down.

When Asher reached the fourth floor, he immediately ran for the safety of the first visible room to the right. He felt exposed out in the halls, surrounded by the repeating squares of black and white tile on the floor, and the stacked, metal lockers covering the walls. The first room was empty, only a painted, gray floor and a stained sink remained. He hurried to the door on the other side, but found the adjoining room to be almost as bare, the large cabinets lining the walls filled with useless relics of the past. Asher was frustrated by the gutted interiors, but as he counted and recounted the floors in his memory, he was sure that he was in the right place. He ran out into the halls again, his mind already wandering the high-ceilinged rooms of the first floor, and dreading an investigation of the cellar—a failed, mold-ridden experiment in penetrating the limestone that lay just below the city's sea-level ground. The climate never changed here. Not even the Eclipse could lift the shroud of Azevin's humidity.

His fragmented musings broke against the wall, as the rest of his body made contact with the concrete. "You call this stealth? I could smell you from the basement. You stink with your desire to die," Jeremy's voice hissed out from between his clenched teeth. He waited for Asher to reply, or to struggle, but his enemy was still, understanding that it was useless to fight against his supernatural grip. Asher's composure only further enraged Jeremy, as he took hold of his poncho again, and slammed him into the steel doors on the opposite side of the hall. "What were you thinking, coming here? This is the third time you've left her alone. You lay claim to her and then let her wander in this world? You'll wish you never touched her." An overwhelming wave of disgust stirred Jeremy and he seized Asher's arm and throat, turning his face towards him, moved by the need to see some reaction in his rival's features.

Just as suddenly, a blistering vision engulfed Jeremy's awareness, and the tighter his fingers grasped at fragments of the real world, the more it fell away. The profound suffering that pulled everything aside—leaving only raw devastation—was familiar, but this time it wasn't his own. That ache ran down his insides in warm rivulets, pooling in strange places, but it left his chest open, to be filled with cleansing air. It was then he noticed that he was holding Kayla against his torso. Her tears spilled down over his body, forging clean trails that he could feel reflected within. He wanted to surrender to this dream, but he couldn't ignore the recognition that this was something he shouldn't be experiencing, not now. This wasn't his. This wasn't his desperate need to protect her. This wasn't his only sense of comfort after so many hopeless, lonely years. This wasn't his fear that he wouldn't fulfill his goals, his obligations, his retribution, his release . . . None of this was his. It was Serafin's.

With a cry, Jeremy loosened his grip and collapsed onto the slick floor. In just one moment, he saw and understood everything about his enemy, but his body rejected that knowledge with every convulsion that kept his trembling form weighted to the ground. "Go. First floor. Tregenne. You won't succeed . . ." he gasped, raising his head.

Asher knelt beside him. "You know what I'm looking for?"

"Everyone knows." Jeremy pulled himself up to stare into the vagabond's eyes. "God damn you. Why didn't you just take her and run? The world ends anyways. You could have pretended you had a future and died peacefully, like everyone else . . ."

"I won't let her world end. And I won't pretend with her. With this one exception: she'll never know the depths of the pain I feel, knowing that it's not me she loves . . . but you."

Jeremy's jaw was set and the words barely escaped. "Just—fucking *go*." He watched him disappear, making sure Asher was out of sight before he let his head drop and allowed his noiseless sobs to leave him shuddering against the linoleum floor.

Asher snaked around the *z*-shaped hallway, his legs unsteady. Both his throat and the area below his shoulder were bruised and bleeding from Jeremy's hold on him, parts of his head and back were marked by their collisions with the walls upstairs, but it wasn't these injuries that left his limbs loose and shaking. How did that boy reach into him? It was a violation on the deepest level. He knew that Saros didn't intend to rip away his armor just to see his soul, but it was exactly the accidental nature of his insight that was terrifying.

He fought to control his breathing as he pressed cautiously through a final set of double doors, arriving in the open area that was once the lobby. It should have been obvious to him that Tregenne would be here, amongst his treasures in the Gallery. As Asher entered this last room, there was no need to consider courage or danger or caution. It was too late for any of that now.

Immediately, that softly impatient voice struck him. "Why, of course it's Asher, come to see me. Who else would have taken the most roundabout path to . . . this? This. I won't put it into words. You'd rather I didn't." Gabriel looked up from his desk, slowly removing his glasses and leaning back in his chair. He had changed since Asher had seen him last, but nothing was surprising after the dramatic transformations he witnessed in Tregenne during the years following the Eclipse.

"I don't care what words you use. Your words mean nothing." Asher watched him raise an eyebrow, but further evidence of his expression was lost in the darkness and beneath his long, graying hair and beard, both unruly and carefully braided. The only thing that ever stayed the same was his stare – forever penetrating and fierce, led sometimes to mild amusement, but always unmoved.

"I've heard stories, Asher. You've lost it." He shook his head, cleaning his glasses as he continued, his once-pleasant voice coarser than Asher remembered. "I recognize the allure of leading a revolution, I really do. Michael understood what that meant. But what have you been doing instead? Wandering? Because of what happened here a decade ago? You're a man now. I was sure that as you matured, you'd see that evolution is not only natural, but necessary. But now you're back for something as disappointing as revenge."

Asher was still. "You know why I'm here."

Gabriel's smile was like an animal bearing its teeth. "Then why don't you ask me nicely?"

"How are we going to do this, Tregenne?" Asher's eyes quickly moved over the interior of the Gallery to gain a more complete view of his situation. Only the emergency lights were on, with the exception of the small lantern illuminating Gabriel's desk. It was another reminder that the Arch's love for technology was only matched by his almost superstitious affection for the romance of the past, no matter how clinically he explained history. The walls were adorned with his trophies: various curiosities from the era immediately before the Eclipse, and other remains from a time even farther removed, back when the past really felt like something safely distant and primitive. Tregenne's desk was almost in the center of the room, in front of a project-ing wall that caused the space to wrap around itself. Gabriel watched Asher with bored fascination, leaning back lazily, his muscles coiled.

"There are a few ways this could end. You have to de-cide which one you can live with . . . if *that* is still important to you. 'How do we do this?' " Gabriel purred, stroking his braids. He was clearly enjoying their exchange. "How did we ever do this, Asher? We fight, or we make a deal. I won't shrink from either, but although our first option favors me, a bargain would benefit us both."

Asher's voice was too even. "A covenant with you means death."

"Most likely. So is that your preference?"

Their weapons clashed somewhere near his desk, as the lantern shattered on the ground. Gabriel's cheerless grin was suddenly close to Asher's face, glinting in the last flare of the extinguished fire as he leaned heavily forward, kicking his chair out behind him. Their bodies collided, skidding along the worn floor and crashing into the wall. Asher felt his kukri catch Gabriel's flesh, but the sensation only left him with a feeling of dread as the short sound

Tregenne expelled was more like a suppressed chuckle than a cry of pain. They struggled in the dark, the Arch slipping through Asher's holds with supple movements, eluding Serafin's attacks as if they were shadows of the actual strike. There were times Asher could feel his knives penetrate flesh, but more often they raked against hard, rough surfaces, or were compelled to change direction by stronger forces. Even when a strike met its mark, Asher experienced a sudden return blow. He felt Gabriel scramble for something that had fallen from the wall when they had made contact with it, and understanding the extreme danger in such a hurried movement from this enemy, he hastily slammed Tregenne's head against the painted, concrete floor.

Gabriel grunted, wrenching his body at an odd angle to weaken Asher's grip. Immediately, the Arch fell upon him and the next impact left him dazed, the pain that enveloped him radiating out from his right hand. Through blurred vision in the dim, red-tinged light, he could see Gabriel rise and stumble to a nearby switch plate. A few florescent bulbs flickered, and Asher struggled to keep his awareness from slipping away. He was pinned to the wall by a spike piercing his palm. He painfully raised his head, squinting in the light to see Gabriel motioning to the sliced fabric around his shoulder. The Arch's skin was smooth, but Asher could feel a sickening, soggy warmth spreading down his own torso before he mercifully fell out of consciousness.

33

Jeremy breathed in the cool air and tried to become a part of the blackness that enveloped him. He was closed up in a small room where no red lights would infiltrate his attempt at oblivion, and there was the added benefit of hiding in one of the few sectors of the building where Tregenne kept the air conditioning running. After Asher ran off, he continued to lay there, face down, for a long time. Eventually, he rolled over, splayed out on the floor, sullenly hoping that Za'in would rouse him or that another Arch would jar him out of this pained stillness. None of those prospects were pleasant, but they were better alternatives to staring at the ceiling, listening for the sound of Asher climbing the steps, returning. When it struck Jeremy that he wasn't waiting for him to come back so that they could continue their fight, he crawled away, hurrying towards the nearest place that might help him forget what had happened between them.

He couldn't shake off those emotions. They weren't his, but he experienced them just as closely as the feelings that had always blindly driven his actions. Those vague thoughts that Jeremy avoided confronting or even naming were now laid bare, through his rival. Serafin took her away and left him with nothing but a reflection of his own desperation. The final insult was the realization that, although they both existed in the same Hell, Serafin kept his Abyss locked away from Kayla, while Jeremy knew he had taken a sickening comfort in bathing her in his own suffering and rage. But she was safe from him now. He clenched up against the tremors that crawled up his throat. He didn't care anymore about being an Arch or pursuing some idea of victory. From now on, he'd leave her out of it.

Jeremy's heavy sigh stirred the air. There was almost peace in his decision, and he felt like he might be able to sleep here in the darkness. It had been so long since he could fall into blissful unconsciousness. He only had to let himself drift. He could do it, now. Now that he settled on letting her go, he could surrender. His body slumped painfully against the tiny closet's walls, but it didn't matter. He would stay here, as long as it meant she'd be safe. From him.

His eyes opened suddenly. A realization blacker than his surroundings left him grasping for a hold on reality, but his bulging stare swallowed only nothingness. Kayla was adrift in that same void, exposed, vulnerable to more dangerous forces than his depraved heart. Jeremy tried to cease breathing, to cease thinking. Any small truth that he finally understood would be easily detected by Za'in. Fine. He had acted without thoughts or plans before. Jeremy kicked the door out and ran disjointedly into the halls, his boots noisily sliding over the tiles. As he stumbled forward, his hands helped him keep balance, sometimes slamming against the walls for support, leaving concrete and drywall dust in his wake. He let the angry, hollow sound of his steps echoing down the stairwell drown out any attempt to consider his next move.

The basement smelled like corrosion and ruin. It flickered briefly through his mind that those two words were a strange description for an odor, so he kept repeating them silently to prevent any other thought from entering. *Corrosion and ruin.* He could keep this up for a while. There was nothing else in the whole world but corrosion and . . .

Jeremy's mantra was shattered by an image that held his aching legs still. That drooping, bloodied form that was tied to the wooden cross, it couldn't be . . . "Serafin?"

"I thought I'd give our martyr what he really wanted. He truly looks the part, doesn't he, Saros?" Tregenne was sitting on the ground, leaning comfortably on one locked arm, with his opposite elbow resting on his knee, pulled close to his chest. He didn't turn to see Jeremy, but kept his gaze on Asher, his eyes moving almost lovingly over the intersecting lines of his handiwork. A hammer rested next to his supporting hand, while the other toyed with an iron spike.

Jeremy fought to keep his body from swaying. "You have orders to kill him? Serafin is mine—"

"Za'in has stopped counting on you, Saros. You've become too unstable," he barked. Tregenne's voice echoed sharply here underground, and the sudden, booming resonance stung Jeremy's ears. He was still shaking the pain from his head when Gabriel began again, softly. "Like a true Arch, I don't take orders, but gladly follow the law of the Universe. This is not just Za'in's purpose, ultimately, but a logical progression. We're messengers of a supreme design. Or at least, that's the idea." He finally turned to stare at the fallen soldier, his green eyes steadily aflame. Tregenne regarded his fetters and the tattoo across his chest. "You wear all of that like an affliction."

Corrosion and ruin and ruin and ruin . . . Jeremy missed much of what Gabriel had said, but he caught the last bit. "That's why I'm here," he said suddenly. "These things are a fucking curse. So you know how to use them right, Professor? Let's have it then."

Tregenne's expression lost its intensity before he turned back to the cross. "Later."

"There is no 'later.' Steelryn is here in Azevin, and Za'in sent me with orders—"

"God damn it, Saros!" Gabriel was on his feet. "Dog fuck your orders. I don't want to hear about it. Azevin is my city; I know what's going on here. Steelryn is taken care of. There are less than three weeks left before the Eclipse, and I'm not going to spend it being your schoolteacher." Tregenne took a deep breath, and then bent to pick up his hammer. When he spoke again, his scathing tone was smoothed over. "I've earned a bit of time to spend with an old friend, together solving the puzzle of a much-debated curiosity."

Ruin, ruin, ruin and . . . 'Steelryn is taken care of . . .' Jeremy's mouth was dry. "What's that?"

"What was the real cause of death for the crucified Jesus of Nazareth? I've often pondered this question myself. The scholars have been unable to come to a conclusion. Partly, this is due to the fact that there were various methods of crucifixion, all of which have different effects on the body, but mostly my former colleagues have failed because they were always too squeamish to do what is necessary. But now, this is too tempting an opportunity. I have Asher here, who has wandered in the desert and, as intent as he was to ensure the world's redemption, has offered himself to me as a sacrificial lamb . . ."

Corrosion, ruinruinruin and corrosion . . . Jeremy's mind was reeling. He had to keep up this internal chant and he was having trouble following Tregenne's tirades. The only thing that was certain was that Asher was going to die and Kayla's fate was even more precarious. Why did Serafin feel the need to come here? For what—some relics of the past? They would be as useless as any other charm against Za'in. *Corrosion! Stay focused.* Jeremy let his feet lead him before he could let another thought escape. "You're a sick fuck, Tregenne. Enjoy the scourging or whatever."

No amount of silent chanting could drown out the sound of Asher's scream as he was awakened from unconsciousness by a spike through his palm. Jeremy kept moving, and this time he traded his repeated words for a blurred focus on Kayla. She would be his shield only now, in this desperate moment. Just her name, her eyes, her voice . . . no other judgments or desires or plans. Without that, he couldn't continue, not through the corrosion and ruin that ruled this place completely, to find his way to this particular gate. Each fenced-in hollow that lined the walls was strewn with papers and objects that spilled out of cabinets and boxes. There was a strange sense of organization here. It was hard to follow, but it existed. He found the Steelryn files earlier that night, searching for . . . what? He didn't know. Something that was hers, maybe. Now wasn't the time to examine the impulse. He let that momentum drive him thoughtlessly now, filling the large pockets near the sides of his knees with whatever he found in this compartment.

Jeremy's legs felt numb as he dazedly shuffled back to the cross, guided towards it by another agonized cry. In the dim light, he could see Tregenne standing on the small ladder beside the cross, his face hidden by his heavy locks. Only his sharp grin could be seen as he whispered viciously to Serafin. Asher's eyes were open, but his head was slightly bowed as he gazed down, his drawn face impassive. Jeremy had never seen Serafin this way. His hair, always pulled back neatly, now hung down over his shoulders in moist, tangled strands, and his body, usually concealed by the dense folds of his poncho, was exposed. The ravages of time were clearly etched over Asher's form—each ghost image of an old injury a visual reminder of everything that assaulted Jeremy's spirit during their exchange upstairs.

His eyes blurred. Jeremy tried to dull his thoughts by recalling the delicate gesture Kayla often repeated to tuck her hair behind her ear. When his mind settled again, Tregenne had moved off the ladder and was calmly studying a book, running his blood-spattered fingers over another spike. The Arch's bare chest and back were marked with unusual formations of Angelic script, loose spirals that began on the inside of his forearms and traced his hardened torso with barbed contours.

Gabriel's unintelligible mutterings dissolved into a short lecture, his voice smoothed over by unctuous layers of flourish, no doubt a vestige of his past profession. "Now you'll see that I installed a *suppedaneum* on your cross—that's the foot rest—and I really do think we should use it. At least for the aesthetic merit. The last I read, it's possible that Yeshua wasn't nailed up in that manner, but with his feet straddling the post, or perhaps even in a fetal position. But since most artistic depictions agree on *this* particular posture, I find no reason to argue with Donatello or Rubens." He gently laid down his book and reached for the hammer.

Jeremy stared at the scene unfolding before him. He thought of Kayla's squared fingertips. Serafin didn't struggle as Tregenne approached. He thought of Kayla's mouth, small with consideration or tight with uncertainty, or trembling, close to his . . . The nail was in place, the hammer was raised. Jeremy closed his eyes.

He tried not to think about his hand closing around Tregenne's wrist and squeezing, causing the Arch to drop his mallet. Gabriel's brow furrowed while a slow smile spread apart the lines in his face. "I can only think of two reasons why you'd do this," Tregenne murmured before he staked Asher's crossed feet with his free hand, without the force of the hammer.

"I can't think of even one," Jeremy growled, pulling out the shallowly imbedded nail and hurling it across the room.

"You'll never leave my city alive." Gabriel's jaw tensed as Jeremy's crushing grip tightened around his wrist.

"Could that be my motivation then, you think?" The lids above his cold, pale eyes fluttered with concentration.

Tregenne's head dropped, his mouth close to Jeremy's ear. "It's useless. Your motivations were determined before you even sensed them. You're caught in a cycle you can't even begin to understand, let alone escape."

The fallen Arch grabbed Gabriel's throat and flung him against the opposite wall. "You think I don't know that?" He coughed, instantly regretting losing concentration. His neck stung and it was difficult to breathe. Za'in must have finally read his thoughts, so he needed to work quickly. Jeremy kicked out the bottom of the cross, breaking it at its base, and swiftly moved to catch it near Asher's shoulders. Easing the cross to the ground, he yanked the spikes from Serafin's palms, careful not to look into his eyes. Some unknown danger at the edge of Jeremy's awareness triggered him to fling his body back around, arms first, causing Tregenne to crash again into his treasures. He couldn't help but notice that his enemy's neck was un-marred by the jagged pressure of his fettered grip. Jeremy touched his own bloodied throat. "This wasn't Za'in . . ."

Of course not. But just because I encourage you to make wise decisions of your own free will doesn't mean that I would hesitate to reclaim my own creation.

Jeremy was immediately summoned to the floor. The blinding pain that coursed through his body held him still, cringing. His muscles tightened as he was denied the usual comfort of knowing that the agony would eventually subside, and he slowly turned his head, only to be faced with the raw, bloody void in Asher's palm. His gaze continued to travel up the gore-streaked arm to meet Serafin's red-rimmed stare. Jeremy choked down the humiliation that spread though him—the source, his rival's empathic eyes. "I know," Jeremy groaned. "One of us has to. If we don't, it won't matter if we survive this."

Asher's nod was a shuddering exhalation. Her name was heaviest now, when it could only be expressed in slight movements, constrained by their injuries.

Jeremy couldn't will his body to rise, even though he knew that Tregenne would recover soon. He had no doubt now that Gabriel's Mods worked to inflict his wounds back on his attacker, and Jeremy no longer felt impervious to destruction as he struggled to free his tortured limbs from paralysis. Everything hurt. Except . . .

He couldn't feel fractured bones in his wrist. He couldn't feel anything beneath his fetters. That was almost always the case; the only sensations that were trapped below those black masses related to unnatural changes in temperature or vague, shooting pains. A wave of hopelessness covered Jeremy. His only armor was a tool that was constantly used against him. Under his fetters, he was dead. If he didn't get up off this floor, Kayla was dead. All of this horror that surrounded him was created by his own spite. He didn't deserve to survive this. Let Tregenne come.

Something warm splashed against his cheek. He shifted his focus to see Serafin struggling to rise, his broken body sliding in his own blood. Asher's eyes were merciless, their constancy only wavering under the strain of speech. "How can you lie there . . . when she's still alive?"

A sudden anger burned the new marks on his back. He could feel the intricate curves and points that formed the bony pattern, spreading from the dense tangle of fetters between his shoulder blades, climbing up and arcing back down over his ribs, ending sharply below his waist. The fetters had tapered off in these areas; instead of thick knots of bone, they formed elegant lines and symbols, leaving the flesh around them able to breathe, open to the air. Now they were inflamed with his ire and longing, even with the destructive power of his spite. That fire spread through the black clots that covered his arms and warmed the sluggish blood beneath. If the pain remained, it was so consumed by this flame that it must have changed form, because he was finally able to rise.

Jeremy avoided even a glance towards Serafin's face as he steadied the man's shaking frame. He looked up to meet Tregenne's eyes, closer than he expected and strangely doused in light and a rare awe.

"I always feel like a fool when I doubt Za'in, sooner or later," the Arch breathed, stepping backward. "So the Saros kid wasn't a complete waste, after all . . ."

Jeremy closed his eyes. He could feel the symbols on his back, spreading out into the air behind him as quivering tongues of blue-edged flame. The looming inferno of sigils sprouting from his shoulders became his wings, and he wanted this whole place to burn. He wanted to shoot up into the stars. He wanted to escape the treachery of his own thoughts . . . and he wanted her to be his, without any consequences.

Not everything he desired could be, so he'd have to accept what was coming. Pulling Asher protectively towards the eye of the storm, he let himself ignite.

34

Kayla stared up at the swooping lines of the curved, striped canopy, slashed sharply with black bars and wires. It looked like a mechanical, open-aired prison cell that held a brightly colored umbrella above her, or maybe those rods were just keeping the canopy from floating away like a balloon, by stretching it into this awkward shape. She slowly shook her head side to side against the wooden floor. It wasn't a cage or a balloon that hung above her, but simply the gaping mantle of the carousel, all the inner workings of the now immobile horses exposed. Her shoulders and lower back were stiff from lying here for some unknown amount of time. She knew it must almost be morning.

She rose up on one elbow, twisting her upper body back towards the little bench that sat between the rows of horses. Kittie was still there, sleeping, her limbs gathered tight to her torso. Ever since the fight with Evangeline, the small girl seemed to require more rest, her injuries both slowing down her body and agitating her spirit. But it wasn't only that. Kittie was troubled. Her thoughts would fall in and out of focus, apparent in the flickering attention of her once steady eyes, and the murmurs that would interrupt and trail from her usually precise words.

Kayla slowly sat up, sliding to the edge of the platform, and let her legs hang over the side, her ankles drooping towards the floor. After Asher left her here, the pirates were quick to carry out their orders. The Captain showed perceptive sensitivity in stationing Vic a few feet from the carousel, ensuring her a night quiet enough to wrestle with her thoughts. Leaving Kittie beside her was a strategy that lent her the comfort of a friend, the tranquility of a sleeping child, and, if awakened in an emergency, another protector. Kayla knew that Fec was perched somewhere above her, hidden on a ledge close to the high ceiling, while Bruno and Kerif guarded her from the perimeter of the building.

Still, she could find no peace. Asher was out there facing the only person he seemed to fear, and here she was, fearing everything. Was it her promise to him that kept her here, useless, as all of this violence circled about her, or was it her own terror that held her still? The most frightening realization was the knowledge that it wasn't really *her* that Za'in sought, or that the world relied on for deliverance. It was an idea. It was the Angel in her. Was that what her identity was reduced to? Did she have no say in all of this? As a Nephil, she wouldn't, would she? Angels were meant to serve, not to choose. Her face burned. Kayla couldn't help but remember standing above the desert, regretting her own humanity, embracing all that Sebastian had taught her, and trying in vain to discard her feelings for Jeremy. Back then, she was avoiding his human heart, but now he was something else altogether. Was it the man in him that was wicked, or was it the Ruiners that tainted him? Was it the woman in her that owned this faithless spirit, or was a

Nephil never meant to find fulfillment in this life?

If Asher never returned, it would be her sins that damned him. Kayla wanted to break through this makeshift stronghold and throw her body into the danger he faced. If she could be his salvation, if every assault could break against her instead, it might erase her actions on the shore that day, when it was the sight of Jeremy on his knees that activated her defenses and caused her to fight off her rescuer. Every mistake, every weakness, every ignorant decision she ever made, now pulled Asher towards unknown darkness. He should have never sought her. He didn't know he was pursuing his own . . .

Ruin.

Kayla's fingers gripped the edge of the carousel's platform. "What . . . ?" she whispered unsteadily.

Corrosion and ruinruinruin . . . fuck! Focus. Corrosion. Corrosion and . . .

The words that pounded against her temples were frantic and jumbled. Her palms ached. "God damn you, what is it now?" Kayla closed her eyes and tried to push him out of her head. "I don't care," she murmured, "I don't care what you're doing, or how you're hurting." Her own mantra couldn't drown out his, since no amount of repetition could convince her of her own words. Kayla's voice broke beneath that pressure, her desperate sounds solidifying into pleas. "I . . . I can't. I can't choose you. Please . . . just release me." Her throat and nasal passages burned as she choked down each wave of emotion that came with every one of his fragmented thoughts.

She drew her legs up under her body, kneeling to stand, but collapsed under the weight of his presence within her. He was insistent, his power raging against a new attempt at control. She lay there, still, until the rhythmic chanting, interrupted by curses and growls, subsided. Kayla began to slowly rise, until a new sensation halted her movement, holding her body in an awkward pose. A warm, gentle pressure began in the center of her hands, playing over her fingertips, then back up through her arms, raising the tiny hairs on her limbs. The nape of her neck tingled before she felt a teasing trail of shivers circle behind her ears, across her cheekbones, only to end on her lips, parting them further with each trembling breath. She exhaled carefully and completely, letting her body wilt under Jeremy's sudden adoration for her. If she didn't fight this, just for a few moments, no one would know. If she didn't let it last much longer, no one could condemn her for forgetting all he'd done, opening herself just a bit further to this subtle sense of rapture. She could feel his gaze was narrowed and evasive, his body weary, his spirit forsaken. She knew the air around him was dank and stifling; she knew his nerves were threadbare and dulled. If she opened her eyes, she'd see him again. The side of her face was splattered with something wet. When her vision cleared, everything she was feeling was now torn away by the unexpected sight of Asher, pallid beneath heavy smears of his own blood.

"No . . . *no!*" she choked out, her veins flooded with her own fire again. "I have you—I know where you are. You won't get away with this. I swear, he won't die before you." Kayla's voice echoed coldly through the carousel's canopy, blunted by betrayal.

Vic rushed towards the girl, his steps hurried but measured. "Kayla. What's happening?" His voice was low as he laid a steady hand on her shoulder.

Her face was tight with barely veiled wrath as she looked up into his face. "That coward. What he did to Asher is because of me. It's my responsibility to end this," she whispered fiercely.

"Wait. Who hurt Serafin? Is it Saros?"

Tears were finally forming above her lower lids. "That bastard. But, Vic, I'm not asking your permission. I'm going."

His grip tightened. "You know Serafin commanded me to keep you here." Vic's dark eyes were still.

Kayla's tears fell as she released both Intercessors.

"Heyheyheyhey! Wha're you *doin'?*" Fec was scrambling towards them, tripping over his own sandals. "Have y'lost yer mind?" He leaned his thin frame between them in an attempt to shield his hulking brother.

"She's not going to do it," Vic said simply, with no disturbance in his usual somber delivery.

"If he kills Asher now as I hesitate, I don't know what I'll do." The sensation of fluid streams of searing liquid glided up Kayla's arms and pooled around her shoulders. Her skin felt like a thin layer of tissue stretched over a boiling current, with sharp bubbles popping at irregular intervals over her back. Kayla ignored the momentary fear of being torn apart and let the heat rise. She remembered Asher warning her that her indecision and capriciousness would rend her asunder, so if this was her end, it would be nothing less than she deserved. A surge of euphoria came suddenly, with all of the rage that was clearly Jeremy's, and strangely, all of the hardened purpose that was Asher's. Maybe this wasn't the time for her demise after all. The warmth around her shoulders intensified with the certainty that a god could never be compassionate. Kayla knew this only now, as she never felt more like her absent creator— that void her angelic blood continually sought. She wanted her flight to Asher to be like the eruption of flame behind her. All she had to do was give rise to everything that she was.

She watched impassively as Vic yanked his hand back with a guttural yelp of pain, holding his burned palm close to his chest. Finally released, she whirled around, running weightlessly to the stairwell. Kayla could hear Kittie weakly calling out to her, and the small girl's breathless and pained cries slowed her steps. Why had Kittie been silent until now? Kayla turned to see the girl, hunched over and struggling to stand, her face contorted, and her eyes wide with familiar knowledge. Jeremy's emotions were coursing through her as well. Kayla turned away. She refused to be infected by his weakness any longer.

She threw open the heavy door and was halfway up the steps before she heard it shut behind her, abruptly cutting off the sound of Fec's siren screams as he called out to his comrades on the outer edge of their stronghold. Kayla came out the other side, rushing through the cool tunnel of the second-story parking garage. She glanced briefly at their truck. The pirates' decorations were neutralized by the darkness, and it almost looked like Jeremy's vehicle once again. No, that wasn't true . . . it was always Sebastian's possession. Kayla turned away. It didn't matter. Even if she knew how to drive it, she would have refused to let this thing bear her to him. They were close enough for her to reach them on foot; she could feel it in every pulsating stab of heat that pressed her forward. It wouldn't be long before she would have to make the stand that Asher had told her countless times was unavoidable. It wasn't what she expected: a showdown with Za'in at the brink of Armageddon, but simply this—cutting her heart off from her last sympathies with the opposing side. She had no chance of victory against the overwhelming force of that ageless being if she couldn't even do what was necessary now.

Kayla's feet slid over the slanting concrete as she emerged from the parking garage, and she felt a vague sense of relief as her skin was now fully exposed to the moist air that preceded the dawn. The atmosphere was cloudy with steam and tinged with orange hues, affected by the flames that now sheltered her body. She blinked in the haze, stumbling as her vision cleared to reveal an apparition at the base of the ramp. His skin glowed white against the murky morning shadows, but dark nests of emptiness collected around his arms and face. Kayla let her shaking legs carry her further. She had to see that blackness take a solid form, so that she could banish from her memory the illusion of his body being consumed by a crawling abyss.

She watched his cold blue irises move upwards to meet her gaze, the pale orbs catching in their sockets with little nervous jerks. Kayla stared hard. She wasn't even quite sure that she saw the trembling movement beneath his brows. Her fists gripped the empty hilts of her Intercessors tightly as she moved closer, determined to keep both her outward and inner awareness focused. "What are you doing here?" she heard her voice call out to him, but she was more intent on studying the angle of his spine as he stood.

"Stopping you from getting killed. Go back inside, Kayla. Tregenne's coming, and out here you're—"

She ran forward, skirting around him by jumping down off the end of the ramp.

"Hey!" he barked, turning hurriedly and grasping her elbow. Kayla didn't struggle, ending her sprint suddenly to notice each pained shudder as he fought to keep his hold on her smoldering skin. He finally let go with a frustrated cry, and she staggered forward a few steps before turning back to him.

"Stop playing games," she murmured. "Masquerading as Saros will only get you killed."

"How did you . . . ?"

"Your eyes don't travel like his and your back doesn't relax at the same point. But, most of all, we share this fire. I don't know which one of us sparked it, but I'm sure it's burning at his back too, and it won't be what hurts either of us."

The simulated, brooding severity dropped from his face, leaving only simple exasperation. As his expression melted into something more innocent, his features transformed as well, and his disguise fell along with a heavy sigh. "What, are these things not even *working* anymore?" Bruno howled, holding his forearm close to his face to examine the three lines of raised flesh.

Kerif stalked out from beneath the ramp. "What are you complaining about? It's my ability that's been useless lately!"

"You saw when that stupid Arch deflected every one of my coins back at me! I thought this would work, though, since I was pretty successful against that deranged blonde chick, with your help. I don't enjoy looking like him, but you give me that psychological edge," lamented the Captain, sadly dragging out the gold disks with the unburned fingers of his left hand.

"Aw hell, Serafin is gonna kill us," Kerif groaned as he looked up to find Kayla gone. The only evidence of her departure was a warm glow in the distance, too localized to be the rising sun.

"No!" A look of resolve hardened Bruno's troubled face. "No," he repeated more softly, grinning at his comrade as he drew out a long chain of silver coins.

Kerif glanced back towards the Mall, even as he ran in the opposite direction, towards the dimming light. "They'll catch up."

The two pirates rounded the corner, following the orange glimmer around buildings with unsteady, stacked stories and beneath sheltering overhangs of scrap metal. They followed the train tracks overhead, and when they emerged from a tight alley, they found themselves facing Kayla's fiery wings. Her flames took the form of strange symbols, bending gracefully around her form. Bruno pushed the patch up onto his brow and squinted both his eyes. Was she being consumed? The same angelic script that scorched the surrounding air appeared to also be etched painfully into her flesh. He closed his eyes for a moment, but bright blobs of light still danced in his vision. The Captain had lost sight of Kerif, and he hoped his comrade would have better luck in catching her if this momentary stupor cost him the chance. He opened his eyes again and shielded them from her brilliance with his singed hand while he flung the string of coins with the other, aiming low. Kayla sensed the metallic rope's approach and, her back still turned to him, immediately side-stepped the attack, all the while continuing her dash forward.

"Damn!" Bruno searched his pockets frantically for another one of his specialized weapons. He heard Kayla's steps halt as his fingers closed around another chain, and he flung it wildly, fearful that this moment of stillness would pass him by if he hesitated even a moment to ensure perfect aim. His gaze followed the line of its trajectory, breathlessly blocking out any sight other than this immediate goal. The head coin pierced the crest of her calf while the rest of the chain circled tightly around her legs, binding them together. She made no sound, and scarcely flinched at the impact. Her hand slowly dropped to pull away what restrained her movement.

"Is this supposed to stop me?" she asked quietly.

Bruno choked, certain she wouldn't be able to easily tear off the chain and fearing she might damage her hand in the process. When her fingers stopped, resting motionless over the coins, he raised his stare to see Asher emerging from between two buildings, stumbling towards Kayla. "Shit," the Captain breathed, his body going limp before he began shuffling in their direction, taking his time as his mind raced for some excuse to offer his hero on his obvious failure to keep the Nephil sequestered.

Kayla sullenly watched Asher's approach. "Don't say anything," she whispered.

Serafin dragged his body closer to her. "Again, you've put yourself, and all of us, in danger! Go back now with Bru—"

"Don't you use his voice!" she hissed. "Can't you stay out of my way, now that he's so close?" She looked down at her bloodied legs. "None of this will stop me." Kayla took hold of the chain, untangling herself from its grip.

Asher's face darkened. "Kayla, Tregenne is in pursuit—"

The fire at her back flared up, and she dropped her head, biting her lip to suppress a cry. When she raised her eyes, the two men were close, boxing her in, and she let the weapon in her hand cut the air with a violent snap.

Bruno was struck still, unsure of what happened until he became aware that his forearm was bloodied with a series of jagged slices. His gaze wandered dazedly to see Kerif's stunned expression as he held his bleeding shoulder with both hands, and it was then he noticed Kayla drop the chain and begin to run again, the red marks down her legs highlighted by the blaze that surrounded her.

"That was *me*, you idiot," Kerif groaned, half-heartedly attempting to kick his Captain. "At least my illusion still works on someone."

"Kerif," Bruno muttered, staring beyond his friend, his eyes fixed in horror, "I wish that was you now . . ."

The pirates watched helplessly as Evangeline pulled Kayla toward her by a handful of hair, her trench knife extinguishing a portion of the Nephil's fire as it carved a slash through the corresponding symbol that marked Kayla's back.

35

Kayla could feel an uncomfortable change in temperature, paired with a sharp, stinging pain beside her spine. That area was numb with cold, while the rest of her burned even more intensely. She struggled to throw off her assailant, but her movements were controlled by her attacker's tight hold on her hair.

"Serafin leaves you with only Tregenne's stooges for protection?" she heard Evangeline giggle. "He really did give up, didn't he?"

Kayla thrashed as she felt her flesh being carved again by the Arch's blade, but her enemy reined her in by her tresses, yanking her into a narrow space between two buildings. "If Asher found him, Tregenne is dead by now," Kayla gasped, her fire erupting from behind her left shoulder, releasing the pressure built up from the channels of energy that Evangeline cut off. She reached out, her hands scraping against plaster walls and planks of wood that enclosed the cramped space. Kayla wrenched her neck back towards the pirates, but the tight entrance to the alley was now choked with fire.

"That's right, you're alone with me now, darlin'," Evangeline whispered. "If Serafin won the battle, where is he now?" She clicked her tongue mockingly before mutilating another glowing sigil.

A numbing sensation washed over Kayla, all of her senses gripped by stillness. Evangeline's taunts weren't idle. Wasn't it her own certainty that Asher was badly hurt and needed her help that drove her out into the streets this morning? Her body sagged. She could sense him still, only a few winding corners away from where she was now being held captive, his life slowly draining out of his body. But he wasn't alone. Pulsating sparks of energy were pulled up her arms like stinging trails of lightning. She knew she was only able to feel Jeremy because of this cursed bond she shared with that child of the Saros. The pressure was building beneath her shoulders. After what he had done, Tregenne meant nothing. And this woman was just another Arch standing in her way.

Kayla's waning strength suddenly surged through her, expressing itself as both a billow of fire from her fractured wings and a notched blade from her Intercessor. Her weight dropped down through her legs as she bent deeply, swiftly stepping backwards, and plunged her blade into Evangeline's thigh. The Arch snarled, leaning forward, but Kayla smoothly grabbed the shoulder of her uniform, and then a quick twist of her body was all it took to throw her enemy to the ground. As Evangeline's back collided with the confining wall of the alley, Kayla sprung towards her, her father's Intercessor engaged. The Arch was dazed, but she still had enough presence of mind to drag her bracelets of bone up over her forearms, the angelic script behind her ears gleaming as she spiraled around to meet Kayla's attack.

The Nephil's weapon caught in her enemy's gauntlet, and she reached for the other hilt still imbedded in flesh, yanking hard to retrieve both. There was a moment of unyielding resistance before the weapons were released suddenly, causing Kayla to stumble backward, losing her grip on her Intercessor. Evangeline's screeching battle cry echoed through the alleyway as she threw her body over Kayla's, pinning her to the ground and prying her father's blade from her fingers. The Nephil jerked wildly as she was disarmed, and the hilt skidded against the pavement, out of reach. Her fire spread out over her head, curling about her shoulders, as her back was pressed hard to the concrete.

Evangeline stretched Kayla's arms up, restraining her movement by pushing her wrists into the broken road stones. The Arch easily rode the waves of her opponent's thrashing, dropping her weight down strategically over each rising movement beneath her. "This is all you could glean from Lord Za'in's teachings?" she whispered huskily with a haughty shake of her head, clearing the pink-tinged hair from her eyes. "You're nothing. I don't know why he thinks he needs you."

Kayla could barely breathe. She could only think of what brought her here. It was the fire that now encircled her and the unyielding serenity that had first come with it. For once, even if it was sudden and senseless, she had been truly certain about her course of action and of her ability to follow through. She had finally felt like the Nephil that was worth seeking and protecting. Where was all of that now? Without her Intercessors, she suffered her human helplessness again. And this woman, how was she not burned by the flame? Kayla stared hard at the symbol behind her ear as Evangeline shifted her weight. Its tiny glow reached out into the air, surrounding her adversary with a faint blue aura. Kayla then felt the familiar sensation of sharp tendrils inching over her hands and clamping down painfully at irregular intervals. Her body shook softly. There was no defense for this, nothing she could do to fight back. Except . . . She struggled to remember the impressions of Evangeline she experienced from her journey into Jeremy's memory, in a desperate attempt to grasp some ammunition.

"Of course you don't understand Sebastian's plans," she whispered breathlessly. "He always said that, among his Spheres . . . the Second Ophan Fiora . . . was still the most detestably human beneath all the Mods." Kayla was weakened from the effort to wound her and she felt herself go limp, even as her will to resist wracked her body with little jerking motions.

Evangeline's grip on her loosened for a moment before an increasing pressure threatened to shatter Kayla's bones. "You think this is about you? You happen to have something Lord Za'in can use, and he's going to take it from you before you die. That's all. There is nothing special about your family, except that they are exceedingly easy for us to kill. Are you proud that Saros follows you? Its *orders* he's following, sweetheart. From the moment you saw his face—oh, what an interesting coincidence that you ran into an Arch on your first day away from home—any shred of charm he managed to scrounge up to hide his disgust and beguile you was just a part of his job description. Lucky for him, you're so easy. If he had to work any harder to get you in the dirt, he might not have had the stomach to go through with it. But I should thank you. I've been enjoying erasing that unwanted memory from his mind for many nights now!"

Kayla's body went cold for a moment. Was nothing hers alone? Those private remembrances that Evangeline perverted and spat out were sacred. Even as she moved wrathfully towards Jeremy tonight, ready to take revenge for Asher's wounds, those memories were a comfort. They held no hope for future happiness, but they were a reminder that broken things once had form, and that, inside her mind, she could keep what she treasured most from being tainted by decay.

The fetters tightened around her hands, and Evangeline's voice sounded distant. A wave of pain flooded over her insides and seeped out her pores. But the suffering wasn't hers. Before she could search for Asher's energy through this familiar conduit, her limbs swelled with the last of Jeremy's wasted vitality. Kayla was completely still, focusing on her struggle within. She couldn't guess his motivations, and even that didn't matter. She didn't want to borrow his strength for any reason. Her entire form stiffened with rejection.

Kayla's eyes opened with quavering lids, and it was the sight of Evangeline's wicked grin that changed her mind. She would end this useless diversion now. She let the heat rise: all the hatred and pain, bliss and adoration, every glowing spark of blue and red, angelic hosts singing spirals of glory around nothing, and human limbs with bonds that allowed toil but no chance of ascension . . .

She pulled her hands out from beneath Evangeline's grip, the fetters undulating and flailing like frustrated, hungry leeches. The Arch lurched forward and Kayla slid out sideways from beneath her weight. As Evangeline caught her balance and turned swiftly back towards her, Kayla drew her body up and threw herself at her opponent, fists first. The fire at her back was so intense that she could no longer feel the flesh that separated it from her insides, as she shot explosive tongues of flame against the walls of the alleyway. She dropped heavily onto Evangeline's torso, one hand gripping the Arch's throat, while she raised her other fist above her head. These bones, beneath their corruption, were of her own kind and she had the right to reclaim them. Kayla willed the blackened fragments to move, gathering in jagged clusters around her knuckles. The foreign force within her trembled warmly with satisfaction as she noticed the still, fearful eyes of her enemy, moments before her fist descended, shattering bone. Kayla's tears evaporated before they fell, her spiny knuckles connecting again and again with the form that lay helpless beneath her. She was an act of nature, of sinful man, of absent God. She was divine retribution, and she was everything that tore them both apart. Blood splattered against her cheek, that sudden, familiar wetness freezing her movements with a choking force that sobered her frenzied mind.

"Asher!" she screamed, her voice thundering like millions of beating wings. Kayla rose to her feet, her gold eyes regarding the bloodied weapons she fashioned from her shackles. In disgust, she passed her hand through her wing, the fetters melting through her fingers in foul rivulets and disappearing into the cracks in the pavement. She endured a brief spasm of vague guilt, but she shook it off with the final remainders of the blackened bones. There was a loud noise from above, and Kayla didn't realize that the fire she set caused a structure above them to collapse until she was on the ground again, a heavy beam weighing down her hips. She coughed, unsure if the ash and smoke was invading her lungs or if she was expelling it. She was no more concerned with her body than she was earlier this morning, as physical sensation took a backseat to her driving inner forces, but still a tiny pang of worry sent her digging her fingernails into the gaps in the concrete in a vain attempt to pull herself from the crush of the scrap pile. She soon gave up on that approach, her hands moving feverishly through the debris in search of something to aid in her escape.

Kayla's fingers brushed against a gnarled and pointed object which she immediately identified by the soothing vibrations it sent through her arm. She grasped her

Intercessor, and urgently engaged the weapon, breaking through the rubble that covered her with a wide arc of her arm. She reached out and stabbed the earth, using that anchor to pull her body forward. Her other hilt was now within reach, and with her father's blade in hand, Kayla was able to emerge from the wreckage. She stood, briefly looking behind her, but the fire at her back was beginning to burn low. That woman was beneath the smoldering pile, not her . . . and Asher was still out there.

Kayla retracted her Intercessors with painful shivers, knowing instinctively that she needed to rejoin with her Angelic bones to bolster her strength. She issued forth from the alley, covered in blood and ash, but her stumbling steps were without hesitation. She knew exactly where to find them. Her eyes found a bright point in the distance: a tall building consumed in flame, glowing in the early morning darkness. They weren't there now, but she was sure that was the place where something terrible happened to Asher. Let it burn. Something within told her it was Jeremy's fire that ravaged the structure, but she tried to ignore the question of what that implied, as she made her way towards the blue glimmer that radiated out from behind the ruins, just a few blocks away. Kayla could feel her wings sputtering out in between painful bursts of explosive fire that momentarily sent her to her knees, but whether she was running or crawling, each movement forward brought her closer to them.

She held her breath as she rounded the next corner, raising her hand to shield her eyes from the cold light. From beneath her upturned palm, she could see Asher's drawn face, gruesomely pale in the blue glare. He was lying on his side, his exposed body tethered to the spot by his own spilled blood. Kayla could feel her heart grow heavy with slow, sludgy beats until she raised her eyes, and then the only fire she felt was the insistent force of whatever pumped maddeningly through her veins. Jeremy stood over him, his frame bent at awkward angles, with more of his body devoured by the fetters than she remembered. A set of blazing sigils hovered behind his shoulders, and her fists clenched with the recognition of how similar they were to hers. The light trembled and flickered while he shuddered, coughing out a suppressed cry of pain, before he began to stoop down towards Asher.

"Don't touch him!" Kayla growled savagely, rushing towards him and extending her right hand to release her Intercessor.

Jeremy paused before he slowly straightened, awaiting her approach, his brow knit above resigned eyes.

Just steps away from him, Kayla choked in frustration, her weapons refusing to come forth, even as she focused her depleted energy on this one action. She stood before him, powerless, her rage fueled even further by his soft, troubled stare. What he did to Asher, that she could understand. With him, that sort of viciousness was expected. But this passively pained expression on his face— adrift, disconcerted, longing? It didn't make sense, and it was unforgivable. She brought her hand up in a last attempt to wound him, not knowing if there would be any effect at all as she slapped his face, the sharp sound of contact resonating through the empty streets.

He closed his eyes for a moment at impact, bringing his fingers up to touch the gash opened by a fragment of her hilt, the only part of her Intercessor she could manage to draw forth from her palm. Jeremy's eyes narrowed, anger darkening his features, while Kayla's heart leapt in nervous recognition, but that instant of familiarity died shortly after he broke the contact of their gaze. He regarded the blood on his fingers with a sound that was somewhere between a

convulsing sigh and a derisive laugh, but then his countenance flattened again into that uncharacteristically vague
expression, even as she could see the gouge in his cheek
begin to close. Kayla's body felt cold, but she tried to warm
it with snarling righteousness. She slashed across his torso,
from hip to shoulder, and drew in close to pierce his throat.

"Kayla, stop!" came a weak voice at her feet.

The world seemed to cease moving. "After what he did
to you?" she murmured.

"No, he Delivered me. It was Tregenne—"

"He couldn't! How . . . ?" Kayla stared past Jeremy's
shoulder into the weakening blue flame. She couldn't
understand why he would save Asher, but the truly
inconceivable notion was that he could act as a Nephil now.
The building was still burning in the distance. She turned
away quickly; his Ruiners smelled like corpses.

Kayla knelt at Asher's side, trusting his words enough to
not fear turning her back on Jeremy. She remembered what
she was able to do for him in the churchyard banyan tree,
but now there was so much blood and too many possible
injuries. "I don't know how to help you," she whispered.
"Last time your wound was small and I had my mother's
tree . . . and like everything else, it was an accident. If it's
safe, I can go get Kittie—"

"Nothing's safe." His eyes were closed with concentration, his breathing labored.

She took his grossly punctured hand and gently pressed
it to the skin above her breast. Kayla could feel viscous
trails of fluid sliding down over her flesh. If it ever
mattered, she had to be an Angel now. She drew the almost-
extinguished fire at her back first around her spine and then
into her chest before pressing the energy through her arms,
but she felt sputtering sparks ending at her wrists. Kayla let
out a tiny cry as she kept futilely pushing, her face contorted

with effort. As her body began to sag, that foreign force invaded her again, reaching into the same points beside her backbone, and surging through her like streams of boiling water. She raised her widening eyes to see Jeremy's wings slowly disappearing into hissing smoke, his tense, closed face turned from her. This was all they had left. Kayla let the energy pass from her hands into Asher's as the world dissolved.

She was roused by a familiar, child-like voice yelling, "brake . . . *brake!*" below the insistent sound of an engine. The tires squealed and she raised her head, groggily watching Kittie jump out from behind the wheel of the truck, while Fec emerged beneath her, tumbling over the pedals and through the doorway. She was lifted from the ground, somehow holding on to consciousness long enough to see Asher being piled into the back seat, sometime before the forward thrust of the vehicle drove her again into darkness.

36

Jeremy's deep breaths gently stirred the blades of grass that stroked his closed eyelids, softening the tight muscles in his cheeks. The night air cooled the grass, but the still-warm earth felt welcoming, and he allowed himself to settle into it. There was an enjoyment to lying here on his stomach. He had spent more than a week in that damn truck, and the fetters on his back didn't allow him to lean into the seats without at least mild discomfort, and sometimes, intense pain. But that wasn't the only thing that hurt.

The first day was the worst, but he had learned to deal with his new situation. Jeremy still wasn't sure why he got behind the wheel to begin with, but once he was there he wouldn't be moved. The only members of the group that were fit to drive were those pirates, and he wouldn't put Kayla in their hands. He didn't understand how Serafin ever did. When they first left Azevin, he yielded to Kit's demands and let the bony, shifty guy sit beside him, so that the pirate could grab the wheel whenever a particularly acute wave of nausea, agony, or illusion weakened his own ability to lead them out of danger.

Jeremy plunged his fingers into the earth, tearing at the roots below. The thought was sickening. Was it Za'in that was torturing him that day? Or was it just the after-effects of what he did, of what happened to both of them? Za'in had been quiet since; it appeared that his suffering simply came from the nature of the fetters. Well, that and . . .

He dropped his forehead to the earth. He was barely able to stand that nervous kid sitting beside him. Between them. Jeremy kept insisting that Kit look after her, but his former Ophan was occupied in the back seat, tending to Serafin's wounds. She assured him that Kayla would be okay, that she was certain of it. But the glimpses of her that he caught from around the pirate's skinny frame brought him no comfort. All he could do was drive faster and try to not crush the steering wheel beneath his tightening grip.

It was useless. His best efforts would only result in delivering her to destruction in record time. Is that why Za'in left him in silence? No one could do this job better. He could drive for weeks on end; he couldn't even remember the last time he slept. But still, Kit made sure they stopped at night. If he ever imagined that there was no fate worse than being trapped beside a human ashtray in a truck that looked like a circus freak's tent, these past few nights were reminders that the universe was limitless in opportunities for degradation. Three such nights passed before she was truly awake to the world again. Jeremy had spent most of that time hovering in the doorway while she lay stretched out on the front seat, strictly watched by a changing guard of dunces that never could have stopped him if he wanted to do her harm. When he sensed his monitors' eyes wandering or drooping, he would let his bare fingers lightly touch her skin. It was an appropriate punishment: a jarring reminder that he was denied the simple, futile gesture of sitting beside her and holding her hand, as an ordinary man would. As Serafin did, in the brief moments that his nurse allowed him to lean over the seat and touch her with his healed left palm.

Often his eyes would flicker to Asher's sleeping form. Jeremy was determined to feign indifference to this man, even with the knowledge of how transparent the effort would be to Serafin. That line of thought always ended, as it did tonight, with him turning suddenly and stalking off, seeking a place to crush his aching chest to the ground, allowing his fetters to breathe. It was Kayla's fault. He never would have seen into Serafin if she hadn't touched his rival so deeply. Jeremy expected those meteoric glimpses of the soul's desires, memories, and experiences when he brought his skin against hers with passion. But he never imagined that through the hateful contact of battle, he would, for a moment, live inside the heart of his enemy, through the one connection they both unwillingly shared. The immediate effects of this union were simple and violent, and inevitably led him here, but he didn't foresee the long-term consequence—this new form of helplessness. Upstairs at Tregenne's, with only a breath to mark the time, he *was* Serafin, and although it wouldn't be a stretch for him to destroy something he identified with, it was against his nature to entertain defeat for any longer than a fleeting moment of self-pity. If their goals were opposing, he'd have to lose on some level. Jeremy flopped over onto his back, wincing at the sharp stings that radiated through his flesh, but then he settled comfortably into the soft earth. This was no different than his connection to Za'in. Whichever goal he worked toward, he'd still lose something. There was no longer an illusion of pure victory, a vision of standing above the world.

He looked up at the stars. They were fixed, their patterns

predictable. Jeremy always felt that those glowing points watched him disapprovingly, so tonight he stared back, unblinking. As the focus of his vision shifted with fatigue, it no longer seemed like the clouds above him were drifting, but instead the stars were streaming by like a flock of lazy, distant birds. He forced himself to continue seeing the stars move this way. It was a small triumph over the lights that had always held dominion over him. For a moment, he would allow himself to feel contented, to bask in the fantasy that he could alter his fate as easily as he could shift the stars.

Jeremy could feel a tiny finger twist a lock of his hair. He froze, then recognizing her touch, sighed heavily. "I'm slipping, aren't I?"

Kittie breathed a humorless laugh. "No, I'm just sneaky."

He didn't look at her, but kept his eyes set above, even as his little deception was shattered and the glittering holes in the sky were still and steady again. "You always were."

She slid down into the grass, her head resting against his. "Things will never be the same between us, will it?"

"Shit has happened."

"I'm sorry about all of that. I really am." Her small hand hovered above the fetters near his shoulder. "But worse things would have happened if I—"

Jeremy sat up abruptly, his back turned to her. "If what? If you would have ran your plan by me first? If you would have . . . stayed with me? All we ever had was each other. And now, why is Kayla so important to you? Why Serafin? This world is fucked, Kit! We never had any illusions about that. We understood that, we used it. Things were starting to go right for us. We had her, we brought her—"

"To Za'in. That's right, we did. And you would have been happy with what he was going to do with her?"

He turned his head, watching her with dull eyes. "We don't know what he was going to do."

Kittie drew closer, not letting him look away now that she caught his gaze. "And to think that I told her you loved her. Was I wrong?"

"What's with all of you?" he exploded, standing. "I don't have to prove anything to anyone. I'm leaving her alone, okay?"

She slowly got up from the ground, her palm pressed against her knee for support. "But you're still here."

"Are you asking me to leave?"

Kittie's sigh was more akin to a growl. "I'm asking you to think! Za'in is staying quiet, isn't he?"

He was speaking before he could question how she knew. "You think I haven't wondered why? Is there some logic I can follow that will cause the world to make sense again? I never believed in Angels, or Nephilim, or God. I never thought Za'in could touch me. So what do I do now?" Jeremy roughly grabbed her arm over the long sleeve of her shirt, pulling them both back down to the ground. "Get on your knees! Let's fucking pray. Jesus, save us! C'mon, I know you remember the words. You're educated in all these damn legends. Now's the time to recite it, before Za'in tempts me again into darkness or smites me for my resistance." His mouth was wrathful, his eyes savage as he mockingly repeated the prayer. " 'O God, Who knowest us to be set in the midst of such great perils, that, by reason of the weakness of our nature, we cannot stand upright—' " He ignored Kittie's tears, holding her arm tighter as she struggled, driving her knees further into the dirt. " '—grant us such health of mind and body, that those evils which we suffer for our sins we may overcome through Thine assistance. Through Christ our Lord. Amen.' " Jeremy looked above him, forcing Kittie's chin toward the sky as well. "Is anything happening? No? So what the Hell am I supposed to do about all of *this*?" He released her, motioning to the cross on his chest with his blackened arms. His sinister, broken grin was gone, his eyes desolate. "In the face of this . . . I can't question why he's silent. I'm just accepting the blessing, with the full knowledge that I'm damned. There's no God to appeal to, no one that will take pity on us and save us."

Kittie smeared her tears away, leaving stripes of dirt on her cheeks. "Just because God has perished, doesn't mean that we're not left an inheritance. There are debts, I know, but there is great wealth in what Man can do. Your soul, even if it's damned, is a spark of the divine. And Kayla . . . she possesses a unique fragment of that lost Heavenly glory. Within her is the defiant, brilliant pulse of a fallen Star. You're connected to each other. I know you are aware of the unusual occurrence that affected both of you in Azevin. And I'm still asking you to think!"

Jeremy's face was frozen, his lips barely moving. "You're saying that now Za'in is in . . . her?"

Kittie shifted her weight to the side and she sat down, pulling her knees up to her chin. "I don't know. But Azevin was a trap. If I realized how that place was going to affect Asher, I would have never allowed it." She raised her head to meet his gaze. "You know what I mean."

He stared back, their eyes both moving slightly with their unspoken communication. After a while, Jeremy turned his head, crossing his arms over his chest as he began to pace. "At Tregenne's, he didn't think he could win. And it's not that it didn't matter, or that he was at peace with it. God . . . damn!" he growled, as he threw himself down heavily on the ground to sit with his back to hers, his arms flying up in frustration and his fingers clamping tightly around his hair. "I can't explain it."

Kittie remained still. "Why do you even care?" she whispered.

"Don't tell me that's the one thing you don't know."

"If I know so much, you could try trusting me some time." Her back sagged close to his, barely missing his Ruiners.

Jeremy's head was bowed, his voice quietly falling from beneath his dark hair. "So what do I do?"

"You want to save her. I know you do. You can't leave her alone, not yet. Azevin was a trap that I doubt we truly escaped, but what you have in your pockets, that was the reason for the detour. I know why you haven't handed them over, but you don't have to be afraid." Kittie's features were gathered tightly together, her eyelids shut beneath a pained brow, but her words were soft.

Jeremy grabbed the treasures he carried, from the outside of his pockets. He shook off his sudden reaction; it was no use wondering how she knew. Kit was Kit. He slowly rose, and looked down at her. "You're right, it will never be the same with us, but some things just won't change. We can't escape these roles. I'll do this. It's like I'm always handing over relics. And it's not that I don't trust you—to have this maddening insight into nearly everything—it's just that when I needed you most, you were gone." He offered her a cheerless smile and turned back towards the truck. He walked toward the vehicle, bathed in moonlight, but he refused to look at the sky again tonight. The stars weren't sailing by. They were fixed and cold and piercing, just as they were the night the tower fell. Every memory of his utter vulnerability that night involved some awareness of their surveillance. Kit was gone, Kayla was gone ... Because they were by Serafin's side instead.

It was the complaining, dreadlocked pirate that was her guard tonight, leaning sullenly against the truck and fiddling with his hair. "She's sleeping," he mumbled, his eyes moving around the landscape in an attempt to show Saros that he was on watch and that the former Arch was no concern of his. As Jeremy continued to approach, Kerif's body stiffened. "Resting. Not feeling well," he said, his voice rising nervously. The pirate scooted out of the way before he could be shoved from his place in front of the door. Kerif tried to regain his composure, taking comfort in murmuring under his breath, "I guess it's better that she's sleeping. You're just gonna give her that creepy stare for hours . . ."

Jeremy hardly noticed the pirate as he leaned into the doorway, making room for the moon to enter and illuminate the girl curled up on the back seat. Her hands were folded into loose fists, resting lightly against her neck. Kayla's face was smooth, only occasionally troubled with twitches of dreamy concern. He watched her features carefully, waiting for a sign of waking to offer him the least intrusive moment to break her slumber and destroy her dreams with more burdens of her legacy.

Kayla moaned softly, her hands gathering her blanket close in a spasm of tightening muscles, and she turned over onto her side, clinging to the seat's support. Her camisole strap slipped from her shoulder, revealing scars that raised intricate lines over her back, forming familiar symbols. His face went numb. Jeremy backed away, choking on the stale air in the truck, and he stumbled out to be cleansed by the cool night, but it offered no relief. He grabbed Kerif by the collar, hissing, "Where is Serafin?"

"Aah! Dude, he's there! *There,* okay?" the pirate stammered, motioning to the dark form beneath a tree at the camp's perimeter. Jeremy released him and stalked wrathfully in that direction. Kerif dropped to his hands and knees gasping, "sweet Jesus!" before sitting down cross-legged and waiting for the shivers to subside.

Jeremy clenched his fists until his fingers bled. He wouldn't relax his hands to allow his flesh to heal. He felt like a fool for not expecting it, and that only fueled his anger. Of course, why didn't he think of it sooner? After Serafin was stabilized, Kit tended to her. He had looked through the rearview mirror and saw her treating Kayla's back. She was practically an Angel; she should have been okay. Before this, he wasn't sure who really set that fire in Azevin, but he was certain now that it was his own doing . . . through Za'in. These things on his arms that now made their way over his back, he thought they were singular instruments of his own personal Hell. But he couldn't entertain that fallacy any longer, not after seeing the angelic script marring her back in the same formation as the fetters that covered him. It was disturbing when he saw her red fire facing the dying glow of his blue wings, but he never guessed what it meant. He had to break this connection before she was consumed by his own certain damnation. This knowledge purged from his heart any dark fantasies he once had of her sharing his fate. Jeremy shook his head. No, he knew all of his base emotions would eventually resurface. He had to hold the image of those scars in his memory. They were a reminder. This had to end.

Serafin looked up at him, his face closed, his eyes unaffected by Jeremy's explosive approach. He gently dropped his glance as the former Arch emptied the contents of his pockets at his feet.

"This is what you were looking for, right? I hope it was worth it! All this fucking trash."

Asher's bandaged hand twitched, but he reached out with the left one instead, running his fingers over the blood-spattered book that lay amidst the other discarded trinkets. "Saros . . ."

Jeremy's swift departure was halted by the sorrowful throb of Serafin's voice. "No, don't. I wanted that place to burn just as much as you did. And this stuff didn't belong to Tregenne or his master. They're hers now."

"We should wake her. Her physical wounds are healing, but I still don't know what happened to her, and I don't understand the nature of her deeper injuries. These objects will no doubt strengthen her—"

"Then bring them to her, dammit, but leave me out of it!" Jeremy turned back angrily to face Serafin, but his rage was quenched by the sight of Asher rising up to his sore feet, clutching the relics to his chest, his unusually sharp gaze now vague and wet.

Asher didn't seem to notice his outburst. "I don't know how to thank you. I had no words for what happened at Tregenne's, but this—"

"Listen, nothing I've ever done has been for you. If you want to thank me, then keep silent about all of this. She doesn't need to know that I gave these to you. Just stay the hero. Kit says that Azevin was a trap. She's your new advisor, so you work out what the hell that means. I can only figure that Za'in has found a foothold in Kayla, and I thought maybe this stuff can help protect her. It's more chance than I ever got."

Asher's eyes regained their keen focus. "My silence will deepen the memory of your noble actions."

"We all have our own delusions that help us endure this shit. Just keep yours to yourself, like any other sane person." Jeremy stormed off into the trees, retreating to a dark spot to watch Serafin carry those ordinary treasures to their heiress.

37

Kayla was adrift, floating in the spaces between worlds. When she found what appeared to be steady footing, the ground gave way and she fell weightlessly into another complex dream. There were moments when she longed to emerge from her internal landscape, but she was unsure of which reality would receive her. Sometimes it was Asher's voice that penetrated the thick air that separated them, and she was torn between her desire to walk upright in his unwavering realm and the impulse to just wander this vague expanse within, safe in the knowledge that he wasn't conquered by darkness. These musings were often interrupted by tiny electrical shocks that would move gently over her arms or cheeks, sometimes lingering around her collarbones or hands. These sensations came from a different source, a different man, and she drew further into herself, unable to face whichever fleeting emotion she would find expressed in his pale eyes.

She was aware of the presence of her companions, but the soothing rumble of their interactions—the product of the comfortable roles they had assumed—was disturbed by his energy. Why did he have to stay? Why did it have to be his will that forced the truck forward? She wanted to remain in this void, worlds away from explanations or apologies or pleas.

But he was unkind, and never let her rest. She noted the passage of days by counting the stretches of darkness, marked by a lull in movement and the force of his attention focused completely in her direction. It was always the same. His gaze burned through her closed eyelids for what seemed like hours before she could hear his voice, pounding in her temples, even as she felt warm, moist air pulsating against her ear. The words were jumbled, his thoughts gathering thickly and then shattering into frenzied gasps.

Wake up, wakeup—God, you stupid fucking girl—beautiful—just, alive, be alive . . . I don't believe you're okay—prove it—I'll kill them, you've got to, I can't stand it . . . what I want, without your eyes . . . it can't be stopped, just stop it, silencesilencesilence . . . Just wake up, God damn it! I hate . . . you don't know I'm here . . . I hate this, this . . . just stare back—like a star/ the sun/ your eyes—condemn me . . . every star, stare back judgment . . . It doesn't matter—I don't know if the world exists if you don't see it, just wake up . . . and see me, damn me, burn out the stars, awake . . .

Kayla could feel the painful, sparking current pass over her closed eyes again. This was the third night of this treatment, and she couldn't bear it any longer. She reached forward, angrily seeking to snuff out the bright, searing explosions that danced before her sight, her eyes fluttering open as her grip tightened around flesh, and she saw his face, choked with surprise. Any words of pain or rage that she had prepared dissolved in that moment, while neither one of them breathed.

His body quietly shuddered, caught in some halted movement. His brows gathered together in resolve before he barked, "Serafin! She's awake." He yanked his fingers from her grip as Asher staggered to her side, and she lost sight of Jeremy's retreat as the pirates crushed in, their declarations of relief and tribute cascading through the jammed doorway.

After that, Kayla was unable to drift with any measure of peace, and she was painfully aware of her surroundings. At first, she feigned a return to the state Jeremy interrupted. It was easier than answering Asher's questions or judging the distance between her and their new driver. She busied her mind with an internal inventory, as her eyes remained closed and her limbs drooped. Kayla's hands still hurt. The bruises that traveled from her palms to her chest were still present from her internal battle with Jeremy en route to Azevin, but beneath the scattered bandages that followed the same path, she could feel thin, burned flesh. Somehow, the joint effort to heal Asher's punctured hand caused these injuries. Kayla swallowed down the guilty shiver of pleasure that came from the memory of that foreign jolt of power bubbling through her arms. Forget that. Both times they joined together this way, whether their wills were clashing or in agreement, it caused her harm. She focused on a more innocent satisfaction that proved the worth of these wounds: Asher's left hand was whole again. In those moments when she first woke, her eyes frantically searching for the white shapes that formed Jeremy's back as the fetters merged with the surrounding darkness, it was Asher's callused palm that was cupped to her forehead, the smooth, new skin in the center providing the gentle force that pressed her to his shoulder. She could feel his lips against her hair, his murmurs quelling the cracking lightning that still drummed faintly through her veins.

That memory allowed Kayla to relax again now. She couldn't remember his words, and she doubted she even understood them at the time, but that didn't matter. She continued to let her awareness wander over her body. Her legs were sliced by Bruno's weapon, and she was spattered with various superficial injuries from her fight with Evangeline. But her attention kept returning to her back. Those weren't wounds beneath the bandages . . . but scars. It had only been a few days since she felt the symbols form and ignite, and although she didn't think they could harm her then, these burns should still be raw. Instead, she felt smooth, raised lines forming sigils, some of which were marred by jagged, slashing marks. She could see in her mind the design of their formation, identical to the fetters that crawled over Jeremy's skin. She thought the last of his fire went into the joint effort to heal Asher, but now she understood that some of his ability was reserved to soothe her blisters. Tiny streams of water filled the space between her closed lashes. Did he know what he'd done?

Kayla couldn't guess what the others expected or what they planned, but to her surprise, no one troubled her for the next week. Asher was slowly healing, laid out on the back seat by day and hovering outside the camp at night. She often felt his eyes on her, but he rarely spoke with anyone but Kittie. The pirates were terrified of the man who steered the vehicle, and they kept sullenly to themselves. They watched over Asher nervously, and although they seemed to have forgiven her for her otherworldliness in Azevin, there was a new sense of caution that subdued their usual warmth.

From what she could see, Kittie was in top form. She tended to Asher, quieted the pirates' agitation, and kept Jeremy on course through questionable territory. She often rested silently against Kayla's side, and she even got Jeremy to smile a few times, although he was also yelling threats in her direction as he grinned. If Kittie ever felt awkward about the similar roles she played for the two rivals who now shared this confined space, she never displayed evidence of it. Jeremy, however, looked perpetually irritated. He drove silently for hours, his gaze trained on the horizon, and at night, she sensed his presence in dreams. She only further exhausted herself when she tried to understand his motivations or attempted to untangle Asher's reasons for keeping him around.

So when her dreams began to invade her waking hours, she thought perhaps it was a result of her evasion and self-imposed loneliness. It wasn't the first time she had vivid visions of her parents, and she couldn't deny that voices had crept into her brain before. She confirmed that she traded thoughts with Jeremy, even over far distances, and there were times that she couldn't tell if that reality was less terrifying than the possibility of insanity. Back in the potter's village, there was a range of normalcy that no longer applied. That was when Asher was just a boy in a picture, and everything else was safely vague and gray. Kayla reached for her heavy locket, buried below her neckline, and held it up tightly beneath her chin. Her desires were simple and that focus dissolved the contradictions floating about her head. She wanted to know. Maybe she hadn't changed as much as she thought.

It wasn't easy to witness, but she couldn't reject the vision of her mother's tears as Kiera held her wrist up to her wet face. Kiera's arm ached; she lost her Intercessor to Sebastian and it left her feeling restless and empty. Kayla began to wonder if this new, reoccurring nightmare was the reason they came to Azevin. Was this emotional image what she required to have certainty, to bring forth whatever it was within her that could stop Sebastian from hurting more people? Was this image of her mother, broken by Sebastian's hubris, her spiritual armor?

Not everything that was revealed was so simple. It wasn't always easy to discern what she should make of her visions, and not everything turned out to be a banner of truth she could wave into battle. Not everything was a dream. Her mother's voice called out to her, shrouded in the wind that shrieked through the spaces around the windows, as the car bore her closer to another Eclipse. *'See, the former things have taken place, and new things I declare; before they spring into being I announce them to you . . .'*

In this new vision, she saw Kiera sitting on the ground with her back to Michael's chest, her toes wiggling as the grass tickled her feet. Kayla recognized the young couple was in a Pre-Eclipsian world. Kiera was reading from a little book while her left hand twirled his necklace around her finger. She was earnestly making some point, her face blissful and her words matter-of-fact, but Michael's expression was distant and troubled. *'I have put my Spirit upon him; he will bring forth justice to the nations . . .'*

Her vision shifted again, and Kayla could see her young father, training at Sebastian's side, as she had. She watched his Intercessor clash against his teacher's, sparking curled tongues of flame and smoke. His weapon cut the air in undulating arcs, cracking like a whip, and firing off fragments at will. With a loud snap he could lengthen the shining white mass of bone and strike from afar with twirling sweeps of his staff. Kayla held her breath in wonder at his graceful movements—even the beads of his sweat projected into the air as if they were missiles launched with precision. But she was even more amazed by the many incarnations of his Intercessor. The few times her weapon took unusual forms were accidental, and the memory was easily buried beneath the pride she took in the limited mastery of her blade. Michael's easy transformations proved she was mistaken in holding on to the concept that their

Angelic gift was primarily a sword, no matter how precious. Her fingers twitched as she pressed against the invisible barrier that kept this vision at arm's length. She longed to experience again the familiar freedom she recognized in Michael as he mirrored his master's movements: the clean, empty rush of energy through the limbs, the warmth radiating from the belly, and the weightless power that bore the body forward and lifted the crushing weight of concern from the mind. The tension she almost always glimpsed gripping his features was now softened by some joyful satisfaction that brought fluid tranquility to his critical eyes.

"Of course it's you." She heard Kiera's voice again before the image of her father dissolved. "For one thing, you're born on the twenty-fifth day of the month. Two and five make seven. The seventh card in the Major Arcana is *The Chariot.* But you chose it anyways, so stop arguing!"

The hint of rapture that relaxed the severity of Michael's eyes was still present now as he lay on his stomach, his head resting along his outstretched arm. He was holding a card limply between his fingers, but his gaze was actively traveling over Kiera's hands, hair, and mouth as she knelt at the side of the bed. It must have been his room they were occupying: a bare space used only for sleeping, study, and training. Kiera stood out as an unlikely inhabitant of this austere world, but her striking presence was subdued by the faded t-shirt that cloaked her form, the sleeves ending around her elbows as it slid off her shoulder, the hem reaching to her knees.

"No, I picked it randomly," he said softly, only half paying attention to the meaning of her words. Michael's bare torso had already acquired some markings. She could see dark symbols scrawled across his upper back, over his shoulders and halfway down the sides of his arms.

"Nothing is without design, and you know that. When

you shuffle the cards, you're putting them in the right order for you. Your soul knows everything already . . . like how to use your Intercessor, or how to breathe in your belly and stand with your skeleton aligned, or how to solve your problems. Our analytical mind and our fears get in the way, but when you relax . . . See, *The Chariot.*" Kiera plucked the card from his lazy grasp, her fingers moving lovingly over its surface as if it was an extension of Michael.

He wanted to laugh derisively, but he liked her answer. It was more interesting now that it wasn't about fortune-telling. "Okay, so what does it mean?"

"It's a card about struggle. A warring or union of opposites. Under a strong will, steered by the certainty of righteousness, these opposing forces can be reined in and compelled to follow your direction. It's a card of victory, but it's hard-won. Travel, motivation, inspiration . . ."

"Don't start adding the nice stuff at the end," he groaned. "So it's saying I'm a conflicted mess?"

"Nope, we're just Nephilim in the end times," she sang happily. "This isn't unusual at all."

Michael's green eyes darkened, the lines around his brow returning. He grabbed her pale wrist and pulled her up onto the bed with him, his arms encircling her protectively while the cards fell to the floor. "I wish Sebastian wouldn't frame it that way to you."

"It'll be fine, Michael. 'Behold my servant, whom I uphold, my chosen, in whom my soul delights . . . he will faithfully bring forth justice. He will not grow faint or be discouraged till he has established justice in the earth . . .' We all want the same thing—Heaven on Earth. It doesn't matter if there's no God or if it's all just useless legend. Sebastian is *our* chosen. He saved us both from our own horrors."

"He's not a god." Michael's voice was hushed, toneless

like a repeated chant.

"He's something better—he's one of us! You don't have to feel guilty about needing him. We all need each other. It's okay to admire someone, to admit that they've saved you. It's not a weakness. Aren't we stronger and healthier than we've ever been? That's the proof . . ." Kiera nestled into his arms, her words dispersing into his chest in muffled vibrations. Her fingers were pressed to the mark of the long-armed black cross.

Kayla struggled to close her eyes, gripped with the inexplicable fear that her mother's hand would disappear into that dark void. She blinked hard, and when her vision cleared, she had taken Kiera's place and was faced with that dreaded mark. Her hands slipped against his flesh as she fought to be released from his tight embrace, seeking refuge from that gaping nothingness. Kayla raised her gaze, a cry rising to her throat, but when her eyes fixed unexpectedly on Jeremy's face her scream fell back into her bowels.

She was pulled from her tormented reverie by Asher's steady hand. The heel of his palm was held tight to the side of her jaw, his fingers crooked behind her neck. Her hands closed around his forearm, and though her body twisted in an attempt to sit up, she refused to let go of her anchor to this reality. Asher supported her back as she rose, and then he slid onto the seat beside her. Kayla's chin craned towards the moonlight streaming through the open doorway; she didn't remember night falling. As the haze that filled her insides began to clear, she noticed that Asher's eyes were red-rimmed and his features were askew with a fragile stranglehold on his emotions. She stared down at her hands, afraid to ask what happened.

"Kayla, we never talked about Azevin," he whispered.

Her muscles tensed. "I'm not going to apologize for disobeying you this time. You don't understand—I *knew* you were hurt. I could see you . . . both of you! And when that fire started, I felt like I could have leveled the whole city. That woman Evangeline tried to stop me, but this time I was different! I couldn't allow myself to lose. Asher, if you died there, I would never have left either—"

"Kayla, stop!" he barked, turning his head and squeezing her hand down against the cushion. There was silence while he took a few shuddering breaths, fighting for control. "You did nothing wrong. Just . . . don't talk like that. We all left that place changed, but I can see that you are still transforming. I won't ask you now; I trust that you will share your burden with me when you can put it into words. Until then, this is all I . . ." His voice broke as he let go of her clenched fist and, swallowing hard, he placed three gifts in her lap with an almost unwavering hand.

Bewildered, she dropped her gaze to consider the worn book, string of beads, and silk-bound bundle that rested on her thighs. She slowly looped her father's necklace around her wrist three times, the cross pendant swinging somberly as she pulled the cloth away from the rectangular object. Kayla wasn't surprised by what was beneath the veil, but she marveled at her efficient movements as she deftly shuffled the cards and cut the pack into three decks before searching each pile for a tingling heat to lick her palm. She snatched up the stack that radiated the most energy and laid those cards out in a crossed formation.

Kayla held up the first and last of the ten cards she organized, shaking her head, the sureness of her hands dissolving into trembling uncertainty. "I don't know what this means."

Asher's unyielding eyes seemed to diffuse, as if they barely could contain their form. "Self . . . and destiny."

Kayla considered the vastly disparate imagery that adorned the two cards. She didn't understand how the tranquil, jewel-like pools of *The Star* could ever transform into the two blazing, intersecting spears of *Dominion*.

38

A little shudder moved through the truck as it came to a halt, and Kayla was jolted awake. Her cards were spilled over the front seat and onto the floor, but her mother's Bible was still clenched tightly in her fingers as the two cards that were the most puzzling protruded from the densely packed pages. She had spent the night poring over the book, trying to find a connection between the lofty words printed on the thin sheets and the surreal pictures painted on the cards. Kayla easily found the instances where "star" was highlighted, just as Asher had mentioned before they even arrived in Azevin, and although that word often seemed to apply to Angels, she noticed no other concrete links between the book and the cards. Frustrated with that pursuit, she searched for the words she heard recited in her previous dream, and received some amount of peace in the discovery of *Isaiah 42*. She read over the sections that Kiera repeated, but found hope in some of the chapter's later verses: *I have called you in righteousness; I will take you by the hand and keep you; I will give you as a covenant for the people, a light for the nations, to open the eyes that are blind, to bring out the prisoners from the dungeon, from the prison those who sit in darkness.* It didn't matter if there was no Lord to carry it out.

Kayla's eyes burned from her repeated readings of *Isaiah*. Was there ever a world where anyone could hear God's voice? Or was it the same when He was in existence? Unable to truly hear and see, were mortals destined to be forever lost on this Earth, unaware of their origins and potential?

She looked up, blinking into the sunlight that streamed in from the other side of the windshield, her eyes quickly focusing on the dark form that stood out against the gleaming rays. Jeremy's face was too twisted into a scowl to be speaking as quietly as he was, and she strained to hear his words or read his lips. He didn't look at her, but it was as if he sensed her scrutiny before he turned his back, the bristling posture of his shoulders and arms still expressing his agitation. Kittie emerged from somewhere below the truck, dark smears running upward from her fingers. Some of the markings were transferred to her brow and cheeks by the clumsy, child-like gestures that accented the usually dexterous motions of her fingers. The little girl frowned, looking hopefully up at Asher who lifted the hood of the truck, and Kayla lost sight of them as Kittie's voice was muffled by the metal barrier.

Kayla stretched her stiff legs onto the seat beside her and slowly bent to collect the spilled deck. She was easily able to place the ten cards she drew last night into their proper order and she slid the little stack between the pages of the book. The rest of the cards she gathered back into the silk fabric, as she silently prepared for her journey to continue in less comfort. The road before her seemed like the line formed by those three cards in her reading's formation: the Suit of Swords that crossed an ominous streak through the image of *The Star*.

She closed her eyes, and the shining blues and purples of that tiny painting still glowed in her mind. Kayla remembered the words she spoke last night to Asher. "So I'm *The Star*. Maybe I understand that now, but what about these Swords that are running me through? You knew my mother. Did she ever read cards for you?"

Asher had closed his hand over hers and pulled it back to rest against his leg, keeping her palm hidden within his own. She felt as if something about her fingers moving over the cards disturbed him. He was silent for a few moments, his jaw tightening as he struggled to swallow. "She did . . . many times. It could be maddening. If you didn't hear what you wanted, you started to suspect her of just using the cards to promote her own agenda. But she was just honest, even in the worst times. I remember the placements, but not the meanings of the cards. There are some I can't forget, though. *The Star* is known as 'the Daughter of the Firmament and the Dweller Between the Waters'—a perfect card for a Nephil, *her* card . . . It's everything I've seen in you both: hope, inspiration, promise. It represents protection, healing old wounds . . . everything opening to a new horizon, a broader experience. Your star was darkened, but now the light is breaking through."

She was staring at the *Three of Swords* that lay across that center card, each blade pictured piercing a heart. "What about this one?"

When she moved on to the next card he let go of her hand, shaking off the spell that had gripped him. His voice came louder, roughly clipping off the ends of his sentences. "The second card represents an obstacle. I can't remember the full meaning of this one, but the symbols are quite clear." He pointed to the tenth card in the formation—the *Two of Wands*, the image of *Dominion*. "I told you that this is a card of destiny, but only if you follow the advice of the spread. It's not a future you're sentenced to; you construct what happens next. This card above *The Star* is known as *Judgment,* and its placement represents an outcome as well, but perhaps the one you most expect, fear, or hope for. The *Seven of Swords* is in the spot of an immediate future, provided your actions continue on their current path."

The door creaked open slowly, the sudden intrusion shattering Kayla's reflective visions. Her memory of Asher's features, skewed with emotion, was now replaced by the present sight of his impassive countenance, affected by only a momentary twinge of tightened muscles. He noticed her neatly arranged possessions, and his voice fell softly, unquestioningly. "You're ready to go."

She nodded, regaining her composure. "What happened to the truck?"

"The Core is shot. It's unexpected, but we should have enough time to make it there on foot if we can't find a new mode of transport." His eyes were on her left hand as it squeezed the Bible, the beads and cross hanging from her wrist faintly trembling. "You can take a minute, if you need it."

Kayla watched the angle of his shoulders slant, the only evidence of the painful shift of his weight from one wounded foot to another. "Asher, you shouldn't—" she stopped herself, and then began again, driving the worry from her voice. "No, you're right, but . . . please sit with me."

He exhaled heavily into a defeated smile, sliding down into the seat beside her. "Do you see more than others, Kayla? Or are you the only one that responds to it?"

Her eyelids fluttered as she looked swiftly downward. "I don't know what everyone else sees." Kayla's hands fumbled with the pages of the book as she took out the cards, arranging the first six into an equal-armed cross, beside a vertical arrangement of the last four. "I . . . I understand some more of the cards today, Asher."

He bowed his head, moving in closer to inspect the little pictures. "Dreams?"

"I don't know. Some things are like this Bible. *Judgment.* The last book here says there will be Angels blowing horns at the end of the world. And see the picture?" She stared at the naked bodies rising up from their coffins, their arms waving joyfully to the emotionless creature hovering above them. "I know there will be a change, a rebirth, but there are crucial decisions that will have to be made. Am I the Angel that heralds the end, or am I the human woman, embracing the new beginning? If there is a choice, is it mine to make?"

Before Asher could answer, Kayla was clutching the *Seven of Swords.* "And this one! I don't know how I know— how these cards know—that I can't trust myself. I'm going to do it again, Asher."

He looked at her carefully, holding out his palm. When she handed over the card, he calmly regarded the image of a thief running off with a stash of swords, a few of the blades falling to the ground, as his burden was too heavy to carry. "Will I be able to stop you?" he asked quietly, placing the card back in the sixth position.

Kayla didn't seem to hear him. "It's all impulse, thought-lessness, dishonor . . . it's everything—" She turned her head towards his shoulder, her hair shielding her eyes from anything she would see on the other side of the driver's window. "Why is he here?" she whispered.

The hissing intake of Asher's breath remained still in his throat as he struggled for a reply.

Her face reddened, her voice rising only slightly in volume, but steeped in sudden bitterness. "Where is he in all of this? Doesn't he deserve a card? If I'm *The Star,* who could he be? The upside-down card there? Or the shining Knight in ninth place? No, he must be my obstacle, my *Three of Swords—Sorrow.* Strife, conflict, upheaval . . . sound familiar? Is this what the cards are saying? Unless I remove my stumbling block, I'll end up in the sixth position? Then *why is he here,* Asher?"

"He is not a danger to you!" he cried.

She choked on any other angry words she had prepared as they stared soundlessly at one another. Kayla was the first to drop her gaze. "You never trusted me with him before. You were right, you know."

"If his presence here sends you running off into the night, then what hope do we have of stopping this Eclipse from forever darkening the world?"

"It's not that! I . . ." She clenched her fists. "I won't insult your integrity with my promises. But I want to choose you."

"Without an alternative, there isn't a choice."

By the time she raised her wet eyes, the door was clicking shut and she could see the line of his shoulders as he walked out into the light, perfectly horizontal and without pain.

Kayla watched with perverse fascination as the pirates tore the truck apart. Without a Core, Kittie explained, the vehicle was useless.

"A lot of people don't really know what it used to be like, so don't feel bad," the little girl went on. "They know what a Core is, but not what it's made up of and how it works. Most of them just know that Za'in controls the only practical power source left. Some don't even understand that! Well, the world wasn't any great shakes before the Eclipse. Most of the Earth's resources were squandered, and people were malnourished too, in spirit and mind. People were desperate. 'Like so many maggots spilling out of a carcass they've already consumed . . .' "

Kayla wrenched her eyes from the truck's dismantling and fixed her troubled stare on Kittie.

The girl gazed back, her brown eyes grim and her mouth small, the corners down-turned. "Those aren't my words, but you've figured that out already. I hate to admit it, but he wasn't all wrong. If he was, it would have been easy to rail against him, but so many of us were pulled in."

"But you . . . you never bought into it, did you, Kittie?" The inexplicable anger that welled up in her gave sound to her fearful whisper.

"When he brought down that profound destruction on the day of the Eclipse, it was easy to seize control. And there were less rats in the cage—"

"You never believed in him. Then why were you in his Spheres? Don't give me your old excuses of loneliness and loyalty; I've had enough of that. What . . . are you?"

A dark form blocked her sight, and when she backed away, she could see Jeremy pulling Kittie to the side by the back of her shirt.

He looked down at Kayla coldly. "Still haven't figured out the big, wide world yet? What do you want to know? Ask me. Leave her alone."

"Jeremy, stop!" Kittie squealed, struggling against his grip. "She just wanted to know about Cores and power sources—"

"Shut up. I know what she asked you." He regarded Kayla with disdain. "You want to know where we came from? The asshole of this world. We crawled out, and we finally got somewhere until you—"

"Saros!"

The wrathful flare of Jeremy's eyes fixed at a point

behind Kayla's head, as Kittie was released from his grasp by a sudden twitch of his fingers. His former Ophan let out a tiny cry, then grasped him tightly below his waist, burying her face into an unfettered part of his back.

Asher met Jeremy's glare with a stern countenance. "Kayla was spared the pain that all of us experienced in our own way after the Eclipse. Please be understanding if she accidentally opens any old wounds."

There was a long stretch of silence before Jeremy bowed his head, gently tearing free from Kittie's embrace, and strode out into the cluster of broken stones in the distance. Finally released from his violence, Kayla found she could move again and whirled around to face Asher, but he was walking away as well, preparing for the rest of their journey. Breathlessly, she turned back to Kittie who was trying to pull up the corners of her mouth.

"He wasn't gonna harm anyone," the little girl whispered.

Kayla experienced only a slight ache in her chest, free from the clutches of the expected sadness and terror. "You're something special then?"

"That suspicion has caused some suffering. He doesn't like reminders."

"You'll tell me some time . . . if it doesn't hurt too much?"

Kittie's forced smile was slowly becoming genuine, her nod almost imperceptible, as she pulled Kayla forward by the hand, following the steps of the pirates as they began walking through the stones and weeds. The boys' pockets were stuffed with various pieces of junk, while sections of the truck were strapped to their backs. Bruno led the way, stumbling every time his eyes lingered too long on the maps that he continually shuffled through. Fec trailed behind him, snatching the curled scraps of paper that fluttered through the Captain's fingers at every grip-loosening distraction. Vic helped support Asher's steps as he plodded forward on wounded feet, and Kerif was saddled with the heaviest load from the remains of the truck. As they passed the rock formation that Jeremy was perched on, he jumped down to join their ranks, muttering something about a 'slower road to their deaths.'

Kayla tried to catch all of Kittie's words, but she was distracted by the sound of Jeremy's heavy boots behind them and the sight of Asher's painful steps leading her forward.

Kittie continued as if there was never a break in her explanation. "So every resource on Earth was slowly tapping out. Oil, coal, wood, water . . . There was still plenty of fear, though, and that's what moved the world. But Za'in wasn't a known force yet—just a quiet presence through the centuries, slowly growing in knowledge, bitterness, and delusions of grandeur. It didn't interest him to stand above a world crawling with humans. So he waited in obscurity, gathering what was valuable, and honing his methods. Everything went as planned during the first Eclipse. Like I told you before, bringing down the void that was once Heaven worked exactly as he hoped—the 'wrath of God,' remember? Millions of filthy humans died in an instant. World geography shifted and skewed. And that's when he rose up. He had real power, after all, since he was the only one that could provide a Core. That little dark lump is an energy source more efficient than any before it, even if it's a bit unpredictable. Za'in was the only one that could light up the world again. But what is it? You've taken a peek. What does it look like?"

Kayla bit her lip, her features gathered together painfully.

Her moment of discomfort was underscored, but allayed, by Jeremy's irritated groan erupting behind them. "Kit, we got the point! Get on with it."

Kittie rolled her eyes. "Okay, fine, a Core looks a little like Jeremy's Ruiners. That's no coincidence. Cores are synthetic Angel bones. Like I said before, most people have no idea what's going on. The words in that book you now carry used to build civilizations, but even in the years before the Eclipse, it was reduced to an esoteric mythology that few scholars studied and that attracted even fewer devotees. No one believed in Angels. But, with a Core in hand, everyone believed in Za'in. If your little tribe could curry favor, then maybe you'd get one. There were rebels, there were pirates, but Steelryn and Serafin—now that was the name for resistance! But that too fell into obscurity, and many doubt if two such men ever existed. Only the dark, looming idea of Lord Za'in remains, imprinted in everyone's minds by that simple black mass. Most everyone is still now . . . it's been eighteen years after all, and humans know how to get comfortable. But in five days everything will change again. In *Genesis,* Angels fell to Earth and the Nephilim were born. So God sent a Flood to kill us all. If, in five days, a new race constructed by a new God enters this Earth . . ."

Kayla waited for Kittie's silence to dissolve into words again, but soon she realized this quiet was more than a momentary pause. "What will happen?" she whispered, cringing at the sound her own voice.

"Has that book anything to say about it?"

Her face hurt and her lips were numb, but they moved anyway. " 'Behold, I will create new heavens and a new earth. The former things will not be remembered, nor will they come to mind—' " Kayla clapped her hands over her mouth.

Kittie's eyes were serene and her nose barely wrinkled. "That's one way to look at it."

Jeremy let out another grunt of disgust before he took longer, faster strides, as if he was determined to move quickly out of earshot of Kittie's history lesson. As he passed them by he grumbled, his mouth forming a mangled grin. "This is the Word of the Lord. Thanks be to God."

39

Kayla's hands felt weightless as they moved over the cards, following the rhythm of a comforting and now-familiar feminine voice.

One, two, three . . . The Star, The Three of Swords, Judgment—you understand. The fourth card is to the right, and it represents your past. The Four of Swords, reversed. What do you see?

She lifted the card and studied it, as her mother requested. Kayla was surprised at how quickly these supernatural encounters had become ordinary and gave her the intimacy of the domestic life that she longed for. Dreams became visions and signs, and soon she found she could penetrate the barrier of past remembrances and communicate with her mother fully, through their Angelic bond.

The card she held depicted the image of a man, lying down, with a sword at his side. Three swords hung above him, and as she turned the card upside-down to view it as it should be arranged in this reading, she wondered if the man was dead or sleeping. The colors were neutral, their pastel tints cold. "This feels like the worst kind of isolation . . ."

It was all he could do, at the end, to see to it that you were safe. This is a card of seclusion, banishment . . . That's not what we wanted, but it was better that you were out of Za'in's sights, in a place where your Angelic powers would be stifled, where no one would be able to sense them—not even you.

"I don't understand. How could the village hide what I was?"

That human settlement in the swamp was once a prison for the Fallen. Before they were judged and extinguished, this is where Azazel and his followers were imprisoned. Spiritual energy will forever be absorbed and neutralized in that place. I doubt you could return there if you tried, and if you did, you would no longer recognize yourself as you are now. Michael discovered the way in for you, but none could follow. I know you suffered much loneliness.

"It wasn't bad, it just wasn't . . . anything. But before that, I was with you, and for a time, with Sebastian, right? I don't remember it. I know he hurt you . . ."

He did nothing to you, Kayla, except use you as a shield. He didn't tamper with your blood or bones because he didn't want to spoil the maturity of your gifts. He's patient.

Her throat constricted painfully as she carefully replaced the card, picking up the next one, *The Moon,* from its place below the first three cards.

This one expresses all your recent circumstances. Can you tell what it means?

She held the card close to her face, examining the impassive gaze that stared out from the ivory circle. The moon hung above a mountain inhabited by animals, their contorted forms straining to the light. "The Moon, night, dreams and nightmares . . . they're all visions. That makes sense. I've seen and heard things that have helped me understand, but some of what I've felt I wish I could ignore."

Yes, that's right. But there's more to it. The Moon is also telling you that although the night may bring spiritual trials and the shadows may hide your enemies, this is a time of creative discovery and you should trust your new insights.

"Hidden enemies," she sighed. "Every step forward brings Sebastian closer—I can feel that. Are there enemies near, staying unseen, or is there one right beside us, in plain sight . . . ?"

You mean Jeremy.

Kayla dropped the card, clenching her fist. "I don't understand why Asher trusts him now! So he saved him from Tregenne. But how do we know that wasn't just a plan to infiltrate our group?"

In Azevin, he aided you as well.

"I didn't ask for his help, Mother!"

Twice. Without him, would you be still in Fiora's grasp? Would Asher have survived?

Kayla frowned. "Would I have these scars?"

Or would those marks still be raw burns?

"Without his 'help,' that fire might not ever have erupt-ed!"

The abilities of a Saros child are unpredictable. I can barely believe he survived; so many of them were slaughtered. But I'm frightened by those bones he wears on his arms. It's bad enough that Sebastian and Gabriel even built those Ruiners, but to use them on one of his kind? The far-reaching effects can't be foreseen!

"Kittie has called them Ruiners too . . ."

She understands things I was around to witness. But you're not wrong to also refer to them as 'fetters'—chains that allow movement, but not flight. He's a prisoner, a puppet. Still, it's foolish to shackle Saros children this way. He's bound, but it's made him stronger. You saw his fiery wings. Did he draw them out from you, or did you lend him power? Is he still human? I don't know what he will become or what it will mean. I don't know what he will do or what it will do to him and the world.

Kayla picked up The Seven of Swords. "If he could bring disaster, willingly or not, he shouldn't be here."

Kiera was silent for a moment. *Sometimes things that should not be, are. But that card, that future, must be avoided. I don't believe Jeremy means you any harm, but that doesn't mean you're safe. The sixth card is a warning. Don't get caught up in any secret plans. And, Kayla . . . don't forget that you love him.*

Her cheeks stung. "Love? No, now we're just bound together by these aptly-named Ruiners. I loved him, I trusted that, and now these intense emotions that some-times move me are just a perversion of my Angelic fire, used as a weapon against me. Why shouldn't I try to forget?"

I'm reminding you of this because your choices will affect your outcome. These feelings, whatever their source, are still there. Reacting against them can be just as destructive as giving in to them. Be aware of your emotions. It will hurt more than denying them, but they will give you the clues you need to avoid danger, whether it comes from without or within.

Kayla's vision began to blur, so she tried to let her tears fall. Her mother's voice was fading, and she realized that her eyes were dry. Some raucous sounds began to pierce the veil of her reverie.

"You can't even get lemon ice in Cormina anymore!"

"C'mon, Kerif, las' summer we—"

"Fec, that was more than five years ago," Vic mumbled.

Kayla blindly groped around for her cards, but as her sight returned, she realized the silk-bound bundle was still in her pocket and she was sitting on the ground, leaning against an incomplete concrete barrier that stood beside the ruined road. She bit her lip, troubled. How long was she out? It was only her second experience of this kind of direct dialogue, and she was so sure at the time that it wasn't a dream. Kayla reached over and tugged on the fabric of

Asher's pants, and he glanced towards her, offering a weary smile. She searched his face for signs of concern, but it seemed that neither one of them noticed changes in the other. Sweat beaded on his forehead, and his breathing was labored; they must have only been sitting here for a brief time to take a break from walking. Kayla tried to smooth the anxious pull of her brow, covering up her worry with a tired grin that echoed his. The loss of time was unsettling, but she didn't want to disturb Asher now.

She took a deep breath before she looked around her, a little shaken by the realization that this reality seemed less familiar than the internal landscape she existed in moments earlier. Kittie and the pirates were gathering around them in a semi-circle, while Jeremy hung back a little further, his stare flickering tensely over Asher's form before he turned half his back to them, his eyes scanning the horizon. The conversation of her companions seemed muffled and distant, and Kayla struggled to catch the plan they were discussing.

"Ponchos? We got those, uh, somewhere . . ." Fec was digging around in his trench coat while Kerif dropped onto his back, but the heavy load he carried kept him suspended above the ground, the backs of his hands hovering over the earth.

"Baaaad iiideeaa, guyyyys," he groaned, flicking a heavy lock of hair out of his face.

Kittie sighed. "Asher and I just have to see how much has changed there before we bring Kayla through. I know neither of us are in top form right now, but we'll take Vic along."

"Cormina blows. Isn't there another way to Velsmere?" Kerif's eyes were rolling back in irritation and exhaustion.

Bruno looked up from his maps. "Yeah, but we'd never get there in time if we don't use the ferry."

Kayla's awareness of her environment was rapidly becoming acute. She turned her back on her companions, focusing her attention on the clearly fatigued Asher. If she checked his bandages and collected his hair back neatly into a long tail, then she wouldn't have to acknowledge the tense watchfulness that kept Jeremy's eyes drifting back more frequently to their wounded leader. What right did he have to wear her concern for Asher's condition in his own expression?

"W-wait! Yer leavin' th' three o' us an' Kayla wi'h *him?*" Fec stumbled away from Jeremy, his wide eyes bouncing erratically between Kittie and Asher, his skewed features pleading for their attention.

Kayla watched Asher's head raise suddenly, his gaze cutting upward until it found its mark, somewhere behind her, his irises vibrating with the effort to keep his target still. She followed the sinking of her stomach with a dropping of her eyes before gathering the will to quietly watch Kittie.

The little girl didn't disappoint. "Well that does pose a problem, doesn't it? How will we know if and when the rest of the group should follow without needless running back and forth? Maybe if Jeremy goes with Asher instead, he might be able to get the information back to me." She looked hopefully in the same direction that Asher was still fixed on.

There was a small stretch of silence before the voice behind Kayla spoke. "I don't know if any of that works like it used to." His dispassionate murmur was pushed out with halting effort.

"Will you let me try?" Kittie whispered.

His dry, bitter laugh was almost lost in the shuffling of his boots along the rocky ground as he moved towards her. Kayla turned her head as he passed by, tilting it downward so that she could watch them from beneath her hair.

Jeremy stood over Kittie for a moment, grinning disdainfully. "Things haven't been going so well, have they? Were you disappointed when you were powerless to see into me?"

Her sharp, tiny chin pointed back at him. "It was no victory for me that I had to wonder if you were dead, only to realize that you were beyond my reach because you gave yourself over to Za'in."

"What else was I supposed to—" he abruptly cut off the rising snarl of his reply as he grasped her shirt above her shoulder and roughly pulled her towards him. Without moving her head any more than she had to, Kayla strained to see Jeremy's mouth as he dropped to his knee and hissed out his words against Kittie's cheek. "It's not as simple as just 'giving over.' If it was, then we wouldn't have to worry about—"

"We don't have to be worried," Kittie snapped, "but if you've suddenly found the ability to suffer that emotion, then be still and let's see if you can let me in." The severity in her voice melted into a gentle sigh as she let her head drop against his. Her almost inaudible words came out in breathy, childlike gasps. "How can you think this is about control? Don't you remember when we started?"

Jeremy seemed to be lulled into stillness by her warmth and he drowsily closed his eyes. There were a few moments of peace before he shuddered and pulled his head away from hers, the grip on her blouse still tight. "I wish I could forget . . . that we threw off those shackles for new ones . . . that we thought we could escape what we were by acting like it was something to be proud of. It's always been a fight for control, one way or another. Let's just get this over with." Jeremy's voice was detached, his inflection nearly paralyzed with resentment, but as he released Kittie and raised his face to watch her back away, Kayla thought she noticed some silent plea in his eyes.

Kittie's features hardened with resolve as she passed her hand over her eyes and then dropped down on one knee, head bowed, steadying her frame by pressing her palm to the earth. She was completely motionless, her small form showing no evidence that she even breathed. Kayla's body froze as well, a throbbing silence clogging her ears. She wasn't sure if Asher and the pirates were also quietly watching this scene or if she was alone in the universe, peering into someone else's dormant reality. Nothing stirred, and after a while her eyes unlocked from their fixed place and moved to Jeremy's crouched figure. A morbid curiosity quickly became a guilty indulgence as she examined the contrast of his pale flesh against the black bones that consumed him. The jagged surface that covered his limbs and threatened to swallow his torso only served to underscore the memory of his skin on hers, the pressure of his hands and arms, the weight of his chest. As vivid as those sensations still were, they belonged to an unreachable past. Those fetters meant that whatever he embraced would now be crushed and torn, and any shred of Angelic energy he grasped would be devoured and perverted. Kayla forced her gaze higher, braving his downcast eyes, but the focus of her vision became lodged in the tension that gathered around the side of his face, curving from his brow down into his jaw. She stayed safely caught in that crescent of pressure, her muscles contracting, mirroring his, the strain squeezing out her troubled thoughts.

Her tenuous peace was shattered as his head raised suddenly, his piercing stare grasping something behind her shoulder. She knew that this time he wasn't looking towards one of their companions or a danger in the distance. His eyes drew from her the sickening revelation that she should have long ago sensed something hovering above the surface of her skin, some invisible force that was too close to perceive as separate from herself. She was aware of Kittie's attention pulled to the same spot. Kayla felt cold, an inexplicable terror barring her from any movement, especially one that would allow her to turn her head to the right. In an attempt to reach for something that could bring the familiar world rushing back in, the fingers of her left hand twitched—the only outward sign of her struggle to clutch Asher's arm.

Kayla could feel heaviness scrape along her back and cup her shoulder, and her body was rattled as her side collided against something solid. Air flooded her lungs, and more distinct sounds began to reach her clogged ears. She shook her head, blinking, and looked up into Asher's clear eyes. He held her closer, both of his arms encircling her.

"What did you see?" he whispered.

"I . . . I didn't—"

Kayla could feel the small vibration that came from Jeremy's hand dropping lightly on Asher's shoulder. "Serafin, there was nothing for her to see. Point is, it worked. Let's go to Cormina before it gets dark, and I'll let Kit know if it's safe to bring Kayla through." The gentleness in his voice drew uneasy shivers from between her shoulder blades, the tiny tremors making it more difficult to breathe the knot out of her stomach.

Asher didn't glance up at him, but kept his eyes trained on Kayla. "Kittie, is this your counsel?"

The girl's round eyes were vague and dark, and although her words came slowly, they were firmly stated. "Things have changed. Za'in won't snatch her up while you're gone, because he's just going to let us come. And the rest of us can handle anything short of a pair of Archs."

Kittie's words didn't have their usual comforting effect on Asher, and Kayla could feel his grip on her tighten as his brow was pulled with tense lines. "Saros, if anything happens here, you'll know?"

There was an unexpected, clumsy hesitation in Jeremy's voice. "Yeah, I think so. But if she tries . . . if she calls, I won't be able to ignore it."

Kayla wrenched around in Asher's arms, but Jeremy's back was already turned. The resistance she fought against was gently released, but not before her protector spoke. "This isn't the split I wanted, but it will have to do. I didn't want to leave you without a strong defense in my absence, but I have to remind myself that the only one stronger than him is you. Eventually, you will have to give rise to everything that you are, but I'm still hoping it won't have to come so soon. Call to him if you need to."

She nodded, fighting to pull her eyes away from Jeremy's bristling shoulders as he wound fabric around his arms, preparing to further conceal his body with the extra poncho and other articles the pirates gathered. Kayla lurched upward, stumbling as she stood, and landed on her feet, close to his side. She could feel his body clench up, ready for violence or flight, and she let out her breath, ready for either. No explosive action erupted. Instead, that potential energy was tightly contained in his eyes, trapped beneath a heavy-lidded downward gaze.

"Don't act so surprised," he whispered. "We've heard each other over distances before. This connection is my fucking torment, but by all means, let's see it through to the end. Why stop now?" Another tiny convulsion moved him before he spoke again, this time more gently. "Okay, he's right. You need to let me know if something happens here, and I'll come for you. But don't listen for a reply. Only believe it's me when you see me. I know you've heard me in the past, but don't trust it anymore. Don't trust any voices, got it?"

Kayla was stunned, not only by his words, but by his

change in manner. Frustration rendered her silent, unable to form a reply, and she was caught somewhere in the process of unraveling his statements and guessing his motivations. She saw no reason to dismiss the purity of her own visions and put her faith in him, but she couldn't ignore the fear that still lingered from his recognition of that unknown presence beside her, within her . . .

There was no need for that conflict to find its way outward now. Jeremy was already a few yards in the distance, supporting Asher's wounded frame through the broken landscape.

40

Asher found a spot near an upper window where the rain didn't fall. There he waited to see Kayla descend from the craggy hills, imagining the damp odor of mildew and rot that seeped into his nostrils transforming into the earthy fragrance of wine that must have once filled this place. Cormina was in worse shape than he'd expected. The town was heaped upon itself, down in a valley that was created during the Eclipse's shifts. Villas were still standing with their lacework of windows, rows of swelling columns, and scalloped, ceramic roofs, but many were incomplete, leaving a jarring contrast of densely stacked elements that ended in sudden emptiness, and staircases that led nowhere. The simple elegance of a town that once thought it could adapt gracefully to a cataclysm had given in to stark decay.

Jeremy joined him in the main vat room and climbed onto the catwalk, the only remaining portion of the second level. He didn't come near the window, obtaining his reading of the outside world by occasional glances at Asher's eyes. "She's close. Unhurt."

"You can sense that now?" the older man murmured.

"Vaguely. Kit got the picture, and I know it put her on the move. It's Kit that can see me; I don't get much back. But I'm not feeling anything now, from either of them. That means it's okay." Jeremy restlessly tugged on the bandages that covered his fetters.

Asher pulled his gaze from the window to regard the former Arch. This wasn't easy for either of them. Jeremy had helped him make his way over the rocks, down into the valley and through what was left of Cormina's streets. Asher had dealt with his enemy saving him in Azevin, but now he had to accept that his body was still too weak and wracked with pain to walk more than a few steps unaided. His hand and feet never had the luxury of time to heal, and that meant he had to lean against his rival, who effortlessly took on the burden of his weight. Asher couldn't gauge the limits of Jeremy's supernatural strength, nor could he tell if Saros allowed his feet to only barely touch the ground in order to keep him comfortable or to make it clear who was in control. Whether compassion was the motivation, or the will to dominate and humiliate, Asher accepted it as a necessary indignity.

But there was something else. As he was dragged along, there would be moments when frightening visions shook his senses. He didn't expect another dose of what happened in Azevin. Although they were both covered up for the purpose of not being recognized in a town so close to Velsmere, he also noticed Saros took extra care to prevent their skin from touching. Still, there were times when lost footing or other sudden movements allowed enough contact for Asher to experience strange sensations—a choking net of black roots pressed close to his face, as he was blinded by dark sludge invading his nose and mouth. He held his body stiff against the illusion, knowing it would pass, and as the tangle of gnarled tendrils and oozing filth began to clear, he could see glimpses of Kittie's eyes and sturdy fingers, her lips moving quickly to form silent, urgent words. Asher was certain that none of his own thoughts and feelings were being pulled from him as Saros was trying desperately to hold in his own sensations, but seeing his rival exposed was just as unsettling as dealing with his own soul laid bare.

It still left unanswered the question of why Jeremy's internal struggles were seeping so easily out of him and into Asher's consciousness. The unknown range of the former Arch's physical powers now seemed like a trivial concern in the face of this. What influence could he have over a mind he connected with?

Asher was troubled by the remembered image of Kittie fighting to make her way through the aggressively churning mire. He had the impression there was something more frightening to witness once it was all cleared away. "Saros. What you saw, back on the road with Kittie . . . Is Kayla—"

"I didn't do anything to her," Jeremy blurted out, defensively. "I don't know why she froze up like that; she was blind to everything . . ."

Asher eyed him coldly before forcing his gaze back to the window, his expression flat. "What happened?" Even though he turned his face away in order to make Jeremy feel more comfortable with making his confession, Asher sensed his companion's muscles tightening in frustration. "Is it Za'in?" he asked quietly.

Jeremy's elbows were planted on his thighs, and his body sagged, his head dropping heavily. "It's my fault. You should have killed me when you had the chance."

"But I didn't. It was for her that I showed mercy. You can't change what you've done, but, for her sake, tell me what you saw."

There was a long stretch of silence before Asher could hear the muffled sound of Jeremy's struggle to swallow. When he finally spoke, his voice was raw, cracking under the weight of his emotions, welling up to form soundless words, and falling back into explanations toneless with apathy. "Kit can see stuff, you know that. She's always been able to see me. I couldn't feel everything like I do now, because of these things," he paused to glance at his arms, "but I always knew she was around, somehow. But after the tower came down, I knew that was over. She was gone. But, fuck it, you know, you all left me to die, but instead I was saved again by being born at a really shitty time in history. It still meant something to Za'in, so I did what he wanted. I didn't think about it, I didn't know what it meant . . . I just wanted Kayla to feel like I did. But instead, I really learned what being cursed was. He was in me. It was strange; I was closer to her than ever, and I wanted it, I wanted her, but he was in the middle. Twisting everything around. I was out of everyone's reach, but he had me.

"Then in Azevin, it hit me. I wasn't an Arch, I wasn't anything, I was grasping at shit . . . and when I saw you brought her into Tregenne's sights, unprotected . . . Serafin, you may have shown me mercy in the past, but that night, your only saving grace was what I didn't mean to see in you. And I can't explain that. I can't explain what came after. But when I ignited, when it all burned down . . . he's been quiet since. It should bring me peace, but you saw her wings, like mine. Who started it? I'm beginning to wonder if it was even one of us.

"But, like I said, silence. So Kit tried, to see if everything could be like it was. For the first time, it wasn't just some vague sense of not being alone—I could feel her reaching into me. But there was something in the way. Black matted . . . wires, or something. Mud. It was smoldering, rancid, suffocating. There was no way she'd make it through that. I don't remember hearing any sound, but there was something piercing, deafening in that silence. My ears stung. I'll admit it, I was scared. But I tried. I wanted her to break through. When I saw her fingers, I felt wind move through the stale air. When I saw her eyes, I felt fluid draining from my ears, from wounds I didn't notice before. She smiled, told me that I wasn't . . . alone . . . and that Kayla needed me now. And then I could feel her nearby, watching me, and I had to turn, to see her, and now that I felt my burden lifted I wanted to tell her that things were different, and I couldn't feel these chains on my arms anymore, and maybe it would be safe to . . .

"But then I opened my eyes and I saw her, and I had some new kind of vision. Maybe it's how Kit sees the world, I don't know, and it only lasted for a few breaths, but Kayla—fucking beautiful—around her, there was a dark cloud, and right above her shoulder it was gathered the tightest. Tendrils of smoke stroking her cheeks, grabbing at her arms, and she had no idea. It's him. That's why he's been quiet. Azevin was a trap. Tregenne was ready for you—that was to be expected. But to guess what I'd do? I can't even do that. So much for free will, right?" He laughed bitterly. "So now you know. It's up to you. I don't know what to do about any of this. All I know is that I have nothing left but to see this through with her, and since I can't be an invisible sentinel, I gotta be one that is barely tolerated. Hated, if possible. You have to be the one to save her."

Asher turned to meet his red-rimmed stare as Jeremy raised his head. "I'm only a man. What can I do without your kind of eyes?"

A broken smile rose and then collapsed under its own weight. "You can talk to her."

Asher nodded, turning again to the window, knowing a sympathetic expression would only contribute to the mangled pile of suffering that built up in Saros. "You believe that I should question her, I should listen, but not warn her."

"I probably gave up too much by telling her to ignore voices in her head, but I don't think he should know we're onto him. And it wouldn't help her to know he's there. It's impossible to stop your thoughts from reaching him, and the fear . . . The fear would get to anyone." Jeremy let out a heavy breath, sniffling and coughing a little as he rubbed his face. Out of the corner of his eye, Asher could see his body straighten, his shoulders returning to their insolent posture—the final detail of collecting himself.

"I understand. I'll tell you what I hear if you tell me what you see. We'll have to trust her to fight for herself. That's what it will come to in the end, when the sky darkens."

"Sounds as good as any plan I've followed lately," Jeremy muttered as he stood, leaning against the railing to stare out of the foggy, barred window into the rainy twilight.

All was quiet beyond the tinny sound of water dropping against metal sheets, and the softer echoes that came from the rain finding other more complex paths down to the ground. They waited, eager to see her come down into the valley, ready to run to her and usher her inside, even as they knew it was a delusion to think that would keep her any safer from what threatened her.

Their momentary peace was shattered by Jeremy's voice rising tensely, "Serafin—"

Asher was on his feet. "Where is she?"

Jeremy held his hand out as if to silence him, dropping his head in concentration. After a moment, he drew himself up as a growl tore through him, some new understanding burning in his eyes. "You're coming. Forget your pride." He grabbed Asher, threw him across his shoulders, and bounded down the stairs, sending rust scattering out from beneath his boots with each booming step.

Asher had no choice but to let his body relax, caught helplessly in an unyielding grip. Deep breathing was his only defense against the fetters as they sent sharp stabs into his limbs and side. Jeremy's agitation and rage were infectious, but Asher didn't engage in a struggle with the fractured, crazed images that assaulted his brain, and instead just let them wash over him. The world flew by, each separate part of the environment now connected by muted streaks of color, the rain stinging his face as he met the drops with reckless speed. He could hear the violent impact of Jeremy's footfalls as he burned through the landscape, but Asher could feel no accompanying jolts travel up to his body.

The journey ended with the ground meeting him in a blinding crash. Asher rolled out of his fall, threw one arm up to protect himself, and waited for his vision to clear. He heard a screeching cry ring out while a dark figure stumbled back, holding its face, and Jeremy stooped down, cradling Kittie in his arms. His eyes darted over the scene, searching for Kayla. He turned to his right to see Fec blowing more smoke into the already large and threatening cloud that hovered in front of him, while Bruno flung his razor coins into the haze. A soldier of Za'in's Spheres already lay bloody and motionless near their feet. Asher painfully pulled himself up to crawl, moving quickly in breathless anxiety. Soon he saw the warm gleam of her hair in the wet, gray night, hidden behind Vic's protective stance. She was crouched beside Kerif, her face closed with intense concentration and her hands gently laid on his chest and shoulder as he grimaced in pain.

Before he could go to her, he heard Jeremy's ragged yell. "Serafin! Get Kit and get them out of here!" The creature

Saros struck earlier had recovered and immediately pounced on him, but Asher didn't have time to watch the outcome of the fight. Kittie was curled up on the ground, the side of her face bruised and bleeding, and he scooped her up, struggling to stand.

A shrill howl stung his ears for a moment before he was knocked to the ground again. The voice was vaguely feminine, but so thick with agony that it was difficult to understand. "No! She's going to pay for what she did. I can't even *hear* Him anymore!" Asher twisted his body as he fell, softening the blow for the child he held in his arms, and then he whipped his head towards the sound. He was only mildly shocked to notice that the deformed creature that caused Saros to collide with him was the Second Arch Fiora. The small, bony Mods she wore on her wrists appeared to have shattered and were dragged up her arms through bloody, jagged paths, leaving pieces of blackened bones imbedded in her burned flesh. Those fetters crawled over her shoulders, wrapping unevenly around the sides of her face, and Asher couldn't tell if that was the cause of her horrifically skewed features, or if the source was internal. Some of the larger shards of bone seemed to fuse portions of her appendages to the tangled mass that gathered on her back, and it rendered her movements limited and jerky.

"Leave her the fuck alone, Ev!" Jeremy snarled, tearing the bandages off his arms and springing forward, knocking her into the mud. He slammed his palm against her forehead, that violent contact with the ground pulling her chin and chest upward. He dragged the jagged bones on his forearm along the exposed flesh of her throat, grinding his weight against her in some instinctive effort to smear her over the rocks.

Asher watched their exchange, and when he saw blood spill into the wet sand, he managed to rise and stumble to

Kayla's side, still protectively holding Kittie's wounded body. The Nephil met his eyes, and he could see the fear in her quieted by purpose.

"I closed Kerif's wound, but I still don't have control of the ability. I don't think I have anything left." Her gaze moved regretfully over Kittie's face, and lingered on Asher's bandaged hand.

"We'll live. Follow me into the valley; it's too dangerous out here." They stood, and he raised a flap of his poncho, beckoning her to find shelter at his side as they made their escape. He was aware of the warmth of her body against his before a loud crack snapped through the air, and his footing slipped as he felt Kayla fall down onto her knees.

Evangeline's triumphant shriek was closer than he expected. "Where are her wings now? She took Him from me, but it doesn't look like He's on her side anymore. This must be a test!"

Asher could see a tangle of blacked bones tightening around Kayla's throat. "No! Don't touch it!" he barked, smacking her hands away from her reflexive attempt to free herself, and he knelt and forced his own fingers between the choker and her flesh. "If these things bind your hands, they'll take everything away." He turned his head to see Evangeline holding the end of the chain of tangled bone that was wrapped around Kayla. The Arch's throat and chest were torn, and blood oozed down over her breasts, staining her tattered uniform.

She set her gaze on him. "Some legend you turned out to be, Serafin. I guess it's no mystery why the resistance failed. I really am disappointed, but without martyrdom all heroes become has-beens, right? If you didn't have the decency to die in Azevin the first time, you never should have stopped wandering the wastelands. Oh well, it doesn't really matter anymore, does it? You can stop fighting over her. She's mine now." A blissful smile flickered over her face, twisting into a grimace as she yanked on the whip. Asher took some of the impact as his bleeding fingers struggled to keep a hold on the fetters, but it was ripped from his grasp as Kayla was jerked into the mud.

A strange clattering sound followed the Nephil as she was dragged, choking, towards the Arch. Asher slid Kittie to the ground so that he could scramble forward, collecting Kayla's dropped Intercessors before Evangeline could snatch them. He slipped them beneath his poncho, and he couldn't tell if they were restlessly stirring at his side, or if he just felt uneasy holding them so closely. Was she being careless, or did she offer these to him in desperate hope?

Two gore-stained hands emerged from the gathering darkness, grabbed the whip as it hung in the air between the two women, and twisted it until it snapped. Jeremy seized the half that Evangeline still held before he slipped behind her, throttling her with her own weapon. Asher was surprised to notice fresh gouges running along Jeremy's face, and even the shadows couldn't conceal the appearance of bloody, mangled flesh stretched across his left arm.

A warm, frantic energy zigzagged up Asher's limbs, radiating from a frenzied heat in the center of his palms. He looked down to the see the hilts of Kayla's Intercessors clenched tightly in his fists, the grip of his wounded hand strong and without pain. Turning his head, he could see her eyes, peering over Vic's massive hands as he fought with the fetters for her breath. Asher understood what she asked of him, and he allowed himself to be a vessel. As he rushed forward, his body suddenly infused with new vigor, he felt the weight he held in his hands shift, and he didn't have to look down to know he would Intercede with kukris now.

"Christ, you're pathetic!" Evangeline spat, flipping Jeremy over her shoulder and slamming him to the ground.

"You were only strong because of Him!" She tore a deafening, agonized scream from Saros as she ripped another chunk of blackened bone from his arm. Evangeline didn't even notice his torment as she gazed wistfully at the dark mass in her hand. "Why doesn't He speak to me anymore? Where is He?" she murmured.

Asher reached the Arch as all of Kayla's resolve and fear surged through him in one last quivering burst, pressing against his skin from the inside until he didn't care if it tore him apart. He never felt such sublime peace as the blades arced down, one following the other like the beat of an exultant heart. Evangeline's body, slashed in two, fell in the same rhythm as his strikes. The blades retracted and Asher's body sagged; all the Angelic vitality that flooded him was now exhausted. Jeremy had pulled himself up, halfway to standing, but he froze, regarding the grisly scene with stricken features. He tightened his muscles to stop their trembling and hurtled to where Kayla was propped up against Vic's chest.

The pirate managed to keep the grip of the fetters from cutting off her ability to breathe, as his scraped and cut fingers pulled outward on the ring of bone, inching the weapon away from her tender throat. Jeremy's left hand was mutilated by Evangeline, but it was free of the parasite that bound him, so he was able to slide his fingers up beneath the choker and grasp it hard, while the other hand yanked the tangled mass in the opposite direction. The ring snapped in two, and he pulled back both pieces as they flailed violently. The fetters quickly crawled up his arms, finding a place to join with him.

Asher's steps were slow and purposeful, concentrating on each movement forward to ensure there would be a next one. He bent briefly to collect the wounded Kittie before he fell heavily to his knees and offered the spent hilts to the

Nephil. The rest of the pirates staggered close, joining their solemn, ragged circle, and Kayla took the Intercessors back into herself, bowing her head and whispering prayers of thanksgiving to her human friends. They all sat motionless, unmoved by the storm, none of them willing to break the comfort given by Kayla's falling tears. They didn't hear the cry of a frightened child, but an Angel weeping for their broken world.

41

Kayla tried to sweep aside the wet, clotted dirt and heavy flakes of rust that littered the floor, but the dust brush she found was missing half its bristles, and the rest were split and curled, catching debris just enough to spread it around. She stayed intent on her task, even though all she accomplished was scrubbing the grime further into the concrete. She enjoyed the sensation of her knees pressed against the hard floor, her toes pulled back, and her weight falling onto her elbows or the heels of her hands, leaving stiffness in her shoulders. In this position, she could stretch out her sore lower back, and twist the ache out of her hips. Her leg muscles could relax, and all the symptoms that came from days of walking could recede, and new pangs of fresh discomfort could soothe her.

But the motions of this little chore couldn't erase the throbbing sting trapped beneath the bandages that bound her neck and shoulder, nor could it soften the memory of what happened outside Cormina. The only thing that brought her peace was the knowledge she was clearing this space for Asher.

He explained that they had to stay here for the night. The ferry wouldn't be active again until the morning, and they should use this time to recover what strength they could. Still, she didn't like this place. Cormina wasn't the rough collection of filth that was proudly Azevin, nor did it possess the unnatural innocence of the potter's village. It was unlike the beautiful desolation of the road, or the stillness of the ghostly ruins that hosted the last Eclipse. Kayla could feel the decay in Cormina. Even now, she was aware of the twisted olive trees outside, their brittle bark uselessly taking in the rain, and she couldn't be the only one that could smell the rot of the vineyard.

The winery had been left to waste away, and it was an uncomfortable place to wait for the sunrise. The skeleton of the structure was laid bare, its shed layers cast aside in ruined shards. It was difficult to imagine what this place once looked like. She had attempted such a vision while she sat at the bottom of the stairs in the emptied vat room, lazily turning the crank that kept Kittie's flashlight burning, but the wood splintered again in her mind when she felt Vic watching her from the door, and she imagined the stones falling back to the ground every time she heard Fec and Bruno shift uneasily on the catwalk above her. The void that connected the two floors kept her accessible to her companions, but her thoughts needed some cover and her body nervously searched for distraction. Kayla cried out a quick excuse and apology, dashing into the little room nestled beneath the staircase.

She paced the small office, rummaging through sliding drawers and struggling with the metal door of a cabinet, painted a muted green. Her curiosity about what was left behind disappeared with the discovery of the dust brush. There was nothing soft and clean about their hideout, but she was determined to change this room into a place where Asher could find comfort when he was through seeing to the wounded. He was in the washroom now—a small, separate building less littered with debris—and he had ordered her to rest and attempt no more healing tonight. He knew she easily exhausted herself with this skill she hadn't mastered, and after what strength she lent him with her Intercessors . . .

Kayla shook her head. Asher was hurt, but he was still there taking care of Kerif and Kittie, and he even was showing concern for Jeremy, who somehow managed to keep bleeding. She forced her hands to release their pressure on the brush, which was grinding uselessly against the floor. It didn't seem possible that his fetters could be pulled off, but even with chunks missing, he still wasn't free. He looked worse than ever.

She flung the brush, letting it skid across the concrete and disappear into a dark corner. She thought about his hand, pulsing and wet, pressed against her neck as he tore the collar from her throat. When Asher cleaned her wounds, she had stared at all the red, searching in vain for some difference that would separate Jeremy's blood from hers.

Kayla stood, trembling, and dusted off what dry cardboard she could find, placing the flattened boxes in the area of the room she had tidied. She murmured prayers to herself, waiting to hear her mother's voice, but Kiera had been quiet for some time now, even when Kayla fingered her beads, gazed at her cards or read her book. Her heart was beating faster as she placed the dry blanket Asher had wrapped around her over the bed she made for him.

The light in the room was growing dim and the pain in her body was returning. She pulled herself up and lay sprawled on top of the cabinet, winding the flashlight more for the distraction than the illumination. She couldn't forget the *10 of Wands*, and she needed to see Asher's face.

Before Evangeline attacked, before they were back on the road, she had some insight to the meaning of the seventh card in her reading. She could see a picture of a man, weighed down by a bundle of rods. The card told her that she strove to do the right thing, but warned that her burden may be too much to carry alone. It was her card, but wasn't that Asher's story too? He had his own load to bear, but he still always came for her, always took another step forward despite injuries, fear or pain, and always steered her back to steady footing. Tonight he took a piece of her into battle, but she didn't lose her power to him. He let himself be a vessel, and then he returned the Angel in her, without any hesitation.

Kayla closed her eyes, but she couldn't blot out the image of Jeremy running towards her, the raindrops rising off his skin as tiny clouds of steam. She called him, and he was there, faster than she thought possible. In danger, he was her first thought. She swallowed hard, remembering the eighth card in her reading, the *7 of Cups*. The placement of the card represented the influences of her environment, and she was warned that she may have too many alternatives closely surrounding her. Grave consequences loomed if she didn't choose wisely, but a mystical experience could guide her way.

She slid off the cabinet, dropping the flashlight and falling to her knees, fingers clasped. Kayla didn't know where prayers should be offered anymore, to the skies or to the earth. She tried to imagine something worthy of reverence, and she focused on the memory of Asher's hands. She let the fire in her cheeks be expelled as warm breath, her lips moving rapidly. " 'Guard my life and rescue me; let me not be put to shame, for I take refuge in you.

May integrity and uprightness protect me, because my hope is in you . . .' "

Cool, calloused flesh rested against her burning cheek, and she leaned into his touch. She kept her eyes closed, afraid to discover if this was real or imagined. The hand lingered along the side of her face before she was lifted off the ground.

Asher's voice was low, but his murmur was so close that she could hear the bruising that lay below the coarse sound, resonating in her ears and brain. " 'How priceless is your unfailing love! Both high and low among men find refuge in the shadow of your wings.' "

The familiarity of his words caused Kayla's eyes to open suddenly with hazy recognition, but her question caught in her throat when she was faced with his gaze. This time, his usual restraint couldn't completely obscure the evidence of his suffering.

He turned his head slightly, gently releasing her onto the blanket. "You've been reading *Psalms*."

Kayla's chest ached, and in her mind she could see branches, and a rooftop . . . She felt foolish for not understanding his eyes sooner. "She read them to you."

His mouth twitched in an attempt to smile. "She had to share it with someone. Michael accepted that he came from Angels, but he wasn't one for Bible study."

"He didn't believe in God?"

"It's not as simple as that. Most people don't believe this old mythology, but then again, they think the Nephilim are also legend. Michael understood what he was, and that was enough to convince him that God had at least crafted his ancestors. But he didn't believe that God had perished when war waged in Heaven. How could that happen to a Supreme Being?"

"So what did he think happened?"

"God abandoned us."

They were both silent, their eyes wandering to the dark corners of the room. She felt his body making small adjustments, trying to settle into a comfortable position on the floor, and she jumped up in sudden embarrassment. "No, please, I want you to rest here," she cried out too loudly, motioning to the little bed.

He glanced up at her, his face composed, showing no signs of his earlier weakness. "I'm fine. You need to prepare for what's coming, more than any one of us. Take the comfort while you can."

"I . . . I made this bed for you. Please."

Asher turned his head, some internal struggle tightening his muscles. Slowly, he raised himself up, shifting onto the blanket. "Thank you. I'm only going to sleep for a short time."

Kayla watched him close his eyes before she sank down to the floor, huddling into herself. She let her gaze travel from his large, tanned forearms to the regular rising and falling of his bare chest. She avoided looking too long on his jaw and brow, and got lost in the strands of his damp hair, forming jagged, curving patterns on the cloth beneath him. Her eyes followed the undulating curls, her palms tingling with the memory of the electricity that swirled through her hands as he held her Intercessors. Energy had traveled through her arms into his in the same twisting waves, and he returned clear bursts of force with every strike he landed, with every caressing adjustment of his grip on the hilts.

When she was helpless in the grasp of the fetters, she could feel his need to protect her. She offered her own bones, and he wielded them by her will. Doubt moved him briefly, so she gave up control for a moment and felt the blades bend into gleaming kukris. She trembled with the certainty that flooded his body, with the freedom of joining with him completely as he allowed her to experience each of his powerful movements as her own.

Kayla struggled to take deep breaths. Asher's eyes were open, and he was halfway sitting up, his attention on her hands. Her palms were throbbing and she reached out to him as another surge of piercing rapture swelled up from her insides. A little moan escaped Kayla's lips as her Intercessors broke through her skin, the release of pressure causing her to tumble forward. He caught her wrist as she fell against him, while her other hand reflexively clutched at his side.

Asher's head was thrown back and Kayla gasped, running her fingers along his ribs, searching for the place where she wounded him. A low sound began in his throat, and she crawled over him, bending to see his face. She whispered his name, but his only response was to release her wrist and press their palms together, his fingers hooking around hers. "No!" she cried out, afraid to stab him again, but as soon as the sound escaped, her body weakened, drooping atop his. A familiar heat pulsed between their hands, snaking over their knuckles and back inside through their arms. It was only then that she noticed her Intercessors weren't in the form of hard bone, but warm light. That clear fire emitted from her other hand, expelling luminous tendrils that clung to his torso. She let those threads pull her closer to him, and as the glow tightly enveloped them she could feel his injuries, deeper and more numerous than she had guessed. Kayla's energy plummeted, scattering everywhere he felt pain, and it left her almost paralyzed, limply stretched across him.

Asher's frame gently writhed as her light entered him and she clung to his chest, pressing her face into his shoulder, wanting to experience his body being made whole again. Pain struck her with tiny shivers, the intensity varying in different locations, but the sensation drove her on. She wanted to take all his suffering from him; possessing his body was not enough. A little sigh escaped her as she released all control to the forces within, and she finally allowed her lips to brush against his throat.

She could feel his entire form respond, as a trembling jolt moved him. She swung her leg over his hips, pressing the length of her body to his, her fingers crawling up his sides with hissing sparks, glowing brilliance gathering around his face as she caressed the back of his neck, his jaw, the soft skin behind his ears. His wounds were distant, almost as if they never existed, but something new was rising within him that set her fire sputtering into more violent bursts and tethered her more tightly to him. This terrible fear that seeped out of his pores . . . could it ever have been his? He was in the shadow of a tall building, and everything hurt. He didn't want to die, but what was left now? This hopeless quest for redemption, it kept him moving, it led him back to this place. He was more terrified the second time. It was as if everything he accomplished was worthless, that he had nothing to show but an older face, owning only more scar tissue.

She saw strong, white teeth, vicious green eyes, and an iron spike. A wooden beam bruised his spine, his arms were stretched out, his head sagged. Those animal teeth parted . . . "*nec spe, nec metu.*" She didn't understand the Latin phrase, but she felt it unlock a wave of despair that washed over Asher. The agony that entered her palms quenched her flames for a moment. She had never heard him scream before.

He kept her image in his mind, he longed for her, and no amount of light she poured into him could heal the solitude that had been silently tearing him apart. Her mouth claimed his and his body awoke, consuming her passion while generating more with each rough caress. He seized her, slamming her back onto the blanket, sending the cardboard beneath sliding. Her blouse was a barrier between them that was easily removed, his hands possessing her flesh with purpose, each touch building on the next in sequence. She wrapped her legs around him tightly, afraid of her own senseless escape.

Soon they'd have what they both needed. He'd make her his, and he wouldn't have to be alone anymore. She wouldn't have to let the world down, and she could face the *7 of Cups* proudly. Kayla pressed her cheek to the skin below his collar bone, unmarred by any black marks. He still hadn't forgotten what happened at Tregenne's. He was seeing that tattoo she feared before he was hurled into a wall; she could see the faces of her two choices, close in battle, bathed in a red light. The fire in her hands began to harden. She wouldn't let that abomination hurt Asher. No, something else happened. It was as if those two rivals reached into each other and found something they could recognize, something that was the same . . . but it couldn't be! The vision dissolved and she could see him back in the basement of that building, the hammer was falling again, but Jeremy was there too, shattering the bones of that frightening Arch, gathering Asher's broken body to his, and he used those cursed Ruiners to make a light that would save his enemy and bring him back to her. It was true, it was all true . . . Why did she have to experience this now?

She held tighter to Asher, moved harder. But still, she could see Jeremy, dropping the book, the cards, and the necklace at his bandaged feet. *She doesn't need to know that I gave these to you.*

It didn't matter! That didn't change anything. Jeremy's actions were just another random impulse. She struggled with the cord that cinched Asher's pants tight.

His hands were on hers. "No."

Her eyes opened to see his sober face, no longer lit with passion. She felt her cheeks grow hot in shame.

"It's not your disgrace to bear, it's mine. It's been so close to the surface, I'm surprised you didn't see it sooner." He untangled himself from her and stood.

"So for once in his life he did the right thing . . . that doesn't mean anything! Please don't go." She stumbled to her feet and grabbed his hand with both of hers.

"I'm not tallying up our deeds in a contest for your love. I didn't do this when he was my adversary, and I won't give in now that we've recognized each other. We're nearly two days from Armageddon, and if all we've been are sad pawns in Za'in's game, then this is our last chance to make our own moves. If we've been thrown together to tear each other apart, I won't participate in his plan." He lifted her hand to his lips and kissed it softly. "It's not that I won't fight for you, Kayla. You know I have, and I will never stop. When this is all over, I still want to be the one you choose. Until then, there are too many changes happening in you, too many forces pulling you in different directions. If I had you now, it wouldn't make you mine."

She pulled her hand back slowly, numb.

Asher nodded gravely and walked to the door. "Thank you for healing my body. Please try to sleep." When she didn't respond, he turned around. "Kayla, if this is about those cards . . . remember that they can be interpreted in many ways. Make sure the voice you're listening to is your own."

When he closed the door gently behind him, she dropped onto the disheveled blanket, clutching her blouse to her chest. Her eyes burned. She tried to hold on to his words, but his abrupt exit still felt like rejection. Her uncertainty was what kept them apart in the past, and now . . . maybe it still was. Was he right? Was she trying to force everything into place according to what the cards told her? Kayla pulled the deck from her pocket and stared at the *7 of Cups*. She could see a woman holding a veil adorned with images of gold chalices, each containing a different object. The choices ranged from a dragon to a child's head. What did it all mean? She tried to listen to her own instincts, but no inspiration came.

That's because a correct choice has been made. It's not any of them you need to follow . . . it's you. You saw how your passion allowed you to see the true nature of your gifts.

"Mother?"

You've finally realized that your Intercessor isn't merely a sacred weapon. It's your Angelic fire made physical. It is what you let it be. Would you have discovered this without the fervor that makes all vision, love, and creation possible? Use that emotion, with restraint, to fulfill your potential.

Kayla remembered Asher's words and Jeremy's warning. This voice wasn't hers, but it did come from within. She looked down at her palms. "This was the first time I was able to heal so effortlessly, unaided, and without absorbing any wounds myself."

Try it again. Make it more precise.

"With who?" she whispered, subdued by Kiera's urgency.

Jeremy seems like the obvious choice.

She pulled her shirt on over her head, sprang up, and grasped the flashlight as it began to flicker out. "I . . . I can't . . ." Her words faltered helplessly, but she turned the torch's crank with angry purpose.

You got carried away with Asher. You were just leaking cures. But if you focus your ability . . .

Kayla frowned. Jeremy's capacity to heal himself instantly was frightening, but she was more afraid of what it could mean now that this power had mysteriously abandoned him. Would there be some catastrophic reaction when a Nephil's gift reached into one tainted by Ruiners? What would happen when their skin finally touched again? When she spoke, she made sure to keep her voice even. "What makes you think this is necessary?"

Notice the ninth card in your reading, the only one you haven't unraveled yet. Remember, this one is your most personal hope and fear . . .

She stopped pacing and forced herself to sit, dropping the flashlight down beside her. Kayla picked up the next card, the *Knight of Wands*. An armored man sat astride a rearing horse, and although the animal's eyes were wild, the Knight appeared at ease, keeping a firm grip on his staff. "Who is he?"

They call this card 'Lord of the Flame and the Lightning.' He represents a man that is charming, but unpredictable. He is passionate, clever and physical, but he is also impatient, wrathful and impulsive . . .

"Fine, it's him. The ninth placement represents hopes and fears, so what am I supposed to do—admit that he scares me? He does, okay? He's just human and hopelessly damned . . . but he frightens me. I don't want to touch him."

He's the last card before The Two of Wands: Dominion. Those two rods are power and clarity. You won't be able to have the success you desire without the wisdom that can only come from experience, from learning to join the energies of opposing forces. How will you face Za'in if you can't face him? Where will you draw your strength from if what you desire and despise is the same?

Kayla bowed her head in angry defeat, her clipped whisper falling from beneath her hair. "I'll call to him." She let out a long breath, imagining that the hissing whoosh silenced the world. It wouldn't be hard to reach him. She simply released the tension that came from avoiding thoughts of his eyes, his shoulders, his mouth. He was close; she could taste blood. There was no message she had to formulate—the honest surrender to their connection was enough. He sensed her need, and almost immediately she heard his voice on the other side of the door.

The angry muttering ended abruptly as the door creaked open and he peeked warily into the room. A look of relief and irritation flickered across his features when he saw her sitting cross-legged on the floor, unharmed, but still he entered, securing the lock behind him and crouching at her side.

"What is it?" he asked flatly, his hard gaze fixed on her, except when he spoke.

Kayla could see that the jagged, red lines scraped across his face were wet with clear fluid, and his left arm was wrapped with seeping bandages, the fetters peeking out between the bloody rags. "Are you okay?" she gasped, squeezing her eyes shut in a spasm of embarrassment at her clumsy words.

"When was the last time I looked okay?" he growled. "You called me in here to ask me that?" Jeremy snatched the flashlight from her hands and stood. "You're going to wear this thing out for nothing. Go to sleep."

"Wait! I can help you—"

He laughed spitefully. "Really? How are you planning to do that? Do all you Nephilim think you're God or is that something just you and Za'in have in common?"

She let his words hit her. It didn't hurt anymore. But she couldn't let him leave without getting the chance to do this thing that was necessary for them both. . . Before he turned his back, she threw herself forward, her cheek colliding with his breastbone, her hands awkwardly pressed to his chest.

Kayla was acutely aware of his Ruiners and didn't allow herself to be snagged. A tremor ran up his body, his arms twitching with a stifled desire to wrap his arms around her, and as she sensed his struggle, her palms flickered with warmth. So many times she opened her memories to glimpse again a smile or a scowl, the distant image of his bare arms, or the way his mouth moved to form her name, but now she just recalled what she saw inside Asher—the evidence of Jeremy's virtue despite the demon that rode him. He was the one that saved them all in Azevin. But before his heroics, he was searching for her, high above the city; he was stalking the dark streets. He was feverish, weary, without hope. He couldn't remember her touch, her face. He was without the comfort of a romanticized past, but he was still drawn to her and repulsed by his own baseness. When he found her, what would he do anyway? He couldn't touch her, not the way he wanted to. Would he feel any relief if Za'in took her? Were any promises ever real?

Kayla's stomach felt loose. She was within him now, and all she had to do was to let the nervous thrill of her closeness to his spirit move her, without losing herself. Her Intercessors were beams of light, penetrating his flesh, and she felt his body tense up, then droop against her, her Angelic fire encircling them in the embrace they were denied. A wave of pain engulfed her and she reeled, swallowing bile. "I'm here. I never wanted to leave you alone," she breathed into his wounds.

He struggled weakly, but his anguish began to recede as he surrendered, taking in her light. That glow branched off into veins, sliding around his arm and burrowing beneath his bandages, thickening into milky pools over his mangled flesh. Kayla bit her lip, but she couldn't hold back a tortured cry. The agony in his arm was limitless, tied to his internal Hell, caught in a cycle of feeding off and fueling his torment.

She felt her brilliant rays crash against a barrier, her flames curling around the blockage in useless billows. Nothing could get past the image of Evangeline, distorted, screaming in the blood-soaked rain. He was staring at her body, hewn in two. His former Ophan was vicious and manipulative; she had made him a plaything, and then set him up in Madeline. She was blindly loyal to Za'in, willingly taking on Mods and trifling with death. But she was human, like he was. Even if it was all on Za'in's orders, there were times she had covered his back in battle, there were moments of tenderness when her body comforted him . . . But she died an abomination. Just like he would.

His limbs flailed, struggling to escape the warmth that invaded him. The roar that was building up inside came out only as a choked groan as he flung Kayla aside and collapsed to the ground. Welts were rising on her skin from where his Ruiners lashed her, but she kept him reined in by her fire and she was pulled back to his side.

"You're not her," Kayla whispered, brushing the hair from his face. "I won't let that happen to you."

He sighed angrily, his brows pulling together in irritation. "What can you—" he began, but swallowed his words as she grabbed his wounded hand, pulled the bandages aside and pressed it to her cheek. There was pink skin stretched taut over his hand and it tingled with forgotten sensation. He pulled himself up to face her, his palm sliding over her soft flesh, his eyes wet. His fingers twitched before he grabbed the back of her head and pressed her lips to his.

Kayla struggled. It wasn't supposed to go this way! Images, words, and emotions rushed between them at dizzying speeds, and she couldn't find her balance. Her brain screamed her mother's name, but the voice was silent. Jeremy saw everything in her, no longer turned inward by the healing light, but not even the knowledge of her exchange with Asher loosened his grip.

He released her lips, but still controlled her movement by keeping a tight hold on her neck. "I was going to give you up," he said quietly, his face close to hers. "I promised I would. I wasn't going to stand in Serafin's way anymore. He's the kind of man you deserve. But I love you, Kayla. I didn't think there was any hope for me. I wasn't planning to survive this. But I want to live. Even if it's only this way, I can still touch you with one hand. I was going to stay away so you wouldn't have to keep getting hurt. I thought Za'in was in you because of me, but you must have driven him out. You're all light."

She couldn't move. Za'in . . . *inside* her? She remembered Asher's words. Were they all his pawns? Her power was meant to be the fire of God, but with the deity absent, her passion was misplaced. What was she doing to these humans? She could see the future that had to be avoided, the *7 of Swords*, and here she was acting impulsively. There were just too many choices in the *7 of Cups*, but as the *10 of Wands* urged, she had to do the right thing, to take responsibility for her burden alone and respond with honorable actions. She concentrated her will, firing up her Intercessors and letting the symbols on her back ignite.

Jeremy's panicked voice sounded far away. "Kayla, stop! Don't do this now!" He shook her by the shoulders, and then held her head in his hands, forcing her to look into his eyes. She could feel his fetters grabbing at her, but the barbed tips melted in the heat she radiated. "You don't know what you're doing! You can't do this alone. Let me fight beside you! He'll do worse than kill you—" He struggled to keep his fingers clamped tight to her flesh as her fire burned him. His eyes were helpless as he was forced to release her. "You . . . said you didn't want to leave me."

"You finally want to live. I want to give you more than two days to do it. If I stay, I'll destroy you all." Kayla closed her eyes, ready to be Delivered. She could hear his voice, too distant to understand the words that gave meaning to his shouting. There was only one voice within her, and she was compelled to follow its truth. Something collided with her body and took her off her feet, but before she could feel the second impact, the world exploded.

42

Kayla's fingers raked against the little pebbles that were strewn across the cold floor. She lay heavily on her chest, her eyes closed, but she was aware of a dim light, flaring up and then sparking out, somewhere in the dark. Parts of her body rested at a comfortable degree, but a damp chill sent shivers over her bare shoulders and ankles, leaving gooseflesh on her forearms. Although her back and palms were heavy with heat, the gathering cold tightened her thighs, bringing a line of tension up to her face, leaving her teeth chattering softly.

Soon, a warm pressure began to glide over the surface of her skin. The temporary thaw brought by the sudden contrast in temperature was paired with little shudders that gently shook her awake. She fought the stiffness in her body, and turned slowly towards the source of the comforting touch. Even in the darkness, that black cross was a gaping void lodged in his chest.

Kayla started, sliding off of his lap. "No . . . no! Why, why did you . . ." she murmured, struggling to stand.

Jeremy grabbed the hair at the nape of her neck, his fingers twisting the strands and jerking her head back towards him. "You know, that was something I was planning on asking you when you woke up," he said softly, holding her still with the hand she healed, controlling her movement with his merciless grip. "Why did you, Kayla? How did you? You knew you'd end up here."

She winced. "Let me go so I can see where I ended up," she managed through clenched teeth.

"I'll save you the trouble," he snarled, pushing her forward onto her knees before releasing her. He stood, pacing nervously, the motions of his lean body resembling a stalking cat. "We're in one of the caves at Velsmere. As if you didn't know."

Kayla looked up at him, absently rubbing the sting out of her scalp. "Then it's fine. This place has been pulling me towards it for a long time now. There's nothing more for you to do here. His attention will no longer be on you."

Jeremy's body bristled in anger, his fist clenching as if to strike the cavern wall, but he left it trembling close to his chest as he battled with his impulses. He choked on his low growl before it could rise, flinging himself down onto his knees beside her. His constrained rage seeped out of him as hopelessness, his eyes wide and pleading as his left hand tenderly grazed her cheek. "You didn't listen to me in Cormina, did you? I'm not letting you go again. Not this time."

"Even if that damns the world?"

He turned his head in frustration. "Kayla, that doesn't even make sense—"

"Even if I don't want you to follow me?"

Jeremy paused, looking sidelong at her before he spoke, his quiet words skidding against the coarse surface of an unspoken threat. "You'll have to do better than that."

Kayla closed her eyes. They both knew why his hands were trembling. She could do this now, now that she could no longer see the reflection of her dying radiance setting fire to his clouded irises. "Forgive me," she murmured as her arm shot forward, a vessel for a channel of flames. A tight constriction in her palm was all she felt of the impact when her light met his face. He cried out in pain, one hand coming up to shield himself, the other reaching behind him as he tried to stand, his boots skidding along the slick floor. Kayla slammed her palms to the ground, forcing her Intercessors through the dirt and stone. She then watched them unearth in front of her in the form of hard, white tendrils, raising the pebbles from the wet rocks as they reached for him. Jeremy kicked her Intercessors, the movement forcing him backward, colliding with the wall of the cave.

In that moment of regained balance, his survival instincts receded while his conscious mind grasped again for control. "Kayla, what the fuck!" His voice was raw, but the cavern allowed his words only a hollow sound. He hadn't yet recovered his vision, but his arm swung out, almost catching her as he lunged forward.

She watched his body jerk back, suspended in the air, its hurtling trajectory interrupted. He gasped for breath, and Kayla did the same, her stare fixed on the way his form responded to the pointed ends of bone that held him, as if he was caught in the gleaming talons of some giant bird. His flesh swelled between the sharp crescents that pressed into him, all feverish skin and straining muscles. But the internal combustion of his humanity wasn't the only force within him. As his energy surged up and threatened to spill over, the darkness that consumed his limbs came to life, lashing out and taking hold of her Intercessors. Kayla's hands shuddered against the ground. She had the power to penetrate this mountain, but she couldn't enter him. Her extended awareness was beginning to grow dim, and she felt like she was slipping beneath a pool of tar. She couldn't allow herself to be swallowed now by those Ruiners. He felt so far away, but she was still within the mountain. She would have to move it.

The stones that surrounded her flaked off in tiny crystalline shapes as she forced herself deeper into the earth. She let her Intercessors grow barbs, catching rocks as they snaked to the surface, then she willed both materials to gather tightly around what almost still felt like Jeremy. Kayla pulled her weapons back, scraping him against the wall and summoning him to the ground. She called to her bones, bidding them to return, but she felt the crystals clinging to her still, as the boundaries of the two very different surfaces seemed to blur. When she lifted her hands from the ground, she could hear the soft clattering of stones to the earth, paired with a sharp pain in her palms. Her fingers twitched in a failed attempt to form fists, but she shook her head and still moved forward, using her stiff digits to catch her balance as she stumbled to Jeremy's side.

She could see him, weakly struggling against the purple stones that tethered him to the wall of the cave. The crystals were cloudy and dense, their subdued glitter lodged in the blackness that surrounded his arms, their jagged edges protruding from his flesh, trailing undulating red lines. As she crouched close to his side, she could make out tiny slivers of white, lacing the stones together. Those rocks gripped him tightly, allowing little movement, and though his head was caught at an awkward angle, his eyes searched for her.

"This . . . might be your last mistake . . ." he murmured, his words fragmented with sharp, pained gasps.

"Let's hope so." When Kayla caught the blue gleam of

his eyes from beneath his lids, she forgot the luster of his stone adornments. She let her fingers brush his lashes, travel across the side of his face, and curl around hanging strands of his hair as she grazed his neck. His brow tightened, but that conflict disappeared into a sigh as his eyes closed. She let her hand drop, and then she stood, turning towards the cool light in the distance.

Behind her, Kayla heard him choke on a broken attempt to laugh. "This changes . . . nothing. I've . . . found my way back . . . to you . . . through worse."

His words were faintly carried to her ears, but their meaning was lost in the rumble of beating wings. She looked up when she reached the mouth of the cave, but instead of being greeted with wind and feathers, there were only giant, purple stones, piled sharply in layered chunks to form a tall, steep hill. The sun was rising somewhere behind her, allowing her to see the shimmering purple granite, accented with tufts of green and the somber geometry of ruins. At the very top was a long, flat structure, and although the details of the exterior were simplified by the distance, she was sure the façade would still be austere when she approached the doors. She ran towards the base of the hill, her body weightless. She only had to ascend. There was no past, except the vague memory of anticipation, of longing, of need. She knew she would find gardens enclosed by colonnaded halls. She knew there would be staircases, unfurling like scrolls, and windows that framed the view as if it was an altar's sacred image. Only the cool marble of this monastery could soothe her burning skin. She would ascend.

'O you afflicted one, tossed with tempest, and not comforted, behold, I will lay your stones with colorful gems, and lay your foundations with sapphires. I will make your pinnacles of rubies, your gates of crystal, and all your walls of precious stones. All your children shall be taught

by the Lord, and great shall be the peace of your children . . .'

The words were carried along the breeze, finding their way softly to her ears. As she began to climb up the steep path, she felt the verses rising from the cold rock beneath her feet, flooding her legs with brisk energy. That promise, it was Kiera's hope. These were her steps too, along this ruined road. Kayla grasped at this fragmented vision, but all she could see was dark hair and slender fingers. It was impossible to tell if she was glimpsing her mother's life before the Eclipse, or if it was her own childhood memory of this place. She paused, kneeling down to scoop a handful of dirt into her palm. Was she ever here before? Small grains of earth sifted through her fingers, leaving a few purple crystals in her tightening fist. She was a part of this place. How many ways did she exist here before now?

Kayla stood and began wandering upwards again. Her feet moved over splintered rock, roots and debris with confidence, with purpose, as if her body was following an often-repeated ritual. The muscles below her shoulders ached, but that pain only quickened her steps.

'*. . . all your children shall be taught by the Lord, and great shall be the peace of your children . . .' That's what all this is for.*

Those delicate fingers were held tightly in a scarred hand. "I don't have your faith," he said.

She could see Kiera clearly now, frustration fitting awkwardly on her peaceful face. "We were children, born without a homeland. We are orphans, who found each other, despite everything. That we're together now—isn't that enough to build faith on for an eternity? But we can't let our child come into this kind of world; you know that."

"I'm not saying I won't do it. I just didn't have any doubts until now. I would have torn the world down before. Now I . . . now I need to be certain." Michael wrapped his arms around her, and she happily let herself be enveloped in his embrace, the sigils on his skin pressed to her bare flesh.

"It will be an adjustment," she breathed, running her fingers over the dark symbols that marked his body. "Change can be painful. But I'm not afraid of this transformation, because it's necessary, and for us, it's natural."

"I don't know. I've been thinking . . . is anything natural for us? We're not Angels. We're part human too—"

"We're not like them! What do we have to see every day? It's not Heaven. It's the drug dealers that hang out by the church, or the sick laying in the street, or the almost healthy ones who are afraid to catch what they have. It's the grieving families of your friends who shipped out to war and never came back. It's the bars on the windows, and it's desperation and squalor and . . . Michael, it's our own mothers. What they did to us was out of fear, I know, but this will take all the fear away. Things will be better for the humans too."

His fingers gripped her. "Am I any better? What about all the things I did out of fear? Angels aren't afraid, but that's because they're content to follow orders. Is that all we're doing now?"

"If you don't want to follow, then *think*. Why did he bring us here?"

Michael closed his eyes. Kayla could feel his awareness dropping through his feet and into the ground. His burden was sinking down, hitting only one barrier before it disappeared beneath the stone.

He sighed, letting his head fall softly against hers. "So that we can be certain. So that, before everything changes, we can feel our connection to the earth, to the sky, to our history . . . I feel it. I can sense the Fall here, even stronger than back home."

"It's the quartzite."

"I know," he murmured gravely. Michael was far away now, his eyes fixed on the purple stone.

Kayla swam towards everything he discarded into the rocks at his feet: his doubt, his mistrust, and all the little evasions that held his world together. She reached for him, for the arms that held Kiera, for the swirls and intersecting lines that kept his energy from bursting through the surface of his skin. Those black marks came closer, and she plunged into their gaping darkness.

Another vision arrived. It was still dark above her, but the boundary of the sky was torn. Contorted, flailing points of light plummeted down, crashing against the dense clusters of crystal, spewing trails of sparkling ash up into the thick air. She barely had time to wonder if this is what Michael saw when he first let the stone touch him. For her, it was more than just a vision; she was one of the fallen stars. Now there was only the sensation of warmth, spilling out into the dust. Her body went slack with pain. Were her muscles so torn and disconnected that they could no longer react by tightening? Every light was going out. She was alone, numb and empty. There was nothing, except the vague sensation of sliding down into oblivion. It would be over soon, if she could just accept the Divine's will one last time. She exhaled.

Something scraped against her shoulders, and she was suddenly aware of her ability to move. The agony that shot through her back was unfamiliar, but as she rolled and twisted her body, she found new joy in motion. A cry of pain escaped her lips, startling her. It was no longer a song of joy or praise. She tried the sound again. It was ugly, but it was hers. The purple stones clung to the new form that cloaked her now-dimmed angelic light. They filled some gaping void; they anchored her here. She rose, dragging her bare feet along the pebbles.

The sun was rising. There were endless possibilities in this new dawn, as if it was the very First Day. Her eyes were different.

'. . . *and great shall be the peace of your children . . .*'

Kayla stopped short. This wasn't a new place, only a new time, a different life. A part of her she had lost. She had heard this verse before, somewhere . . . but in her memory, that sound was lighter, clearer, than it was now. "Mommy?" Her own voice was that of a child's, without the glory of a Star, without the suffering of the Fallen.

"See all of this? It was my mistake. But I was thinking of you . . . Shouldn't that have made it right?" Kiera's eyes were large and deep set, staring beyond the view from the purple mountain. Her thin fingers absently rubbed her palm.

"Mommy, don't be sad." Kayla threw herself into her mother's lap. She wasn't afraid. Daddy would come get them. He taught her the rules of games like this. She was starting to think that maybe everything was a game, or that nothing was.

Kiera didn't seem to hear her. Sometimes she was very far away. But she stroked Kayla's hair as those familiar verses spilled out, her voice serene and even, and they were both again soothed by the constancy of her anguish. " 'How you have fallen from Heaven, O morning Star, son of the dawn! You have been cast down to the earth, you who once laid low the nations! You said in your heart, "I will ascend to Heaven; I will raise my throne above the stars of God; I will sit enthroned on the mount of assembly, on the utmost heights of the sacred mountain. I will ascend above the tops of the clouds; I will make myself like the Most High." But you are brought down to the grave, to the depths of the pit. Those who see you stare at you, they ponder your fate: "Is this the man who shook the earth and made kingdoms tremble, the man who made the world a desert, who overthrew its cities and would not let his captives go home?" ' "

The vision faded. Kayla found herself standing in front of a dull, faded wall, punched with tiny windows and topped with a slanted, tiled roof. She lifted her chin to the sky. The peaks of intricately carved towers were barely visible, climbing up from somewhere on the other side of the wall. She walked along the perimeter of the stone barrier, allowing her shoulder to brush its irregular surface, and hoping her feet wouldn't stray from its shadow. Kayla turned the corner, and found that this side of the wall gave way to an open, towering arch. She ventured in without hesitation. This place was hers. She'd been here before, in so many different forms. Kayla suffered a tiny pang of regret that she didn't find her way here sooner, but she finally understood that there was no shortcut to the inevitable.

The stones under her feet became smooth and rounded as she entered the courtyard. The simple exterior began to slowly acquire ornament, and as she moved forward, she was able to make out a short stairway leading up to another entrance, surrounded by carved relief columns and large sculptures of draped figures. An iron cross balanced atop the high wall, above a set of two bells in an open niche. Kayla's eyes were focused skyward for a few long moments before she stumbled on the cobblestones. When she caught her balance, she found herself closer to the stairs than expected, and she peered into the shadows that gathered around the closed double doors. A figure sat at the top of the stairs, leaning comfortably in the doorway. She knew he'd be here, and her feet never slowed, her path never faltered. When her toes touched the bottom steps, he rose, and her shoulders tightened with some distant memory, but the emotion that loosened her legs and constricted her throat was unfamiliar and insignificant.

When she landed on the highest step, Sebastian moved suddenly close to her, his dark eyes pressing her hard. Even with the intensity that shone in his gaze, she wasn't surprised that his words were simple and gentle. "What did you find when you wandered in the world?"

Kayla's eyelids closed slowly with effort, an exercise in fighting the sudden impulse to be very still. "Emptiness."

His breath stirred her hair. " 'The earth was formless and void, and darkness was over the surface of the deep . . . ' "

" ' . . . and the Spirit of God was moving over the surface of the waters—' "

"Ah, but something is missing."

She squeezed her eyes shut tighter, struggling to recall a nearly forgotten image. "No. No, I've felt it before, somehow . . ." Somewhere in her memory, her neck was craning towards a warm light, and there was something waiting above with an outstretched hand. Her heart leapt then, and how many times since did she feel that sacred wonder set her on fire? Steam hissed across the sigils on her back.

"You feel it here." Sebastian gently grasped her wrist, tugging it closer to the marble railing, and then released her as her palm touched the cool stone, guiding her fingers lightly around its curving surface.

The Angelic script that trailed down from her shoulders burned softly. Her awareness spread from her palms, into the marble, and then the crystal below . . . across the hills and caves, catching glimpses of a former world through blazing eyes. "We Fell here too? I thought—"

"So much time wasted. You traveled across an entire, sprawling continent and still you know little more than you did in the exile of your youth. Time passed differently in

Heaven, and we were cast out across the Earth under a series of Eclipses. Something unusual occurred *here*, however. This mound of quartzite reacted with Angelic bodies in an unexpected way. The natural quality of this stone is to regulate change, and so more Angels survived the Fall while retaining their attributes." Sebastian paused, smearing away a bit of the purple dust that clung to her fingers. "And there's more. But you've experienced some of that yourself."

Kayla shuddered, her hands clenching the rail. "Jeremy . . ." she gasped as she spoke the word that she promised she would keep silent, the name she somehow forgot during her journey from the cave. The oppressive weight of her body returned; her legs felt weak and her back ached. She couldn't remember what she did to him. Her cheeks burned with the memory of the simple ecstasy that moved her to this place. Now that it was gone, she felt more human than ever, and it seemed absurd to think she could touch divinity. The script on her back was just a series of cold, raised scars. She felt Sebastian's body behind her as a towering pillar of heat, and she struggled to keep her breathing even.

Kayla maintained her composure for a few moments, but she soon found herself coughing, her chest swelling with the effort to draw in air. She remembered that the sun should be rising, but her eyes were growing bleary in this expanding darkness. Her hands still gripped the marble balustrade as her legs began to give out, buckling underneath the weight of her fragile and breathless form. Before she slipped away, she felt Sebastian's disapproving voice envelop her in endless ripples: "You've felt the elation of your Angelic mind, but still, even the vaguest thought of him can drag you back down to what you still consider your 'self.' "

An unfamiliar, coarse purr echoed from somewhere close by. " . . . Interesting."

43

Kayla watched the tops of the cypress trees bend as they yielded to the autumn winds. She shivered. The earth below her was warm and inviting, but the cold air stiffened her skin. How long had she been here in the garden, staring off over the tiled roofs, past the distant purple hills, to the troubled sky? Her body was heavy, but her head swam through the thin atmosphere, and although so much didn't make sense, she had the suspicion that for once, she understood everything that really mattered. She knew she was in the innermost courtyard of the monastery, but she couldn't remember how she came to be in this place. Something happened between her last lesson with Sebastian out in that seabed desert and her most recent memory of his disappointed eyes. Kayla gazed at the sun's rays breaking through the clouds as the shining star let itself sink closer to the horizon, and there was something familiar about her attention being focused on those tiny points of light. Her chest ached with longing. She knew she was lost.

Very soon, that same sun would go dark, high up in the

sky, and everything would change. She was afraid, but not for herself. There were others, somewhere . . . There were people she loved. The pain in her breast sharpened and she let her body fall to the earth. Were they already dead? She couldn't remember their names, their faces . . . Kayla pressed her cheek into the dirt and crystals. They had to be long gone. She was alone, except for Sebastian.

She thought about the tattoos that crossed over his torso and down his arms. The symbols blurred in her recollection as a mass of dark, chaotic strokes. She closed her eyes and went deeper into her memory. There was a sharp line that dipped and changed direction, then hooked around a tiny curve. Beside that mark was an inverted, diagonal cross that trailed a two-pronged spike. The shapes weren't random, they weren't decorative—she recognized them now. The first symbol represented a "B," then an "A." *Baltoha.* There was more. Twisting, bending lines, swelling and constricting. I-Z-I . . . *Izizop. Baltoha. "From the highest vessels." "For my own righteousness."*

Kayla held her breath. When did she learn to read this language? It was just another thing that she didn't remember understanding. All the beginnings were missing. She fought to recall her first meeting with Sebastian. Light was filtering through large windows, and there he was—dark eyes, dark hair . . . Something moved, and they were left alone. Who led her there, that very first time? His image was distant; she couldn't see his face. There was only a pair of shoulders, thrown into a posture of reckless apathy, set above a thin back, its strong angles lashing together sets of curves that seemed ready to bend, explode, or change direction at any moment. Those features were so familiar. Kayla could feel her heart beating fast against the earth. Was this someone who she loved or feared? She remembered his fingers bruising her wrists, her arms; she remembered him inflicting darkness on her, and poison; she remembered his hair brushing her face, his warm breath . . . "Jeremy."

He was nearby. She knew he was hurt when she found herself wincing with every attempt to draw in air. Kayla tried to ignore his thoughts, but he was insistent, and he only had one desire: to ascend just high enough to reach her. She sprang up and began running across the courtyard, trailing glimmering dirt, but it wasn't until she passed through the marble walkway into the adjoining garden that she considered the direction of her flight. She stopped suddenly in front of a fountain, carved with images of two winged beings. What sort of human was he, that he could inspire this breathless sort of fear, and still drive her to rush, not to end it, but to let it endlessly continue? Kayla planted her palms against the rim of the sleeping fountain and stared into her own reflection in the water. She had a past, and he wouldn't let her forget. There were scrapes along the sides of her face and blood-blisters scattered over her shoulders and chest. She pulled the bandage away from her throat to reveal wounds that were beginning to scab over. What happened on her way here? Did he do this? Kayla gazed into her own eyes, their radiance dulled by the dark skin below them. She dipped her fingers into the cold water before attempting to smooth her hair and smear away the grime that clung to her flesh. Here, in this place, she was suddenly aware of her body and regretted her disheveled appearance. She examined her reflection again as the water settled, and she adjusted her rumpled, sleeveless blouse. As she pulled the straps of her top straight, she noticed a little white line circling above her collarbone and disappearing down beneath her neckline. Her hand moved in a reflexive spasm to clutch her locket, but it was gone. A cold shiver of recognition struck her before she began frantically searching her pockets. Her mother's cards and Bible were missing, and her father's prayer beads were no longer wrapped around her wrist. She closed her eyes. How long had she been without them? When did she see them last? She could only remember the weathered hands that had first dropped the keepsakes into her lap, trembling almost imperceptibly beneath the pressure of their own strength. It was only through great suffering that she obtained these relics. She forced the gaze of her memory upward so that she could again meet those eyes, forever unmoved by the chaos that dazed the rest of the world.

"No!" she cried out, slamming her hands down along the edge of the fountain. "Asher . . ." How could she forget why she was here? How could she forget him?

Jeremy's voice exploded in her mind, sending urgent blasts of force against her skull. He was screaming their names. He wanted her to remember.

"Kittie . . . Kittie! Bruno . . . Vic . . ." She clapped her hands over her mouth. A sharp pain in her stomach nearly pulled her back down towards the ground, but she fought to stay standing. These were the people she lost; they were her family.

He did worse to your family. Jeremy's voice stung her brain.

"Stop . . ." He kept flinging images at her, smearing his cruelty over the spaces of her mind that were once soothed by sweet words. Where was her mother's voice?

Is that what shut me out for so long? Since Azevin, you thought you were hearing her? Jesus, Kayla, that was Him.

"What? No . . ." She gripped the marble, concentrating on the quiet moments between his words. When he didn't force his thoughts on her, there was no past and there was nothing to remember. Was there anything that she could trust as truly hers?

The gentle pressure of a warm palm between her shoulder blades drew her back towards external reality. This time, sound reached her ears before her brain. "Are you still so lost? What do you suppose it will take for you to finally find your bearings?"

Kayla turned, determined to find her own answers in Sebastian's face. His eyes were still and his features were relaxed, disappointment only slightly pulling his brows, and she saw no evidence of malice tightening his mouth. She could still feel Jeremy's distant influence as he thrashed against his bonds, some desperate warning in every roar he expelled. Should she be afraid? Kayla peered deeper into Sebastian's clear, black eyes. His energy was forceful and probing, but she couldn't see any threat hidden in that veiled intensity, only expectations. She lowered her gaze, wrestling with her failings as an Angelic being and the sudden desire to watch that face soften with approval. Her eyes searched for a place to secure her focus, and she noticed the symbols marking his forearm—sharp, angled characters alternating with delicate, curving ones.

"*Iadanamad . . .*" she whispered, astonished again by her ability to read the script.

"'Undefiled knowledge . . .'" Sebastian's fingers brushed against his tattoo before they lifted her chin, not allowing her to avoid his gaze. "Is that what you've been searching for all this time? The purpose of your training was to answer those questions you have about yourself, your past, your world. Now we have such little time left."

She could barely breathe. "But . . . it's not too late."

"Not even two days of training to prepare you for a new Earth . . ." He closed his eyes, but he didn't release her. "You don't know what you're saying. How could you?" Sebastian moved closer to her and a tiny tremor moved his features. "The world has finally touched you. Even now, I can smell the decay, the hopelessness, the savagery. On your skin, I can smell them . . . and him."

Kayla tensed her jaw and pulled away from his touch. "Then shouldn't I be able to do the same?"

"You've picked up another human trait." He opened his eyes, but they passed over her now, looking to the architectural adornment with the same interest he once bestowed on her. "Have you noticed how they demand what others have? They desire the fruits that spring only from diligence and toil, but they want an effect without a cause. You see them search for a shortcut, and if that can't be found, they'd rather take a poor imitation, a little fix, than do what is necessary to create their own glory."

"I've seen humans move with resolve. Would an Angel stay still until the Divine calls her? Where is the power that guides the Nephilim?"

She was worthy again of his gaze. "*Iadanamad* again? Could it be possible that all this was your way of seeking? You weren't wrong to think there really was something to find, despite all that emptiness that surrounded you. Then who am I to deny you a glimpse of it now?"

Kayla let her breath leave her as she was enveloped by darkness. She wanted all her confusion to trickle down into the void, but she realized she wasn't completely adrift. A suffocating warmth felt like cotton against her eyes, her mouth; it tangled her hair and caught the backs of her arms. She could feel the fire inside her chest leap, then plummet down below her stomach, and she knew this black abyss was the comfort of his arms. Last time she felt closeness like this, she was sure something else significant occurred as well. Her hands burned.

The scraping of purple stones along her back was a familiar sensation by now. He was still so close to her, but she couldn't make out the boundaries of his body. She heard his voice, but it was images that reached her. There was a red flower, spreading its four petals, and her thighs clenched in recognition of the heat it generated. She felt exposed. Stars were falling and people were afraid. But something emerged from those extinguished blazes . . . beautiful, mysterious, tragic. The Heavens fused with all that was profane below, and now there were new lights to move across the surface of the Earth. There were those that fell to their knees and offered what poor gifts they could, and the Stars, so like gods, found splendor in the fragility of Creation and accepted the touch of urgency and the taint of death. This joining of the divine and the mundane resulted in offspring: new creatures that glowed brighter and burned faster than any before them. These Nephilim were hunted, and it was necessary for them to seek isolation, to hide their brilliance from an avenging God, mad in His death throes, and swarms of humans, wild with the terror of autonomy.

The flower's red petals were turning inward, as the plant began to consume itself. Kayla tried to open her eyes to the present reality, to escape memories that were not her own, but that heat still churned below, and it dragged her back down into its core. That fire wasn't limitless, however. Nothing was. Even the sun could be quenched again, and last time that happened, the world exploded.

At least that's what we were all told.

Kayla felt her heavy limbs twitch. She couldn't distinguish the exact moment when her thoughts broke from Sebastian's and Jeremy forced his way through.

We didn't see an Eclipse, and if we did, we had no memory of it. We were guiltless, innocent, and never given a chance. Humans didn't do this. He did.

She couldn't catch her breath. The stars she saw this time only appeared in brief, blinding moments of pain. No one mourned the loss of the trees or lamented over the barren ground, but there were machines that would never move again, and that was enough reason for Jeremy's stars to return, quickly and without warning. There was nothing beautiful in this new world until that child's eyes recognized him.

Cool, clean air flooded her lungs. Humanity didn't have to be brutal, senseless. With Kit, he wasn't alone. Kayla's muscles began to loosen, but this new atmosphere of peace was threatened by another image, looming right outside her range of vision. A sense of dread began to settle with the knowledge that no man could escape his beginnings. Original sin wasn't dealt out equally, and that girl couldn't lift his portion. But she tried.

A burst of white light cleared everything away. Not even the red flower remained. Sebastian's spirit stirred restlessly within Kayla, grasping at the last image she received. Soon, she could feel him regretfully abandoning his curiosity about what caused that explosion, but as she began to open her eyes to cypress trees and ivory marble, the world went dark again beneath the choking strength of his grip.

"I thought he told you not to trust the voices in your head." Although she couldn't see Sebastian, his breath warmed the side of her face. Kayla struggled to swallow a wave of guilt. "This is real. I'm here. I am only doing this because you desire it." A flower with six orange petals reached out for her. "You are Nephilim. You want to ascend, but you need a solid place for your steps to land. You have been separated from your legacy for too long, and this is the only way, now. I'm going to continue to open the gates of energy in you that have been forced closed." The fire between her legs was thrust into her lower abdomen. "You'll experience our collective memories as this happens. When I'm done, you'll have your 'undefiled knowledge.' You'll be clean, light, and ready to see the connection between the next change and all that has come before. Then the last hours of this era will truly mean something . . ."

The flaming petals swelled and his voice drifted away. The warmth that radiated out from within her hips drew his presence closer, and she could feel the weight of his chest against hers for a moment before it passed through the boundaries of her body, and his energy trickled down to meet the ball of light below. A dull ache squeezed her heart, but it wasn't any familiar sense of hopeless longing. This new pressure opened up her lungs and awakened her sluggish blood. Her nerves tingled and her hands were alive with pulsing sparks. Kayla breathed deeply, to take in as much of Sebastian's sensations as she could, but there seemed to be no limit to the amount of air she was now capable of filling herself with. Lost in his vision, she let his feet lead her towards the object of his fascination, gasping with pleasure at the electric jolts that coursed through her arms. He was aware of these feelings, they were his after all, but for Sebastian there was no mystery to this agitated bliss. He was merely being drawn to the light of another Star.

Sebastian's steps quickened, moving curiously over uneven ground, but Kayla didn't notice the environment he navigated through. There was no place, only his body—her body—and even that was just a vessel for this fervor, this need to join again with something that was theirs all along. Kayla's sight began to clear, revealing a pair of wide eyes, and the heat that was building within her hips was suddenly released, setting her entire body on fire. Those eyes, so familiar, met hers, and it was recognition that softened their fear-rounded gaze and loosened the tight mouth below. Sebastian reached for the Angel in the tree, and Kayla let her senses dissolve into the serenity of the flames within. The world was nearly dark again, but she could see Kiera's mouth bare its teeth and open in a silent scream. She felt Sebastian's limbs respond, and although he didn't let the vulgar creatures he struck down steal his focus from the

Nephil, Kayla couldn't ignore their energy. She didn't notice the presence of those humans before, but now she choked and shivered, cringing away from their desperate and brutal imaginings, grotesquely fragmented in their crippled subconscious. She clung to Sebastian's strength as he silenced their vicious thoughts and the rocks stopped flying. Kayla felt the Nephil's touch, and there was peace in her fire, as it flowed in tranquil billows from one conduit to another.

She sighed, allowing the orange petals to return. Love was recognition and it was without pain. This was her natural state. She let the ball of light between her hips expand with a deep inhalation.

This isn't your peace.

Kayla coughed spasmodically in an effort to exhale. "No . . ." Why was Jeremy's voice still within her? Why couldn't she sever this connection?

That's not what you want. You meant what you said in that tower. I understand that now. And I . . . I didn't know until now what all that pain meant. Yeah, there was pain, but there was recognition too. Don't tell me you didn't see me . . .

The stars were falling, but Jeremy held on to her admission of love. It was what he wanted. She said the words, but it would never have to be tested, so it couldn't wither or be destroyed. The world would end—*his* world would end—and those words were the trumpets to herald the coming darkness. It was what he wanted.

Why did it even matter? He asked that of himself so many times since he first saw her frightened face peering up at him. She had tried then to hide her innocent eyes beneath the forced pull of resolute brows. Why did it matter that she was beautiful, that when he touched her, he forgot all those that called him *Saros*? She didn't have a past. She didn't see tidal waves and famine in him. Every stretch of desert or swamp didn't move her to mourn what once was. Za'in would give her past back to her, and here he was, caught in a futile battle with his own helplessness.

Kayla couldn't will her throat to complete the motion of swallowing. In a few dizzying moments, she traveled across the wastelands again, but this time, inside Jeremy. This wasn't the harmony of Angelic love, spiraling cleanly from one vessel to another, leaving nothing behind beside intensified warmth and understanding. Human passion was fragmented and it didn't wind in predictable patterns. It led her through endless nights in the desert, when his skin was whipped raw from the wind and sand . . . through ruins where Za'in echoed so loudly, he couldn't remember his own voice. Through the filth of cities, and the desire to be able to just bleed again . . . She was there with him now, but she was there then too. Every mercy and every sin he committed was in her name. There was no hope for the future, only the eternal desire for her gaze, her touch, her words.

Her tears burst forth so suddenly that they seemed to have jagged edges. She and Jeremy both were holding on to a hurt that could be healed so simply. Why did she ever do anything but tell him honestly, tell him everything, as many times as he needed to hear it? The light, the flowers, none of it mattered. She'd break through and free him from beneath the mountain, from beneath the weight of eighteen years after the end of the world. "Jeremy, I—"

Exploding sparks of light blinded Kayla as the air was forcefully taken out of her. A yellow flower with ten petals appeared, but she didn't have the energy to tear it away, as she struggled to breathe the sting out of the tender area above her navel.

"Have you learned nothing?" Sebastian spat. "Even you have the ability to read the intentions of those humans that attacked your mother. What do you think would have happened to her if I didn't Intercede? Have you forgotten the outcome of the last time you gave into that human, Saros? You barely survived, and now you've been tethered to his darkness as he sucks your vitality. The Nephilim are the divine, plagued with the taint of human weakness. Nothing is more dangerous. It's necessary for us to cultivate our higher essence, and to eliminate the base impulses that threaten from within."

Kayla could feel her tears evaporating from her feverish skin. There was nothing she could do. She had one foot in the material world, but the other had already begun to transform. As a human, how could she ever overpower Sebastian? And as an Angel, her will was the whim of a higher power. She felt his hands high on her stomach.

"You'd do well not to resist me. If we don't move quickly, you'll burn up before we've finished."

Kayla winced as the sphere of light expanded, pressing out against her ribs and skin. She experienced his impatience as a sudden barrage of emotions, devoid of words and simple in imagery. She tried to step back, to separate from him, but she faltered, unsure of which memories she should discard. Maybe all these were hers, and she was just discovering them again. The thought patterns seemed foreign at first, but perhaps they were the structure that came before her fears and desires pulled her adrift.

The sky was very clear. The vibrancy of the blue hue was without variation, and staring at it too long hurt her eyes. She was dying. They all were. There was a time when the idea of extinguishing was noble and romantic, but now it was just another indignity she didn't have the patience to endure. Not anymore. It wasn't an accident that she was here, and it wasn't a punishment. This world was her inheritance. It wasn't made properly, but that was no reason to surrender it to her murderers.

How could something so weak bring her to this? This shouldn't be her last look. She groaned, reaching out for the Intercessor shard that lay motionless, a few feet away. It wasn't hers, but she wouldn't let those creatures take what was left of her kind and use it to fuel their superstitions. This was forbidden, but soon there would be no one left to condemn her. She took the sharp end, once a gleaming white, and dragged it along her inner arm, from her armpit to her elbow. *C-r-o-o-d-z-i.* This was her vow. *The second beginning of things.*

She watched the red lines of Angelic script expand before her blood completely obscured the form and meaning of the word. *The second beginning of things.* Her intentions pooled in her upturned palm. Reverence for God, regard for Man, even her devotion to her brothers brought her here. The only way to survive, to find a real life, was to swear her only allegiance to her own will. She stirred the blood cupped in her hands with the Intercessor shard. *The second beginning . . .*

The pain in her palm caused the light within her to fluctuate wildly. Deeper. She didn't cry out. Push it in deeper. She clenched her teeth, tightening her throat against a wave of nausea. Her Intercessor stirred, involuntarily lurching outward, but the shard met its forward thrust, sliding between the layers of bone like a slick needle. The moment of pain before her entire left side went numb continued to throb in her memory. She closed her eyes. They were coming. Her muscles loosened, allowing her head to swim up into that piercing blue sky, even as her heart beat heavily into the earth. They were coming back, to take what they could. When they returned, she would show them divine retribution. This time she would have the chance she was never given, because of course, this time she created the opportunity herself.

The yellow petals were small and fragile, defenseless even in this mild breeze.

She woke to a vibrating pressure opening thousands of tiny wounds in her chest. Her eyes fluttered open, her fists clenching. This couldn't be avoided. She fixed her stare on the scars across his arm as he marked her body. Those symbols were familiar, but she couldn't decipher them.

"I haven't done one of these in a long time. There hasn't been a need."

She started at the sound of Sebastian's voice, but only felt an uneasy intimacy when she heard Jeremy's words issue from her mouth. "I'm . . . grateful, sir."

"You're not the first Saros child I've encountered."

"I know, Lord Za'in." Her eyes moved over her skin, and she attempted to identify these features as belonging to Jeremy or herself, but her awareness kept slipping to other places. The vibration. The sigils. The fear.

"You've survived me. And I have plans for you."

She tried again to read Za'in's scars, but she could only think of that other boy's face. That dead soldier who brought her here. "Is this punishment then? For killing him, I mean."

"He was a Malak, and you'll do more than replace him. I wouldn't consider that a punishment, but an opportunity."

His name was Nathaniel. She remembered that, at least. She didn't know him, but still she experienced a cold twinge in some imagined hollow beneath her breastbone. Her defeated opponent was intelligent, powerful, but he didn't matter either, not even to his Lord. "How come that Malak knew about me?"

Sebastian pressed down harder with his needle. "It's sometimes very useful how these marks affect *humans* so differently . . ."

She didn't like the strange way he used that word. "So

this tattoo made him psychic?"

"He was assigned to do what he was able."

"But I can't do that, so—"

"The Malak might be dead, but he's still in service to me. Your abilities will be different, but your fate is the same. You're now a part of something greater than yourself."

She closed her eyes. She remembered giving in then. It wasn't comfortable, but she was the one that lived, not the Malak Nathaniel. And this way, she could take care of Kit. That was part of the deal. But soon she could feel Za'in trying to find his way inside, and she discovered that the others felt it too, but they were unable to resist. They told her that no one could escape it. It was a part of taking the mark, or any other Mods. It's not like they didn't have their benefits. She found that now her body could effortlessly perform once strenuous tasks, her reflexes were instant and her heightened strength gave her a very solid sense of freedom. The new joy she found in movement almost made her forget. But she didn't want to share it with Za'in. The others said there was one man that couldn't be reached into, one man that kept his free will and his soul . . . Michael Steelryn. If he could do it, she'd find a way to keep Za'in out too. The fire in her stomach burned hotter with the pressure of constant vigilance.

The world went black, and her arms jerked in an attempt to find her bearings. A green flower began to appear and she tried to turn from it, to let the darkness return, but the heat rose high into her chest and she was confronted with a six-pointed star nestled between the petals.

"Kayla."

"Yes, it's me . . ." She moaned, dropping her head.

"I apologize," Sebastian murmured. "It was unfair to give you my experiences without a veil to separate you, without a ledge for you to step back on. It obscured your identity just long enough for him to take advantage and split you further from yourself. Kayla, come back. But allow me to continue. Your potential, your Angelic nature . . . even your fragile human consciousness depends on the completion of our journey here."

Kayla's eyes scanned the blackness that surrounded her, but there was no escape. Her limbs were heavy and weak, as all of her vitality joined the fire rushing around her heart. She thought of Jeremy, but she couldn't even gather a sense of betrayal to fuel her. Sighing, she collapsed into the center of the flower as she was enveloped by its petals.

"I wasn't as cruel to my soldiers as he made it appear." Sebastian's voice gently stroked her threadbare nerves. "Michael understood the urgency of our cause and didn't take personally the sometimes harsh realities of this path." He paused, but still his whisper faintly wavered. "He was my first Arch."

Kayla raised her head suddenly, moved by the restrained emotion that weighed down his last five words. She searched for his face, his eyes, but he wasn't there. Instead, there were banyan trees and crisp air, her feet crunching over dead grass and hardy weeds. Michael was sitting in the clearing behind the church, leaning against an abandoned concrete tube. His head was thrown back, eyes closed, and his young face was pinched with frustration. As she approached, she could see nearly a dozen discarded books surrounding him, in various states of use and mutilation.

"You said I was an Angel or some such shit, but none of this makes sense," he muttered, kicking at one of the paperbacks as the rest of his body remained stiff and still.

"We're Nephilim, Michael. Descendants of Angels," Sebastian said gently.

"It doesn't explain anything. It's just a line in *Genesis*. Do I look like a giant? There's the *Book of Enoch*, but that's even more confusing. There are ancient aliens and *tennyo* . . . and none of this tells me why I'm here and why I'm this way." Michael opened his piercing eyes. "God failed, didn't he? Couldn't quite wipe us all out with the Flood before he fled and left us all here to rot . . ."

"This isn't a curse."

He sprang up, kicking around dirt as he paced. "Do you even know why I came away with you? I've hurt everyone . . . everyone! And not just potential step-dad deadbeats and other guys that ask for it, but people I actually like too. You know I tried to start a band?" He laughed bitterly. "I couldn't even argue with them about stupid shit without this thing getting in the way!" His voice lowered as he grasped his right wrist. "Angels walking around, stabbing drummers—yeah, real Biblical. And I can't even have a girlfriend. Because I'd . . . I'd hurt her too. This one girl, she must of really liked me, because she never told anyone that I . . . cut her. And I wasn't even mad, I was just, I just . . ." Blood was running down his arms as he tried to push his Intercessor back inside. He looked up at Sebastian, helplessness softening his green eyes.

Za'in stepped forward and gathered the boy into his arms. He gingerly untangled Michael's rigid fingers and eased his weapon back to its resting place. "I know. It's not what you deserved. But I can show you how to control your passions, to ensure that you only strike when it's necessary. I'm not giving you this gift so that you can waste it caterwauling in a garage or playing house with a human girl that will inevitably bore you. The purpose of your training will be to develop the tools to rise above the needless brutality and forge a world that you can be proud of."

Michael looked up at him through his tears, his eyes already narrowing again. "Prove it. I can read, and nothing in those books back up what you say. The closest thing to

your story is the *Book of Enoch*, and you can't even get that
fairy tale straight. Angels fell *here?* Wrong. Mount Hermon.
And you said they fell more than once, in more than one
place. There were two hundred that came down before God
imprisoned them and killed their offspring. Nothing about
eclipses, time-lapses, or survivors. You could at least study
the bullshit you're selling."

Sebastian smiled. "Parables."

Michael didn't realize he was knocked to the ground
until the shooting pain in his shoulder left him unable to
move. He looked up to see Za'in standing over him, a
twisted and barbed channel of bone issuing from his palm
and penetrating the boy's flesh.

"You're going to have to look below the surface,
Michael. God didn't fashion the universe in six days and
mold you from a tiny ball of clay. Yet, here we are. The
superficial details may not line up, but I see you feel my
divine influence. These books were created by man, to serve
purposes only man could devise. I found you, desperate and
lost in a bookstore, and you're continuing that futile search
here? Your answers aren't in those pages."

Michael closed his eyes, leaning into the agony that
radiated through his chest and arm. "Teach me," he
managed through clenched teeth.

Sebastian waited a moment before he retracted his blade
and knelt at the boy's side, his brows drawing together
softly. "This path isn't without pain," was the almost
inaudible murmur that escaped, before his mouth tightened
in a spasm of remorse. A warm light began to form in his
palm, and he pressed it to Michael's wound.

The young Steelryn pushed Za'in's hand away. "I know.
So leave it."

Kayla closed her eyes. She didn't need to dissolve into
Sebastian in order to feel this. She was still a part of it.

Am I the only one that isn't moved by this?

She cringed at Jeremy's thought. He shouldn't be here, inside her. It wasn't safe.

Good, you should be scared of him. The things he's done to Nephilim, the things he's done to Archs . . . I was set up, and so were you. It wasn't an accident that I found you, out there near Madeline. They left me to die, but I met his expectations and had a sufficient ability to heal. Mods that were killing Tregenne's experiments wouldn't finish me off so quickly. So I was the perfect one to find you, even if I didn't know it then. I knew I was supposed to ensnare you, but I didn't expect what you'd do to me. Well, I didn't, but he did. He threw us together because his guesses for an outcome are based on knowledge we haven't lived enough years to imagine. I don't care that what I feel for you was a part of his plan . . . at least I got to feel it. But I see now that's why I was made an Arch—just so I could become an abomination that would be compelled to hurt you, hunt you, and force you to grow, so you could return to him a more useful creature. I exist only because I have the strength to survive these fetters, just long enough for you to mature into what he needs you to become. At least I got the chance to figure it out and tell you: don't give in to him. It was all his will. None of this was an accident, or even fate. Not your parents meeting, not your birth, not their deaths—

Her heart lurched into her throat, and with it came the heat and light that had already filled most of her body. She choked as pale blue petals flew at her face, blinding her. "Jeremy!" Kayla held her breath. He was too reckless and he knew it. He wasn't even fighting visions with visions anymore. If all he had time for were a few panicked confessions . . . She had to go to him. Kayla tried to remember what happened before the light started to fill her. There were purple stones at her back. She gulped a mouthful of air and then pressed her shoulders hard into the earth. Sharp points of crystal dug into her flesh and she cried out, her eyes opening weakly to the real world. The sky looked strange. Kayla rolled over and rose onto her hands and knees before her limbs gave out and she collapsed against the ground. The earth was shifting sickeningly below her, and her entire body trembled with cold.

"So you'll die for him? You'll surrender your potential and give up all you've developed within yourself? Is that what you want?"

"I . . . want him . . . to live."

She felt Sebastian scoop her into his arms. "You must let me complete this process or there will be nothing left of you to fight for him. Tell him to let go. If he didn't interfere, you would be whole already. He is dangerously prolonging this. Demand that he yields!"

"Jeremy, I'm sorry . . ." was all she could manage. She felt sick and needed the flowers to return. A tightness grew in her, like a rubber band slowly stretching, but she was denied the release of it all ending in a sharp snap. Instead, the sensation slowly diffused and left her with an uneasy feeling in her stomach.

Sebastian was satisfied. "This path isn't without pain, but Michael never could accept that the pain would end. It will, if you will only let it subside."

The blue petals surrounded her, four times four. She stepped around them lightly, but they followed, stroking her arms and cheeks, and she felt the weight leave her body. There was peace here, but she knew she couldn't remain as she was indefinitely, warm in this illusion of safety.

"Why does shelter and comfort seem so distant to you?" Sebastian's quiet voice enveloped her. "Shouldn't a steady foundation be given, instead of constantly pursued? And you have so many assumptions. If the end was coming, then why would I urge you to develop your abilities? Of course there will be a change when the sky darkens, but it is inevitable—as natural as any other cycle of life, and as just as consequence. But while Nature is indifferent and vicious, casually leaving you to a life of mediocrity where your untapped gifts offer you nothing but confusion and isolation, I want to give you the chance to be whole. I want to equip you not only to survive this global change, but to thrive and allow your light to nourish all that touches you."

Kayla felt the heat in her throat push out the words. "I don't know what it means to be a Nephil."

"Of course not. You've only learned tricks. And they haven't been without sacrifice." His finger traced the scars on her back.

She drew away from him. "I had no control over that. It was my connection with Jeremy—"

"You are not chained to him! There is something there that must be severed, but you are unlike him. This link you perceive is only the consequence of his theft and misuse of one of my Modifications."

She clenched her fists. There were times when she wanted to blame it all on those Ruiners, but now she longed for it to be real, without the taint of darkness.

"A Nephil isn't tied to one mortal. She's a part of everything, attuned to all there is. Just open your eyes. You'll feel it."

With an exasperated sigh, Kayla prepared to raise a defiant gaze, but she was blinded by the light in her throat as it was expelled with her breath. When her vision cleared, she could see the moon, glowing brighter than any night in her memory. She sat up quickly and glanced around before springing to her feet. "This is real," she murmured, turning back to smile, astonished, at Sebastian.

He was silent, sitting comfortably in the dirt, his elbow crooked around his knee. His eyes didn't leave her, but he dropped his chin into his arm, not quite concealing the upturned corners of his mouth.

Kayla noticed thousands of tiny purple flecks glittering brightly across his clothes, his hair, his skin. She looked down on her own body, and was surprised she didn't notice, until now, the intensity of the quartzite's sparkle. Her gaze was pulled away from the little stars as a cool wind was dragged along her bare arms. She shivered, sighing, feeling as if she could easily be carried away by the gentle current, even as she imagined raising her arms and clawing the gust of air back to her. She let neither urge move her, passively watching the purple dust lift from her form and float away. Kayla wondered if it was unusual that she could sense each blade of grass or slab of marble where the stone flakes landed.

She stepped forward, following the flight of her shimmering adornments. Her pace quickened as she realized how lightly she moved over the earth, but soon a nearby musical sound grasped her curiosity, causing her to pause. She turned her head, searching for the source of the lilting notes, but it was the vibrations that accompanied the fire in her throat that caused her to recognize her own laugh. The sound continued, louder, this time accented with the satisfaction of knowing that the music she heard belonged to her.

Kayla was running again, completely unencumbered by the weight of her body, her senses her only guide and delight. She caught the sharp scent of grapes growing somewhere outside the walls of the monastery, and her flight changed direction. Her excitement grew as she glided up the curved staircase, and when she thrust her head through the pointed arch of the window she was rewarded with a brisk rush of wind and recognition. Wild grape vines crawled up a pair of crooked trees and she could taste a pleasant bitterness on her tongue. Kayla closed her eyes. It wasn't just the wine she could imagine, but there were the flavors of the soil that nourished the vines' roots, cut with the dull taste of rainwater. The earth was deep, spicy, dense, and it seemed to continue on forever. Her senses dropped down through the bottomless mountains, echoing through dank caves, empty except for traces of . . . herself. Kayla's brow furrowed as she followed the winding threads of bone, braided with bits of quartzite, that tunneled through the ground and arced up into the cold subterranean air. They coiled around something breathing, sinewy, and not only filled with fire, but ravaged by it. She tightened her grip, inhaling salt and desperation.

I've tasted you too.

Her eyes went wide, but her view from the window was gone.

Sometimes cinnamon, almonds, lime. I don't know if it's you changing or me.

She dropped her head into her hands.

That's the trouble with being at one with the universe. Not all of it is beautiful or obedient. But your spiritual guide there cut me off last time. Ask His Benevolence what happened to your parents. Let's see that vision.

Kayla could feel the heat in him subside, then rise again, burning his insides.

Listen. I might almost know what it feels like to be an Angel, but it's only because of you. I'm human. You're made to ascend, but I don't think even these fetters are going to pull me through this one. I won't be able to be your reminder, so make him show you. Hold on to it. Don't let him get away with it.

Her fire plummeted through the mountain, yearning to cradle the blaze that devoured him with her own healing light. But instead she was seared by a channel of flame that ran up the center of her body, pressuring the space between her brows. Sebastian's voice softly landed on her forehead, as cool as the two indigo petals that soothed her burning skin.

"This process has been about banishing your misgivings and putting an end to your ignorance. I will show you why Michael and Kiera laid down their lives, what we waited for, what we saw in the distance. That dream isn't so distant now, through you . . ."

This new sensation that gathered above the bridge of her nose began to not only numb her face, but also her awareness of both the outside world and her inner thoughts. She allowed the glimpses of another world to become her reality.

Michael didn't want to open his eyes. He could feel the tired earth beneath him, defeated and bearing weight. The sky above was open, and he could hear the air whistling through vacant channels as he rested in the rift between a profane and perished world. His body was heavy, detached. He wasn't tired of fighting, no more than he was weary of the rise and fall of his breath, but he knew he didn't want to build anymore. The stronger he became, the clearer his mind . . . the more powerless he felt. Everything Sebastian taught him, all they worked toward, it all seemed futile as each day the world grew sicker. With all they were capable of, even they couldn't make this world Heaven. It didn't want the change.

A squeezing that began beneath his down-turned palm splayed his fingers out and pulled his mind back to its resting place in the grass, beside her. "Kiera . . ." he breathed. She relaxed her hand, and he was forced to let his muscles go slack so that he could feel their palms pressed tightly together again.

The world inside her was serene. Michael breathed deeply, inhaling bits of stars and scripture. In her, he could see the stacked concrete slums dissolve into a field of wildflowers and mystery. The worn highways, littered with refuse and clogged with the blind and hysterical, were now clean passages where the enlightened glided to their eventual destinations. Instead of the suffocating jumble of matter and existence, there was space . . . finally, empty space. Kiera's reality had them lying in a wide, lush meadow beneath a boundless sky. He didn't want to open his eyes and acknowledge their position on this tiny strip of grass, trapped between towering, hastily constructed buildings and lidded with buzzing power lines.

"What you think is real is only a fleeting vision," she murmured.

"Yours is an escape, a fantasy—"

"It's within and it's eternal."

Michael wanted to pull his hand away in anger, but he couldn't bear to lose her star-filled sky. So much was wrong with the world; how could a vacant Heaven heal it all? He thought of his mother, fragile and flawed. He wasn't able to save her. Michael let his pain seep into Kiera's palm. Every violent mistake, every fearful action—didn't he do as much harm as any human? With all his power, he was still impotent. His work with Sebastian was for the purpose of controlling his impulses, utilizing his gifts, and sharpening his abilities. The Nephilim were the closest thing this world had to gods, and still he was helpless.

The space between their hands caught fire, and Michael gripped her fingers protectively. Kiera's visions seared his consciousness, and he couldn't ignore her past. A beautiful Angel, convinced she was unholy, and striving so hard to be a saint. While he tried to protect his mother from her own weakness, it was all Kiera could do to defend herself from constant attempts to extinguish her light. She was hospitalized, medicated, exorcised. She had cried out to God for deliverance, but it was Sebastian who answered her prayers.

" 'He brought me up out of the pit of destruction, out of the miry clay, and He set my feet upon a rock, making my footsteps firm.' "

Michael grit his teeth. That's exactly what Sebastian did for them. But soon even the Heavens would plummet and the Earth would slide beneath them. She wouldn't understand. Did she even know?

Sebastian was right. She had to be protected from darkness, even if it was necessary, even if it was their own. He would use the gentlest words, instead of giving sound to the desolation that haunted him. Michael slowly untightened his jaw, preparing to speak her language. " 'When the foundations are being destroyed, what can the righteous do?' "

Kiera rolled onto her side, drawing nearer to him. Her face was lit with the thrill of his voice forming those familiar words. She pulled his hand to her cheek and he felt his cold skin awakened by her breath. " 'Nevertheless, the righteous will hold to their ways, and those with clean hands will grow stronger.' "

He didn't know if his hands were without blame, but they felt lighter now that they were caught in her guiltless grasp. For her, he would go forward, endlessly. For what she carried inside her, he'd build something beautiful atop the ashes of everything that ever hurt them.

Kayla could feel the heat in her brow extending through her body as a shaft of light, only escaping through her palms and the blazing sigils on her back. She was sprouting wings of cool, white fire, dripping indigo tongues of flame. She waited for a familiar darkness to pull her back down into uncertainty, but that influence was so vague and distant, it might have been imagined. Still, there was something she wanted to remember.

The last time she saw Michael's face, he wasn't this wistful boy, clutching withered blades of grass. He was a vision that she couldn't imagine forgetting for eleven years, but somehow she had been separated from this moment for so long. Sometime between then and now, she had caught a glimpse . . . his somber mouth, forming urgent words, kissing her goodbye. His eyes had changed too. The bitterness was gone, and any pain that was present was too tethered to understanding to be recognized as suffering. What did he tell her then?

At first, Kayla could only hear him muttering as he knelt before her and dug through his pockets. "It makes sense. From the beginning, this was your world. It should be you." He found the tiny box and thrust it into her hands. "You did well, little one. Take this and close your eyes. You'll wake up somewhere peaceful."

She didn't obey. He was pressing a white, gnarled spike through his hand. "Will you be there too?" she whispered.

Michael circled his arms around her, and she felt heat rising between his hands, behind her back. He rested his forehead on her shoulder. "This will only be a dream. You'll build a new reality, Kayla. I've done all I could. This was inevitable. This was why . . . everything . . . everything . . ." His eyes were shining when he raised his head, and he smiled now as words failed him.

"Will I be alone?"

There was a whirring sound coming from behind her, and she pressed her face to Michael's neck to shield herself from the blinding light he was generating. His voice was her comfort, easing her fears with one of her mother's favorite prayers. " 'If I go up to the heavens, you are there; if I make my bed in the depths, you are there. If I rise on the wings of the dawn . . .' "

Kayla slowly stepped back, allowing herself to stand inside the fire between his hands as she recited the words with him. " '. . . If I settle on the far side of the sea, even there your hand will guide me—' "

Kiera cried out somewhere in the distance, but Michael's stare forbade her to turn her head. He raised his voice, " '—your right hand will hold me fast . . .' "

His eyes broke from hers for just the span of one breath, and in the stiffness of his features, she recognized a glance meant just for Asher, even if she couldn't read its content. Michael's gaze grasped her again as they both mouthed the words. " 'If I say, "Surely the darkness shall fall on me," even the night shall be light about me; the night will shine like the day . . .' "

The fire erupted, and she could feel the light shooting straight through the crown of her head. Inside her, every stain was burned away, leaving only silence, and she opened her eyes to the night that fell on Velsmere. Her flames were cascading back to earth like a thousand white petals. Kayla could see the days ahead of her as infinite paths stretching out and over the mountains. They all led back up to the sky, to the moment when the sun would go dark. The earth below her was black, dormant, waiting to be awakened by her touch. She was the star that would light the world again.

44

Jeremy held his breath until he couldn't help but gasp for air, and after a few shaky inhalations, he started the cycle again. This was the only way to keep from losing himself. He could feel his grip on reality slipping, now that he could no longer perceive it with his senses. Even his internal awareness was blunted. He couldn't feel her at all. Was she still alive? He was certain that if she was destroyed by that fire, he would experience her loss as some prolonged and conscious evisceration, rather than this vague impression that he'd been gutted. Jeremy allowed his breath to return, so that his lips could form her name. His mouth trembled, not knowing where to begin.

"I believe the word you're searching for is 'Kayla.'"

He shuddered at the sound of Tregenne putting on his professor voice. Still, his fear subsided with the mention of her name.

"Should I not have uttered that combination of sounds? I was charged with dividing you two, after all. Ah, well, you won't remember it long. Go ahead, Saros. Tell me who you're yearning for."

Jeremy's mouth was tight. She had disappeared again so suddenly from his mind. Her name, her face, her voice . . . gone. There was nothing he had to hold on to, beyond his driving need to find her, to possess her, but without the knowledge of her identity or the comfort of her memory, he found no ground beneath him, no calm center in the rising panic that threatened to devour him.

"This is Hell, Saros," Tregenne murmured. "Complete separation from the Divine."

Jeremy swallowed a nauseating wave of despair before forcing his face into an expression that, despite his best efforts, was more grimace than grin. "I thought my punishment was listening to your shit. But you've fallen too. While some new world is being built, you're stuck down here with me. You're an Arch. Wasn't there anyone else to—"

"No, Saros. They're all . . . occupied. This duty was my humble request, of course."

"Fucking with me is more entertaining than what's going on out there? Yeah right. So what's this really abou—"

"Suffer quietly!" Gabriel growled, the smooth layers finally torn from his voice.

Jeremy choked as a blow struck the cluster of bone that wrapped around his throat. His limbs jerked against these new fetters, but he was allowed little movement beyond the clenching of his fists. This was nothing like being trapped beneath the mountain. There, he was bound and consumed in fire, but those chains, those flames, they were hers. He was ready to accept both the certainty and finality of death; those qualities of his demise were a comfort beneath all his regrets.

But then Tregenne had come and his world went dark. The new fetters the Arch clamped around his head were different from the ones that crawled over his arms and kept him tied to her. These bones took his sight and left him without any recognizable foundations, severing his connection to what, for so long, had been his closest glimpse of purpose. It was hard to say what came next, but he had the sense that the hardened shell that covered much of his body devoured the flesh beneath. Even with that lack of sensation, he knew he was grasped by his armpits and dragged through the wet pebbles of the cave. The stale air lifted and he felt himself caught in a steep ascent, his lower back scraped by stones and prickly weeds. He had no strength with which to struggle, and his mind was too occupied to protest. He'd rather burn the last of his energy uselessly defying the Ruiners from within by not abandoning the search for the memory of her eyes.

The raw skin above the waist of his torn pants was suddenly pulled along a slick, cold floor. His back made contact with a wall, but instead of the fetters piercing and tearing that surface, he could feel them join with the barrier, fusing his body to the structure by his shoulders and spine. He didn't know how long he sat there, sightless, moved by dreams and illusions, waiting for breaks in his transparent hallucinations. Those moments were opportunities to piece together what events led him to this place, but any clarity he reached was briefly held.

It was then that Tregenne's voice broke through his fragile web of memories, just as Jeremy reached deeper into that tangle in search of her name. That sound pulled him from his feverish pursuit, and his mouth followed old patterns to keep his fear at bay. Tregenne's responses were of the expected variety, and it was a small comfort that some things were unchanged, even as Jeremy now willed his bruised throat to complete the motion of swallowing. He knew Tregenne struck him because he probed too insistently, but if he remained still, if he waited, the old professor would win out over the savage. Gabriel was intolerant, vicious, but he liked to instruct before the slaughter.

Jeremy willed his breath to slow, his muscles to uncoil and go limp. He felt the effects of his exhaustion expressed as patience.

Just as he began to drift into an uneasy state of near detachment, Tregenne spoke again. "That's better. Some work requires silence. Other tasks benefit from discussion, but even you must admit you have little to offer there."

"Because you're already sucking my memories with this thing?" Jeremy muttered, weakly shaking his bound head.

"There is nothing you know, remembered or forgotten, that isn't already old news for us."

"Yeah, I got that. I'm not a threat," he laughed bitterly. "But it's more fun for you if I know why this is happening, what's coming, what you're going to do to me . . ."

"Correct. If there can be no stimulating exchange of ideas, I'll take the consolation prize." Tregenne's voice faded and grew louder again as he moved through the room. His steps only sounded occasionally, but the rustling of papers and heavy, metallic clinks gave away the continuous movements of his hands. "Did you ever think you were a threat, Saros?" he chortled. "Hmm, that could be the Ruiners talking. You've been a tool, kid. Don't try to make sense of it all. You were a curiosity, a possibility, and it was just a process of elimination that drew you into a larger plan. Don't make the mistake of thinking it was woven around you."

Jeremy could feel Tregenne's fingers probing his chest below his collarbone. "But now . . . it depends on me."

Gabriel was still for only a moment. "You've been acquired. There are no more acts of obedience for you to perform. You even managed to return her in a more desirable condition than the one you found her in." He paused, expelling another dry laugh. "Not familiar? I might have to adjust your Mods. You aren't supposed to forget her completely, but just enough to make this interesting."

Jeremy frowned. Memories were falling away, but his passion hadn't waned. His captor had misread the tightening of his muscles. Did he really give her over to them? If he betrayed his brightest light, then wasn't he to blame for being cast into this all-consuming darkness? His thoughts were interrupted by something cold and wet swiping circles across his skin, followed by a sudden, piercing stab in his chest. He struggled to inhale, but that only underscored the sensation of the needle penetrating his flesh.

"Don't move!" Tregenne barked. "I'm not going to waste any Lidocaine on you, so you'll just have to take it." His voice dropped again into the almost pleasant drone of a lecture. "I've accepted that this might not go the way I imagined. I'm content to see the events unfold as they must. I'll speak as if you still have the capacity to listen and understand, and I'll sort out the effects of these Ruiners on the brain of a Saros child later."

The pressure on the outside of Jeremy's body remained still and constant, but he could feel a tiny wire moving deeper within him. He kept his breathing shallow, promising the shadow of her memory that his surrender would only be temporary.

"The coming storm won't kill us all," Tregenne continued, "in fact, some of us will adapt. But not without help. I've developed various Modifications for both humans and Nephilim, but even you've seen how some of those ended. Za'in has been slowly fortifying his body with sacred blood and Angelic script, and it was his method of grafting foreign Intercessor shards that inspired some of my projects, including my input on Core development, and the Ruiners, of course. But there were setbacks. I was disappointed to see most of my early experiments destabilize, mutate, and either destroy themselves or need to be put down. I had to start over. Start small. Tiny slivers of bone embedded beneath the skin were generally successful, but most subjects couldn't take on any more than that. For instance, we both know what happened to Fiora."

Jeremy's body was moved by a quick spasm, and Tregenne briefly stilled his hands, chuckling. "You remember that one, do you? It's funny what sticks. At any rate, your 'fetters' haven't restrained you much. Yes, you were tied to Za'in, you were steered, but instead of being consumed by the power that clothed you, you were improved. Stronger, faster, impervious to injury . . . you required very little sustenance or sleep, and your means of perception were, for the most part, sharpened. You also were able to be a conduit for divine energy, which, for me, was the most exciting aspect of your transformation. Still, none of this was singularly unique. But every time I thought you'd join the others and burn out, you would find your equilibrium. Now this experiment wasn't strictly scientific; you weren't the only variable. The young Steelryn was our second wild card. You've been a fascinating pair to observe."

A small, but deep, slice joined whatever punctured Jeremy's flesh, and he felt something wider than the needle begin to burrow down into his chest. There was pain, but he felt strangely detached from these precise, violent sensations. Fluid ran down his ribs as Tregenne continued to force those instruments inside, pausing at times to press something soft against his skin, leaving sticky smears around his wound.

"However, now we're in the end times and there is little

room for pleasant diversions. Your actions in Azevin allowed Za'in to enter your Angel, and although that gave you the benefit of some deserved silence, you probably noticed some of your new strengths have weakened. Za'in may be as close to God as we have encountered, but his energy is not limitless and his attention can only be focused in so many directions. You won't last long. But a part of you will.

"As you can see, Saros, Modifications do not an Angel make. You are strong enough to survive these devices, but you're certainly no specimen of divinity. What Za'in is constructing won't be without flaws, but you'll be surprised what a little sacred bone and quartzite can do to a human body under the right circumstances. And your blood will ensure that our test subjects survive their rebirth."

"Are you doing the same thing to her?" Jeremy breathed through stiff lips. Something was tugging at his skin, drawing the exposed end of the invading tube tight to his chest.

"Of course not. She has a more active part to play. This is your fate alone because this is all you can offer."

Jeremy's veins awakened with a cold rush, then immediately began to slowly thaw, his energy fading with the returning warmth. "Take what you want now," he whispered. "You won't keep me here long."

"Don't you think that sort of bravado is pathetic at this point? How do you propose to escape and rescue her?" Tregenne paused to regard Jeremy's subdued silence before erupting into laughter. "It can't be . . . you're hoping that she saves *you*? Really, Saros, you could at least display the dignity of an Arch before death. Regardless, these Ruiners work both ways. You have disappeared from her thoughts, but she won't experience the conflict you suffer because she has no reason to fight to regain her memories, to hold on to some ghost sensation of attachment. She doesn't want to remember you."

Jeremy felt his face relax into what was almost a smile. Even with these fetters, he didn't forget that there was something that lifted the senselessness from what he endured, in penance or in sacrifice. There was darkness, but he wasn't the only one standing between it and the end. She was what he needed to reach, but there was another that shared his torment, and the will to keep going . . . "You went through all this to keep her from me. This prison for my weakness—is it strong enough to hold her? You better be sure because I'm not the only one you have to erase."

"Serafin?" Tregenne snorted. "He died in Azevin ten years ago."

"Yeah. And that still didn't stop him."

The almost musical sound of glass vials softly colliding with one another was muffled by Gabriel's hand as he rose from Jeremy's side. "That sort of persistence you admire is exactly what led you into this position."

Jeremy listened to Tregenne's echoing steps disappear behind the heavy slam of a door. He was finally alone. He let his head hang, almost enjoying the sensation of gravity pulling the lower part of his face in the opposite direction of his Ruiners. He knew it was hopeless, that Serafin couldn't win. Behind that great warrior was an army of four kids, armed with novelty Mods. Jeremy inhaled sharply, his head painfully snapping back. There was another. An intense energy, tightly contained, thinly shrouded . . . and so familiar. Why couldn't he remember? He swallowed hard, clinging to the comfort that although his connection to anything higher was now severed, and the holiness he constantly condemned, but always desired, was now forever out of his reach, some aspect of it was at Serafin's right hand, and however it ended, it would end here.

419

45

Asher kept his back to the wall and his eyes craning up toward the window as he sat crouched in the ruins of Velsmere, waiting for night to fall. He had been too reckless. This was his last chance to atone for yesterday's actions, and he needed to be patient and approach the monastery with stealth. He released the handle of his kukri to pull the wrinkled and bent card from beneath his poncho. *The Seven of Swords.* His thumb traced jagged circles over the card's surface while his watchful gaze remained focused on his surroundings. Did she mean to leave this behind? Did she realize what she'd done?

He regretted his weakness. In those moments with her when he allowed his grip to loosen, he still didn't experience the surrender he thought he desired. Instead, his isolation was even more apparent. She had turned her face towards him, searching for light, but found only the shadows of an unresolved past. He wasn't a man. He was flesh, animated by some purpose that grew vaguer with every lonely year that passed. She woke the hope that slept deep within him, she sent energy rushing into his legs, but she also reminded him of everything he tried to drown beneath his single-minded goal. When she touched him, she saw the desperation he sought to conquer . . . and she saw Saros.

Asher returned the card to his pocket, his trembling fingers grasping his weapon again with an unyielding grip. He had no choice but to leave her then, to find his balance, but little time passed before he heard raised voices and smelled her fire charging the stale air of the winery. He beat down the door in time to see Saros fling his body into the heart of the flames, and although the force lifted Kayla from the ground, throwing her back, nothing human could stop her. They were gone. All that remained was the flashlight rolling to a stop, settling in a crack in the concrete, illuminating a card that lay face down.

He had fallen to his knees, gently lifting the card to see the *Seven of Swords* revealed. It was such a short time since she read him this warning, and he tried to strengthen her with his faith, but still she chose to disappear. He felt the edges of the card press painfully into his palm and fingers before it was crushed in his grip. He wasn't blameless. It was the third time he faltered, allowing his desires to give rise, and how many other countless times had his glance, his touch, spoke less of duty and more of need?

It was then Asher remembered feeling the presence of the others behind him, not staring with bewilderment into the empty room, but tensely looking to him for guidance. He held his breath, slowly rising to his feet, and then he abruptly turned and forced himself through the doorway, shoving aside the huddled bodies that blocked his path.

"Serafin!" Bruno's voice called out behind him. "What should we do now?"

Asher kept walking. He only escaped the alarmed and plaintive sounds that followed him when the door of the winery closed at his back. Asher stood in the rain, stilled for a moment by the sensation of wet droplets stinging his cheeks, but soon he was moving again, making his way in the dark through unfamiliar streets.

"Asher! Asher, stop!" Kittie's cry halted his steps. "What are you doing?"

His head was bowed, his hair hanging loosely around his face. "The same thing as always. Chasing after Steelryns and their ghosts."

Kittie approached cautiously. "Yes, I know," she whispered, gently slipping her hand between his heavy palm and stiff fingers, "but let's return to the winery, stay together, and stick to your plan—"

"My plan?" Asher raised his red-rimmed eyes to regard Kittie and the four boys who sloshed towards them through the mud. "We've been running towards our deaths this entire time. Is that a plan? You want us to stay together?" He threw her hand back at her, his voice growing suddenly louder. "I never asked any of you to follow me! I didn't want that. Either way, my failure damns you to die, but you never needed to know the reason. And I don't want to see it." He turned away from their shocked stares and stepped blindly forward.

"It doesn't matter what you want!"

Asher's balance was almost taken by a strong hand grasping his arm and yanking it back and down. He twisted around, stooped, to face Kittie, who wouldn't release her grip.

"It doesn't matter what you want," she said again, her voice dropping. "We're soldiers, both of us. I'm through standing by and watching it all happen. I can't do that anymore. But I'm stuck in this kind of body and I can't go alone. You're not leaving me behind."

Asher felt her eyes holding his still, even as she let go of his arm, and he swallowed a rising pressure in his throat. "I'm not a soldier anymore. I'm an avenger. I couldn't fill Michael's shoes and I couldn't fight beneath anyone else. Under my leadership, the Resistance was slaughtered. And they were soldiers. These boys are not."

Bruno stepped forward, tearing his eye patch from his face and flinging it into the muck. "I know I'm just a scared kid. I know I'm not strong like you or all berserker like Saros. But if life as we know it is almost over, I'd like mine to mean something."

"We kind of have to, right? I mean, we accidentally helped Tregenne in all sorts of twisted shit, I'm sure—" Kerif gulped. "Uh, yeah, sorry about that . . ." He stopped fidgeting with his jewelry as he allowed his words to slow and voice to deepen. "I want to make up for it. Really."

Fec forced his face into the most serious expression he could manage. "We've been protectin' M'ss Kayla this long—we can't aband'n 'er now! C'mon, Serafin, we don' screw up *all* th' time . . ."

Vic entered the circle, laying his hand on his brother's shoulder. "We can't just start wandering again, not now that you've given us purpose."

Asher watched them silently before closing his eyes. "I wouldn't know where to lead you," he murmured. "I don't know where Kayla went."

Kittie braved taking his hand again. "But I do. I can sense Jeremy. He's beneath the ground, in a cold, hollow place—"

"Where?" Asher asked urgently, his eyes regaining their usual composed and observant focus.

"I . . . I know he's close, to the west, but it feels really weird. I can't keep my concentration on him for very long," Kittie said, her voice quavering.

"But Kayla is with him still?"

"I think so. He's . . . afraid."

"Then they're in Velsmere." He tightened his grip before he released her hand and began to hurry through the streets again.

"What about waiting until morning?" Kittie called out as she trailed him.

Bruno was quick to follow. "What about *us?*"

"If you insist on following me, you'll have to accept that the strategy is unsound," he muttered in answer to both of their questions.

The pirates shrugged, unconcerned, while Kittie trudged on, her face grim. Vic lifted her onto his shoulders as they passed her, hurrying to match Asher's swift pace.

It was still dark when they reached the marina. There were several small boats docked and bobbing in the sludgy water, but the pirates ran to the only one that appeared to have a motor. Asher stared out into the darkness, his eyes searching the leaning watchtowers and the spaces between the warped boards of the surrounding structures.

Kerif roused him from his silent vigilance. "If there's anyone out there, they won't see us."

Asher turned around to see him raise his hand towards Fec, as the scrawny pirate expelled a cloud of smoke that engulfed the row of boats. Within moments, that suspiciously dense fog diffused into a delicate haze that gently obscured the sight of anything beyond it. Asher began to walk towards the gloom, but almost immediately he was lost and disoriented in the thick air.

A hand gripped his shoulder and Kerif's voice reached him again. "That's how they'll feel." The raised lines on the pirate's arm pulsed and the illusion faded.

Asher didn't glance at his companion, but freed himself and ran into the spreading miasma that surrounded the now visible boat. When he was on board, he looked to Bruno.

"Is there a Core? Can you get it started?"

"It's definitely been adapted, but it looks like they must take the Core out at night."

"Shit, we can't take a rowboat out there! It would make more sense to wait for the ferryman," Kerif complained.

"I'm not sure he's still in business," Vic said quietly, looking back at the sagging buildings near the shore.

"Do I 'ave t'do *ev'rythin'?*" Fec yowled out the side of his mouth. He thrust a small object into Bruno's hand.

"Where did you get this?" the Captain breathed, lifting a fold of the stained cloth that wrapped the black mass.

"Tha' crazy lady pulled't off Saros. Looks like'a Core t' me!"

There truly was power in that tangle of bone, as it soon enabled the boat to skim over the water in little upward jerks. Asher couldn't see Velsmere in the distance, but he glanced back towards Cormina to watch the sun rise over the broken and glittering roof tiles of a sunken civilization. He let his gaze sweep over the empty horizon as he sped towards this final chance to keep his promise to Michael. His companions remained quiet and distant, barely breathing while dawn unfolded.

The tense peace the ocean's beauty brought him was shattered by the sudden lurching of the boat, and he lost his footing, his body colliding with the gunwale. The vessel bobbed restlessly, but no longer moved forward.

"It's dust!" Bruno cried as the pirates pressed in close around him, all protesting that they could squeeze more fuel from their power source.

"The energy his fetters contain is more intense and brief than what is expected from a Core," Kittie whispered near Asher's side.

"But it's not completely extinguished," Vic intoned. Clumps of ash and splinters of bone were cupped in his dirty hands. He gingerly brought his palms together, the ridges below his wrist swelling. When his hands parted again, there was a tiny, dark lump resting between the deep creases of his weathered skin. "I'll strengthen what power is left in these remnants," he said as Bruno dropped the nugget into the Core chamber.

The motor sputtered to life again and the boat dragged itself forward. Vic's eyes were closed in silent concentration, his Mods flushed and throbbing. Their progress was slowed, but they were moving closer to her. Asher watched the pirates—a surreal display of quiet purpose. The Captain was confidently guiding their craft to Velsmere while his crew focused their attention on the tasks their Mods allowed them.

Kittie clasped her hands around Asher's and urged him to sit beside her. "At this rate, it will be a few more hours before we get to shore. You might not get another opportunity to sleep."

"Perhaps not." His words were clipped and short, and there were too many concerns that kept his eyes from meeting hers. "Do you have a location on Saros yet? Anything you can sense about Kayla?"

"He's still in that cave. I can feel us getting closer."

"And Kayla?" he asked sharply.

"She . . . trapped him there." Kittie nervously circled one of her braids around her finger. Her voice was quiet, her words halting. "She's gone, and he's . . . calling out to her."

"God damn it. She went to the monastery alone, didn't she?"

Kittie didn't answer.

"When we get to shore, I want you to free Saros. He'll be able to tell us more about her location, her state . . . And if I fall, I know he'll—"

"What must I do to make you sleep?" Kittie interjected,

her face suddenly pale and close to his.

"There are no promises that can do that."

"Threats, then? If you refuse me now, you'll have all five of us trailing behind you, without Jeremy's strength. I'll leave him there, I swear."

Asher's shoulders shrugged in silent laughter. "Is this how you got things done with him?"

"He's like you. Tears and violence turn the world, but they can't bend his will. So I have to sink lower."

Asher felt her lips against his forehead before he was enveloped by a brief moment of bliss, followed by dreamless darkness.

A heavy boom and metallic screech shook Asher awake, and he fought to stand as the boat pitched and swayed beneath him.

"The Core, it ruptured. But still, this shouldn't have happened! I don't know if the chamber was cracked, or if it's 'cuz it belonged to Saros, or if Vic lent it too much strength." Bruno was pulling on his hair. "God, what am I saying? We should never have used it—it wasn't even a *Core!*"

Asher noticed that his feet were wet and the sun was in the wrong place in the sky before he could acknowledge his hand gripping the boat's railing so that he could remain upright, while the stern dipped below the surface of the water.

"As'f we never sunk'a boat b'fore," Fec coughed.

"Yeah, we know the drill," Kerif sighed wearily as he swung his legs over the rail and jumped down into the sea.

"We're about a mile from shore. We'll make it." Vic's words were expelled with some effort, his Modified arm visibly bruised and limp at his side.

The sun had set when they all gave up the ferry. Asher

swam with Kittie on his back, slowly, so that the exhausted pirates didn't fall too far behind. "What did you do? You took the entire day from me."

"Do you think I didn't notice that you haven't allowed yourself to really rest, especially since Jeremy joined us? You can't live like you're not human. You can't always be there to watch them, and you can't will yourself to match the powers he now holds, especially not without the curse that comes with those abilities. If you want to save Kayla, you need your body to cooperate. If you were awake, you only would have weakened yourself further with anxiety. You couldn't have made the vessel move any faster than Vic pushed it. And look at the boys now. A full day of driving their Mods to the limit. Only the Captain suffers from the weariness of ordinary men."

Asher turned to see his companions trailing far behind him, struggling to move forward on their tired limbs. In the distance, the boat was turned on its side, sinking quickly into the darkness. He knew she was right, but that didn't make it any easier to accept what she did. He always sensed that he was shown only the mild fringes of her abilities, but until now he felt confident that the understanding between them kept him safe from the direct effects of her power. Perhaps she was simply becoming bolder, now that the dwindling days were bringing her closer to a moment where she would have to reveal her true nature, whatever that might be.

He unclasped her hands and pulled her arms away from where they draped around his neck. "Let's hope you have another trick up your sleeve that will keep them from drowning." Asher swam back towards the pirates and offered his strength to his weakening companions.

When they finally collapsed against Velsmere's sands, Asher flopped onto his back, panting, and looked to the moon as he waited for his limbs to regain their warmth. "Kittie," he gasped, "has anything changed? Where are they?"

"He's . . . gone."

Asher turned his head to see her huddled face-first in the sand, her knees drawn up to her chin, her little fists balled close to her ears, catching handfuls of hair. He barely recognized her when she raised her head.

"They killed Jeremy," she whispered.

"Are you certain? There was another time that you couldn't sense his presence—"

"Serafin!" Kerif screamed as the waves pushed him to shore on his hands and knees.

Asher twisted his body up to see the pirate collapse in the sand, his jeweled fingers weakly reaching for the needle protruding from his neck.

Kittie didn't notice. "Swear to me that you'll make them pay . . ."

Fec was the next to fall as he rushed to his comrade's side, and when Asher rose to his knees he noticed a dart in the sand where he once lay.

Bruno was sending his coins out into the surrounding rock formations while Vic stumbled towards his fallen brother.

"I'll bet it was just as much Tregenne as Za'in. I'll kill them both myself . . . I'll find a way!" she screamed. Her skin sparked, setting the air around her ablaze. Three needles shot out from the darkness and pierced her chest, but she only glowed brighter before they dropped down into the sand at her feet. Two men, dressed in the armor of Za'in's soldiers, emerged from the cliffs and ran towards them, weapons drawn. Kittie shuddered at the sight of their dark uniforms and cried out again, a wordless expression of grief and wrath.

Asher fell down onto his elbows, blinded by an explosion of her brilliance, his ears ringing. He kept his head lowered as he crawled towards her, waiting for the darkness to return, but when his hands found her soft form nestled in the sand, his vision began to clear. The two soldiers had collapsed just a few feet away, while more were now issuing forth from their hiding places. Asher turned his head back to the shore and watched Vic dragging his fallen friends towards the shelter of the towering rocks, protected by Bruno's projectiles. Gold and silver sliced beneath masks, severed straps, and opened red streams at points of articulation. But there were too many soldiers. As they closed in, Asher tried to draw his kukris and stand, but something held him still.

"Serafin!" Bruno shook his head, his panicked eyes searching for his leader, but even as he looked towards Asher, there was no recognition in his stare before he was chained and gagged.

Asher struggled to move, to speak, as his friends were taken, but he was helpless. He looked to Kittie, and the world dissolved.

"They can't see us," she said quietly. "No one can."

"You're Nephilim? Why did you wait so long to—"

"No, I'm not. I had to hide the truth from Za'in, but there is no way he missed feeling me now . . ."

"What are you, Kittie?"

Her smile threatened to tear her face in two. "Powerless, unnecessary, extinct . . ."

"You're an Angel."

She flinched, her mouth forming soundless words before her defeated voice reached his ears. "I'm nothing. Promise me . . . just promise me you'll kill them."

"Kittie . . ."

"I wanted to save Creation, because that's what my God

wanted. I never thought about what *I* wanted before. I had no desires that weren't His. This was why I first protected Jeremy—he would grow to be a crucial player, so I had to ensure his survival. I became this," she motioned to her small frame, "so that he might trust me, but I lost something along the way. Without God, without my natural form, soon it was no longer about saving the humans' world. There had to be a world left, simply so that Jeremy could live in it. That was all. I loved him. I loved him more than anything," she sobbed. Her light flared and her form flickered. She was a lion, an armored warrior, a golden woman, a pillar of fire. "I know you want to stop the darkness from forever descending. I know you want to save Kayla. These are my goals too. But there is one thing I can't do. Without His command, I can't end human life, no matter how tainted it has become."

"You told me that you did take a life once."

"An Angel. I killed an Angel. And I became the last." Kittie didn't avoid Asher's wide stare. "Humans weren't the only ones that feared Saros children. And although we can take very little direct action, my Brother in Fire was influencing humans to murder Jeremy. He was just a child. No, he wasn't innocent, he never was innocent, but I saw hope in him, and beauty. I took him and ran. I tried to save him every way I knew how until there was no other way. It changed me. I must have looked like a monster to Jeremy then, but he was unshaken. He nursed me back to health and never asked questions. So you see, Asher, I am truly helpless. What can I do alone?"

Asher moved suddenly, taking her into his arms. "I can make no promises. I will do what I can for Kayla, for Michael, for Kiera . . . and your Jeremy. But you know the score."

"Za'in by a landslide. I know." Her laugh was half a sob,

and when her tears landed on his shoulder, he could feel warmth flooding his body. "Whatever you can do, you won't do it alone. I'll lead the rest of the soldiers away from this place before I try to rescue those poor boys, and you'll ascend to the monastery after. I can't sustain this form for long, Asher. The source of my power is gone, and now that I'm exposed, I'm vulnerable to Za'in. Still, when you face him, when you face Tregenne, you'll have as much Angel in you as I can manage."

His eyes blurred as the heat within him began to rise, and he thought he heard Kiera singing. He fell into the echo, and when he raised his head again, he had to shield his face from a fierce light. His head throbbed, just as it did on the first day after the end of the world. "Michael?" He stumbled to his feet before his eyes cleared, but soon he could see that it was morning and he was alone on the shore. About this time tomorrow, the sky would be dark.

Asher found Velsmere to be in much the same shape as Cormina, but as he neared the rocky, towering hill that supported the monastery, he could see that structure was untouched by the decay that spread over the land below. Still, this was no time to climb those heights. He'd have to wait in the ruins for the sun to fall into the last ordinary night.

He was alone again, for the first time since that day when he battled Saros on the dried-up seabed, that day he first saw Kayla's face after so many years. The boys joined him then, and it wasn't long before he stormed Za'in's compound and claimed the reward of her presence beside him for each day that followed. But now they were separated and it was as if his ten years of isolation never ended. One of his companions was already dead and the rest were captured.

Asher tightened the grip on his kukris and watched the sky. No, this wouldn't be like before. He wasn't leading the Resistance this time. He had stopped resisting. This wasn't the explosive human will to rebel or revolt. Instead, he was simply a vessel of divine retribution, a herald of a needed end.

46

There were swirls of green and blue, tiny explosions of stars and the mysterious inner workings of machines all revealed to Kayla's consciousness when she closed her eyes. She blinked lazily, enjoying the contrast of the sun's orange glow against the cool tones of her internal landscape. Other than the temperature of the colors she perceived, there wasn't much difference between the two realities that existed on opposite sides of her eyelids. Both worlds were hers.

She clutched the book Sebastian had given her. No, that wasn't quite right. One world was hers and the other would join with her soon, once her light resurrected tomorrow's black sun. She rested her cheek against the cool marble of the window jamb and looked down at the valley, encircled by purple hills. The surrounding mist made it impossible to tell where the sky ended and the rocky cliffs began, and that soft haze obscured the disorder of the overgrown fields, littered with the ruins of a village of stone and tile. How would she improve this already beautiful world? Her heart swelled at the majesty of her view, but the tears it brought to her eyes were melancholy.

"Lonely, isn't it?" Sebastian joined her beside the window, and gently wiped a tear from her lower eyelid with the back of his knuckle.

"No, it's lovely. My ear is to the cool earth below and I can feel all that echoes beneath. My arms are as wide as the fog and my embrace drapes over each tree, each rooftop. My adornments are quartzite, glittering over every surface, each sparkle a blink of my eyes as I survey our kingdom. In everything, I see . . ." She trailed off, surprised to find herself wiping away fresh tears with trembling fingers.

"Yourself. You see yourself. Yes, that's beautiful, but a mirror is lonely company. That's what we shall change. We'll bring the Earth to life by making its inhabitants worthy of its glory."

Kayla's eyes drifted from her view and landed on her abandoned studies. "How?"

"You have been diligent in your training and your reading, but there is no substitute for experience." Sebastian closed her book and placed it on the ledge of the open window. She quickly slipped it into her pocket before he took her hand and led her away from her perch in the tower, through the warm, open-arched halls that overlooked the inner gardens. Everything that her gaze touched was transformed by his palm pressed to hers. She could see through his eyes, feel through his skin. Each slant of the surrounding architecture existed as two angles simultaneously, with the added perception of eyes that stood a head above and a step ahead of her own.

"The wonder in you is dizzying," he murmured, laughter in his voice.

He opened a door into a darkened chamber and she followed, ascending a staircase, holding tight to the arm he crossed behind his back. She could see the spiraling steps echoing before a piercing light shot through the patterns beneath her. He lifted her through the opening in the ceiling, and her feet landed lightly on a ridge of roof tiles. The wind stirred her hair. She turned her head left and right, noticing the crisp, geometric shapes that composed the inner gardens and the unpredictable rhythms that formed the wilds on the opposite side of the monastery's gates.

"But you do have someone to share it with," Sebastian said, suddenly.

Kayla turned to face him, her question dying on her lips as she saw his eyes, merging with her own in his gaze.

"You don't have to say it aloud." He squeezed their palms more tightly together. "I feel it. For the first time, you can really see the beauty around you, but even as it fills you, there is a place of emptiness that it can't touch. If you want to light the world again tomorrow, you must be without the darkness of grief and doubt."

Her brows drew together as she searched his face. "Was there someone? Someone who was a part of me . . . someone I lost?"

He turned his head. "Tomorrow, so many brothers and sisters will be born—"

"It's my emptiness then, my sorrow. Even with that tiny void, I am still Nephilim. Let me keep it. A tribute to what I left behind." She squeezed his hand, defiant in the face of his avoidance, determined to find answers through their Angelic senses. A painful shiver crawled up her arm and for a brief moment she was confronted with a pair of glowering blue eyes.

There was a loud smack and she tasted blood. She didn't know if the illusion was shattered at the moment that he broke contact with her palm or the instant his hand struck her cheek.

"If you are not ready for the new Earth, it would be a mercy for me to just end this now." Sebastian's dark eyes were clouded with some unfamiliar emotion.

Kayla looked to his right hand and calmly took it again into her grasp. In the heavy throb of blood in his fingers she could feel his desire to bruise her arm and force her beyond the roof's edge. She slowed her heartbeat and allowed herself to be helpless in his fantasy so that he might be unable to detect how clearly she sensed this intention. She closed her eyes and breathed in the autumn breeze as it whipped nervously near her face. "Is your wound graver than my own?" she whispered, pity driving out her fear.

"My burden is." His pulse slowed and her violent visions dissolved as he walked her a short distance to the opening of a shallow dome. He motioned towards it with his usual assurance that answers would be revealed if she only stepped closer.

Kayla crawled towards the oculus and peered down into the chapel. There was an empty altar below her, surrounded by a stone floor inlaid with designs like bright sunbursts. She held the back of her hand to her nose. There were corpses below. "How awful. Why are you showing me this?"

"Use your true senses."

She gripped the edges of the dome's eye and allowed her awareness to drop down into the cold, stone chamber. The broken bodies of these humans were like petals, fallen from withered blossoms. It was a sad fate, but their destiny nonetheless. A little tremor loosened the hold of her fingers. Her light would go out too, someday. She would be a felled tree amongst these tiny flowers, but she wouldn't pass peacefully into the soil. She would be reclaimed, her power no longer hers, chained sleeplessly to the earth.

Kayla understood this now, as she looked deeper. The

stench of death wasn't coming from the humans. A few were separated from their souls, but most were still alive. The chained creatures below, all of them without fail, were fitted with fragments of divine bone, whether they were embedded beneath the skin or clamped tightly around their flesh. It was grotesque. Each human was the captor and prisoner of the Angel he donned, blind to the spiritual rewards and dangers at his fingertips.

"But what if the Angel conquered?" Sebastian's voice was very near.

She closed her eyes. Kayla could see slivers and knots of bone burrowing deep into organs, bursting forth from flesh. When the entire figure was consumed, it shone brightly. It was a body no longer, but a vessel for divinity. The eternal spirit was the focus, the driving force, and the form was just an expression of the soul. The fragility was gone, the fear was gone, and every division was lifted. Even she would be whole, without the emptiness that troubled every moment of peace she grasped. She could feel her roots digging into the earth again, her trunk straightening and her branches climbing to the light. She wasn't in a forest, but there was contentment in existing as a sentinel in this garden, safe in the shadow of a great banyan. All that came before was buried beneath the soil and served the purpose of fueling them all.

"What must I do?" she whispered.

"Spend the remainder of the day in meditation and the night alone in the presence of the stars. You will stay within the walls of the monastery. Although you will not see me, I will be very near. Sleep will come to you before dawn and there will be a few hours of oblivion before the sun wakes you. When it does, you will find me in the innermost courtyard."

Kayla turned from the dome and gazed down at the

ruined village in the valley. The beauty she had witnessed there, just moments before looking into the chapel, was now obscured by an overwhelming sense of decay. "And then?"

Sebastian tapped the book that protruded from her pocket. " 'When you give rise to that which is within you, what you have will save you. If you do not give rise to it, what you do not have will destroy you.' "

Kayla's toes dragged along the purple stone walkways that glittered in the light of the moon. Her bones felt restless. She had practiced her breathing exercises, taking in bits of the universe with the cool air. It filled her, but also made more room within her body as she expanded. Her exhalation was warm, blessing all of existence with her hopeful intentions, her invisible kiss received by the plants and the sky. She practiced the movements Sebastian taught her, the sequence of postures that reflected her internal motion. She felt weightless then, her body simply following the flow of her spirit.

Still, she was unable to quiet her mind. The spaces between her thoughts were filled with the image of those cold eyes she glimpsed in Sebastian's memory. Kayla touched her cheek. He never meant for her to draw that vision out—it was private, it was painful, and he didn't expect her ability to reveal it. Was that enough explanation for his violence? Did he realize that she saw the other thoughts that lay beneath? Kayla looked up at the stars. She had to admit the true cause of her unrest. She needed to see those eyes again.

She allowed her feet to drift without her consciousness leading them, and she found herself at the entrance to the domed chapel. The doors were locked and she could hear the altered humans stirring uneasily within. She let her forehead fall against the marble. The bones and blood of her kind were trapped on the other side of the wall. Could that explain the flash of recognition she felt the night before? No. That bright burst of divinity was unlike these perverted relics. Sebastian felt it too. He had run to her then and found her safe, but he left troubled.

Her feet were moving again, pulled towards the opposite end of the monastery. She pressed through a set of double doors and held her hands out as she groped in the darkness. She continued to step forward, her legs more certain than her apprehensive arms. Soon she could see faces emerge from the shadows, in the warm tones of inlaid wood portraits. Kayla turned, looking for the source of the light, and then realized that the symbols on her back were aglow. There was something waiting for her here.

She fell onto her hands and knees, her palms sliding over the little trompe l'oeil boxes on the painted tiles. The sets of white, gray, and black diamonds created the illusion of stacked cubes. Her fingernails found a deep groove and she pulled up a chunk of the floor. Jumping down below, she noticed the darkness was thicker and her sigils blazed brighter. Kayla stepped softly through the underground tunnel until she reached a heavy, metal door, but it wouldn't open for her. She closed her eyes. The stench of death that wafted up from the chapel was mild compared to what she sensed on the other side of this barrier. Still, her hands ached and her back burned. There was something here she was searching for. She pressed her palm against the keyhole and willed a fragment of her Intercessor to enter and spring the lock.

As she stepped into the cold chamber she could barely breathe, a heavy shiver coursing through her when the door closed at her back. Her gaze swept over the room, landing on tables strewn with books and papers, and other more ordered surfaces topped with shiny instruments, and vials of thick, dark fluid. Some of the glass containers felt familiar and she shuddered, remembering that forgotten vision of Sebastian collecting the essence of his kiss with Kiera. She stepped deeper into this lair of science and magic until she saw a limp figure slumped against the wall, his arms and bare torso chained to the stone behind him, while his legs sprawled helplessly along the floor. She stared in horror at the fetters that bound his arms and head—bones blackened by more hatred and pain than anything she witnessed in the chapel. She didn't recognize this creature, but she was certain she sensed traces of herself, twisted and mangled, running through his bonds.

Kayla was unsure if it was mercy or wrath that pushed her forward, but she knelt at his side, her palms drawing close to the black mass that swallowed his head. She angled her face to his and she could see he was still alive and breathing; his nose, mouth and chin were exposed beneath the heavy hang of his head. Was this the result of a man attempting to steal from an Angel so that he could become more like a god?

"This should not be, even if this is your own doing." She doubted the last part of her statement when she glanced down to see the set of tubes that protruded from his chest and the dried blood that streaked down his ribs.

His form jerked when she spoke, the small movement seeming to exhaust his weakened body. The fire at her back sputtered, and then burst into two curving, red flares. The light flickered, and tongues of flame issued from her palms, those burning tendrils wrapping around the fetters that bound his head. Kayla grit her teeth. The black mass began to lift from the man, reaching for her wrists, her face, but her fire coiled even more tightly around the corrupted bones. She refused to cry out, even as piercing wails of agony and rage shook her spirit. She wouldn't let the darkness conquer. The remains of her kind were not meant to exist in this perverted state. The sigils burned white and she focused her will on one thought, straightening her body and aligning her internal passageways of energy. She exhaled and allowed her heat to rise.

Kayla choked on the failed attempt to inhale, her back and palms now cold. Instead of meeting a dark force, her flames disappeared into a void. She fell forward, her cheek colliding against his chest, and she could feel his heart racing. There was something familiar in those savage beats.

"Hey," she whispered, "are you still in there?"

"Mm."

"Then help me kill this thing."

His lips twitched, almost forming a smile. Kayla raised her head and willed her fire to rise again, a growl forming in her throat. She straddled his slumped body, now tensed with whatever was left of his defiance, and she pressed her palms directly against his fetters, pushing his head back into the wall.

Kayla held in a scream as the bones threatened to invade her flesh. She willed her flames to wind around her fingers, swelling to form fiery claws, and she tore at the dark mass with wild strokes. Charred lumps splattered against the wall and fell to the floor, but there was still a tight, black net clamped to his face. In the spaces between the web, she could see his eyelids, forced closed, and his tight brow. Her heart leapt. Kayla brought her lips close to his forehead.

"Let him go," she breathed.

The tangle reached for her and he opened his eyes. Her breath caught in her throat with a strangled cry, thick with tears. That was the same gaze that couldn't be slapped out of her memory. She laughed, her joy bringing tiny sparks to the edges of her flames. With her fingertips, she lit the black threads like eager fuses, her red light winding along their paths before they fell from his head in clumps of ash.

They stared at each other, the returning flood of memories holding them still. Her hand passed over the burns and scratches that marred his face, tears falling from her eyes for every wound she closed. When she attempted to heal his bruised eyelids, he stopped her, grabbing her wrist with his one unfettered hand.

He swallowed, speaking with effort. "I don't want to lose sight of you again."

Kayla pressed her lips to his, one hand stroking the back of his neck, dragging up through his hair, while her other arm trailed down his side. His mouth opened and she felt his tongue seek hers, but soon his body tensed in a painful spasm as he was denied the movement he sought. She took her hands to the wall behind him and released a tremor through the stone. The vibration shattered the bones that attached to the fetters of his upper arms and back, and he was free from what chained him still. Immediately his limbs lifted to hold her, but he froze, close to her skin, and she could feel pain and frustration well up inside him. The sigils at her back flared, curling around his arms and drawing them close to her. The light formed a thin barrier between them, keeping her safe and giving them both the ghost sensation of the other's touch. He held her tightly, acceptance soothing his torment.

She wanted to heal him, but she had to admit that wasn't all she wanted. She was beyond the confusion of her journey. Now she understood the difference between the ecstatic fire necessary to act as an Angel, and the human passion that she desired to express only to him. The space between these emotions was narrow, with blurred borders, but she felt as though she finally had the control of choice. She could heal him now, without a taste of his lips or the satisfaction of his fevered moan, but she needed this as much as he did. How many times since they first saw each other did they battle for dominance, for safety, for release? How many times were their minds clouded, unsure of their goals and wishes, unable to tell the difference between captivity and freedom?

"You saved me a long time ago," she murmured into his ear. "You brought me to life. It's my turn. What you need . . . is to know that your life means everything to me."

His eyes were wide, but her kiss silenced any questions or rough words. Kayla brought her palms over his eyelids, erasing his injuries without protest, and then her right hand slid down to the tube that sprouted near his heart. She pressed her body against his and he responded, squeezing her harder, leaving no space between them. A shard of white bone cut the sutures and her fingers gently removed the tube, her sigh of pleasure easing his pain before her light closed the wound.

There was still so much suffering in him. He was thinking of that night beneath the banyan, the last time their skin touched with no barriers, and how he wanted that memory to be beautiful and unmarked by darkness. A wave of guilt loosened his grip.

Kayla pulled back from him and held his gaze. She untied her blouse, carelessly throwing it to the side, and presented her body to him. "That can't be changed. Even this won't be without shadow. But it's ours. I'm yours, Jeremy."

He turned his head. "I fucked up, Kayla. So many times—"

She silenced him with her fingers on his lips, her other palm tilting his face back to hers. There were no other words she could use to replace his regret with the solace she found here with him now. She let her hands caress his neck, move unwaveringly over the tattoo below his collarbone, and tenderly graze his ribs, stomach, and hips. Kayla touched her cheek to his throat, slowly turning her head to breathe cool air on his skin before he felt the wetness of her kiss. Her hands lingered on the waist of his pants, and then moved lower, disappearing beneath her skirt. She gasped, burying her face into his hair, her wings expanding with the convulsive jolt that moved through her body.

His limbs went slack for a moment before he gripped her hard, forcing her closer. His depleted strength surged through him as he tightened his hold, his crushing embrace stealing her breath but not stilling the movement of her hips. The fetters reached for her, breaking through her glowing second skin and tearing her flesh. She cried out, her fire spreading with tiny explosions that enveloped them both.

Kayla weakened, her head falling against his. The bones were winding around them, tethering her to him, and she could feel him surrendering. Soon the battle would be over and they would be together.

"No! Not like this," she whispered. "Peace isn't for us. If you want it to be different this time . . . then fight!"

Jeremy let out a pained breath, a blue light glowing at his back. Kayla's fire reached for his, and when they joined, the divine heat was transparent, distorting reality like floating whirlpools. He kissed her, breathless and trembling, concentrating on her warmth, her rhythm, and not on the demon she would take from him. She could feel his terror, the uncertainty of being separated from something he despised but forgot how to live without.

Thick tongues of flame surrounded his fetters, and although chunks of bone began to lift and dissolve, the light was becoming increasingly streaked with ash and blood. She felt as though she would be torn asunder, but she held tightly to him, quivering atop his body, her position no longer guaranteeing her the dominant role. Kayla looked at his shoulders, half freed of the fetters, but the exposed flesh was mutilated. "Jeremy . . ."

His eyes were closed, his face distant, his hands viciously clutching her backside and thigh. More black knots were lifting, each sending a shudder through him, and the light grew thicker with blood.

"No, stop! It's killing you—"

"Ssh. It's okay, Kayla." His expression didn't change.

Her body stiffened. "You can defeat it, but not this way!"

Jeremy growled, pushing her to the ground, never breaking his hold on her.

"Look at me, Jeremy! Be here with me."

He opened his eyes, fear narrowing his gaze. "That's what I want. But there's always something in the way."

"Then let's burn it." Kayla's stare was intent, a smile spreading slowly over her face.

He squeezed both of her palms to his, pressing the backs of her hands into the ground. Jeremy kissed her softly, watching in awe as her features tightened and relaxed again with pleasure. He dropped his face into her neck. "Let's burn it."

Kayla felt his weight bear down on her, his fire, his blood. Her muscles were taut, just as his were, a choked sigh shared on their lips. Their light was purified again, and in a brilliant flash his armor was shattered and thousands of black scabs fell to the earth.

47

The chill of the underground chamber made Kayla's toes curl and her limbs clutch Jeremy's body more urgently for warmth. She woke slowly, her fingers stroking his bare arms, her head resting above his heart. When her eyes opened, her past deeds and all of the future's phantoms scratched their old marks into sleep's clean slate. She shifted in his embrace and saw that his features were untroubled. She wondered if he had ever rested at all beneath his fetters. Kayla closed her eyes, breathing in one last moment of stillness here with him. This was what she had longed for. With this impossible intimacy finally reached, she could elaborate on her fantasy, and for just an instant, they were in a place of their own, in a world where the sun could never fall.

A voice from somewhere above struck her with the force of reality. "Any of that fire left for today's festivities?"

Before she could move, she felt Jeremy grab her and then she was flung aside. Kayla slid along the floor, colliding with the leg of a table.

"Get the fuck out of here," Jeremy snarled at the man that stood above his crouched form, but she knew he was telling her to run.

"That's right, Steelryn, go." The stranger watched as she clutched her blouse to her breasts.

Kayla met his green, vulpine eyes. "You must be First Arch Tregenne. I apologize for the intrusion of your . . . study." She stood, crooked at first, tying her top around her, but she slowly straightened and walked towards them, holding her hand out for Jeremy. "Sebastian allowed me free reign of the monaste—"

"*Lord Za'in* didn't give you this freedom so that you would lie down with his dogs. Now leave. The cur stays."

She stood between them, her Intercessors engaging. A sharp pain moved up her arms and Kayla fell down onto one knee.

"Out of juice? I'm not surprised. It's a rare Nephil that possesses the power and understanding necessary to break Ruiners, but it's never without a price." Tregenne lifted her chin with his finger. "I'd still gut you for spare parts. But by Za'in's orders, you have a job to do. Go do it."

Jeremy's whisper stilled her impulsive will to strike Tregenne. "His Mods are powerful. If you try to hurt him, you'll be the one that feels it."

Kayla growled quietly, pushing the Arch's hand away as she stood and began to walk towards the door. The heat in her palms was finally rising and she spun around to face him. She knew that she couldn't be burned by her own fire, whether it was here in her hands or from a redirected blow. A channel of flame shot forward, but Tregenne was already going for Jeremy. Gabriel's boot collided with his target's bare chest before pouncing on him. Tregenne smashed Jeremy's head into the stone floor, and then slid beside him, pulling him up by his neck, pinned between Gabriel's forearm and shoulder.

Kayla watched in horror as Jeremy struggled weakly against him, dazed. There had to be a way to deal Tregenne some damage. She felt for the Angel in him. Winding over his body were familiar, delicate symbols, laced with the blood and ash of her kind. She followed a trail that curved up from his ribs, over his chest and along his arm. Each set of characters translated into a lyrical phrase. *Trussed you together . . . with two-edged swords . . .* The light in her hands squeezed up through her finger and she traced the script in the air. *"Commah . . . napta . . ."*

Tregenne's sigils glowed and he expelled a roar of pain, releasing his grip on Jeremy. The Arch fell onto his hands and knees, but continued to stumble in her direction, knocking objects off tables as he careened around them. Kayla collapsed, clutching her arm. She could see the end of the trail of tattoos. *The strength of men . . . a bitter sting.* Her finger completed spelling the ancient words against the floor. *"Vgear . . . grosh!"* she gasped, all of her intention focused on stilling his movement by seizing control of his Mods.

Tregenne landed close to her, prone, his fingers weakly grasping her wrist. "That's a good girl. You're strong enough for this to actually work." He coughed out a rasping laugh before his hand went limp as consciousness left him.

Kayla's shoulders heaved with unshed tears and empty gulps of air. She pulled herself along the ground to reach Jeremy, who had already crawled a few feet in her direction. She sat up, shaking, and eased his bloody head into her lap. "I hate to say it, but I was so used to the powers the Ruiners lent you."

"Yeah, me too." He attempted a smile, but his facial muscles awkwardly disobeyed.

She tried to gather her energy, but the center of her

being felt cold. Kayla could feel his life force weakening. She had to admit that she was out of her depth when it came to the fetters; their properties and the consequences of their use were not known to her. It was pure will, pure fire, pure love that tore them from him, but was there another way? Some method that wouldn't have left him drained and helpless? Perhaps it was unavoidable. His body went through weeks of abuse, pushed beyond limits that he was unable to feel. The Ruiners quietly took everything from him, cruelly disguising his slow death as the birth of a dark god. Now the Eclipse was at their heels, and she could see no other option. Without the time to cultivate her healing energy, she would have to use Za'in's methods to ensure Jeremy's survival.

"The Eclipse . . . it's about to happen, isn't it?" he murmured. "There were times I thought it would always stay some distant threat or promise. I was supposed to be standing today."

Kayla held her breath while she shifted out from beneath him and hooked her hands beneath his armpits. "We have to get out of here before he wakes up," she whispered shakily, dragging him through the doorway.

"Leave me here. You have to run."

"No. I'm going to meet Sebastian."

"You can't be serious, Kayla . . ."

She let go of him and rested by his side, panting. "When I felt human, I wanted to stop him. When I mistook myself for an Angel, I wanted to help him. But you remind me what I really am. Being a Nephil is no different than being anything else. I can't make decisions based on what I think my parents would want or what might be best for the world. I can't foresee that future. I only know that every time I tried to forget you, I was divided further from myself. I'm not going to let you die." Kayla brought forth her Intercessor with effort; her palm felt thick and swollen. Her entire body tensed as she held her breath and snapped off a tiny piece of white bone. "Before the sun is fully obscured, take this into your body. It will save you." She dropped the fragment into his hand, closing his fingers into a fist around it.

"Shit. I guess I have no other choice. I'll be right behind you." He closed his eyes, wincing and swallowing. "Just don't get yourself killed, beautiful."

Kayla's cold lips sought his, their union a promise that the fire would rise up again. She ascended the ladder, eager for her last look at this sun.

Michael burst out through the doors of the church, the sunlight causing his hair to blaze like flames of righteousness. The man he chased disappeared behind the tightening semi-circle of soldiers that surrounded the leader of the rebellion. His Intercessor engaged, whipping a bloody arc across the line of men in black before it contracted tightly around his knuckles and down his forearm. His barbed fist smashed into the face of his first opponent, his opposite arm knifing the bowels from an attacker that entered through his blind spot. The next warrior he felled received a blow from the back of his arm, a descending strike thick with barbs. His left hand followed the rush of that wild circle, his blade catching deep in the chest of another assailant. Michael dropped to the ground, falling below a swinging sword, his long legs taking the root out from under two other soldiers. His body spiraled, landing on top of one of the felled men, swiftly snapping his neck. Michael's palm made contact with the temple of the other, his Intercessor penetrating and contracting in an instant.

He sat up among his felled enemies, his face grave, to

watch Asher approach. Serafin's face was softer, his beard thinner. He dragged a bound man along with him, a kukri to his throat.

Michael stood, searching the soldier's pockets until he found the relic. He stared at the unusual bone formation in his hand.

Asher saw the conflict in his mentor's face. "You have to do it. It's the safest place to keep it from Za'in."

He bowed his head, red braids swinging, and thrust the shard of bone through his right palm. He suppressed a cry, his fingers twitching as he grasped his trembling arm. "Fine, it's done," Michael said between clenched teeth. "One less weapon to be used against us."

Kittie stayed hidden behind the concrete barrier and tugged on Jeremy's arm. "He's strong. We should see if we can go with him."

The boy shrugged off her fingers, accustomed to bossing the older girl around. "No."

"You said we need to be on the winning side."

"We will be," he breathed, watching as Michael and Asher ran towards the falling radio tower in the distance. Steelryn and Serafin were strong, but it was Za'in that was on top.

Bruno's eyes fluttered open as he awoke, the vision shattered. "The relic was a diversion!"

"If that tower was functioning . . . it would have been more potent than any of Za'in's magic," Vic murmured.

Kerif groaned, leaning against the chains that held him. "Did we just have the same dream?"

"Ev'ry time I clos' m' eyes, I'see Kittie." Fec rubbed his sore limbs. "Whattaya think they did t'er? What'll they do t'us?"

"They already *did* something to us." The dreadlocked

pirate looked down at the bandages around his elbows, and his bruised, lumpy forearms.

Vic scanned the chapel and its prisoners, over one hundred in number. "Looks like we all have Mods. Everyone that's taken comes back with bandages, and those with external Mods come back with purple bones, instead of black." He touched his swollen arms. "The stones on the cliffs . . . why are they putting them inside us?"

"This Eclipse isn't about destruction . . . it's about creation." Bruno looked up at his friends with wide eyes, quickly narrowing again with resolve. "We can't let this happen. I don't know how he's going to do it, but *we're* the 'new race' Kittie was talking about."

Kerif tugged on his chains. "Ugh. Us? Talk about de-evolution."

"Not if Za'in switches out the parts of us he doesn't want," Vic whispered.

"With what?"

There was a stretch of silence before Fec spoke, his eyes closed and face peaceful. "I had a'dream tha' Kittie was surroun'ed by fire. She didn't look like 'erself, but I knew it was 'er. She had wings, two sets of 'em. An' she roar'd like a lion, an'er eyes were eagle-sharp, an' I could feel 'er strength . . . she was practic'lly an ox! She tol' me—"

"This world is ours . . ." Bruno said softly, remembering.

" . . . but we fight with God's will behind us, through his last messenger," Vic concluded.

Kerif straightened, his head snapping up. "Oh Christ— she's an Angel, isn't she? It makes sense! It makes so much sense! First Gabriel turned out to be an Arch, and now *this?* We catch onto these things really slow, don't we?"

The massive double doors of the chapel were slowly parting, opening the room up to morning's warm light. The pirates felt their Mods, at once more powerful, but restrained and sluggish. Their eyes darted between each other's gazes and the two figures that were meeting in the garden, as they waited for the moment their tiny flames would attempt to outshine an inferno.

Kayla squinted in the sunlight as she walked towards the dark form that cut a void into the morning's brilliance, deeper than the small chip in the sun's disk. He stood tall, his shoulders only slightly stooped beneath the weight of his purpose, his black clothes just as simple as always on this fated day. Sebastian turned as she approached, his brow tensing at the sight of her torn clothes and the blood and dirt smeared across her skin. He snatched her wrist and pressed their palms together, searching for answers.

"You . . . whore!" he bellowed, striking her across the face when he saw into her most recent memories.

Kayla fell to her knees, her voice rising softly from beneath her hair. "Was it forbidden for me to love?"

"It's not love. It was a part of your training. It was the biology of the Ruiners—"

"We destroyed those fetters."

"Then it is a blessing that today everything will change, so that you will be spared the slow decline of human love. If life just went on in some routine fashion, what would become of this love between you? Will there ever be a more intense situation, a peak experience beyond this? No, romance can't maintain that fury for long, and so it would become as mundane as the rest of reality. You will grow weary of that face you now long to see once it becomes a constant companion, and what's worse, his boredom will wound you, even as you try to evade the truth that he no longer holds any mystery for you either."

Kayla raised her face beneath his shadow. "It doesn't

frighten me. I am not going to destroy something beautiful because one day it might wither. He is mine; this is my choice. I'm going to do what you want simply because I want him to live."

"At this point, it doesn't matter if you're willing." Sebastian pulled Kayla to her feet, his hands clamping around hers. "You've forsaken your training at the most crucial hour and squandered the energy we've been cultivating in you. You have nothing left to freely give."

She felt something invade her palms, and both Intercessors reflexively engaged, pressing back against the incoming force. Her breath came heavy between her teeth as he tugged on her Angelic bones, sending sharp pangs up through her skeleton. Kayla looked down and saw white spurs, dark at the tips, spilling out from his palms and tethering their hands together. Purple stones were woven between transparent layers of bone, and she experienced their shimmer as blinding sparks and little cramping bursts beneath her skin.

Kayla's body felt weightless, and she wasn't sure if she was even standing anymore. Her eyes were rolling back, her limbs were faltering, but she fought to bring her gaze to Sebastian's face. He was luminous, serene, terrifying. He was a god, and she was his sacrifice. Kayla closed her eyes. If it meant Jeremy would survive, she wouldn't resist.

"Is that what you think? I have never asked for sacrifices. Energy will be redistributed, but it won't be yours that will wake in so many new vessels . . ."

She gasped, turning her head. The doors of the chapel were wide open, and she could see a large grouping of ragged humans, chained in purple and black. Their bodies were restless from within, blood churning and crashing up against their insides in waves. She felt the insistent force of Jeremy's presence, but she couldn't locate him. She looked to her left, and there was a pile of pink, glittering quartzite, stacked high in the center of the fountain. Bone fragments carved dark paths through the stone, gathering in the center of the cairn. There in that nest, there was a mass of swirling light, flaring up and falling back down into the dark tangle. Sometimes the glow would solidify into a wing, a hoof, a claw. Kayla looked deeper and glimpsed a pair of brown eyes.

"Kittie!" she cried, pulling back against Za'in's merciless hold. "She's a, she's a . . ."

"You didn't think I'd simply empower undeserving humans and raise them out of their condition so that they could again bring this world so low? Those imperfect souls must be extinguished, and their improved bodies will be animated with a new fire."

Kayla tried to free herself, but the bones and crystals that bound her to him climbed higher up her arms. Her ears stung with a sudden silence, and she looked to the sky. The sun was reduced to a thick crescent. That daunting sight just underscored the knowledge that this plan condemned Jeremy's spirit to oblivion.

She allowed an angry sob to escape. "Why are you making me do this? You don't need me, unless cruelty is your motivation."

"All births require a mother."

Kayla closed her eyes, slammed by a wave of nausea. "I don't understand how this could have been your plan all along. So much time . . . so many things that could have gone wrong . . ."

"The trees yielded their expected fruit. And if they hadn't, I have other orchards. I thought you recognized how many years I have walked this Earth. I was among the first offspring of the Fallen, both of God and Man. That weight comes with patience, foresight, changeability . . . but this is the ideal arrangement of these events. And when we walk in the majesty of our new world, ourselves too changed and filled with glory, I am confident that you will no longer see me as wicked, but as destiny's last agent."

Everything, from the grass, to the marble, to the quartzite hills beyond, were all darker, duller to Kayla's eyes as she stared desolately beyond the creature that was tethered to her. The sky was violet, deepening somberly in the west. Sebastian was no longer considering her, but instead was turned inward, his energy compressing and expanding, boiling up and over, washing himself clean of any stain left by this world. She could feel the deep reserves of her power being drained, but in return, he lent her the strength to remain conscious and standing. Her head lolled to the side, watching Kittie's flickering form with regret. This isn't how the last Angel should be extinguished.

Nothing should end this way and nothing should have its beginnings here.

"Kittie?" she sighed weakly.

Hush. He won't hear me. He never could. His Fall was not a matter of his birth, but a choice he made in God's absence. How foolish, to obey God as if he was a tyrant, a jailer, and then when the divine whispers fade, to react like an overindulged child. How can he expect to now hear a messenger of God?

There are no new revelations for me to announce. There haven't been for so many years. I wandered as a ghost, a bird, a hermit. And I forgot. But when Za'in shook the entire world with his blasphemy, I had to awaken. Some time passed before Jeremy's soul screamed out to me. I didn't know what it was then, but I followed his call. What is left of God is in all of you, and I learned I had to pay close attention if I wanted to hear His voice. So I took the form of a child and stayed by Jeremy's side. But I had never lived as a human before, not this way, not for so long, and things became complicated. It was hard to tell the difference between His will and my new desires for Jeremy's happiness.

Eventually, I lost aspects of my sight and was unable to change.

Then you came around. All those vague memories began to resurface, but you knew nothing of your heritage and I couldn't teach you what you needed. If I revealed myself, Za'in would feel it. I have limitations. My fire isn't the active urgency of humanity, but the watchful influence of Heaven. It was a risk to allow your enemy to be your teacher, but I am a being of faith.

Still, Za'in knew about me . . . somehow he knew! He prepared this place for me, and in my grief, I inadvertently gave myself away. Those Ruiners that separated Jeremy from you, they worked with me as well. I thought he was dead, but I know now that you saved him. You're not the same; none of us are. But we're all here. We can do this together. This is the way it has to be.

The sky was dark now, except for the band of orange near the horizon. Kayla held her breath as the burning sickle of the sun was continuing to be engulfed. An ominous black disk was emerging, even as a defiant beam of light bubbled along its edge. Her body trembled violently as that gaping abyss settled over the warm, flaming star. Still, the white light refused to be completely swallowed, now crowning the darkness with its halo.

She could feel the rays touch her back, and her wings spread out behind her, the sigils shining brazenly in the gloom. Her eyes were still seared by the Eclipse's afterimage, but she could see Sebastian's Angelic script intersecting that ghostly circle, glowing in curving arcs through the air around him. Kayla's sight left her as a blinding flash of Heavenly glory passed through her body, leaving the following darkness blacker than the moments before. She took a breath before the sensation returned, again and again. Kayla noticed that Sebastian's form shuddered seconds before each wave, and she turned her head first towards Kittie's rapidly dulling light, and then back to the chapel. It was happening.

A pale figure was emerging from the open doors, crawling at first, and then slowly finding his way to his knees. In the shadow of the moon, his skin was ashen, his clothing iridescent. As he stumbled closer to their light, Kayla could see there was no flesh, no fabric, but a body made of translucent crystal, interwoven with slivers of bone. Shimmering sigils appeared beneath the thin outer layer of stone, but the symbols changed and disappeared before she could decipher them. Behind his eyes, she could see fire, wonder, and the restlessness that arises moments before understanding settles. The creature looked to Sebastian with patience, struggling to hold himself upright. Soon more beings were finding their way out of the chapel, forming a glowing circle around the Nephilim. As more power flowed into the quartzite man at her side, Kayla watched the stone skin soften, flickering with light, then solidify again. Out of the corner of her eye, he shifted form, taking on the appearance of her vaguest memories. What were these beings and what would they become?

"The Anakim," Sebastian breathed. "Our children."

Kayla watched helplessly as they approached, her body wracked with continuous blasts of divine fire, her limbs fused to Za'in's. She tried to redirect the energy, to collect it deep within her and release it as hers, but it was too strong and too brief to hold. Her body softened in despair, but that surrender was only momentary. She wasn't able to borrow this power, but she wouldn't lose her own.

She tightened her muscles, locking her joints. Fire still leaked through these clenched gates, but the flow was lessened and the light that pooled beneath her stomach began to expand. Her arms were restrained, so the only place to send the force was up. Kayla's loaded scream pierced the unnatural silence, disrupting the energy that moved through the others. Before they could regain their equilibrium, there was a sharp crash, the shattering of something delicate.

For a moment, she couldn't breathe, and she watched the flare of Kittie's spirit rise up and then fall to the ground, her childish appearance returning. The quartzite and bone cairn was collapsing into fragments, and Asher slid down over it as he withdrew his gleaming weapon from that crumbling prison. Their eyes met for a moment, but he quickly turned from her and attacked Sebastian's progeny. Kayla noticed bright silver streaks racing through his body and disappearing when she stared harder, searching for earthly sense in the holy fury that somehow moved through him now.

The Anakim seemed weaker than they were moments ago, disoriented, and Asher hacked through their crystallized skin, yanking the Angelic bones from their bodies before they fell. She was infected by his urgency and fought harder to crack her bonds, but soon she lost sight of him. Something brushed heavily against her and she leaned toward Sebastian, an orange flash glimmering at the edge of her vision. When she looked up, there was a gap in the ring of creatures that circled her and it was Michael that joined Asher's assault on the Anakim. There was no place in her that could question how her father could be there now; she was too filled with awe. Here was Steelryn and Serafin, not imagined or glimpsed in visions, but *here*. Their faces were so alike in this moment, both held still by cold purpose, but their movements gave away their distinct hearts. Asher cleaved through rows of Anakim, one after another, with little variation in his fluid strikes. As he systematically worked his way through his enemies, his partner snaked through the ranks of towering figures. Michael's attacks were creative, but he moved too quickly to consciously consider the best expression of his Intercessor. He simply followed the necessity of the moment. If an Anak found itself too close to Michael's trajectory, it was drawn in and felled.

Kayla watched breathlessly as Michael approached, wrath in his muscles and his eyes. She could see him move to strike Sebastian, but just as he did, a loud shot stung the air and Michael dropped to his knees. Another bullet followed before he was face down in the dirt. Kayla screamed, her eyes growing wider as Michael's form faded, revealing dark hair and a broad, tanned back. His forearms were bloody with purple and black fragments shoved through his skin.

"Vic . . ." Her voice was choked and almost inaudible.

"Enough. Barely two minutes left of totality. Let's finish this." Tregenne's words came from behind her, and she turned her head to see him drop his gun and wrap a dark and glittering mass of barbs around Kittie's throat.

The surges of energy and light resumed and Kayla struggled to stay conscious. Her eyes were fluttering closed, but she still fought for her sight, searching for Asher, but he was nowhere to be seen. Many of the Anakim were rising up again and more were issuing forth from the open doors. It was as if Vic's heroic actions meant nothing. She dropped her head in despair, her eyes closing in an attempt to stop her tears.

"Yes, Tregenne, let's finish this."

Asher's voice sent a surge of adrenaline through her limbs as her head snapped up, her eyes wide. He swung both kukris at Gabriel, and although the Arch was able to block one attack, his grip on Kittie's leash slowed his defense. The hand that held the Angel fell to the ground, cleanly hewn from Tregenne's arm. He growled, spitting, his teeth bared, his forehead smashing into the bridge of Asher's nose. They both went down, but as Asher was blinded by his own blood, Tregenne grabbed a shard of quartzite and shoved it through his old enemy's chest. Asher fell and Gabriel crawled a short distance away, struggling to maintain consciousness.

Kayla screamed Asher's name again and again, but he didn't stir. Her muscles strained against her bonds, but her rage was impotent. She was taken by a wave of exhaustion and her body sagged helplessly. Her awareness was weakening, but she could feel something calling her from within the chapel. There was one last point of hope somewhere in that darkness and it called her to raise her heavy eyelids. She could see a pale figure lingering in the doorway, but it wasn't in the form of the luminous Anakim. Jeremy looked towards her, holding the sliver of her Intercessor that she had given him. He was dirty, bloody, stooped with pain, but if he just shoved that fragment beneath his skin, she could move through him, even though that Angelic power might burn off the last of his weakened human body's animating force. Still, there was no other way. If Za'in succeeded and he lived as one of the Anakim, the Jeremy she knew would be gone. She coughed out a weak nod and dropped her head, bracing herself for the sensation of a part of her body entering his. The impact sent a stabbing throb up through her arm, connecting to something dark within herself, something restless, but striving for redemption. The extension of herself rushed through the gloom, and she felt his force connect to her back, reaching around her to place pressure on her bound wrists and shatter the fetters that joined her to Sebastian. As the quartzite and bone exploded up and out, she was able to separate the sensation of fire from the visual reality of Jeremy standing behind her, his palms to her forearms. The moment she was free, he tightened his arms around her and dropped to the ground, rolling to the side before releasing her and crouching protectively in front of her limp body.

"It's too late," Sebastian proclaimed. "There are many strong Anakim and I still have enough time left."

He snatched from the ground the end of the leash around Kittie's neck, and Kayla watched as more Anakim arose, all growing brighter than before. The child's body was disappearing again, and even the light that still formed her winged silhouette was fading away.

"No!" Kayla screamed, flinging herself towards the Angel and her captor. She didn't have time to consider if she had the strength, but she experienced a cool rush of comfort when she glimpsed the tattoo along Sebastian's bicep. *Amgedpha. I begin anew.* She clawed his skin, her palm pressed to his sigils, while her other hand reduced Kittie's chains to purple dust. Kayla fell forward, holding Kittie to her chest, willing her fire to join with the wounded Angel's failing embers.

The heat in her arms dissolved as four wings spread up into the sky, surrounding a brilliant form that could only be described in terms of beast or Man, though it was neither. Kittie shined so brightly, it was almost as though the Eclipse had ended and the sun was lighting the world again.

The Angel reached out a glowing arm, her four heads shrieking a painfully beautiful tone. Beneath that sound, Kayla could feel the words: *this is not yours.* The sigils began to lift from Za'in and Tregenne, rising off their skin and into the air, the blood and ash that composed the tattoos completely disintegrating before they reached the flames. Gabriel seemed to have lost consciousness, but Sebastian stumbled to the fountain and leaned against it, refusing to let himself fall, even as the fortifications he built for his mortal body were dismantled.

Kittie's heads roared, this time with a more sonorous quality. Both arms were flung wide, like rays of the sun, and she called back everything that was stolen from her. The eyes of the Anakim lost their light first, as empty as the Eclipsed sun, and slowly their entire bodies faded, falling to the earth like broken statues. She pulled their scavenged bones in next, the blackened masses cracking and burning away as they neared her fire.

Kayla held her forearm to her brow as she tilted her head up to the sky, squinting in the Angel's glory. She could see a glowing jewel in the heavens, swelling and separating out into a series of diamonds that soon merged to form a thin crescent. The Eclipse was coming to an end. She brought her attention back to Kittie, gasping as her dwindling light fell slowly back to earth. The eagle, the lion, the ox, and the cherub were all silent now, their eyes grave and tired. Kayla and Jeremy crawled towards her, even as Fec and Bruno emerged from the chapel, their bandaged arms supporting Kerif's wounded frame, his limbs covered in gashes as numerous as the shards that were forced into Vic's arms. Tears were washing the pirates' red faces clean, but they trudged quietly forward, obeying the overwhelming need to be together again now, all of them reunited beneath the expanding sun.

Kittie was shrinking as if she was the shadow of the moon. *This was it,* her voice resounded in their minds, *this was why I was still here, even with everything I forgot. We won. God's will was fulfilled.*

"Stop being so dramatic," Jeremy said harshly. "The world didn't break in half, great. So we keep living in it."

"No, Saros, it doesn't work that way," Za'in murmured behind them.

Kayla sprang to her feet, both Intercessors engaging, and threw herself between Sebastian and Kittie's living ghost. She raised her right arm over her head to deflect his weapon while her body twisted so that the Angelic blade on her left could be thrust out deeper. The world disappeared and she wondered for a moment if she had stared too long into the sun. The heat at her back was unbearable, but she forced it through her internal passageways, weakened as they were by the overuse of her Angelic abilities. Still, the humanity in her wouldn't accept failure, even if it was a sentence from the Divine. There was suddenly bliss in her blindness as she felt Kittie's radiant light fill her and move vengefully into Sebastian's Intercessor. Kayla thought of her mother's cards and how they led her here. She was *The Star*—she accepted that a long time ago—but this moment, this was her entrance into *Dominion,* the throwing off of every doubt, every fear, every promise. She would act now as herself, as someone who is part woman and part Angel, the daughter of Michael and Kiera, Sebastian's student. She was the girl who was in love with Jeremy and admired Asher, who traveled the world with her friends, her new family. She would no longer be a shield or a weapon, not a burden or prize. Her destiny was her choice. She would be free, sometimes in chaos, sometimes in darkness, but never beneath the weight of another's will, thirsty for his approval, clinging to his judgments.

Dominion, The Two of Wands. She saw that pair in the bones she held in her hands, the two branches of her heritage. The twin rods were the fires she could set with Jeremy, or that sacred union of moving through a human, as an Angel moved through her now. It was the world that came before and the Earth that was now hers.

Sebastian's Intercessor, that monstrous mass composed of countless Nephilim, burst into splinters and every shard of divine power he possessed, whether it was borrowed, stolen or inherited, was consumed in fire until there was nothing left but a memory of Heaven.

48

Kayla woke beneath the sun's warmth with the knowledge that the danger hadn't passed. She had chosen a world of uncertainty. The sound of tears reached her before the wind or the birds, and she rolled to her side, rising up to meet the sorrow without hesitation. They were still in the courtyard of the monastery, and she noticed her friends huddled in two close groups, bent with grief.

She wanted to reach her arms out to them, but she felt far away, separated by a clouded screen. The only thing that was clear was the vision of Sebastian at her feet. He was lying on his stomach, his body twisted, his clothing singed and torn, his bloody hand held tightly to his chest. She could see his tattoos were gone and his scars were now just clean, white lines. For a moment, Kayla wanted only to pierce his heart with a shaft of her own bones, but when she thought of the absence of his Intercessor, of the hollow ache that must be coursing through his being, pity stilled her hand.

"Both you and your Arch must leave this place," she said

quietly.

"Tregenne isn't my Arch anymore. There is nothing left of that kingdom."

Kayla stared at him, stunned. "The Anakim . . . was that all that was left of your army? There was so much that you owned and controlled. Did you let everything go?"

"I never intended to live as some mortal dictator. The last eighteen years were always meant to be a temporary construction. This path ended today. Don't you see how many others are open?" Sebastian looked up at her with the same expectations as always, as if no Eclipse ever cast a permanent shadow over their relationship.

"Wherever you're going, you'll be alone," she whispered.

"And so will you," he replied, rising slowly to his feet. "You will start a new life with your human companions, but something will be missing. The excitement, the fire, the tragedy, they were my creations. Without me, there is no Saros. When you realize it was the fallen Arch that fascinated you, not the ordinary Jeremy, then perhaps we will see each other again."

"I don't want a purpose beneath your design. I don't want a love beside your ambition. This ordinary life you fear is going to be mine, and I'm not afraid to find the divine in a world without you."

He eyed her softly glowing palms before he spoke. "A world without Sebastian Za'in . . . very well." His dark eyes met hers one last time before he turned and walked towards the courtyard's gate.

Kayla watched as he made his way through the marble walkway and then the towering entrance of the monastery, disappearing into a row of cypresses. She turned her head towards where Kittie was once imprisoned, but the only remaining sign of Tregenne's presence was his spilled blood.

"Asher!" she cried, rushing to the huddled form that lay

beside the dark puddle. Kayla sat beside him, cradling his head in her lap. "You're alive . . . you're alive! How could you be so reckless, attacking Tregenne without knowing I had neutralized his Mods? Oh God, Asher, we really did it, and it's over . . ."

"I heard what he said to you," Asher whispered, "and he's right: it's never over. But you're right too. Today the light triumphed. That's all we can ask for. I was able to fight with Michael one last time, and you . . ."

"Ssh." She pulled the crystal shard from his chest, closing the wound with her warm palm.

" . . . and you have the one you love returned to you, freed of his demon."

"Asher, I—"

"I know. You could have loved me, but your heart was already his by the time I tried to hold it." He turned his head and looked out to see Jeremy on his knees, resting heavily against a simple marble bench, his shoulders softly trembling. His hunched back blocked the light that glimmered faintly above the bench. "He needs you now."

Kayla embraced Asher when he sat up to meet her arms, and when they pulled away, she allowed her eyes to meet his, holding his gaze for a long moment before she stood and made her way to Jeremy's side. His voice reached her before she crouched beside him.

"Go ahead and yell at me; tell me it's my fault. I should have listened to you from the beginning, I know . . ." Jeremy whispered, his fingers grazing Kittie's cheeks before they fell through the barrier of her skin as her form disappeared into a mass of light. He choked, then pushed himself back from the bench, his voice rising. "No, fuck this! You didn't die last time. You think I didn't see what you did back when I was ten, when you fought for me? You grew heads, wings and eyes; you screamed and caught fire.

You were death and glory. Are you glad that I didn't try to figure it out? I didn't want to. I wanted you to be you again, with me. I'd kill anyone if they tried to unravel your secret and cause you to explode, or take you away. That time was darker than this one, and you made it through, so pull yourself together now. Haven't you figured out yet that there's no point in us being apart . . . ?"

Kittie's familiar form returned, and the little girl smiled at him from her supine position on the bench. "Were those days darker? I remember drawing pictures with you in the dirt and climbing utility poles. We'd eat whatever we could steal, but you'd always go out of your way to find me something jarred in vinegar, even though you never liked slimy things in bottles. I don't remember darkness. Even now, I can see your arms are free, and I always thought you were cute when you were bleeding. It's all okay now, Jeremy."

His tears fell, and he clenched his jaw to stop any weak sounds from escaping.

Kittie was pure light now, rising up from the bench, and it was difficult to distinguish her brilliance from the rays of the sun. *What I lost in Heaven you all have returned to me. Each one of you, you helped me to remember, and in each one of you I see* . . . Her light separated into smaller shafts, shimmering defiantly. *Hold on to your joy, because you're the proof . . . you're the proof . . .*

The sun was shining, but silence reigned. There was no longer anything in the air they could recognize as hers.

"Proof of what?" Jeremy finally asked, his voice hoarse.

Kayla squeezed their palms together, her eyes holding his before looking to her fallen comrade, the somber faces of the three pirates that hovered over him, and finally to Asher's steady gaze. "The darkness has lifted, and we're still here," she said softly. "I see the same thing Kittie did. This

469

isn't a profane world, made in the image of the Fallen. There is something beautiful here, sacred. It's the home of our light. The divine can't abandon us; we can only ignore our connection to it. Don't you see what we meant to her? We're the proof that God isn't dead."

ACKNOWLEDGMENTS

I'd like to thank everyone that believed in this project from the beginning. Mr. Bayer, you encouraged my creativity, even when it was crude or ridiculous. This story began in your class. Nicole, thank you for being my cheerleader (and for rooting for Jeremy, when no one else did). Thanks to Tiffany, Michelle, Rachel, Mom, Dad, Ray, and Sifu for listening, reading early drafts, and every small favor that made the next steps possible. And, of course, thank you Grant for all the edits, late-night discussions, and critical questions. This little world is real to you too, and I couldn't ask for a greater declaration of love.